Dick —

CODE

of the

FOREST.

Happy reading!

S.

CODE

of the

FOREST

a novel

JON BUCHAN

JogglingBoardpress

Books—In the Spirit of the South

Joggling Board Press books may be purchased for educational, business or sales promotional use. For information, please contact sales@jogglingboardpress.com.

First edition.

Jacket design by Torborg Davern; Interior design by Shanna McGarry.

Excerpt from *The People, Yes* by Carl Sandburg, copyright 1936 by Harcourt, Inc. and renewed 1964 by Carl Sandburg, reprinted by permission of Houghton Mifflin Harcourt Publishing Company.

Library of Congress Cataloging-in-Publication Data

Buchan, Jonathan E., Jr.
    Code of the Forest: a novel / Jonathan E. Buchan, Jr. - 1st U.S. ed.
    ISBN 978-0-9841073-5-3

For my father, Jonathan Edward Buchan, who encouraged me to be a reader, and for my mother, Margaret Alice Liles Buchan, who encouraged me to be a writer – with love and gratitude.

To be nobody but yourself – in a world which is doing its best, night and day, to make you everybody else – means to fight the hardest battle which any human being can fight, and never stop fighting.

– e.e. cummings

Only connect.
– E. M. Forster

PART I – GEORGETOWN
1995

1

Ducks in the Freezer

Senator Buck Ravenel hunkered in the chill of the Low-country dawn, pondering ducks and politics. There were always ducks at Bowman's Forest. And there was always politics.

He glanced at the man kneeling beside him in the duck blind and smiled.

"Do-Good, you still got that nice pair of cowboy boots I gave you your first year in the legislature?"

Judge Dupree Jones, squirrel-cheeked, bushy eyebrows at parade rest, squinted toward the tops of the longleaf pines lining the pond's opposite shore. He warmed himself with a sip of Maker's Mark from a metal hip flask sporting the South Carolina state flag, silver crescent and Palmetto tree against a dark blue background.

"You know I do, Buck."

Ravenel had given Jones the snakeskin boots – custom made by Ravenel's favorite Texas craftsman and soft as a puppy's belly – fifteen years ago. The nickname came with the boots, right after Jones had voted for a fellow the senator had promised a judgeship.

"Helping you out put me in a pinch with some of my folks back home, but it all worked out. Made you happy."

Ravenel reached for the flask of whiskey and took a sip.

"You did good, Dupree. I can always tell which of the new

young bucks understand how things work and know the right team to be on," he said. "I like looking around the State House and seeing those boys wearing my boots. And I like giving out those names."

Judge Jones sucked in a sharp bourbon breath and wiped his lips with the sleeve of his camouflaged hunting jacket.

"We're 'bout to see some thirsty damn ducks coming this way," he said with a laugh. "When they spot this pond, they'll come right at us. It'll be the last letter home, Momma."

He patted the senator on the shoulder and surveyed the peaceful setting.

"Got-almighty, what a perfect morning," the judge said.

Two hundred yards away, two score or so mallard ducks, quacking and jostling, the drakes' iridescent dark-green heads bobbing, waddled through the open gate of their ground floor pen. They headed up a wire-enclosed ramp that sloped gently higher, spiraling up and around the three-story wooden tower hidden in the pine forest.

The Superintendent of Game for Bowman's Forest had raised these ducks himself, breasts plumped by ample corn, for a day just like this January morning. Since the sun last rose, he'd given them neither food nor water.

When the duck parade reached the tower top, the superintendent deftly herded the first six ducks into an outside wire pen. From there, they could see Paradise through the tops of the pine trees – a freshwater pond baited with tender millet. Sweet Lord, here we come across the River Jordan! They whacked their wings against the sides of the pen, desperate to escape. They were still out of sight and sound of the hunters.

Judge Jones shifted his stiff legs in the duck blind. He blew his warm breath on the cold fingers of his trigger hand.

"Buck, what's been bringin' you to Georgetown so much

these past few weeks?" the judge asked. "I haven't seen you in my courtroom."

The senator was quiet for a moment.

"I've been helping out some old friends with that phosphate plant they want to build over on the Waccamaw River," he said finally. "It'll be a great deal for Georgetown. Damn good-paying jobs, the kind of company that gives back to the community and all that sort of happy crap."

He grunted and spat.

"But right now, all those tree-huggers are trying to stop it, having little wine and cheese fundraisers to get everybody all worked up. Some piss-ant reporter for the Georgetown paper is fishing around like he's after some big ole trophy bass."

Ravenel checked the chamber on his 12-gauge.

"Well, we'll get it all straightened out, though, I'm not worried about that."

"Don't tell me more than I need to know, Buck," the judge said.

Ravenel gave him a tight grin.

"Don't worry, Dupree, I'll tell you just enough, just like always."

They listened for a moment in the silence, hoping for the sound of ducks. Nothing yet.

Ravenel rested his shotgun across his knee and scratched the head of the judge's chocolate Labrador retriever Muddy Waters.

"Dupree, you know how I first heard about Bowman's Forest? It was 1970. I was a year out of law school, and I had my first case set for trial in Marion County. My client had slipped on a wet spot in a grocery store and slammed his head on the floor. He was never quite the same, lost his job driving a long-haul truck. Buddy Beeson was the lawyer for the grocery store, and its insurance company wouldn't offer us a nickel to settle. Said it was the man's own damn fault for not watching where he was walking."

"Beeson – he was the senator from Marion County back then?" Judge Jones asked.

"Yeah, but I didn't give a good goddam about that. I was too green to know any better," Ravenel said, peering straight ahead at the tall pines across the pond. The early morning sun had begun to burn away the mist rising from the water.

"I had a damn good case. This was no 'wino actor with a chiro-practor' kind of whining plaintiff. This was a hard-working man who had really been hurt. I just wanted a jury of twelve good people to hear my client tell his story and explain how his life had been taken away. Trial was set for the week before Christmas. You know how generous juries are around the holidays. The insurance company lawyers use every excuse in the book to avoid those Santa Claus juries. I was sure we could get a couple of hundred thousand dollars in damages.

"When we got to the courthouse, I was one ready son of a bitch. I had my exhibits to show the jury. I had a specialist from the medical school set to testify about how my client's mind had never recovered. I had the wife ready to testify how her husband was a different man, a lesser man, after his accident. My client and his whole family were there."

The quiet morning exploded with quacks and whistling that sounded like gridlock in Manhattan. Ravenel's eyes caught the first flight of six mallards as they cleared the green tops of the pines. They were flapping for all they were worth, the leader setting the pace, necks stretched straight, lusting for the food, the water, the peace in the pond. Muddy Waters heard the racket and began to fidget.

"Got-almighty-damn," exclaimed the judge. "Here we go!"

Jones stood, pocketed his flask and released the safety on his own shotgun. Shots exploded from each hunter's gun, but Muddy never left his spot. Two more groups of mallards, and eighteen shots later, the carefully trained, soft-mouthed retriever – better pedigreed than most race horses – had returned a dozen ducks, still warm to the touch.

There had been a time when coastal South Carolina's winter skies were darkened with thousands of migrating ducks. The modern take at Bowman's Forest was a mere nod to that era.

"You didn't finish your story," said Judge Jones, as he rubbed his proud puppy between the ears. "What did Santa Claus bring you?"

Ravenel was counting the ducks, dividing them up. Finally, he spoke, shaking his head at the memory.

"Before we could start pickin' a jury, the judge called us back to his chambers," he said. "I sat down across from the judge and started to tell him about my case. Beeson, he just leaned back in his chair and propped his feet up against the edge of the judge's desk. He asked the judge about his family and about how his daughter was enjoyin' her first year at Clemson. Then the judge asked Beeson if he was takin' folks down to Bowman's Forest that winter to go duck huntin'. Told Beeson how much fun he'd had on last year's trip. The judge said he'd eaten his last duck from that trip just a few weeks ago, at Thanksgiving."

Ravenel shook his head and laughed.

"I had no damn idea what they were talkin' about. But then Beeson dropped his feet to the floor, slapped his thighs and said, 'Judge, I gotta few of those ducks left in my freez-ah. I'll bring some over to you this weekend. And we need to go huntin' again.'

"The judge smiled at Beeson. Then he frowned at me and

said, 'Mr. Ravenel, I've read your trial brief, and I believe your case has some problems. I think Mr. Beeson's motion to dismiss has a great deal of merit. Now, I suspect he's about to offer you thirty thousand dollars to settle this case. I suggest you go out there and have a come-to-Jesus meeting with your client and help him understand why he should accept that offer. You can tell him the judge appears to be on the verge of dismissing his lawsuit, in which case he'll get nothing.'"

Ravenel reached down to pick up his share of the ducks. He put his hand on the judge's shoulder.

"I left that room pretty shook up. My client couldn't believe it. He knew how much we had prepared. I had told him the day before that I thought the case was worth at least a hundred thousand dollars. But he needed money bad, and thirty thousand dollars would at least pay some of his overdue bills. I cut my fee to almost nothing, but the whole family was crying when I left them.

"I tell you what, Dupree. I walked out of that courthouse hating the law, hating politics, hating judges and hating the state legislators who appoint them. I was just beginning to understand how things work.

"As I headed down the courthouse steps with my tail between my legs, Beeson came hustling up beside me. He threw his arm around my shoulder, all buddy-like and chuckled, 'You know, Buck, that case of yours wasn't half bad. But you know what your biggest problem was?'

"I said, 'No, I guess I don't.'

"That sonovabitch brayed at me like a mule: 'Buck, your problem was, you didn't have no ducks in yo' freez-ah!'"

Ravenel lifted his three brace of ducks, their gray bodies and green heads dangling limply at his ankles. He smiled at Judge Jones.

"Do-Good, my friend, that was twenty-five years ago," Ravenel's blue eyes were wide and twinkling.

"As they say in the country, I realized I needed to move up closer to the main road and start subscribing to the newspaper. I wised up some. And now here I am at Bowman's Forest. My Senate committee picks the judges. I got ducks in my freezer. And I win most of my cases."

2

Kate Stewart

In the dimly lit Georgetown County courtroom, Kate Stewart could not read Judge Dupree Jones.

She had heard he was hard on what he still called "lady lawyers," but she had never seen him in action before. And today's hearing was not going well.

"Your Honor," she said firmly, "With all due respect. . . ."

She struggled to hide the sarcasm that almost leaked from her lips onto the word *due*.

"The State wants to tell the jury about a burglary conviction my client had six years ago. If my client takes the witness stand during his trial next week, the State may properly question his credibility by asking him about that conviction. But if he elects not to testify, the State cannot simply argue to the jury that his other burglary makes it more likely he committed *this* one. Rule 404 prohibits that."

Judge Jones rocked slowly in his chair behind the bench, his eyes locked on Kate's. Decades of South Carolina's Lowcountry cuisine had helped him fully fill his judicial robes. His hair was the gray of the Spanish moss that hung like giant spider webs in Georgetown's oak trees. At 65, the judge's cheeks had grown puffy, giving his eyes a slitted, sleepy look that disguised his mental acuity.

He watched Kate Stewart carefully, like a feral cat eyes a cornered mouse. Kate was clearly quick on her feet, but the judge knew he was going to win.

"Ms. Stewart – do I have that right, or is it Mrs. Stewart? – the rule is not as clear cut as you and your client might like it to be."

Kate tried hard not to stare at Judge Jones' massive white eyebrows. They swept up onto his forehead and leaned toward his temples. When he was angry, they took on a life of their own, dancing like agitated mice. When he widened his eyes, every hair in his eyebrows stood erect, like soldiers at attention. She wondered if he had trained them to do that.

"The State relies upon the exception to Rule of Evidence 404," the judge continued. "If the State can demonstrate that there appears to be a pattern, a similar *modus operandi*, then the prior conviction may be introduced whether your client takes the stand or not. The Court will instruct the jury that it cannot consider the defendant's other burglary conviction as evidence that he was more likely to commit *this* burglary. But the jury *will* get to hear about his burglary conviction."

It was a fine distinction, lost on jurors every time. That's why the exception was sometimes called the "Prosecutor's Delight." Kate knew that once the jury heard that her client had committed a prior burglary, he was toast. The judge's "limiting" instruction to the jury would just call additional attention to her client's earlier crime.

The judge peered down at her over the top of his reading glasses.

"I'm going to let that evidence come in at trial. It's a week away. That's plenty of time for a smart young lawyer like you to figure out how to explain it away."

"Judge," she said, in a voice firm but pleading. "I ask the Court to review the two cases I have handed up. They squarely support my position that the law does not permit the jury to hear about the prior conviction unless my client takes the stand."

"Ms. Stewart," the judge responded sharply, "It's a little like that old country song. What part of 'no' do you not understand? Your theory is not the rule in my courtroom. I do not go easy on criminal defendants. The legislators of the State of South Carolina elected me to administer justice. I leave it to God to dispense mercy. If you want a different result, you can consider Rule 521-dash-378."

Kate's cool almost cracked, and she felt her stomach knot. Ten years of practicing law, and she had never heard of Rule 521-378. She took a slow sip of water from the paper cup on the counsel table, stalling while she whirled silently through her mental Rolodex of legal principles. Before she could respond, the judge gave her a tight smile.

"It's not in your law books, Ms. Stewart," he said.

He was squinting at her now, his eyebrows quivering like porcupine quills.

"I mean you should take Highway 521 until you get to Highway 378. Then you take 378 to Columbia. That's where the South Carolina Court of Appeals sits. If my esteemed colleagues on that lofty bench agree with you, come back and we'll talk about this some more."

The judge's eyes darted to the government-issue clock on the back wall. He took a quick glance around the courtroom and gave a satisfied nod at the prosecutor and at Kate.

"Looks like there's nothing else to be heard," he said. "It's 5 o'clock. Bailiff, please adjourn court. Have a nice weekend, counsel."

His eyebrows relaxed and lay down, like old dogs after a long run. As the bailiff spoke, the judge gathered his robe and disappeared through the wood paneled door behind his high-backed leather chair.

Kate spoke briefly to her client and patted him on the shoulder of his orange jumpsuit before he was shuffled away by the deputies. She slid her legal pad and her files into the large leather briefcase and snapped the brass clasp shut. The briefcase had been a law school graduation gift from her father. Over the past ten years it had weathered to a deep tan, the color of a well-cured tobacco leaf.

She reminded herself that every case is a long war, and you don't win every battle. But it was clear that the learning curve for representing criminal defendants who couldn't afford to hire a lawyer was steeper than she had anticipated. She could hear her father reminding her not to get discouraged. He had always told her to be as stubborn as a snapping turtle: "Don't let go until it thunders."

*   *   *   *   *

Friday afternoon happy hour at Sliders Oyster Bar was a local ritual, and Kate had quickly made it part of her weekly routine after moving to Georgetown from Columbia. The small bar and restaurant opened onto a waterside courtyard shaded by four ancient live oaks, stunted by decades of heat and hurricanes but elegant in the unpredictable curves and angles of their wandering limbs. Visible from the courtyard was a long row of docked shrimp boats – ancient, low-riding wooden tugs with names like Stormy Seas, Geoffrey's Gem and Ellie Belle, sea-scarred, patched and painted bright white, full of hope for the opening of shrimping season.

As Kate entered Sliders, the long table against the west wall was already getting rowdy. It was reserved on Fridays for the POETS Society, an informal alliance of young assistant prosecutors, Legal Services lawyers, and reporters for the *George-town Pilot*. They shared, over pitchers of beer, their sharply cynical political and social commentary. The name stood for their Friday night rallying cry: "Piss On Everything, Tomorrow's Saturday."

Kate waved at a couple of the lawyers and made her way through the tables to her favorite spot by a window overlooking the water. From there, the fading February sunlight gave Winyah Bay a serene, glassy look that always had a calming effect on her.

Kate settled into her seat and discreetly slipped off her shoes under the table. From behind her came Bobo Baxter's familiar baritone, not quite Ray Charles, but not far off.

"*Hey, good-lookin' ... Whatcha got cookin'? How's about cookin' somethin' up with me?*"

Bobo, Sliders longtime proprietor, could make anyone smile, including Kate on a bad day.

As a young lifeguard in the late 1950s at Ocean Drive Beach – O.D. to that generation – he had survived on a diet of beer, chili dogs, and Krispy Kreme doughnuts, appreciating every detail of South Carolina beach life. By day, he had rented canvas floats, beach chairs and beach umbrellas to the resort town's summer tourists and enjoyed the flirtations with each week's new crop of teenaged girls. By night, he haunted The Pad, the South Carolina strand's best-known den of young adult iniquity. As Bobo had watched the state's most talented shaggers quick-step, spin, shoulder-slide and dirty-bump across The Pad's sandy concrete dance floor, he had soaked up the lyrics of hundreds of beach and rhythm-and-blues songs.

Bobo quoted song lyrics the way a Southern Baptist preacher cites scripture. He had been known to give a wink to an attractive woman seated at his bar and softly sing, with a Buddy

Holly hiccup and a Mick Jagger hint of abandon, *"My love's-uh-bigger than a Cadillac,"* and wait for her reaction. Or watching a patron's subtle shift of affection from the man she had arrived with to the one she would soon leave with, he'd shake his head and quietly moan a little Percy Sledge: *"Lovin' eyes can nev-er see-ee-ee."* Every good song held a parable for him, every good lyric a life lesson.

"Evenin' Counselor," Bobo said, with teasing in his voice. "It's Friday night. You want the Goose with Ice, right? And you're expecting someone?"

"That's just what I need, Bobo," she smiled back. "Thanks. And Carolyn should be here shortly."

"Back in a flash," he said and headed to the bar.

Her Friday night standard soon appeared before her, as welcome as an angel: a Grey Goose vodka martini, easy on the vermouth, with ice on the pond. That thin coating of ice and the frigid bullet behind it quickly separated Kate from the tensions of the week. And it put a little distance, for now at least, between Kate and her doubts about her recent choice – walking away from the large Columbia law firm after ten years to start a solo practice in Georgetown.

Kate glanced at the door, keeping an eye out for Carolyn. She was always in a hurry, but seldom on time.

They had met at the University of South Carolina their freshman year and become fast friends and sometimes quiet competitors. Kate had pledged Zeta, and Carolyn had joined Tri-Delt. Kate quickly became an academic star. Carolyn was a strong student, but her good looks and easy way with people had propelled her into campus politics. They had both dated SAEs and KAs, and had sometimes ended up on group week-ends together at the beach or in the North Carolina mountains. By their junior year, they had eased away from the Greek scene and shared a house off campus. Kate had graduated *summa cum laude* in political science, and Carolyn was student body president her senior year. Carolyn moved to Charleston after graduation, working her way up the ranks of the state's environmental groups. Within five years, she was state director for the Sierra Club, pushing the group into some of the toughest environmental battles in the region. Her energy had attracted more members and donations than the group had ever known. The national Sierra Club leaders had teased her with a bigger job in California, but her love for the South Carolina Lowcountry kept her anchored there.

Kate's goals in law school had been more traditional. She had figured out that South Carolina's rapid growth and development would spawn increasing environmental regulation and litigation. She devoured every environmental law class the University of South Carolina law school offered. She studied environmental law with the intensity of a medical student absorbing organic chemistry.

One summer during law school she interned at a large Manhattan law firm. She enjoyed the glitz and acquired a taste for martinis, but found New York too fast, too loud, too brusque, too much concrete, just too damn much. She spent her second summer working at the Devereaux law firm in Columbia, and the partners there quickly recognized her mastery of environmental law and her ability to explain it to clients and judges in a practical way. They offered her a job.

Kate made partner at the politically well-connected law firm in just five years. The pace was grueling, but her hard work won her many loyal clients. She helped some of the state's most powerful industries stay just inside the clear lines of environmental regulation and blurred those lines for some who might have strayed beyond them. The work had created

some tensions for Kate and Carolyn over the years, but mostly
they had put their friendship ahead of politics – until the fight
over the Georgetown paper mill that had come up two years
ago. Kate and Carolyn ended up head to head, and it had almost broken their bond. Kate had hoped that when she moved
to Georgetown, they would find a way to put the issue behind
them. A Friday night dinner at Sliders seemed like a good way
to get their issues on the table.

When Carolyn arrived, she descended on Kate's table with
her usual high energy. She was now the county-appointed
Riverkeeper for the Waccamaw and Pee Dee rivers, which con-
verged at Georgetown, along with the Black River, the San-
tee and the Sampit, to form Winyah Bay. On weekends, she
earned extra cash by guiding kayak and canoe trips along the
rivers for visitors to the coast interested in more than beach-
sitting and porch-rocking. Carolyn's company, Five Rivers, introduced them to the estuaries, where the fresh water rivers
draining southeastward through the Carolinas meet the rising salt tides of the Atlantic Ocean. She taught them about the
intricate food chains: dying spartina grass becomes food for
fiddler crabs, which are gobbled by mullet and puppy drum,
which are feasted upon by dolphin, osprey and bald eagles.
Along the way, she pointed out the lingering elegance of
Georgetown County's ancient rice plantations.

Carolyn was a pretty, athletic blonde whose candor and
take-no-prisoners humor kept even her friends off-balance.
When she rushed into Batten's Fish and Game to grab a cold
drink after a day on the river, the old men would look up from
their beers and video poker games, nodding and smiling. Even
the crickets in their wire and wood hutches seemed to chirp
a little louder. With two ex-husbands in her wake – both still
drinking buddies – she kidded that she was no longer looking

for Mr. Right, just Mr. Right Now.

Tonight she wore jeans and a tight blouse unbuttoned to reveal more than a hint of her breasts. As she sat down, Bobo appeared from nowhere. He had a smile in his eyes.

"Carolyn, I love it when you wear those Biblical outfits – low and behold, '*You Are The Wonderful One*,'" he said with a wink and a grin.

Carolyn picked up a napkin to throw it at him. He backed away laughing.

"Okay, that will cost me a free beer," he said. "What can I bring you two lovelies tonight?"

Carolyn ordered a Corona and a half-dozen raw oysters. Sliders boasted the best raw oysters on the Carolina coast, hand-picked straight from the oyster beds of McClellanville, a tiny fishing village 15 miles south of Georgetown. January and February had brought little rain to the coast, and the dry spell had improved the quality of the local oysters. It made them plumper, saltier, tastier. Some thought the dry weather gave the oysters a better "chew." Kate ordered crab cakes, Tabasco on the side, and a Corona. One martini was her limit.

Carolyn read Kate's glum face and gave her a sympathetic frown.

"Tough day with Judge Eyebrows, huh?" she asked. "Don't take it personally. He's never going to give a criminal defendant the benefit of the doubt. You're lucky he pretends to presume they are innocent. And we know he doesn't think much of lawyers who weren't born with the male equipment. Remember, the twentieth century hasn't dawned in all parts of South Carolina."

Kate gave her a small smile.

"He's a peach, I'll tell you. He asked me if I preferred to be called "Ms." or "Mrs." I almost held up my ring finger to show him it was empty. Good thing I didn't. He might have thought I was giving him a one-finger salute and put *me* in the jailhouse."

As Kate told Carolyn more about the day's hearing, the beer, crab cakes and oysters arrived. Carolyn squeezed the lime slice into the longneck, hooked her thumb over its mouth, deftly flipped it upside down, sending the lime slice to the bottom, then slowly righted it, all without losing a drop.

"Try an oyster," she urged. "They're great."

Kate grimaced, and pulled her brown hair back into a long ponytail. She looked younger than her thirty-four years.

"I've never been big on raw oysters," she said. "There are only two things I remember my father absolutely refusing to eat. Stewed okra was one. A raw oyster was the other. He always said he wouldn't eat anything so slippery it swallowed faster than he could."

Carolyn nodded and slurped down another milky oyster. Kate swirled the martini residue in her glass and speared the olive. She was clearly thinking hard about something, and Carolyn waited for her to break the silence.

Kate swallowed the last of her olive, then dove in.

"Carolyn, since moving here I've been thinking a lot about those paper mill hearings again. We had a lot of tension between us and never really worked through it. I think we should talk it out and get it behind us. Can we do that?"

Carolyn stared down at the Corona as though the label would give her the answer.

The conflict between them had started in the wake of mounting evidence that dioxin from the plant's bleaching process caused cancer. The federal Environmental Protection Agency had come down hard on the Georgetown paper mill, threatening to close it until it ceased discharging the chemical into Winyah Bay. The state's conservation groups – led by Carolyn – had joined that fight.

Months before hearings on the issue, Carolyn had bumped into Kate in a Columbia restaurant and talked with her about the case. Carolyn told Kate that the expert witness she had hired to help the Sierra Club was angry. His daughter – who had worked for a public relations firm helping the paper mill – had been fired from her job because of her father's criticism of the paper mill's management. The expert witness thought that was dirty pool.

Six weeks later, the CEO of Georgetown Pulp and Paper Company had approached Kate, told her he was unhappy with the law firm that was representing the company, and asked Kate to take over the case. It was the first time a big client had sought out Kate directly instead of one of her older partners. Being the rainmaker had increased Kate's stature in the firm, and she had worked day and night to get up to speed quickly on the case.

Midway through the hearings, Kate used the information Carolyn had shared with her while cross-examining the Sierra Club's expert witness. Kate then argued to the hearing panel that because of his daughter's termination, the expert witness had given testimony biased against the paper mill. Kate contended that the incident had colored his testimony and he should be disqualified as a witness. Kate won her point and the case. But the victory had almost cost Carolyn her job and Kate her close connection with Carolyn.

Carolyn finally looked up from the Corona label, her eyes guarded.

"Kate, I didn't understand then, and I don't understand now, how you could use that information against our witness, when I had not given you permission to do that," she said.

"That's not how friends treat each other. Maybe that's okay under your code of 'legal ethics' but it isn't okay under my code of friendship."

Kate could see the hurt in Carolyn's eyes, and thought for a moment before responding.

"Carolyn, you know that was a tough case. The plant was changing its bleaching process to eliminate the dioxin. And even though the EPA didn't like the amount of dioxin in the water, the paper mill's measurement showed it was within the federal limits."

"*Barely* within legal limits based on the *company's* questionable measurements," Carolyn said quickly.

"Yes, but still technically within legal limits. The key was I wanted the EPA to let the plant stay open while it put in the new equipment and keep those folks employed," Kate said. "It's not like there were a lot of ten dollar an hour jobs in Georgetown County."

"You're missing the point, Kate," Carolyn said. "You traded on the information I gave you as a friend. I don't understand why you don't see how wrong that is."

"That was information I got honestly and legally, Carolyn. You know that. I got it long before I was asked to represent the plant. I had a duty to use it to defend my client."

"I hear you," Carolyn said, drawing a wet circle on the table with the bottom of her beer bottle. "But I think that's a bullshit answer. Not using that information would have been unfair to your ambition, if you ask me. Look, Kate, I admire you, and we go way back. But I learned then that your friendship stops at your job. It was a tough lesson for me."

Kate poked at her uneaten crab cake with her fork.

"I don't know what else to say," Kate said, looking up. "I've told you before I'm sorry that happened. Can we just agree to disagree and move on? I'm out of that line of work now, anyway."

Carolyn sipped her beer and focused on her remaining oysters.

"Well, I can't say I'm sorry you left that big law firm. But I do wonder whether this criminal work really suits you," Carolyn said, shifting the subject. "Lord knows we could use you leading the fight against this phosphate mine. It's an environmental disaster heading straight at us - massive fish kills, no more blue crabs. Winyah Bay will end up like the Dead Sea. Senator Ravenel and his cronies are pushing it hard. We'll never beat it politically. It will take a hard-fought lawsuit to stop this thing."

She speared an oyster with her fork, dipped it in a bowl of drawn butter, and held it up.

"If that damn phosphate plant gets built, nobody will ever want to eat the oysters from around here again. I know these poor criminal defendants you've been representing need a good lawyer, but I wish you would focus on what you know best - only this time on the right side."

Kate knew where Carolyn was heading. They had danced around this issue ever since Kate had announced she was leaving her thirtieth floor office at the law firm. From that vantage point, Kate had been able to look west to catch a glimpse of the Congaree River as it flowed slowly past Columbia, and from her other window, she could view the majestic dome of the South Carolina State Capitol building. Neither the river nor the dome had changed much in the past hundred years, except that both were dirtier. Kate had begun to worry that the very companies she represented on environmental matters had contributed to the decline of the Congaree, and plenty of other rivers. When Kate had announced she was leaving her comfortable position at the firm, her colleagues had been shocked. She had explained she wanted a change – she wanted to represent people she felt really needed her legal skills. She wanted to be more like Atticus Finch.

Carolyn leaned across the table and caught Kate's eyes.

"Kate, our issues aside, I'd love to have you helping us on the phosphate fight. Why can't you? Maybe I don't even really understand why you left Columbia and came down here."

Kate took a deep breath and decided to offer Carolyn more.

"There were two reasons. When I joined the Devereaux firm in 1984," Kate said, "there were twenty lawyers, all men. The only woman they had ever hired fled after a few months of trying to fit in there. But it was the best law firm in the state, and I was determined to make it work.

"One of my father's best friends, Cathcart Cooper, was the firm's star trial lawyer, and he took me under his wing. He was the lawyer every client wanted on its side in court in a bet-the-company case. He knew I was a thorough researcher and a good brief writer, but he forced me out of that comfort zone. He hauled me into courtrooms all across South Carolina those first two years. He made me stand up and talk to judges and juries, with my knees trembling and voice shaking, until it got to be a natural thing."

"I met him a couple of times," Carolyn said. "He was the tall guy who wore the bow ties and smoked cigars, wasn't he? Didn't look you in the eye much?"

"Not until he had to," Kate said. "Like most trial lawyers he was a little quirky. He loved being in the middle of a complicated fight, with hard legal issues and unpredictable witnesses who might go either way. He taught me that most lawyers we think are good on their feet are simply well-prepared for every question that comes their way. He always found an angle on

his case that let him believe his client deserved to win. Once
he found that, he could look any judge or juror in the eye, tell
his story, and win them over almost every time. Even wearing
those damn bow ties."

She looked down at her plate and shook her head.

"I learned everything I know about trying a case from him."

"About five years ago Cart had a brain hemmorage while
whitewater kayaking. I had always thought kayaking was the
perfect sport for a trial lawyer. It was like physical chess - putting himself in danger just to prove he could get out of it.
But he couldn't outthink or outmaneuver the aneurysm. He
somehow managed to paddle himself to shore, but died that
afternoon."

Kate looked back at Carolyn.

"To this day, whenever I'm in a tight spot - in court or in
life - I think to myself: 'What would Cart do?'"

Kate's fingernail absently peeled the wet label from the
beer bottle in strips.

"After I joined Devereaux, I made a point of getting to
know every lawyer. I knew every lawyer's wife, or current girlfriend. Sometimes both. We worked hard and watched each
other's backs. We went jogging together, we played softball.
Sometimes we got drunk together. Before we merged with the
Phillips law firm from Atlanta, our firm had doubled in size,
but I still felt like I knew everyone there. But three years later,
we had 225 lawyers, and it was a different place. The managing partner in Atlanta brought in consultants who told us we
had to work harder, we had to bill more hours, we had to raise
our rates, we had to bring in bigger clients.

"They didn't tell us we couldn't do *pro bono* work, or serve
on bar committees or coach softball teams. They just took
away most of the time and energy we had to do those things.

They got us focused on who brought in the biggest new clients, who was managing the next merger, who billed the most hours. They wanted our associates to be like young Rumpelstiltskins, spinning billable hours into gold. I felt like I was measuring out my life in six-minute increments: one-tenth of a billable hour."

"You worked longer hours than all those guys with wives and girlfriends and golf partners waiting on them," Carolyn said. "I used to hear about that from our Columbia friends."

"Even in college, you reminded me of what folks said about my grandmother who grew up on a farm: 'Your idea of resting is hoeing in the shade.'"

Kate smiled.

"In my first five years of practicing law, I never heard the Devereaux partners argue about dividing up the profits," she said. "I heard a lot about that after we got big. Maybe my expectations were just unrealistic. I thought we had a great thing, practicing law and playing together. I guess it's like Camelot, lost in the ancient mists."

Kate stopped and watched the last of the shrimp boat mates come ashore for a night's rest before heading back out at dawn.

"I finally decided I was going to represent individuals who really needed my help and who might actually be grateful to me. But I'm not ready to do a 180-degree turn and start fighting the companies I used to represent. It's just too soon for that."

Kate's hazel brown eyes, almost golden in the early dusk and candlelight, looked away.

"Sorry about the filibuster," she said.

Carolyn finished her last oyster.

"And the second reason you left?" she asked.

Kate shook her head.

"It's about my dad. You know he died right after that dioxin fight. Just before he died, he told me some things that made me rethink how I wanted to spend my life. But that's a story for another day. "

The lights had come on in the bar and the restaurants lining the docks. Several yachts and sailboats, over-nighting in the bay as they made their way north from Florida, twinkled in the dimming day.

"I look forward to that day, Kate," Carolyn said. "In the meantime, I want you to know that I'm glad you're here."

"I'll be happier once I learn the ropes of this place and how to read Judge Jones' eyebrows."

"I want you to be thinking about this," Carolyn said. "We need you right now, right here to help us stop that phosphate plant. Remember what Thomas Jefferson said – we own the land only in trust for those who come after us. Arch Stewart and Cathcart Cooper would want you to be on the right side of this fight."

3

Wade McNabb

Wade Hampton McNabb leaned back so far in his battered wooden desk chair that its ancient spring moaned. It had been his father's chair when he had owned the *Georgetown Pilot*, and it had squeaked even then, despite liberal doses of 3-in-1 Oil. When Wade had purchased the foundering daily from the Brackett newspaper chain two years earlier, he had discovered the familiar chair in a storage room, cleaned it up, and eased it behind his editor's desk. He liked the way it fit.

Wade crossed his well-worn cordovan penny loafers on the corner of the desk and gazed across it at Sandy Anderson.

"What do you know so far about Senator Ravenel and this phosphate plant?" he asked the young reporter.

Sandy was an odd mixture of youth and tradition. At twenty-four, he occasionally sported the blue and white seersucker suit and bow tie of someone thirty years his senior. He was serious beyond his years. He had studied southern politics at the University of North Carolina and knew the subject cold from Ben Tillman to Jesse Helms, at least in an academic way. He was just beginning to learn how politics worked in the real world.

"Eight months ago, Carolina Phosphate Company applied to the state Environmental Resources Agency for a permit to start strip mining for phosphate on a 4,500-acre tract of land along the Waccamaw River about a mile and a half upriver from the bridge at Highway 17. Most of that is state-protected wetlands that can't be mined or disturbed."

"I know exactly where that is, about a thirty-minute boat ride from my house," the editor said.

"The usual suspects among the Green groups immediately started screaming," Sandy said. "The Coastal Conservation League, the Sierra Club, Wildlife Action, the Waccamaw River Keeper, the loggerhead turtle people – they all got their backs up. They pointed out the problems Carolina Phosphate had run into in Louisiana. They had air pollution violations and wastewater releases dumping thousands of pounds of phosphorous into the river every day. Really bad stuff for the food chain. The Greens say the mining in Louisiana released cadmium from the soil into the water there. That just about killed off the blue crab population, and it ain't so healthy for humans either. The algae blooms from the extra phosphorus sucked the oxygen right out of the water and caused massive fish kills. Created some serious concerns about eating anything that came out of that salty chemical soup."

"I have to admit," Wade said, "that I've hesitated a little these past few years before eating fish that came right out of this bay. That dioxin fight over the paper plant discharges gave me some pause. What are the phosphate folks saying?"

"The company and its P.R. folks have been pretty quick to get their spin out," Sandy continued. "The usual stuff – they have cleaned up their act since the Louisiana problems; they are bringing in 400 good-paying jobs with a $30 million annual payroll to one of the state's poorest counties; they would ensure we had good jobs *and* quality of life; it's a critical source of phosphorus for fertilizer, blah, blah, blah. Scaring off this company, they say, would send a bad message to potential new industries thinking about coming here. You know what they always say: stopping the plant might hurt the 'bidness' climate."

"The environmental folks have been fighting back hard," Sandy added. "They showed some pretty ugly photos of the company's phosphate strip mines in Louisiana at the public hearings last month. They brought in marine biologists who said the loss of wetlands and the phosphorus spills could disrupt the ecological balance of our whole bay. They said the company should be banned from mining in the wetlands and stick to the phosphate reserves further inland. The Environmental Resource Agency staff is still studying it."

Wade knew this was a tough issue for Georgetown. The waterside city already had a smelly paper plant and an ugly, aging steel mill. When the paper mill belched out its rotten-egg aromas, the beach tourists held their towels over their noses. And the dust from the steel mill left everything with a layer of red metal pollen every few days. You couldn't even read the water tower anymore – "Welcome to the 'Seapo t of orgtown' it looked like. Georgetown could use the phosphate jobs, but he feared it might be the last coffin nail for the waters of Winyah Bay.

"What do you think is going to happen with the permit?" Wade asked.

He walked over to the small refrigerator behind his desk and pulled out a Diet Coke. He held one out to Sandy, but the reporter shook his head.

"My sources in Columbia say the ERA staff is leaning hard against the permit, and the phosphate folks are pulling out the big guns to get it issued," Sandy said. "Carolina Phosphate is all over the ERA director Tripp Ravenel. The skinny is that he's determined to make the permit happen. I'm trying to find out who's pulling the strings, and his daddy – Senator Buck Ravenel – is right in the thick of it. It has the aroma of last week's crab bait, if you ask me."

Wade dropped his feet from his desk and leaned toward Sandy.

"What's the rest of your Friday afternoon look like?" he asked.

"It's okay," Sandy said. "I was hoping to meet with Kate Stewart, the lawyer who moved here a few weeks ago from Columbia. She's a different bird. She represented the paper mill in that dioxin fight a couple of years ago. I checked out those stories in the paper's library. But now she's doing criminal work down here. I've heard she thinks the local lawyers appointed to defend indigent criminals have gotten way too cozy with the D.A.'s office, not representing their clients zealously enough. Too much 'Meet 'em, greet 'em and plead 'em' going on. She's already managed to piss off some of the criminal lawyers here by raising that issue with the judges. I thought I should find out what's on her mind. But I take it she doesn't like reporters too much.

"When I asked her to talk with me, she flat out refused. She said good lawyers don't talk to the press. She said that lawyers tend to explain things in paragraphs, and reporters like to quote them in a sentence, over-simplifying everything. Seems a little prickly to me. Sounds like she got burned by the press somewhere along the line."

Wade looked at the ceiling and said nothing for a little while.

Sandy had worked at the *Pilot* for about a year and a half. It was his first newspaper job, and he had already figured out that a reporter learns a lot more when he's listening than when he's talking. Thoughtful silence and an attentive look are productive interviewing techniques. He sat quietly and studied some of the editor's favorite wisdom framed behind his desk: the First Amendment, all forty-five words of it. Over several beers one night, Wade had made Sandy commit it to memory. Beside it was a piece of calligraphy that read: "The duty of a good newspaper is to comfort the afflicted and to afflict the comfortable."

Sandy kept his own favorite quote typed and folded in his wallet as reminder of why he became a reporter:"The news is what somebody, somewhere wants to keep you from publishing. The rest is advertising."

"Sandy," Wade said finally, "you're a little young to know much about lawyers, so let me give you a few clues. The lawyers I've known are usually more clever than the average guy, and they know it. They figure out early on - especially the gun-slingers who make their living in the courtroom - that they have to out-think and out-maneuver the lawyer on the other side. They learn the art of smooth talk, saying just enough to make their point to the judge or jury without revealing something that will hurt their client's case.

"There's a lot of crap out there about telling the truth, the whole truth and nothing but the truth, but lawyers don't do it, and they sure don't coach their clients to do it. Lawyers are the masters of the half-truth. I've never had a lawyer lie to me as far as I know, but I've learned to listen carefully for what they choose *not* to say. That's usually where the trick is."

Wade gazed out his office window for a few seconds before continuing.

"And most of them can't help using that same way of thinking and talking in their personal lives. The really good lawyers I've known can make you feel like their best friend after five minutes of conversation. But don't ever mistake a lawyer looking for a favor for a normal person looking for a friend. In my experience, lawyers are usually just looking for an edge, an angle, a slight advantage they can leverage, trying to rearrange reality to suit their clients' needs. I don't know this Kate Stewart, but I doubt she's any different.

"Personally, I'm with Shakespeare – you know what he said: "First thing we do, let's kill all the lawyers.""

Wade took a deep breath.

"On the other, more practical hand, I've always found it mighty helpful, as a reporter, to have a friend with subpoena power and an interest in sharing. A lawyer like that beats the hell out of anybody's public records statute. Just remember, defense lawyers and prosecutors never share the secret stuff unless they think the publicity benefits them or their client. They always think they have the upper hand, that they are using us. But we have the final say – we don't have to print anything unless we think it ought to be out there for everybody to see. But sometimes, it's pretty damn hard to know who's zooming who."

Wade's mind seemed to suddenly switch gears. He stood up so quickly the wooden chair had no time to squeak.

"We're going on a field trip," Wade said. "Meet me at my house in thirty minutes. Jeans and boat shoes. No seersucker, no bow ties. We're taking a little boat ride up the river. Pick us up a beer or three, something ice-cold and domestic, none of that exotic stuff you say you like. Come on, I've got something you need to see."

4

Quid Pro Quo

Wade's house was a three-bedroom cabin his father had built in 1950 on a sandy bluff overlooking the Great Pee Dee River about a half-mile before it joins the Black River and flows toward the Highway 17 bridge into Winyah Bay. He had chosen the most scenic spot on the last ten mile stretch of the river. The property had once been part of an old rice plantation named Nightingale Hall.

After his parents died, Wade had left town and the house had been rented out for years. Upon his return to Georgetown, Wade had fixed it up and moved in. He had even restored the old tin roof. As a boy, he had played countless games of solitary baseball, tossing a hard rubber ball onto that roof, catching it as it ricocheted off at odd angles, announcing each hard-fought play in an excited sportscaster's voice. His team always won in a miraculous bottom-of-the-ninth play.

He had spent hours on the screened porch reading Sherlock Holmes stories and books about baseball and basketball, listening to the rain dance against that tin roof, like his mother's hard-polished fingernails tapping the kitchen table. In the years Wade had wandered the country working for different newspapers, he had never found a better spot for viewing sunsets than the porch of his cabin. From that perch on a westward-looking bend in the river, he had often watched the dark, tannic acid-stained waters of the Pee Dee turn almost purple just before the day's final slight earthturn hid the setting sun.

When Sandy arrived, they quickly loaded the cooler onto Wade's 15-foot Boston Whaler. Wade knew these rivers and the connector creeks between them as though they bore familiar street signs. Within twenty minutes, they had maneuvered from the Pee Dee, through Jericho Creek, and headed up the Waccamaw, 300 yards wide this close to its Winyah Bay mouth. The Waccamaw was deep enough to serve as the Intracoastal Waterway from the North Carolina border, sixty miles upstream, paralleling the coastline all the way to Georgetown. Ten minutes later, Wade slowed the boat and pointed out a long stretch of high ground, heavily wooded, on the river's west side.

"That's Wright's Landing," Wade said, popping a Budweiser. "You may have heard of it. Until the Civil War, it was part of Rice Heart plantation, one of South Carolina's most successful rice plantations. It was started in the early 1700s by Heyward DuBose. His father came here with the French Huguenots who settled a good bit of the Lowcountry."

The South Carolina rice culture had been brutal on the African slaves brought there to build and work the rice fields. Rice-growing was labor-intensive. It had taken one slave to cultivate two acres of rice as late as the first part of the 1700s. By 1730, the rice growers had begun building complex hydraulic systems of dikes, canals and floodgates that used the tidal flows of the coastal rivers to irrigate the rice fields. The remains of many of the canals and floodgates were still visible along the rivers.

Wade pointed out one of the old wooden floodgates to Sandy.

"Thousands of slaves died building these hundreds of miles of dikes and ditches out of the malarial mud. Once it was built, though, the new system was incredibly productive – one slave could tend five acres of rice."

As a boy, Wade had heard many of the romanticized tales about the glory of the old rice plantations and the brilliant men who ran them and made tons of money. It was only in college that he had learned the truth behind those lies. The English and French settlers had no history of growing rice before they settled in South Carolina and knew little about it. They learned most of what they knew from Africans who were captured in the Senegal-Gambia area of West Africa – where rice was the life-sustaining crop – and sold as slaves. The tidal irrigation systems introduced in South Carolina in the 1730s had long been used on those African coastal rivers.

The South Carolina rice planters had eagerly sought out slaves from that part of Africa for their rice fields. By 1775, almost two-thirds of the slaves arriving in South Carolina were from the Gambia area. By 1850, Georgetown County had a population of 20,000, and ninety percent of those people were slaves working on the county's 175 rice plantations. Until the Civil War, the white population of Georgetown County had the highest per capita income in the country. The only place in the world that produced more rice than Georgetown County was Calcutta, India. After the Civil War, the rice plantations died out quickly without the slave labor force to keep them productive. By the turn of the century, the rice culture was dead.

Wade pointed to a tall oak tree at the river's edge, about forty yards away. At its top was a three-foot tall, seemingly random jumble of tree limbs and sticks, bleached gray by the sun. Peeking over the edge of this unlikely nest were two fuzzy heads, baby osprey that had hatched just weeks before. One of their parents, a large, brown-winged, white-bellied raptor, perched on the edge of the nest, a freshly caught mullet in his talons. He began methodically feeding the babies, holding the fish down with one yellow claw and using his sharp, curved beak to peel off strips of fish flesh for the fledglings.

Wade slid the engine into idle and let the boat drift toward the river bank for a closer look.

"They are amazing birds," he said. "They return to the same nest each year. And they mate for life."

The fish hawks had almost died out in the 1970s because of the effect of DDT residues on their eggshells. With the banning of that mosquito-killing pesticide, the osprey population had recovered. The sight of an osprey's fluttering wings just before it began a heart-stopping sixty-foot vertical dive into the ocean after a mullet or Spanish mackerel was now common along the Atlantic coast.

Sandy reached into the cooler for a beer and glanced at Wade.

"Who owns the property around here now?" he asked.

"It's not easy to say exactly," Wade replied. "Right after the Civil War, Rice Heart's owner – the widow of one of Heyward Dubose's descendents – got religion on the slavery issue and gave several of her freed slaves this piece of high ground near the river. One of them was Isaiah Wright, hence the name Wright's Landing. Other former slave families bought up some of the adjacent land. All told, they accumulated around 750 acres. Twenty or so families, all descendants of the plantation's original slaves, still live here. Over the years, the property has passed from generation to generation, usually without the benefit of a will. Most of those children and grandchildren and great-grandchildren who inherited a legal right to some part of the property have scattered all across the country. Hardly anyone had clear title to any piece of property in the whole area.

"Over the past ten years, some of the community leaders have hired lawyers to try to track down all those far-flung owners and to clear up title to this 'heirs' property' so those who wanted to sell their interests could," Wade continued. "They have made a lot of progress, and there's a plan to develop some of the land for a marina and a riverfront community. It would make some of these folks pretty damn rich.

"Now look just north, up the river from here, near that line of tall pines running from the river westward as far as you can see. That's where the Carolina Phosphate land begins. If the permit goes through, the property at Wright's Landing won't be worth a damn thing," Wade said.

Wade cut the boat motor off. The sun was slipping behind the trees along the river, the wind had died and the water was calm. Wade didn't set the anchor, and the boat drifted slowly downriver with the current.

"What do you really think is going on with Tripp Ravenel and the phosphate folks?" Wade asked.

Sandy hesitated and looked away at the crab pot buoys bobbing in the brackish water.

"I think they are going to get their permit," he said finally. "Carolyn Brown and all the other environmental types say the fix is in, but they don't know any details. They think Carolina Phosphate owns both Ravenels, and that they can make this permit happen. They say money is changing hands somehow. I'm trying to find out how. I'm shaking the trees as hard as I can."

Wade scratched his chin for a few seconds, thinking.

"Bribery's a damn tough thing to prove in court," Wade said, "And it's even harder to write about it in a newspaper. The way it used to work was simple. Most legislators had a few natural buddies who were friends of folks who needed political favors. They might need help getting a highway paving contract, or a tax break for a utility company or some other damn thing before the General Assembly or a state agency. A lot of well-paid lobbyists were just that – longtime friends of powerful politicians, natural go-betweens.

"So when they ended up together at a Friday night dinner at the country club, or at a Saturday football game at USC or on a little boat fishing for bass on a Sunday, it all seemed pretty normal. And when that envelope full of crisp Benjamin Franklins changed hands at the end of the day, it was just a touch of the green salve passing between friends, soothing some of the pain in a sometimes hard and unfair life. A life of service to the public, after all. No witnesses, no records to trace. These days, a lot of it is right out in the open in the form of campaign contributions. And who's to prove that any particular decision gets made because of the money changing hands?"

"Well," Sandy said, "I guess sometimes you can prove the *quid*, and maybe you can prove the *quo*, but it's pretty damn hard to prove the *pro*."

"Smart people don't pass cash that way any more," Wade said, shaking his head. "The politicians get cut in on a business deal that no one can trace or their law firms get paid huge legal fees. That's what Chicago Mayor Richard Daly always said – 'Never bribe a lawyer, just send him a retainer fee.' Nobody needed to bribe Lyndon Johnson when he was in the U.S. Senate. They just made sure that all the advertising time on his wife's radio stations got purchased at handsome rates."

"I think that's exactly what's going on here," Sandy said quickly. "I understand that Senator Buck Ravenel's law firm is part of the phosphate legal team and getting paid big bucks. And the rumor is that Tripp is going to be well taken care of, too. I'm digging on this as hard as I can, but it's tough to get anyone to talk. Buck Ravenel might have some political enemies out there, but they don't want their footprints near any newspaper story about him. He's a powerful guy."

The boat had drifted almost back to the cut-through creek, and Wade leaned over to restart the motor. Trios of orange-beaked black skimmers were gliding silently along the top of the river's glassy surface in the twilight, mouths open, scooping up minnows and creek shrimp for dinner, leaving long, thin lines in the water behind them.

"That's a great story if you can get it," Wade said. "But that'll be tough to nail down. Go at it hard, but you need to be sure you get it right. We can't afford to screw this up. Don't make any assumptions. And remember what they say in j-school: 'If your mother says she loves you, check it out.'"

"Boss, you know I didn't go to journalism school, but I'm all over it, like kudzu on a junked car," Sandy said. "I promise."

"Well, right now, you're in the Wade H. McNabb School of Journalism, and you'd better not blow it," Wade said with a smile.

Sandy reminded Wade of himself in his mid-twenties: the enthusiasm and energy of a Boykin Spaniel puppy, but sometimes lacking the judgment needed to see the forest for the trees.

Wade paused before pushing the start button, and watched the skimmers for another few moments.

"Sandy," he said finally, "When I was in Chicago, one of our most experienced reporters bungled a big story on kickbacks on a state construction project. It took two editors a full day to craft a "we were wrong" to try to fix all the mistakes, a whole damn column down the front page of the Business section.

"I ran into the reporter at his going away party a few months later, deep into his third or fourth drink. He looked at me real sad, hung his head and said, 'I had always hoped I could get through my newspaper career without publishing a correction longer than my dick.' Not a great feeling."

Wade paused and seemed uncertain about whether to continue.

"You don't have any reason to know this, but my father lost this paper twenty-five years ago because he published things that pissed off some powerful people. It ultimately killed him. It ran me away from here for twenty years. I'm all for letting this paper speak truth to power, but when we do, we'd damn well better get it right. I'm not going to lose this newspaper again."

The motor cranked on the first try. Wade let it idle in neutral for a minute and stood in the boat looking around him.

"This is amazing country," he said. "Most of the life in the ocean starts right here, with the spartina grass, the fiddler crabs, the creek shrimp, the menhaden, the mullet, the tides that flow in and out twice every day. It's a complex life chain. You weaken it in too many places, and the whole damn thing might break down."

Wade took a slow, deep breath, inhaling the entire scene around him, pulling it into his body, making it almost a part of him. He shook his head, smiled and turned back to Sandy. "I'm never more at home than when I'm right here on this water. You know what Mr. Keats said – 'Oh ye whose eyes are vexed and tired, feast them upon the wideness of the sea.'"

"But let's get you home. You've got a lot of work to do."

5

Amici Usque Ad Aras

The late May sun in the blue Virginia sky was just warm enough to let Buck Ravenel peel back the canvas top of his silver BMW convertible. It was his kind of day – a Friday road trip, winding through the two-lane backroads of rural Virginia, headed to his prep school alma mater for a board of trustees meeting, his old friend Vince Stone, always good company, dozing just now in the passenger seat.

The board was set to consider admitting girls as students – ending the institution's century-old history as an all-boys boarding school. Most of the best boarding schools – Exeter, Andover, Groton, and even Westminster Forest's arch-rival Episcopal High School – had long ago made that change, and there was concern that Westminster was losing some of its best candidates to those schools for that reason. Vince was third generation Westminster, with his oldest son about to introduce the fourth generation the next fall, and the Raleigh lawyer was dead set against the change. He and Buck had discussed it for the first few hours of the trip. Somewhere near Fredericksburg, Vince had closed his eyes for a nap, and Buck navigated the final rolling hills, enjoying a quiet cigar, thinking about his years at Westminster.

He and Vince had met there in 1957 and had shared a dorm room their senior year. They had stayed close these last three-plus decades. Buck had not fully appreciated his parents' decision to send him away from his public high school in South Carolina, where he was happy and comfortable. His parents had first considered a military school, but a friend had steered them toward Westminster, a traditional boys preparatory school in the heart of Virginia horse country, along the Rapidan River between Charlottesville and Washington, D.C. Westminster Forest School had been founded after the Civil War by a Confederate soldier who had ridden with Captain John Mosby's fierce-fighting Partisan Rangers.

By the time Buck and Vince had arrived in the late 1950s, Westminster Forest had 250 boys in grades nine through twelve – "Third Form through Sixth Form," the school called it in the best British boarding school fashion. It had served as the grooming ground of choice for the sons and grandsons of this century's captains of commerce and industry in the Carolinas, Georgia and Virginia – the second and third generations of the New South entrepreneurs who had built the textile mills, the tobacco companies, the furniture factories, the export companies and the insurance and financial institutions, those striving families from Richmond, Charlotte, Charleston, Greensboro, Winston-Salem, Raleigh, Atlanta, Columbia, Savannah and Greenville, and from smaller towns like High Point, Fort Mill, Thomasville, Roanoke, and Aiken.

The boys came for different reasons. Some were sent to escape a bad situation at home – an alcoholic parent, a marriage on the rocks, a rough time at the local high school. Others were sent to experience a tougher discipline than loving but soft parents were willing to enforce at home. Most of these parents knew their children would get a better, more focused education that would help them make it to a good college, or, for those boys whose genes had been stretched a little thin over the last generation or so, into some college.

Most of all, these parents knew their sons would find the right connections at Westminster. They would meet the sons of other successful families and get to know them – in classrooms, on football fields and soccer fields and wrestling mats, in late night dormitory bull sessions, and on spring breaks and summer vacations. And these boys would know each other later – at the fraternity houses at Mr. Jefferson's University, at Chapel Hill, at Davidson, at Duke, at Washington and Lee. Some would venture to college or law school or business school in the Northeast and return to find their Westminster friends at *the* country clubs and driving clubs and yacht clubs back home. Along the way, they would meet the sisters and cousins of their classmates – attending Chatham Hall or St. Catherine's or Madeira – and invite them to the Fall Prom or the Midwinter's formal, dance with them, smooch with them, take them to football games, serve as their marshals at debutante balls and, if all went well, marry them, merge their assets, have sons who would come to Westminster and start it all over again.

* * * * *

Nothing young Buck Ravenel had ever seen in the South Carolina Lowcountry had prepared him for his first glimpse of Westminster Forest School. When the Ravenels set out from Conway on that mid-September morning in Buck's father's tightly packed brand new 1957 Buick Electra, summer's sultry heat still lingered. They spent that night in downtown Richmond at the John Marshall Hotel, the grandest establishment Buck had ever visited. He was so excited about this new adventure, he could hardly sleep. He was what his mother had always called "journey proud."

The next day, at mid-morning, as they turned onto the narrow road snaking through a canopy of oaks, black cherries, and maples, Buck noticed the hints of yellows and reds at the tops of the trees, autumnal changes weeks away in South Carolina. As the dark blue Buick rattled over the steel bridge joining the banks of the gently flowing Rapidan River, he could already feel a tinge of fall crispness in the Virginia air. Two sweeping curves later, they emerged from the woods, passed two brick entrance pillars and faced, 125 yards away, the three-story tall Walker Building, the school's main dormitory and administrative office. Built in 1899, its four massive Ionic columns set atop a story-high staircase radiated history and tradition.

The check-in, drop-off, unload-the-trunk, comfort-the-parents, and brave-goodbye routines were handled firmly and swiftly by the school staff, veterans at gently prying mothers' hands from boys' shoulders and, with confident, cheery smiles, assuring them their sons would be fine. By dinner time Buck was settled into his fifteen-by-eighteen foot room in a corner of Turner Hall with his new roommate, another first year student. Like Buck, he had no prior Westminster history to draw upon – no father or older brother or cousin or even hometown family friend to provide a little skinny about the lay of this new land.

Their room, like all Westminster rooms, was Spartan: two metal army cots with thin mattresses – the savvy quickly learned to buy sheets of plywood in town and put them under the mattresses to eliminate the inevitable sag of the wire screen supports. Two wooden desks, two chairs and two chests of drawers, two closets, a steam radiator and a trash can. It would be 1960 before fifth formers were permitted a radio, which on a clear night could pick up a station or two in Charlottesville. Sixth formers, as their reward for such patiently delayed gratification, were allowed record players that same year.

Buck quickly learned the school's inflexible regimen. Each day began at six-forty-five a.m. with the demanding clang of the dorm's wake-up bell, and there was hardly an unstructured minute until bedtime. The first year students – dubbed New Boys – were required to handle chores for the seniors. For those sixth-formers, New Boys were the next best thing to an English valet – New Boys were required to make up the seniors' beds when fresh sheets were distributed each week, and to sprint to the school store during study hall breaks for Cokes and snacks. While every student wore a coat and tie to meals and classes each day, New Boys were required to wear a black tie to signify their fledgling status. During the school's three "dance weekends" each year, New Boys won the privilege of wearing, for those brief shining hours, a "colored" tie.

Westminster Forest was not a military school, but it did impose a strict, usually unforgiving, routine and discipline that most boys' home lives did not. It taught a straightforward lesson. Life had certain basic requirements. They were non-negotiable, and there was no soft-hearted parent to whom one could appeal for sympathy or leniency. Some rules were truly absolute. A drinking scandal in the early 1950s had ushered in a new, tougher headmaster, Andrew Roberts, and a discipline code that made drinking or possession of alcohol a dismissible offense. Westminster Forest allowed no second bites at that apple. Violation of Westminster's stiff honor code – no cheating, no lying, no stealing – sent boys home for even technical violations, swiftly and with little due process. The teachers – "masters" in the prep school parlance – were required to enforce those rules upon everyone – New Boy or senior, football captain or dork – with neither malice nor sympathy allowed.

Classes met daily until lunch, followed by study hall, then

an afternoon of athletics. After showers, students were back into coats and ties and into the main dining room for dinner – that large, high-ceilinged room on winter evenings reeked of damp wool and Atomic Balm. Every night but Saturday, there were two hours of study hall, punctuated by a fifteen minute break. The school required students to be in their rooms studying or in the library, and for those two hours, the campus was silent. Study hall ended at 9:40. Students could use the next twenty minutes for whatever leisurely pursuit they preferred, but at 10 o'clock, third formers' and fourth formers' lights had to be out. Fifth formers could keep their room lights on until 10:30. Sixth formers could stay up as late as they wanted.

Saturdays brought a half morning of classes, and on non-football fall Saturdays, students could get "town permission" and catch a cab into Orange, a sleepy town of about four thousand souls. Diversions in town were slim – a trip to Grymes Drug Store to buy a copy of *Playboy* and deodorant and a visit to the tweedy clothing store Crafton & Sparks, where New Boys could look at brightly colored ties and dream of dance weekends to come.

It was mid-March of his senior year – the Saturday before Spring Break – when Buck had finally understood how the Forest network, and maybe all good-old-boy networks, operated.

Buck was the prefect on Turner Hall his sixth form year, a return to his New Boy roots. His roommate Vince Stone was an outgoing, never-met-a-stranger Greensboro native who was repeating his senior year after a losing battle with Zippy Zirkle's physics class. Zirkle's Physics Train had left the station the previous spring with Vince – never an ambitious student – standing trackside. Vince had thus joined the elite Westminster Century Club – that group of students who needed

more than four years at the school to earn their diploma. The
Century Club's group photo always appeared in the yearbook,
ironic and unexplained, along with the likes of the Investment
Club, the World Affairs Club, and the Audio/Visual Club.

Vince, as sports editor of the school newspaper his first
sixth form year, had achieved minor fame by quietly changing
the volume number on the front page of the newspaper from
LV (the fifty-fifth year of publication of the *Oracle*) to LXIX,
invoking the adolescent sexual humor attached to the number
69. Arthur Bunsome, the elderly English teacher who was the
faculty advisor to the newspaper – long-plagued with serious
eye problems and unable to read small print – distrusted the
students implicitly, as he had learned to distrust many of their
fathers decades earlier.

"You think you're clever," the chubby, white-haired bach-
elor would mutter under his breath. "But you're not, and neither were your fathers."

He required the student editors to read to him aloud all
of the editorials and satirical articles for pre-publication approval, demanding removal of anti-Westminster heresy and
phrases bearing scatological or sexual innuendo. Bunsome
had never, however, thought to check out the Roman numer-
als on the front page. It was weeks after publication of the first
Volume LXIX before a young faculty member had summoned
the courage to explain the prank to Bunsome. He promptly
banned *all* numbers except sports scores from the paper for
the rest of the year, and he checked even those carefully with
the younger faculty, adding them and rearranging the most
innocuous numbers in search of a sinister insinuation.

Vince had a strong Westminster heritage. Two uncles had
graduated from Westminster, and his father, also a graduate,
was a current trustee and chair of the school's capital fund-

ing campaign. Vince's grandfather – himself a Westminster grad – had built a successful photography business, taking and printing school photographs for nearly half of the public schools in eastern North Carolina. That business, handed down to his three sons, had boomed in the 1950s as even the poorest parents found the cash to purchase their children's annual school photographs. The Stones had shared their good financial fortune with both Westminster and the University of North Carolina at Chapel Hill.

The baseball diamond had brought Vince and Buck together the previous spring. This year, Vince was the returning starter at shortstop, and Buck had made the cut at second base. Vince's baseball hero was Luis Aparicio, the All-Star shortstop for the Chicago White Sox. Aparicio had gutted his way from Venezuela to the major leagues with speed, spirit and Spanish-flavored English. Vince admired Aparicio and played shortstop with the same hustle and abandon. Buck set out to emulate Nellie Fox, the Sox scrappy second baseman and an All-Star in his own right. Vince and Buck had spent hours fielding grounders on concrete-hard, orange clay infields, practicing double plays, seeking the perfect – quick but soft – toss across the bag and the clothesline throw to first, until darkness would steal the baseball and end the double play ballet. It was the essence of individual effort and teamwork: each had to field the grounders independently, but the toss and pivot depended on perfect timing from them both.

March in central Virginia is an unpredictable month. Sunny mornings can dissolve quickly to grey and damp afternoons, bringing a chill to outdoor events. A baseball caught in the palm of the glove instead of the web or fingers leaves a sting that is father to a bruise. A pitch mis-hit off the bat handle shoots an electric tingle from the pinky to the wrist, with a burn like a sharply banged funny bone.

Buck had decided to skip a late March Saturday's practice game and take a quick overnight trip to the D.C. area to visit his Uncle Bob and Aunt Sister, both school teachers in the Washington suburbs. On Friday afternoon after practice, he tried to persuade Vince to join him. Their senior year was quickly slipping away.

"Aunt Sister will cook us a big pot roast with rice and gravy and buttermilk biscuits. Maybe a little banana pudding. We can catch a movie, stay out a little late, sleep 'til noon. They'll get us back by dinnertime on Sunday."

Vince hesitated. He loved Aunt Sister's biscuits, and a little escape from the rigorous Forest schedule was appealing. But he was worried about falling off the Physics Train again. That just couldn't happen. His father would kill him.

"No," Vince replied, "I have a physics project to finish. Zippy has us doing an experiment to measure the mass of an electron. I've got to work on that Saturday night and Sunday. Otherwise I'd love to join you. Tell them I said hello."

Buck left campus after Saturday morning classes, sharing the cost of a cab ride to the D.C. area with three other students. It was great to see his aunt and uncle. Blessed with four brothers, Buck's aunt had been known her entire life simply as "Sister." Bob and Sister's children were grown, and the couple always showered Buck with attention. His Westminster-honed manners – now operating on automatic pilot – with 'yes ma'ams' and 'yes sirs' liberally scattered throughout his sentences, along with a tendency to stand up whenever any woman entered or left a room, still impressed other kids' parents.

It was just after 11 o'clock Saturday night - the roast aroma still reminding them all of a great comfort meal - when the telephone rang. Their oldest son had just checked into the hospital with appendicitis. They needed to drive to Charlottesville that night, and decided to drop Buck by Westminster on their way. It would be late, but he could let himself into Turner Hall even in the morning's wee hours.

Bob and Sister let Buck out just in front of the Walker Building. He had a short walk – about a hundred yards – back to Turner Hall. There was no moon, and the clear sky had let the day's sun-warmth escape, leaving a chilly but windless night. It was nearly 2:30 a.m. and the dorm windows were dark except for the occasional bathroom light left on for the evening. The campus was as silent and peaceful as a country cemetery. Buck was surprised to find himself thinking that he might actually miss this place next year. He had emerged as one of his class's leaders, but he had never become comfortable with the slight, unspoken social divide between students like himself whose parents had a decent income and students like Vince, whose parents has significant assets.

Buck let himself in the back door of Turner Hall, climbed the stairs and stopped by the bathroom. Heading to his corner room, he stopped just outside and undressed swiftly, hoping to slip into the room and into bed without waking Vince, a light sleeper. Vince had placed his "Quiet, Do Not Disturb On Pain Of Death" sign on the door before hitting the sack. That sign – and Vince's famously quick temper – usually won him all of the Z-stacking time he needed. Buck desperately did not want to be the bump that knocked Vince Stone off this year's Physics Train. He gave the doorknob a silent turn, slipped in the room, and shut the door quickly behind him, extinguishing the brief shaft of hallway light.

"OH MY GOD," came the distinctly female gasp from Vince's bed.

"Shh, shh, shh. Shit, shit shit," pleaded Vince's unmistakable voice, a North Carolina drawl barely accelerated by his sense of panic.

"Who the hell's there?" he hissed.

"Vince, it's me," Buck said. "What the hell is going on here?"

There was a stunned silence from Vince's side of the room. It was a good ten seconds before Vince's irrepressible social graces kicked in. Buck's eyes had begun to adjust to the dark.

"Buck, I'd like you to meet Marjorie Chandler," Vince said very quietly. "She's a senior at Orange High School. You know her brother Jimmy – he's a fourth form day student this year. Marjorie, this is my roommate Buck Ravenel, whom you have heard so much about. You know, the one who was not returning until tomorrow. Buck, you already know me. I'm Fucked. Maybe the prefect board will refer to me as Mr. Fucked when they send me home."

Buck could just make out the two bodies now sitting up on the single cot with a blanket pulled in front of them. A faint scent of a sweet perfume teased his nostrils. He nodded at Marjorie.

"I'm pleased to meet you," Buck said. He couldn't think of anything else to say. He felt a little odd standing there in his underwear, holding his clothes. Vince took up the slack.

"Marjorie, the cab is going to meet you outside the infirmary at 3 o'clock," Vince said. "It will drive up with its lights out and flash its parking lights once. What the hell, let me just walk on down there and wait with you. You gather up your things. I'm sure Buck will turn the other way for a minute while you get assembled. I'm very sorry about this."

Marjorie didn't say a word. She wiggled quickly into her skirt, buttoned her blouse, and pulled her sweater over her head, giving her short blond hair a quick comb with her fingers. Tucking a pint bottle of George Dickel bourbon into her large purse, Marjorie threw her shoulders back and slipped her arm confidently through Vince's. He, too, was dressed by the time Buck looked again. She was cool enough to give Buck a warm smile and look him right in the eye.

"Nice to meet you, Buck. Sorry if we scared you."

She looked over at Vince.

"C'mon, sweetie, let's go."

Vince peeked out into the hallway, walked down to the stairs, returned, and gave her a thumbs-up. And then they were down the stairs and out the back door without a sound.

Twenty minutes later, Vince slipped in the bedroom door.

"What the hell was that all about?" Buck said immediately. It was a difficult discussion to have in whispers.

"Don't you see the spot you've put me in?" Buck asked. "I promised when I agreed to be a prefect to enforce the rules here, at least the serious ones about lying, cheating and drinking. What do you think I'm supposed to do about turning you in for drinking and bringing a girl to spend the night in our room?"

Vince quickly displayed the verbal agility that would one day make him a highly sought after lawyer.

"Buck, listen to me. First, she was not spending the night. We had planned to take a blanket and fool around in the grass bunker behind the eighth green, but it just got too damned cold. Since you weren't here, I decided to sneak us into the room. And I'm not an idiot. I didn't have one sip of the bourbon. She brought it, and she drank some, but there's no way I would do something that would get me kicked out of here this close to graduation. I couldn't face my dad again if that happened."

Buck's eyes strayed to the two paper cups sitting on the edge of Vince's desk, near his bed. One was empty. The other still had a little brown liquid in it. He looked back up at Vince.

"Buck, she poured some for both of us," Vince pleaded. "I swear I didn't have even a sip."

Buck gave Vince a tired, sad look.

"You know that I have to at least bring this to the prefect board for them to consider," he said. "The whole board may agree with you, but they have to hear about it. How do we know that no one else saw Marjorie sneak in or out? What if she tells her brother about this, and it gets back to the prefect board? Then I get kicked out for covering for you."

"Buck, please don't take it to the prefect board," Vince begged. "There are some guys on there who will be gunning for me. We've butted heads for three years. They'll do anything they can to send me packing."

Buck thought about this for a few moments.

"I'll tell you what, Vince. I'm going to sleep. When I wake up tomorrow I'll think about it some more, and by tomorrow afternoon, I'll have figured out what I have to do. I don't want to talk about it any more tonight."

Buck slipped under his covers, plumped his pillow, and began his silent sleep-inducing mantra: he was lying on a beach just before sunset, facing a quiet ocean with small breaking waves on a rising tide. Heading south was a long line of brown pelicans, swooping low across the Atlantic Ocean, gliding inches above the outside shoulders of the slow-breaking waves. Buck started counting them backwards from one hundred – 99, 98, 97, and before he could reach 80 he was asleep. Just as leaning forward to sip water from the opposite lip of a glass always cured his hiccups, the backward count of pelicans always put him to sleep.

Vince was less lucky. He was still tossing from one shoulder to the other seeking the cooler side of the pillow when the sun pried its way around the thin bedroom curtains on Sunday morning.

After chapel and a quick brunch in the dining room, Buck changed clothes and headed to The Residence where Headmaster Andrew Roberts lived with his wife and two daughters. Buck knew the headmaster usually reserved Sunday afternoons to read the Sunday *New York Times* and hang out with his family. Buck hoped he could catch the headmaster before he settled in too comfortably. Within seconds after Buck pushed the doorbell, Mr. Roberts appeared, the Sunday *Times* crossword puzzle in one hand and a pen in the other. He was a confident crossword puzzle solver. He quickly read Buck's worried face, signaling a serious problem.

"Mind if I come in for a few minutes, sir?" Buck asked.

He has spent many hours in office chats with Mr. Roberts over the years – talking about college, about responsibility (and its often inverse relationship with popularity) and about the balance between discipline and spontaneity. But he had never visited the headmaster at The Residence.

"Come in, Buck," the headmaster said. "I could use some help on this crossword puzzle. There are sports references that escape me that you probably will know immediately. Can I get you a Coke?"

Roberts was forty-eight years old. He had been a successful Richmond banker. At forty, he had decided he wanted a different kind of life. He had accepted a position at Westminster, teaching history and economics and coaching basketball. When the trustees had realized two years ago that the school needed new leadership, they had quickly focused on Roberts. He was tall, decisive, grudgingly respected by the students and could hold his own with the board of trustees, a group of successful men used to getting their own way.

Buck and the headmaster sat down on the front porch, in a spot warmed by the afternoon sunlight and protected from any light gusts that might remind them of winter. Buck took a sip of his Coke.

"Tell me what's on your mind, Buck," the headmaster said, looking him right in the eye, and offering the tone of one willing to listen while reserving judgment. Roberts agreed with Scott Fitzgerald: reserving judgment is a matter of infinite hope.

Buck told him the story without omitting any details. The headmaster let him finish without injecting a single question. Then he asked just one.

"Buck, what do you think we should do?"

"I'm not sure, sir," Buck said after a moment. "I don't think Vince drank any of the bourbon. He said he didn't drink any. He didn't act like he had been drinking. I was close enough to smell it on his breath, and I didn't smell anything. He might not have even known she had brought it until she pulled it out of her bag. And I don't think having a girl in the dorm is a dismissible offense like drinking or cheating. I never even thought anyone would be brave enough to bring a girl to a dorm room."

Mr. Roberts doodled in the margin of his crossword puzzle, sketching elaborate geometric designs. He was clearly deep in thought.

"The rule is not crystal clear," he said finally. "It's hard to prove a student's been drinking, and that's why possession of alcohol on campus is a reason for dismissal. After all, we don't want to have to take blood samples to prove drinking. But I guess Vince would say he wasn't really in possession of it. I don't know. It's hard to say what the prefect board would do. They could decide to kick him out."

Mr. Roberts glanced at his watch.

"Make yourself comfortable for a few minutes. Let me make a telephone call."

He went inside.

Buck picked up the crossword puzzle. Except for a couple of obscure baseball clues, he made little progress in the thirty minutes the headmaster was gone. When Mr. Roberts came back through the door, he sat down across from Buck and pulled his chair closer, so that their knees nearly touched. He leaned forward, and his low tone implied that what he said was meant to be kept in confidence. Somehow Buck knew this was man-to-man stuff. Buck thought that if he were just a little older, Mr. Roberts would have poured each of them a short glass of whiskey.

"I just had a long talk with Vince's father," Mr. Roberts said gravely. "Things are not good in the Stone household. Vince's mother has a bit of a drinking problem, which has caused her to stray a little in her marriage. Vince's parents are about to separate – they have been holding it together until Vince graduates and gets to college. It's not a pretty scene there."

The headmaster tapped Buck on the knee, then leaned back like he had just had a bright idea.

"Buck, I think Vince would be a lot better off here, busting his hump to please Zippy Zirkle, than he would be going through the twelfth grade for the third time in Raleigh next year. Vince's father, I don't mind telling you, broke down and cried when I told him what had happened. He's afraid getting kicked out would crush Vince."

Mr. Roberts looked briefly over Buck's left shoulder at the Blue Ridge mountains in the distance behind the school's seemingly endless athletic fields, as green as youth itself. He took a long, slow breath through his thin, high-ridged nostrils, held it for a moment, then let out a loud sigh.

"Buck, let me suggest something. What say we give Vince the benefit of the doubt? We don't think he was actually drinking. We keep this incident among ourselves. Vince stays in school. You and I will keep him on a tight leash for the next two months. It will be the best thing for him."

Buck was a little torn. He wondered if the headmaster would have offered him as good a deal if he had been the one caught with his pants down and a bottle of bourbon beside him.

"I guess that works," he said finally.

He looked down at his hands and twisted the gold Westminster senior ring with the turquoise stone on his left ring finger.

The headmaster seemed to need more complicity than that.

"Buck, you've got to be comfortable with this. If you're not, I'm okay with you taking it to the prefect board."

Buck looked up, and the headmaster's eyes were locked calmly, unblinking onto Buck's.

Buck knew what to say.

"I'm comfortable with it, sir."

The headmaster leaned back a little in his chair, clearly relaxed.

"You send Vince up here this afternoon. I'll wear him out. And he won't know it, but this little tryst of his may help us pay for the new student theater. At the end of our conversation, his dad mentioned that he had been meaning to tell me that he and his brothers would make up any shortfall in the fundraising for that building. Right now we're about $250,000 short."

Buck thought, but could not be sure, that he saw the headmaster's right eye give him a quick wink.

"I'm going to tell Vince about our decision," the headmaster said. "I'm going to tell him that I wanted to turn this over to the prefect board and that they would have kicked his butt all the way back to Raleigh. I'll tell him that you argued his case for him and convinced me that he had not been drinking and that having this girl in the dorm room was not a dismissal offense. I'm going to tell him you saved his ass. He'll be grateful to you for the rest of his life, and you'll have a damned good friend when you need one."

The headmaster glanced at the puzzle sitting between them.

"I don't think you added too much here, though, Buck. Why don't you head back and tell Vince I'm up here waiting on him."

They stood up and shook hands. The headmaster tapped the Latin inscription on Buck's Westminster ring.

"And Buck, don't ever forget the Code of the Forest – *Amici usque ad aras* – Friends until the end."

* * * * *

As Buck Ravenel's BMW approached the Rapidan River Bridge, the dogwoods were shimmering white and pink on either side of the snaking road, and Ravenel could catch a hint of honeysuckle in the air. He straightened the orange and black bow tie he wore just for Trustees meetings and gave Stone a nudge.

"Wake up, Night Owl," he said. That had been Buck's nickname for Vince since their senior year dorm room incident.

"You don't want to miss the turn into the long drive and that glorious view of the Walker Building."

Stone shook himself awake quickly and gave Ravenel a big smile and a pat on his shoulder.

"Sorry I slept so hard. We still have lots to talk about. You still with me on the coeducation thing, right? I think we've got this deal wired, but I need your support on it."

Buck didn't hesitate.

"No Girls Allowed," he said. "At least for now."

"Good," Vince grunted. "And on the way back, we need to nail down a meeting to talk about the Carolina Phosphate permit. Can we set up a meeting with Tripp for early July? That's when the critical time is."

"Sure thing," Buck replied. "I'll set us up for a couple of days of fishing down at Bowman's Forest, right before July 4. We'll have plenty of privacy there."

They turned through the brick pillars and into the magnificent view of the school's main building, framed by an avenue of dogwoods in full bloom.

"You're a good man, Buck Ravenel. Thanks for being a good friend all these years. You always watch my back, and I appreciate it."

Vince reached over and held out his palm for a high five.

"Remember – *amici usque ...*"

Buck smiled back and gave Vince's hand a soft slap.

"*Ad aras.*"

6

Let's Kill All the Lawyers

Sliders was busy for a Saturday lunch hour, but Kate claimed an empty stool near one end of the bar, a quiet spot where she could eat a quick sandwich and read her newspaper in peace. She laid her copy of the *Pilot* on the bar and reached for a menu. Before she could pick it up, Bobo appeared. He leaned down, put his elbows on the bar and his face in his hands, looking right into her eyes.

"I only have eyes for you-u-u," he sang softly with a smile.

"I know that one, Bobo," Kate groaned. "The Flamingos, late 50s, great do-wop. And I bet you say that to all the girls."

"No, baby, only the smart and pretty ones who wear their hair in Saturday morning ponytails, like you. What do you want this morning? The best bloody Mary in town? Pancakes with fresh blueberries straight from my cousin's farm?"

"I want to try that world-famous BLT Carolyn Brown has been talking about. I'm beginning to think she has a little crush on you, the way she brags about your cooking."

"Ah, would that this were true, sweet Katherine," Bobo sighed. "As the late great Mr. Sam Cooke might say, she sends me. Alas, she seems immune to my charms. Hasn't stopped me from trying, though."

Bobo surveyed the restaurant, nodding at the mix of patrons. Several from the sailing crowd had docked the previous night in the harbor on their way up the Intracoastal Waterway, along with a few tourists who had heard Sliders was the Saturday morning place to be. One newlywed couple staying at a nearby bed and breakfast, having finally come up for air, was holding hands across the table and playing footsie beneath it, hoping the tablecloth would give them cover. The rest were mostly locals, hankering for their regular Saturday fare but curious about what Bobo may have cooked up special for this pretty June day. Bobo nodded at folks he knew, seeming to enjoy the gathering place he had created.

"Now about that BLT," he said, looking back at Kate. "Those tasty heirloom Cherokee Purple tomatoes are just coming in from John's Island, near Charleston. The Romaine lettuce is from my cousin's garden. The thick sliced, apple-cured bacon was sent to me by a fishing buddy in Montana, the best bacon I know, fries up so lean and crisp it just crumbles when you bite it. And the wheat bread was baked at Kudzu before the sun came up this morning. I'll toast it up for you, and if you don't love that sandwich, Bobo Baxter pays for it himself. How's that for a deal?"

She smiled at Bobo and handed him back the menu.

"Who could resist that?" she said. "Bring it on. And chips and a pickle on the side."

Bobo headed to the kitchen, and Kate thought for a minute about her morning run along the waterfront. She wondered if she was about to eat more calories than she had just jogged off. She lifted the USC cap from her head and smoothed her ponytail – still damp from her shower – through the loop in the back of the cap.

Kate turned to the *Pilot's* editorial page, and the headline on the editor's column caught her eye: "What Are They Hiding?" She folded the paper with a crisp pop, almost grazing the man who had just taken the seat beside her. The editorial chastised the Georgetown County Attorney for refusing to turn over environmental reports filed with the county by Carolina Phosphate Company. She had just read the part where the writer complained that the county was hiding behind a "legal technicality" in the public records law when Bobo reappeared with a BLT the size of a small flounder. He nodded at the man in the baseball cap sitting next to Kate and put the platter on the bar in front of her.

"Here you go, counselor. My modest opinion is that it's the best BLT in the known world. Now I don't really know much about the world beyond South Carolina and a few Montana fishing streams, but you tell me what you think, okay?"

"I will, I promise," Kate said. "The truth, the whole truth, and nothing but the truth. And I won't hide behind any 'legal technicalities.'"

She shook the paper at Bobo.

"Did you read this stuff? Listen to this: 'Personally, I'm with Shakespeare: Let's kill all the lawyers.' Maybe this guy should try actually reading a little Shakespeare. You know what they say about editorial writers – they come down onto the field after the battle is over and shoot all the survivors. They leave the heavy lifting to the ones on the firing line every day. Bobo, who does this pompous ass think he is?"

Bobo stood motionless, giving Kate a funny smile, a bright twinkle in his eye. He seemed very amused. He leaned down close to the bar and whispered loudly, for all around to hear.

"I don't know. Why don't we ask him?"

Bobo beamed at the man sitting next to Kate, who was turning slightly red in the face.

"And just who *do* you think you are, Wade McNabb, my good friend? And while you are thinking about your answer, I'll order up that Saturday pimento cheeseburger you like so much. I thought you two knew each other, but apparently not.

"Katherine Stewart, meet Wade Hampton McNabb, our local newspaper editor," Bobo continued with a smile. "Wade, this is Kate Stewart, the best new lawyer in town. I'll be right back. Don't start without me. I don't want to miss any of this."

Kate looked back down at the newspaper column spread out on the bar counter in front of her. The by-line on the column said "Wade McNabb." She squinted at the thumbnail photograph beside the by-line - a forty-ish man wearing a tie and a serious expression on his face. She looked back up at the man to her right wearing a white polo shirt and a baseball cap with a springer spaniel on the front. He was smiling at her.

Bobo stood a respectful distance away, his bar towel slung across his shoulder, observing quietly.

The man leaned his head sideways toward Kate, then looked up and caught her eye in the mirror behind the bar. He gave her a conspiratorial wink and turned his head toward her again.

"You are a very astute young woman," he said, nodding at the photograph beside the column. "Wade McNabb *can* be quite the pompous ass, but he takes a sabbatical every Saturday from that line of work. And if you are, as Bobo suggests, a licensed member of our esteemed South Carolina Bar, I hereby issue an immediate retraction: I was wrong. We should most certainly not kill all the lawyers."

He swept off his cap and held out his hand.

"My pompous ass name is Wade Hampton McNabb, of the late Civil War general's lineage. As late as we are in the current century, I just go by Wade around here. It's my job in this county to comfort the afflicted and to afflict the comfortable. The photo there of me - with all that dark hair - was taken before I had experienced these past couple of years of angry advertisers, readers complaining about my choice of comics and columnists, and brides upset because their published photos weren't as pretty as the young lovelies think they are.

"And truth be told," Wade added, "I was right proud to find that quote from the Bard to use as a kicker on my column. Shakespeare really did say that, at least according to Mr. Bartlett's wonderful book of famous quotations."

Kate's lips were smiling at him, but her eyes weren't.

"Actually," she said, "Shakespeare simply put those words into the mouth of one of his evil characters. The man's name was Dick the Butcher. He was leading a mob bent on destroying the rule of law and creating anarchy. Right after he urged the mob to 'kill all the lawyers,' they hanged a man for the simple crime of knowing how to read and write: 'Hang him with his pen and inkhorn around his neck,' they cried.

"I think journalists in particular might want to keep the 'kill all the lawyers' comment in its proper context. When the mob decides to replace order with chaos, the first two groups they're coming after are lawyers and journalists. You and me. That's what Mr. Shakespeare was trying to tell us."

Wade pondered that for a moment, sensing the frost on her words.

"Well, I guess it's possible I was gilding the lily a little there," he said, "I'll have to work on my Shakespeare."

Kate opened her mouth to speak, then seemed to think better of it.

She had once used the "gilding the lily" phrase in court. Cart Cooper had sent her a note later with the actual Shakespeare lines, gently chiding her, pointing out how the phrase really goes: "To gild *refined gold*, to *paint* the lily, to throw perfume on a violet, to smooth the ice is wasteful and ridiculous excess." That was what Shakespeare had actually written. She decided to let it pass.

Bobo arrived with a platterful of cheeseburger and hot sweet potato fries, and Wade busied himself with the ketchup and mustard.

Kate seemed about to say more, but she didn't.

"Actually, Carolyn Brown has told me about you, and I'm glad to finally meet you," Wade said a few moments later. "We're always glad to have some new points of view in this town. People here can get pretty set in their ways - especially that pompous ass Wade McNabb."

Wade leaned back to get a better view of Kate.

"Now, I'm curious about what lured you to Georgetown," he said, smiling. "The pace of life here is a little slower than the fast lanes of Columbia."

"An early mid-life crisis," she said, shaking her head. "I wanted a different kind of law practice, was tired of the business of big law firms. I decided I could start something different in Georgetown. I'm learning my way around the courthouse and trying to figure out how to read the local judges. I'm getting some small clients and learning about something besides environmental law.

"Some days I'm representing folks with traffic tickets - the ones who've had the iron in their blood turn to lead and settle in their right foot. I'm trying to get the word out around here that I know my way around a courtroom. I'm enjoying being on the side of David - I spent a long time representing Goliath."

Kate stopped and gave herself a mental kick for talking so much.

"And, anyway, it's beautiful here. How about you? Have you been here long?"

"I grew up here, but wandered away for a long time. Been back a couple of years. I love it here. I bet you will, too, once you learn the personalities and the quirks."

Wade finished his burger and sneaked a glance at his watch. He signaled Bobo for the bill.

"Kate, I've enjoyed the conversation, and I'm sorry I have to go. I promised to meet one of my reporters in a few minutes to talk about tomorrow's paper. It's not every day I get a Shakespeare lesson, plus a scolding from a pretty lawyer, all before lunch. I look forward to hearing more about your impressions of Georgetown."

He took both their bills from Bobo and swung down from his stool.

"Welcome to Georgetown. I'll pick up this tab in exchange for the writing tip, and I'll be sure Bobo gives us the local rate, not the confiscatory prices he puts on the menu for the tourists."

7

Bowman's Forest

Bowman's Forest was one of the most exclusive good old boys' clubs in South Carolina. Legislators, lobbyists, judges, and businessmen, older politicians with power and younger politicians with promise were invited there to shoot birds, fish a little, drink some brown liquor, tell stories and make each other laugh out loud. Political friendships were forged. "Bidness" interests lined up quietly with political aspirations.

If you were a regular at the Forest, you were part of the inside game.

In 1878, the Carolina Railway & Canal Company had purchased fifty thousand acres of sandy-soiled pine forest, just inland from Winyah Bay near Georgetown, fronting the Great Pee Dee River. William Mosby, CR&C's president, saw the sprawling forest as a ready source of fuel for the railroad's locomotives and a steady wood supply for replacing crossties and bridge supports. By the end of the century, when engines were burning coal and the use of wood preservatives decreased the need for replacing ties and wooden bridges, the new paper plants springing up across the southeastern coastal plain created a strong demand for pulpwood. That demand made CR&C's seemingly endless acres of pines a profitable investment.

In the mid-1940s, CR&C's President Mosby Bowman, William Mosby's grandson, turned twenty thousand acres of the land into a hunting and fishing preserve where he entertained the company's best customers, and softened up the federal railroad regulators and the politicians who looked after the railroad's interests. He built twenty-five two-bedroom log cabins and a two-story main lodge building with eight bedrooms, a spacious dining room and a kitchen. It had hardly changed in the five decades since then.

Bowman's Forest was a rustic paradise. There was no sign announcing the entrance off Highway 521 near Georgetown, just a turn-off to a gravel road marked by a street sign that read "Shad Row." A few hundred yards down that gravel road was an unassuming gate where guests were met by an always polite, but careful, guard who made sure the visitor was on the invitation list. Bags were dropped at the cabins and drinks served on the screened porch of the main lodge any time after noon, The welcome desk offered "white wine" – gin, vodka and vermouth – and "brown wine" – scotch, bourbon and brandy. Many nights you could find a Mason jar of clear, high test, untaxed corn homebrew. Folks in many parts of the Palmetto State still thought of corn as a whiskey bush.

Dinner had a distinctive South Carolina flavor. Shad roe – Lowcountry caviar – during spawning season, when that freshwater delicacy was available. That unlikely marriage of rice, chicken and sausage known as chicken bog. Pan-fried quail over grits. The quail were the real, wild thing, and you had to chew carefully to avoid breaking a tooth on a piece of birdshot. Venison steaks, fried bream and catfish, oyster stew, froglegs, McClellanville crab cakes, all served family style in the dining room on rows of polished wood picnic tables. The chief architect of these somehow elegant feasts was Dewey Wright, a 65-year-old Georgetown native whose dark black skin and Gullah-tinged speech marked him clearly as a local.

His friends knew him as Dew, and two generations of Forest guests had affectionately called him "Mr. Do-Right."

Gracing the walls of the main lodge's vaulted ceiling was evidence of the Forest's abundant wild game. Several twelve-point buck heads. A magnificent stuffed tom turkey – with tail feathers flared in full strut and a stiff ten-inch black beard protruding from the top of his chest. Over the two huge stone fireplaces, perfectly mounted quail and pheasant on the eternal wing. Open-mouthed bass and rainbow trout, the lures that tempted them still dangling in their lips. Near the bar, a bobcat and a red fox faced off, silently snarling at one another. A seven-foot long rattlesnake skin, black diamonds prominent, a fifteen-joint rattler still attached, hung just above the double doorway between the screened porch and the main dining room. Each trophy had a small brass plaque with the name of the conqueror and the date of conquest. Under one pheasant the tarnished brass read: Rep. Francis Marion "Buck" Ravenel, 1974. It had been Buck's first visit to the Forest, and his first term in the South Carolina House of Representatives.

The general rule at the Forest was "No Girls Allowed." But for special guests, some of Charleston's most accommodating late-night talent would arrive quietly around midnight and leave just as quietly before dawn. Years ago, some guests had made discreet evening visits to the Sunset Lodge just south of Georgetown, run by a no-nonsense madam named Hazel Wilson. Her young ladies were known for their country good looks and for their playful attentiveness. She required each of them to display a doctor's certificate of good health under the glass tabletop beside her bed.

Hazel had worked out the necessary accommodations with a succession of Georgetown County sheriffs. She hired no local girls, ran a quiet house with no late night brawls and contributed generously to the sheriffs' favorite charities, including their campaign funds. Patrons used only their Christian names, and Hazel kept no list of her clientele. Greenbacks were the only legal tender. Before her establishment closed in the late 1960s, the occasional visitor to the Forest, arriving later than anticipated, would explain with a wink that he would have been there sooner but had tarried in Georgetown to "catch the Sunset."

Whatever the nighttime revelry, at dawn the duck hunters were up and shivering in their duck blinds. The late night poker players who slept in could nurse their cigar-scented hangovers and still have a chance later in the day to head out with hunting guides. In one field, cleared of the corn and sorghum planted to attract deer, were several three-sided bird blinds, made from the metal doors of railway freight cars. In one of the blinds, two or three hunters gathered, shotguns ready. From another blind, one of the black gamekeepers would ask, "Gentlemen, what would you like to shoot today? South Carolina quail, Montana pheasant, or African chukka?" Then from the hooded cages at his side he would take the guest's chosen bird of paradise and on the loud count of three, throw it high over the side of his blind toward the center of the clearing, hear it flap wildly toward freedom, and wait for the thunderclaps from the shotguns.

For the fishermen, Mosby Bowman, who had spent much of his youth fly-fishing for rainbow and brown trout in the gin-clear mountain streams of North Carolina, had dug an artificial gravel-bedded trout stream. It ran for half a mile through the property. In the winter and spring, clear, cold well water was pumped through the stream, stocked with big-shouldered rainbows the size of small salmon. Except for the Spanish

moss in the live oak trees, it could have been a North Carolina mountain stream. For the devout trout fisherman this
was sacrilege, instant coffee instead of fresh-brewed. But for
newcomers to the art it was a thrill to see a twenty-inch streak
of silver and red flash from nowhere, splash at a white-winged
Royal Wulff and dive away, fighting, with the fly hooked in
the uppermost curve of what had once been the trout's smile,
stripping off fly line with a whine like a dentist's drill.

Whatever a guest caught or killed, he left on the cabin
porch when he headed in to shower and change. It showed
back up on the morning of departure, cleaned, dressed and
packed in dry ice in a cooler with the CR&C logo.

It was in these duck blinds, along that trout stream, on
those quiet cabin porches, that the necessary conversations
took place. Or maybe they never really took place at all, at least
in the memories of the participants. If anybody asked about
the visit, they chuckled and said they had shot some "buuds,"
drunk a little "likker," laughed too loud, and stayed up too
late, just cuttin' up. They didn't talk much about who they
were with, and they didn't recall promising to do anything
for anybody. But when these players, these strivers, those sure
of their place and those hustling to claim it, returned home
from the Forest, they knew what was important and what was
expected.

They understood the Code of the Forest.

And they all had ducks in their freezers.

8

Power and Influence

The baking July heat was just beginning to fade at 8 o'clock when Senator Buck Ravenel eased over to the bar at the end of Bowman Forest's dining room and asked for a glass of Knob Creek on the rocks. The bartender splashed a generous amount of bourbon over a few ice cubes and passed it across the bar.

The Senator was decked out in South Carolina summer casual dress: cotton khaki pants starched to a razor crease, a coral LaCoste polo shirt, polished cordovan penny loafers, no socks, and a navy blue blazer with shiny gold buttons adorned with his monogram: "FMR." He wore his RayBans on a Croakie around his neck, cheeks flushed from a full day of fishing in the sun.

Carolina Railway's chief lobbyist always took special care of Ravenel. When the Senator needed a discreet spot for a private meeting, the Forest was always his for the asking. And when it was available, Ravenel stayed in the private railcar of CR&C's former President Mosby Bowman, which was usually parked on the sidetrack just across the highway from the driveway into the Forest. It was the most private spot on the property, and the trysts that had occurred there were legend among the Forest regulars.

This weekend, Ravenel had arranged for a quiet meeting with his old friend Vince Stone to discuss the Carolina Phosphate permit.

The kitchen's padded door swung open, and Ravenel spotted Dewey Wright giving orders in the kitchen. Dewey Wright had worked at Bowman's Forest for more than twenty-five years. Born near Georgetown, he had finished high school there, then hired on as a dining car cook for the Carolina Railway & Canal Company. He quickly found he had a natural culinary bent. Within five years, he'd won every cooking contest the railroad sponsored for its cooks all across the southeast. Mosby Bowman had discovered him at one of those cook-offs, decided his shrimp and grits and his seafood chowder were the best he'd ever tasted, and made Wright the chef for his private rail car. For ten years, Wright had traveled all over the country with Bowman's luxuriously appointed personal rail car, cooking for his guests and picking up tips from other cooks. When Bowman retired in the early seventies, Wright confessed that he was a little tired of traveling himself. The head chef job at Bowman's Forest was open, and it was just what Wright was looking for.

Wright had watched two generations of business executives, railroad employees, politicians and their friends pass through the Forest, some to shoot birds and some just to shoot the breeze. If Wright was impressed by any of the big names who summoned him from the Forest's kitchen to praise his cooking, he never let on. His years on the railroad had given him a formal, somewhat dignified bearing. He treated everyone around him with a quiet respect and expected the same in return.

Ravenel waved the bartender over.

"Tell Mr. Do-Right his old buddy Senator Ravenel is here and wants to check on dinner."

The bartender disappeared and minutes later a tall, bald black man emerged, wiping his hands on his long white apron and smiling at Ravenel. Ravenel grabbed Wright's right hand with his own right hand, slid his left hand up to Wright's elbow, and pulled Wright's dark face close to his own, like a politician sharing a secret with a longtime supporter.

"How you doin', Dew?" Ravenel asked. "You lookin' go-oo-od. Stayin' trim. Must not be eatin' your own cookin'."

Ravenel leaned back and looked up at the taller man's head.

"Your hair ain't turnin' grey, but I think it might be turnin' loose."

Wright laughed with him.

"Well, the women still like this bald head of mine. They like to rub all over it. Say it brings them good luck. Maybe it's a look you ought to try," Wright grinned. "I hear you still like to chase the women, but they say you can't catch none."

Wright's slow and careful speech still contained a strong hint of his Gullah heritage. "Hear" came out like "he-yah," "that" sometimes became "dat." His words landed softly on the ear, like a cotton ball on spun sugar.

"All right, old man," Ravenel said. "Whatchew fixin' for dinner? I got a couple of fellows here never had the pleasure of your magic."

"Yessir, I'm gonna start off with a small helping of sautéed shrimp and grits. The shrimp came in this morning from McClellanville. They the big white roe shrimp. Sweet as a Maine lobster. I'll slice up some venison sausage and cook 'em with butter and garlic and just a little bit of hot pepper, then squeeze a lime on them. For the main course, fish stew. Got some fresh bream I've been cookin' in a tomato sauce. That tender white meat is just fallin' off the bones. For dessert, peach shortcake. Got O'Henry peaches from McBee. They my favorite, just started comin' in this week. And this dry summer has made the sugar rise right up in them peaches. Couldn't be no sweeter."

"Damn, that sounds better'n sex, Dew. Hell, I've probably just forgotten. Anyway, we'll be in the private dining room," Ravenel said. "Come in later and let me introduce you to some nice folks."

The regular bartender was attending a wedding in Charleston. Dewey's nephew was visiting from Columbia, and Dewey had put him to work behind the bar. Dewey had been a little hesitant about having him fill in, but he needed the help. The young man had no tolerance for the kind of off-color and sometimes racially tinged banter that passed among some of the Forest regulars and their guests.

"You just take the drink orders, mix 'em, deliver 'em, and don't make eye contact," Dewey told him. "Don't let nobody's glass get dry. No small talk. Just smile a lot and bob your head every now and then. Some of these guys still like that shit. Do this one for me, okay?"

Dewey thought he recognized two of the three men who joined Buck Ravenel at the bar: Tripp Ravenel, the Senator's son, and Senator Arthur Long, Chair of the Senate Finance Committee, and for that reason, almost as powerful as the state's governor. The other one, he didn't know.

Minutes later, Buck Ravenel led his afternoon fishing companions to the small round table in the pine-paneled private room at the back of the main lodge. Tripp had shared a boat with Senator Long. Over three decades ago, Long had introduced Tripp's parents to each other at a fraternity party at the University of South Carolina, was best man in their wedding, and when Tripp was born, became his godfather. Senator Ravenel's fishing partner had been Vince Stone. For the first fifteen years of his legal career, Stone had been a fierce, combative courtroom lawyer, but in recent years, he had played an even more important role as counselor to some of his biggest clients, helping smooth the way for their most significant deals. Stone's name seldom appeared in the newspapers, but he knew just about everyone who held important public office in the Carolinas and how to get them to return his telephone calls.

Just as they had taken their seats, there was a knock at the door, and Dewey Wright's smooth forehead poked into the room. Senator Ravenel waved him in.

"Guys," he said, "I want you to know that Mr. Do-Right here is the finest cook I've ever known. I can say that safely since Tripp's momma is not in the vicinity. Dew here, he could take some tough old tom turkey, nothing but bone and gristle, never eaten nothing but ugly bugs, cook it for a while in just the right sauce, and you'd think you were eating grain-fed pheasant raised for the King of England. This man is a kitchen magician."

Dewey Wright shook his head and tried to wave off the compliment.

"Gentlemen, when Senator Ravenel isn't in the courtroom or on the Senate floor, he feels free to stretch the truth just a bit. But I hope you'll enjoy your dinner. I think it's gonna be real good. The shrimp are fresh and sweet, and we caught the bream for the stew just yesterday, right out of those same ponds you were fishin' in today.

"I'm gonna have your dinner brought on out in a few minutes. Call me if you need anything."

Wright smiled and headed out the door.

"So that's why Art and Tripp didn't catch a damn thing all morning. Dew's boys caught all the fish," Stone laughed. "I thought Art had forgotten to tie a hook on his line."

"Just took us a while to get goin'," Long said. "We ended up with a good mess of fish, some bass and some bream. A few of those bream were right nice size, too, what we used to call titty-bream."

Long looked over at Vince.

"Vince, a city boy like you probably don't know what a titty-bream is, do you?"

Stone smiled and shook his head.

"When my boys were about ten or twelve, they'd fish in the pond behind our house. They'd take off their shoes and shirts and wade out as far as they could, trying to fish some of those deep holes with their cane poles. When they caught a smaller fish, they could hold it with one hand and unhook it with the other, avoiding that sharp fin on the back. But when they caught a real big one, the size of both hands, they'd have to clutch it against their flat little chests for leverage in order to get the hook out. I can see them right now, running back up to the porch and shouting, 'Daddy, Daddy, we caught us a big ole titty-bream!'"

Long leaned back in his chair and put his hand on Buck's shoulder.

"Buck, you ever told Tripp our bourbon story, how we ended up at Mary Baldwin College early one evening with a station wagon full of inebriated young women?"

Buck beamed at the thought of having an audience for one of his favorite tales.

"Let's see now, Art and I were freshmen at the University of South Carolina, and we knew a good many girls who were students at some of those fine Virginia schools. Sometimes we'd take a weekend road trip, hitting one college right after another. This one spring weekend, we met up with some lovely young ladies at Hollins on Friday night, drove over on Saturday night for a dance at Sweetbriar, and on Sunday afternoon stopped by to visit some sweet young girls we knew at Mary Baldwin.

"We'd all gone out for a picnic, and the girls were supposed to be back on campus at seven. But we had gotten a little bit lost, and I must say, there *had* been just a little drinking involved. At about 7:30, we came roaring up the driveway to the main administration building, ten of us squeezed into that station wagon. The girls were supposed to sign in at the main building. There on the outside stairway stood this tiny sparrow of a woman, her grey hair pulled back on her head in a tight little bun. She had thin, bony arms and tense, beady eyes peering over a pair of glasses way down on her nose. She had her clipboard clutched tight against her chest. My God, she had central casting 'Dean of Women' written all over her.

"She looked stern, like she had been on a diet of fresh limes. I bet she hadn't smiled hard in the last five years. Bless her heart, she looked like someone who had never had any fun, and wanted to be sure no one else had too much of it."

Long couldn't stand it and jumped in.

"I will tell you, that was one nervous group of boys and girls. I pushed Buck forward, figuring if anybody could talk us out of this situation, he could. He was really our only chance. He stepped right up, flashed those blue eyes at her and brushed his hair back from his forehead. He gave her that big smile and started talking."

"I tried my best to warm the ice," Buck laughed. "I said something like this."

Buck launched into full story telling mode, channeling himself back several decades.

'Ma'am, I need to tell you first and foremost that our untimely arrival this evening is in no way the fault of the young women your fine college entrusted to us. I was in charge of the vehicle. The simple truth is that we ran into several problems, ran low on gasoline, had trouble finding a filling station open on a Sunday afternoon in this *beautiful Virginia countryside. It is truly God's country, especially in the springtime, isn't it? Ma'am, I would ask you not to inflict any punishment upon these fine young women, because their late arrival is not their fault. I was in command of the car, and I am the one who failed them. I am prepared to take full responsibility.'*

Buck paused in his story and took a sip of the bourbon the waiter had just delivered to him.

"I could see that the Dean of Women – today she no doubt would be a criminal prosecutor, ice water in her veins, lasers for eyes, a goddam rock for a heart, happily seeking the death penalty for a misdemeanor – was wavering just a touch.

Buck mimicked her brittle, chilled voice.

'Where are you young men enrolled in school?'

"I told her we were all privileged to be students at Mr. Jefferson's University. But she was ready for me. She whipped a pencil from the top of her clipboard."

'I will have you know that I am very close friends with the Dean of Men at the University of Virginia. In light of the circumstances, I will need to report your names to him. Young man, what is your name?'

"Well, there we were. What could we say?" Buck said, smiling around the table at his three companions. "I didn't miss a beat."

'Ma'am, my name is Evan Williams. Allow me to introduce my companions. This gentleman in the burgundy sweater is George Dickel'.

"She immediately wrote down those names," Buck said.

'The one next to him, with the moustache, his name is James Beam. The one leaning against the car – don't slouch, Henry – is Henry McKenna, of the Richmond McKennas. You may know some of his people, fine citizens of the Commonwealth.'

"For a second there, I couldn't come up with a fifth name. Then I remembered my mother's brother Billy, who was *bad* to drink on the weekends, and my Aunt Tilly always hid his whiskey from him in her closet. I could see that bottle right before my eyes. I turned to the Dean of Women, gave her the biggest smile I had, pointed to Art and said '*And the gentleman wearing the Panama hat is Ezra Brooks.*'

"She carefully inscribed each of those names on her clipboard and advised me with no uncertainty whatsoever that she intended to report our names and the unfortunate circumstances to the Dean of Men at the University of Virginia and leave it for him to deal with us. Our lady friends, in the meantime, had slipped away to their dorms.

"I have always wondered what the Dean of Men at the University of Virginia – can you imagine, *the Dean of Men*? What century was this? – must've thought when he reported to him the names of what were most certainly his five favorite brands of bourbon. And to this day, Art here will occasionally refer to me as Evan Williams. And I have been known to address him as Ezra."

The easy banter hid the serious purpose of the evening. As the busboy removed the empty dishes from the table – with scarcely a trace of the fish stew remaining – Vince raised a hand toward one of the waiters, signaling for another round. Buck Ravenel waved him over closer.

"This occasion calls for something a little special," he said to the group. "Young man, would you be so kind as to take this key and retrieve from my locker in the bar the bottle of The Macallan and bring it back with some fresh glasses?"

Senator Long raised his eyebrows, caught Tripp's eyes and smiled.

"Damn," he whispered. "I love it when the big guys call out the twenty-five year old single malt, don't you Tripp? That's flying with the goddam eagles."

Buck Ravenel grinned at Tripp.

"And you can't put any ginger ale in this stuff, son. They don't even make branch water pure enough to mix with this scotch. Maybe an ice cube or two, but that's it."

When the bottle of scotch arrived, Senator Ravenel poured two fingers of his favorite drink into each of the four glasses. He slid their glasses to them across the table.

"There you go, boys, straight up. I learned a long time ago not to put water in another man's whiskey without his permission."

The whiskey and the stories – both well-aged – were political foreplay, easing the men toward the evening's more important business. Beneath the light-hearted banter, a careful calculation was about to unfold. With a nod from Senator Ravenel to Vince Stone, the talk turned serious.

"Here's the plan," Stone said once their drinks were freshened. "Next month Osprey Corporation will purchase 5,000 acres of prime frontage on the Black River for about five million dollars. The current owners can't do anything with it because they can't get permits to develop some of the wetlands areas. We are well-connected to the people who can make those permits happen. That's our added value. Osprey will hold onto the acreage for a couple years and then sell it to a developer once we've got those political issues worked out. It should be a prime high-end golf course community."

Stone looked at his old friend Buck Ravenel.

"You and Tripp and Art will be in on the ground floor of this one. It'll be a sweet deal for you," Stone laughed. "A great investment opportunity – no risk, high return."

His voice turned business-like again.

"Osprey is a North Carolina registered corporation. On the public documents, my secretary is the president, two of our paralegals are officers of the company and the three of them make up the Board of Directors. We aren't required to file anything that will show who the shareholders are. James Sullivan, the President of Carolina Phosphate, will own one third of the shares, I will own one third and a company called Bluefish, Inc. will own the other third."

Ravenel and Long were nodding slightly. Tripp's furrowed brow showed his puzzlement. His glass tipped a little in his hand and a rivulet of brown liquid edged down the outside of his glass.

"You better lick that up before it hits the table, or I will," laughed Long. "That elixir costs four hundred and seventy-five damn dollars a fifth. If there's a better scotch around, it's in heaven, or maybe hell, but it don't exist on this earth."

Tripp licked his hand, and could detect a faint scent of citrus.

Stone winked at Tripp and continued.

"Bluefish is a North Carolina corporation we organized last week. Same officers and directors as Osprey show up on the public records. Buck, you own one third of Bluefish, Tripp owns a third and Art owns a third. The names of the shareholders don't show up anywhere. So each of you will in effect own one ninth of Osprey Corp. and will get one ninth of any profits it makes. Here's how that's gonna work.

"Sullivan and I have each put $500,000 into Osprey so it will have cash for a down payment on the property. Some of our friendly bankers who want to see us build the phosphate plant on the Waccamaw near Georgetown have given us a pretty sweet loan for the other four million. Once we get the wetlands issues worked out, we think the Black River property will be worth three times the purchase price. So in two or three years, we sell it for fifteen million dollars or so to a developer who knows what he's doing. We pay off the five million dollars or so we have in it. That leaves Osprey with a profit of nine or ten million and each of you should get one ninth of that. If the deal craters, you've got no money in it and the only personal guarantee on those loans will be Jim Sullivan's. He's good for that and a lot more, so he's not worried. That is, he's not worried as long as Carolina Phosphate gets that permit for the Waccamaw project taken care of."

Stone glanced up, found Buck Ravenel's eyes and then Long's. Neither looked away.

He turned to the younger Ravenel.

"It's a done deal," Tripp said. "I've taken care of it."

Stone smiled and drained his glass.

"I knew you'd do the right thing. You got the genes for it," he said.

The bartender was waiting to see if they needed anything, and Stone waved him off.

"We wanted to cut Art in on this one, too," Stone said, nodding at the Senator. "Art, when you were student body president at the University at South Carolina we picked you out as a fellow who would go far. You're plenty bright, and you want good things for this state. But I've never thought that just because a man was committed to public service it meant that his children couldn't get a good education, and he couldn't share a little in the good life. I know that insurance business of yours has had a tough couple of years. I hope this gives you a good nest egg and that you take care of it."

Ravenel smiled at Long.

"Hell, we're probably gonna run you for Guv'nah one of these days, Art, if you keep your eye on the ball. I think you got what it takes. In fact, we might just put you up for the Light Gov spot next year."

Stone handed Buck Ravenel a manila folder.

"This has the shareholders' agreement that each of you

needs to sign for Bluefish. There's a chart that sets out the ownership of Osprey Corp, showing the three shareholders, including Bluefish. And then it shows who the owners of Bluefish are, and how we hope the financial end of this will work out for everyone."

"I'll look this over tonight," Buck said. "I'll have Tripp and Art sign it and give it back to you tomorrow morning at breakfast if that works."

"That sounds good to me."

Buck waved at the waiter, standing just outside the door, quietly waiting for direction.

"I'll have a nightcap, boys, if you don't mind," Buck said. "I wore myself out catching all those fish today, and kissin' a little whiskey helps my muscles rest. How about bringing us each a glass of port, young man, if you would."

The talk drifted back to stories. Stone told Art and Tripp about the time Buck had accidentally caught him in their room with a young woman at Westminster Forest. Thirty-five years later, the incident was drained of its tension, and the four of them laughed hard at Stone's story.

Stone downed the last of his port and rose.

"I'm leaving right after breakfast tomorrow, so I'm heading back to my cabin to pack and get some shut-eye. It's been a great day."

Stone singled out Buck and looked him in the eye with a mixture of affection and gratitude.

"Buck," he said. "You know you'll always have a friend in me. I'll always owe you."

Buck tipped his glass at Stone and smiled.

"*Amici usque . . .*" Buck said quietly.

"*Ad aras,*" Stone finished the phrase and nodded. "Friends until the end. That's the Code of the Forest."

"Vince," Long said, "If you're headed back, I'll walk with you."

Tripp waited while his dad sipped his second glass of port. He wasn't sure just how many glasses of brown liquor the Senator had drained earlier. Five or six, and two glasses of port, he figured. He always worried when his father had this much to drink.

"Son, I'm proud of you, you do know that."

"Yes, sir, I do. I just hope all this works out the way Vince says it will. I can't help but worry about how this would look if it all ended up on the front page of some newspaper."

"You worry too damn much, son. It ain't gonna come out. There's no way anyone can track this down because our names won't show up in any public records. Vince is doing this because it's his way of feeling good by doing something nice for an old friend. That's what friends do for one another in this world. They open doors of opportunity for each other."

Tripp had heard this refrain his entire life, and had never questioned it. It had certainly served him well. He had not been an ambitious student in high school, more focused on sports and on weekends than on his schoolbooks. A phone call from his father to a friendly trustee of Clemson University had opened a door that – on grades and SAT scores alone – had appeared to be nailed shut.

Tripp had majored in environmental science at Clemson and had gone to work right out of college at the Baruch Marine Biology Laboratory near Georgetown, on the old Hobcaw Barony land. He had made a name for himself on the environmental issues most relevant to South Carolina – air and water pollution. He had friends on the business side of those issues and on the environmentalist side, mainly because he was a straight shooter who paid attention to facts, learned the details of any dispute, tried to work with both sides, but ultimately stood his ground.

At twenty-nine, he had been appointed by the governor to be head of the South Carolina Environmental Resources Agency. There was grumbling on the editorial pages of a few newspapers about "nepotism" and "inheriting public office," but it had blown over quickly. Now, two years into the job, he was getting good marks for his handling of the agency. He had asked his dad once if he had gotten the job because he was the son of Senator Buck Ravenel.

"Well, of course you did," his father had told him. "Doesn't mean you weren't at least as well qualified as the other two guys that wanted it. They had some friends helping them out, too, you know. But you had me, and my Senate committee had a judgeship or two in its pocket that I'd been saving to trade in for just the right thing. This was it."

The Senator tipped back his head and downed the last few drops of port in his glass. He rubbed his chin and gave his son a serious look.

"Tripp, tell me now, you do have the wetlands permit for the Waccamaw phosphate property under control, don't you? Vince seemed a little worried, and he's got pretty good ears in state government."

"I've got it taken care of, Dad. The project manager assigned to handle this issue turned out to be a little rigid. You know what I mean – he just didn't see that there was room to bend a little and find some good middle ground. He worked up a draft report that was clearly coming out the wrong way. I gave him a good promotion, heading up my new "clean air" initiative, and we've got another fellow taking over the phosphate project. I deep-sixed the first report, and the new one will come out the right way. The new guy understands how this needs to work. Don't worry about it.

"All right, then, just keep your eye on the damned ball. I think we've got it wired, but we need to stay on top of it," Buck Ravenel said.

He leaned away from the table and smiled at Tripp.

"Son, I've been impressed by the way you've handled all of this. I like the way you moved that guy who wrote the first report out of the way to a better job. That was a nice touch. He's happy, you're happy. Vince is real damn happy."

Tripp smiled back.

"I have learned that there are two ways to get people to do what you want them to do," Buck said. "You can ask them nicely and try to persuade them, maybe offer them a carrot. Or you can be tough and mean and try to bully them. You don't know which way might work on that particular fellow, but if you do it in the right order, you get two bites at the apple. Always try nice first. Looks like that worked for you this time."

Buck pulled out his pocket knife and began cutting the end off of a fresh cigar. He had learned that democracy is not like they teach it in eighth grade civics class. It doesn't run like some automatic good government machine. It takes people who are willing to go to the trouble of busting their butts to get elected to office. A few of those folks really do it just because they believe the government ought to provide the most good for the most people. Goo-goos, Buck called them. But most folks get involved because they can get something out of it – usually a little personal power for themselves and their friends.

He puffed hard on his cigar, making it glow a bright red. He removed it from his mouth and pointed it at Tripp to emphasize his point.

"Getting elected to public office is a pretty interesting game. I figured out a long time ago that voters around here don't want to hear too much about big ideas. I always let the other guy talk about that. I talk to the people's hearts, not to their heads. I talk about the jobs I can help their sons and daughters get, the better schools we can provide for their children, and why I love this land of opportunity for every man and woman.

"Once you're elected, once you're on the inside, you come up against other folks who understand a helluva lot about getting and using power. For most of them, it's all about dollars and cents and how their piggybank gets full. Somebody's got to get the highway contracts and build the schools, and design these fancy new public buildings, and own the land where the next big beltway cloverleaf around Columbia or Charleston's gonna go. Politicians and the people they appoint decide who gets that work, who gets those chances to make a good buck. And guess what? The people who get those opportunities know they have to pay to play. Backs get scratched. Favors get returned. The memory of man runneth not to the contrary."

The brown wine had clearly loosened the Senator's tongue.

Tripp nodded, but somewhere deep, he worried about the culture of favors. When it had been opening a door of opportunity to give him a chance to prove himself up to the job at hand, it had seemed harmless enough. He'd never given much thought to the high school student who didn't get into Clemson because Tripp did, with a little help from his father's friends. But as the favors had gotten larger over the years, he knew the paybacks from him were getting larger, too. And lately, it was pretty clear that once you were in favor-debt, you couldn't say "no" to the next seemingly friendly ask.

Dewey Wright leaned back into the dining room, wiping his hands on his apron. The kitchen was quiet except for Wright's final tidying up.

"Senator Ravenel, I'd be glad to give you a ride down to the railcar when you're ready," he said. "I can take you now if you'd like."

"Dew, that would be fine," he answered. "But I can wait 'til you're finished. It will cost you a glass of port, though."

Ravenel thanked Wright for the fresh glass and sipped the port thoughtfully for a moment, taking the measure of his son. Tripp looked younger than his thirty-one years tonight. At fifty-three, Ravenel harbored a mixture of pity and contempt for those who tiptoed through life as though determined to leave no footprints behind.

"Tripp, you have to learn when to compromise to get what's best for the people who support you," the Senator said after a short pause. "Sometimes you make political trade-offs that make your head and your heart hurt, but you do it because in the long run, you get what you think you need, what your constituents need. Right now Georgetown County needs the jobs this phosphate plant will bring. As a bonus, it will help our friend Vince and his people. And they will help us a little. Every-dam-body wins."

The Senator lifted his glass of port toward the duck-head sconces casting a low light on the wall behind Tripp, and swirled the dark liquid, deep in thought.

"You will learn that the desire for money is a pretty common thing. We all want at least a little. But I learned something about myself a long time ago. For me, it's not the money I like so much. When I was younger, I thought it was power that I liked, being able to make people do what I wanted.

"I love it when there's someone in this state who needs a favor, and they come to me and ask for my help, and I can make it happen. It might be their son whose heart is set on law school and needs a boost. It might be a nephew who has got-

ten into a scrape with the law in some little county and needs
a break. It might be a company like these phosphate folks who
need a little help with a state agency. I like it when people ask
me to help.

"And what you need to understand is what it's taken me
years to learn. It is *influence*, not power, that really provides
the grease to get the right things done. I don't lean hard on
the Dean of the law school to let that young man in. I call the
trustee I appointed ten years ago, and he figures out just how
to approach the Dean. I don't have to call the solicitor in that
little county and suggest he exercise a touch of prosecutorial
discretion and reduce the charge for that nephew. I call the
state senator in his county who helped the solicitor get elected
last time, and he'll know the best way to make that suggestion.

"Power is a blunt instrument. No one can use it well for
long. It gets those who use it into trouble sooner or later. Eventually they step over the line, force a result that is too wrong
or too harsh not to be dragged into the sunlight. Influence is
more subtle. It operates at the edges where our political system
lets those in the right positions exercise their discretion. There
is room in the political system for a certain amount of body
English."

He looked right into Tripp's eyes.

"Son, in the end, it's all about having the right connections. That's what life is really about."

The Senator drained the last of his port.

"I've spent twenty-five years sharing my good fortune with
others because having a network of friends and allies depends
on it. I've never been greedy, and I've put many other folks in
positions where they have influence of their own. Men who
think they have power are reluctant to share it. People who
understand *influence* know it's a system of sharing. It's kept me

connected to the world in so many ways."

Tripp nodded at his father, wondering if his father would recall this port-induced, rambling soliloquy in the morning.

"Okay, Dad. Let's go to sleep. I've signed the papers Vince left with us. So did Art. They're in the folder on the table. Let me take you back to your room."

"Nah, Tripp, you go on to sleep. I'm going to sit here in the quiet, have another half-glass of this fine port and finish my cigar. My buddy Mr. Do-Right will get me back to the railcar. Good night, son."

9

Sandy's Source

Sandy Anderson let the door to Sliders swing shut behind him, straightening his bowtie and letting his eyes adjust from the bright August sunlight to the restaurant's cool shadows. He nodded at Bobo Baxter behind the bar and searched the booths along the far wall. He thought he spotted the man he had arranged to meet here – a young African-American whose eyes were already fixed on Sandy.

Sandy gave the man – he looked to be in his mid-twenties, Sandy thought – a brief wave, then headed toward the bar. He could hear Bobo muttering to himself under his breath, as he often did.

"Bobo," Sandy said, "I'll take a Heineken. And, by the way, you're talking to yourself again."

Bobo didn't look up. He reached into the cooler for an iced mug and stuck it under the wooden tap handle.

"Sometimes that's the only intelligent conversation I get all day," he said, smiling more to himself than to Sandy. "Have a seat and I'll bring your beer over in a minute."

Sandy made his way over to the corner booth.

"Don't get up," he said, as the young man rose slightly from the booth's padded cushion and shook his hand. "I'm Sandy Anderson. There's no formality at Sliders, and certainly none with Sandy Anderson."

"Bill Wright," the young man said coolly. He leaned against

the tall wooden back of the booth and took a slow sip of his iced tea. From that spot he could see everyone who entered Sliders front door.

Sandy tossed his blue and white seersucker jacket onto the seat and slid in across from Wright.

"Thanks for meeting me here," Sandy said. "Hope I haven't kept you waiting."

"Not a bit. This is a safer spot for me to meet you than Columbia would be. And I have family in Georgetown, so I can hang out with them while I'm here."

"You know," Sandy said, "I've thought a lot about your phone call last week. I'm very interested in learning more. This is a very important story, especially for folks here in Georgetown."

Bobo Baxter leaned down and put an icy Heineken in front of Sandy.

Baxter's sautéed shrimp with Andouille sausage, served over Carolina Gold rice from Georgetown's only working rice plantation, was his signature dish. The snacks at the bar were Ritz crackers with homemade, jalapeno-laced pimento cheese and – the beer drinkers' favorite – bowls of fresh boiled peanuts. The peanuts were wet, salty and tricky for the inexperienced to eat. He called them South Carolina escargot.

Baxter placed a bowl full of them between the two men.

"You guys need anything else?" he asked. "If you do, let me know. I've got some fresh dolphin that came in off the boat yesterday. I'm grilling it in a lime and dill sauce, real simple. It doesn't get much fresher than this."

"Thanks a lot, Bobo," Sandy said. "I think we're okay for now."

Sandy turned back to Bill Wright.

"What made you call me last week?" he asked.

"When I saw in the Columbia newspaper that the Environmental Resources Agency had approved the permit for the phosphate plant on the Waccamaw River, I knew I had to call somebody about this," Wright said. "Folks I know in Columbia have told me before that you've paid more attention to this issue than anybody in the state. I've checked out what you've written. It's been pretty much down the middle –harm to the environment versus good jobs and all that kind of stuff. But you are really missing the political angle. And that might be the only angle that counts in this deal."

Wright looked around the room, checking out the faces at the other tables. He took a deep breath, put his hands on top of the table, leaned forward and spoke quickly in a low voice.

"I have some interesting stuff to tell you. I'm a paralegal with a law firm in Columbia. I can't afford to be mixed up in this. It could cost me my job. So I want you to promise that you won't tell anyone where you got this information. If you can promise me that, I think I've got something you might find valuable."

Anderson looked around and assured himself that no one could hear them.

"Well, I definitely want to know what you have to say. And you need to know that it's tough to publish a story these days based just on a confidential source. I can make you that promise now, but we may have to talk a little more about this if I want to be able to persuade my editor to put what you tell me in the paper."

Wright leaned back, stroking his chin and studying Sandy.

"The people you are dealing with are very powerful," he said finally. "I'm just a paralegal, trying to save money, hoping to get into law school one day. If my name came up in this, I'd lose my job in a heartbeat, not to mention any chance I might have of getting into law school in Columbia."

"This could put you in a tough spot. What's in it for you?" Sandy asked.

Wright eyed him calmly.

"You newspaper guys don't have a monopoly on wanting to do the right thing," he said. "I don't like the way this decision went down, and it's not right. And I do have a stake in how this turns out. If the plant gets built, all that property at Wright's Landing along the Waccamaw might as well be a garbage dump. I don't know what that property is worth to my dozens of cousins and me if the title to that land got cleared and it was developed into something nice. But I do know this – it won't be worth shit if this plant gets built there."

"Okay," Sandy said. "I won't tell anybody but my editor Wade McNabb where I got this information. It doesn't go any further unless you give me specific permission."

"You can't tell *anybody else*, not your editor, not your lawyer." Wright said. "The legal community in South Carolina is pretty damn tight. Most of them went to law school together and gossip like teenage girls. Information has a way of getting around, and this whole stinking mess involves lawyers."

"I have to tell McNabb or the story goes nowhere. That's his rule. But just the two of us, nobody else."

Wright sipped his tea and popped a boiled peanut into his mouth. He cracked open the shell, sucked out the salty water, pulled the wet nuts out with his teeth and dropped the shells back in the bowl. He seemed to be pondering his options.

"Is McNabb a straight-up guy? Can I trust him?"

Wright looked Anderson dead on, and the reporter didn't flinch.

"Straight as they come. And he's tough as tree bark. He's a guy you'd want in a foxhole with you."

Wright looked away, staring in the distance, conducting his

own calculus on the risks of talking further. When he turned back to Sandy, he gave no hint of doubt.

"Well, then, here we go," Wright said.

He took another glance around the room, then leaned forward and lowered his voice.

"I've got two stories to tell you. The first one is about a conversation I heard at that railroad hunting lodge outside of Georgetown the first weekend in July. I was bartending there, helping out my uncle – he runs the dining room there. It was a Saturday night, not too many folks at the lodge. Four men were having dinner back in the private room off the dining room. I was going in and out, getting drinks, bringing in food, clearing out plates, shuffling all around, you know, like a good colored boy."

Sandy looked at Bill Wright's eyes and couldn't tell if he saw humor or anger. Probably both, he decided.

Sandy pulled his skinny spiral reporter's notebook out of his jacket pocket and began scribbling rapidly. Some reporters still called them "Sitton" notebooks. Legendary *New York Times* civil rights reporter Claude Sitton had taken the spiral-topped stenographer's notebooks he had always used and cut them in half lengthwise so they fit in his inside suit pocket. That way he didn't stick out so much as an out-of-town reporter when he was covering the civil rights movement in Alabama and Mississippi in the early 1960s.

"I heard them talking about the phosphate plant on the Waccamaw River and how the plant had to get approved," Wright said. "That caught my attention because I'd been following this thing. I heard my uncle say that night that one of the men was Tripp Ravenel and the one that looked like an older version of him was his daddy Senator Buck Ravenel. I heard one of the other men say he worked with Carolina Phosphate. I didn't catch the fourth man's name. I heard them call him 'Senator.'"

"Now, I didn't hear all of it, but I was in the room a few times. You know, to most white folks, black people are still invisible, especially when we're serving them. It's like they think we're too dumb to understand what's going on.

"They told some stories about drinkin' and women, just some guy talk. There was some conversation about ospreys and bluefish.

"The youngest guy there, Tripp Ravenel, said that somebody in the wetlands section of his agency had written a draft report on the phosphate permit that came down against it, but he had gotten rid of the guy who wrote the draft, got him a promotion or something. Tripp Ravenel said that he'd be sure the permit got approved. He said it was taken care of – a done deal. Then the Phosphate guy talked about some property all these guys were buying together, some kind of sweet deal for the Ravenels and the other guy. I heard the Phosphate guy say something about – 'great investment, no risk, high return,' and they all laughed. He said the key to the investment was getting the permit for the phosphate plant. They talked about signing some papers, and who would own how much of some company."

Anderson nodded and knew to stay quiet as long as Wright was talking.

"Oh, yeah, later the Phosphate guy said something to Senator Ravenel about some kind of code of the forest. I didn't have a clue what that meant."

"Second story. There's a group of guys I play basketball with Friday afternoons at the YMCA. One of those guys works in the Environmental Resources Agency. I asked him casually that next week if he knew anything about a shake up in the wetlands division there. He thought about it a minute and said that a man named Frank Myer had been recently promoted out of that division. He said he remembered there'd been some raised eyebrows about that, but he didn't know any details.

"I called the Myer guy the next day, and when I asked him about his promotion, he sounded scared to death. He clearly did not want to talk to me about it. I gave him my name, told him where I could be reached, and why I was interested in the wetlands issues. He said he did not want to talk about it at all. I figured that would be the end of it. But, a few days later, I received in the mail a plain brown envelope, with no return address. Inside was a copy of a thirty-page report on the Waccamaw River site for the Carolina Phosphate plant. It was written by Frank Myer. And it was dated June 15, two weeks before the meeting down at the Forest.

"That report – it was marked "DRAFT" at the bottom of each page – concluded in no uncertain terms that the phosphate plant should not be built on the Waccamaw site because it would hurt the water quality and the wildlife on the Waccamaw and in Winyah Bay. I called Myer two or three times to see if he had sent it to me, but he never returned my phone calls."

Wright drummed his fingertips on the table top.

"So, Clark Kent, that's what I know," he said. "What do you say?"

"The timing is interesting," Sandy said. "I heard in late May that there was an agency report recommending against issuing a permit. About that same time, I heard that Buck Ravenel's law firm was helping Carolina Phosphate with its project. You say the draft report was dated June 15. The dinner you are talking about was the first week of July. The ERA announced the granting of the permit on August 1. This does begin to add up. Could I have the copy of that draft report?"

Wright gave him a tight smile.

"I'm sitting on a copy of it right now. When I get up to leave, it'll stay right here. You can say you found a copy with your seat-of-the-pants reporting techniques. But you didn't get it from me. You found it somewhere, right?"

"Bill, let me ask you this. How did you know who the men at that dinner were?"

"My uncle told me who the Ravenels were. He's worked at Bowman's Forest for twenty-five years, and he knows the regulars. He and Senator Ravenel are old shit-swapping buddies. And I heard one of the guys – I think they called him Vince, but I didn't catch his last name – say he was with Carolina Phosphate. He was a tall guy, maybe mid-fifties or so, in good shape, sort of distinguished-lookin', polished-lookin'. The fourth guy was another Senator, but I didn't get his name."

Wright hesitated.

"I want to keep my uncle out of this. I didn't talk with him about what I heard in the dining room. This could screw up his whole life."

Wright started sliding to the exit side of the booth.

"I paid for my tea already," he said.

He stood up and glanced quickly around the room, satisfied that there was no one there who knew him.

"Good luck, Mr. Anderson. You do the right thing."

Then he walked away without looking back.

Sandy slid over to Wright's side of the booth and picked up the envelope. He sat for several minutes reading the report. He jotted down comments in his spiral notebook, filling in a few spots as he remembered details Wright had told him.

Bobo Baxter came over to pick up the bowl full of empty peanut shells.

"Sandy," he said, "I couldn't hear what y'all were talking

about, but it looked pretty damned serious. You be careful. Remember that Marvin Gaye line: *'Believe half of what you see, son, and none of what you hear.'* Pretty good words of wisdom, 'specially for somebody in your line of work."

Sandy pulled on his suit coat, slipped his notebook into his inside pocket, and tucked the envelope under his arm. Heading for the door, he thought he could hear from the jukebox, faint and in the distance, the low, bass beginnings of "I Heard It Through the Grapevine."

He smiled, changed direction, and walked over to the bar, signaling to Bobo. Sandy leaned over and spoke in a low voice.

"Don't worry, old buddy-ro. You know what they say in the newspaper business: If your mother says she loves you, check it out."

He winked at Bobo.

"I'll be careful."

10

The Story

Wade McNabb leaned back in his desk chair and stroked the back of his head, reading Sandy Anderson's draft of the phosphate plant story.

> Six weeks before the South Carolina Environmental Resources Agency granted Carolina Phosphate Company its permit to strip-mine phosphate along the Waccamaw River, the ERA staff had recommended that the agency deny the permit, citing "extraordinary potential" for harm to local wetlands and Winyah Bay's water quality.
>
> Frank Myer, the ERA staffer who wrote the June 15 report, was transferred to another ERA job in late June, the *Pilot* has learned. Myer did not return numerous phone calls from the *Pilot*.
>
> The *Pilot* obtained a copy of the June 15 report from a source last week. When the newspaper subsequently requested a copy of that report from the agency, it was told the only report in the agency's possession was a July 20 report recommending approval of the permit. It said any prior drafts would have been discarded in accordance with agency records retention policies.
>
> ERA Director Marion "Tripp" Ravenel said the June 15 document was a preliminary working document

which did not address fully all of the issues critical to the decision-making process.

"Any preliminary draft is just that," Ravenel said. "It's an early document designed to get all of the issues on the table. It's not meant to be a final decision. I think you are blowing the significance of this document way out of proportion."

Citing personnel privacy laws, he would not comment on why Myer was transferred to another job immediately after writing the June 15 report opposing the issuance of the permit.

Opponents of the phosphate plant claimed the sudden reversal smacked of political influence overriding the ERA staff's decision.

"This is South Carolina cronyism at its worst," said Coastal Conservation League director Charles Pinckney. "There's a huge conflict of interest in Tripp Ravenel making this decision directly affecting his father's client's business by tens of millions of dollars. You have to wonder just what Senator Buck Ravenel's fee was for all this."

The June 15 report included the following comments in a section labeled "Conclusions:"

• The plant should not be built in the wetlands area;

• Locating the plant there is likely to result in significant phosphorous discharges into the Waccamaw River and into Winyah Bay, leading to massive fish kills;

• Strip-mining of the phosphate reserves in the wetlands area could release cadmium from the existing soil and endanger the area's crab and crustacean population.

The "final" July 20 report notes these issues had been raised, but that marine biologists working with the ERA had determined that the impact on the water quality and marine life would be minimal if the company followed state-of-the-art mining and water treatment techniques.

Carolina Phosphate officials have vigorously lobbied state and local officials in seeking approval of their permit request. Those efforts included a private dinner in early July at Bowman's Forest near Georgetown where a Carolina Phosphate official met for several hours with Senator Buck Ravenel, Chair of the Senate Judiciary Committee and Vice Chair of the Senate Appropriations Committee, ERA Director Tripp Ravenel and at least one other state official, the *Pilot* has learned.

Neither Senator Ravenel nor his son Tripp Ravenel would comment on whether such a meeting occurred. Carolina Phosphate also declined to comment.

The *Pilot* has learned that during the dinner the Ravenels discussed with the Carolina Phosphate official a possible private business investment opportunity that would be "no risk, high return." Both the Ravenels and a Carolina Phosphate spokesman denied that the company has discussed any business investments with either of the Ravenels.

"It sounds to me like you've got some bad information from some of the wild-eyed opponents of this plant who will say anything to prevent these

good jobs from coming into our community,"
Sen. Ravenel said this week. "I greatly resent the
implication in your story that the agency's decision
to grant this permit was the result of some kind of
payoff to me or my son from Carolina Phosphate.
I hope you talk to your lawyers before you publish
this story."

McNabb read the article twice, making notes in the mar-
gins with a red pen. Sandy Anderson sat across the desk from
McNabb, nervously clicking his ball point pen and re-reading
his own copy. When McNabb finally looked up at Anderson,
he wasn't smiling.

"Does your source have a dog in this fight?"

"He's got at least a puppy," Sandy said. "His name is Bill
Wright, one of the dozens of heirs to the property at Wright's
Landing, that big bluff on the Waccamaw River you showed
me a few weeks ago. If the plant goes in, the property won't be
worth much. He told me that right up front. He didn't have to."

McNabb was in full serious mode now, no kidding around.

"Have you been able to verify that the Ravenels were at
Bowman's Forest on the night of July 1?"

Sandy had prepared himself for just this type of cross-examination.

"I did a Freedom of Information Act request for Senator
Ravenel and Tripp Ravenel's travel and mileage expenses since
May 1. Both have their expense reimbursement requests current through the end of July. And guess what? They both got
payments for travel on that weekend to Georgetown. Doesn't
say where, just says 'legislative strategy meeting.'"

"I also called Bowman's Forest and talked to their administrative office. The young lady there very coolly explained
that they were a private institution and did not give out the

names of their guests. So I struck out there.

"I left messages for Bill Wright's uncle, who runs the dining room. He never called back."

"What have you been able to find out about this 'investment opportunity'?" McNabb asked.

"All we know is what Bill Wright told us. Carolina Phosphate's public relations folks are adamant that the company is not involved in any kind of investment with either of the Ravenels and threatened to sue us if we reported that it is involved. I've checked out the Carolina Phosphate organization chart from their annual report, and I can't find any person in a high level position whose first name is Vince.

"Well, I've heard loud and clear from Tripp Ravenel and from Buck Ravenel," McNabb said with a long sigh. "They both say we've got it flat wrong. And they both told me to be sure I had plenty of libel insurance if we suggest that they are on the take from Carolina Phosphate. The Senator said he was looking forward to owning the *Pilot*."

McNabb doodled on his copy of the story, thinking.

"So, it's our confidential source against all that. I guess this is gut-check time," McNabb said.

He stood up from his chair and paced around the room in silence for a minute. Then he looked back at Sandy.

"Okay," he said. "I need to meet your source. Get him up here tomorrow."

*   *   *   *   *

At mid-afternoon the next day, Bill Wright met Sandy in the Piggly Wiggly grocery store parking lot. Wright locked his car and slipped into the passenger seat of Sandy's Honda Accord. They headed inland to McNabb's house on the Pee Dee

River, where McNabb thought they would have more privacy.

Ten minutes later the three men were seated at McNabb's breakfast room table. A draft of the story, the June 15 report and a banker's box of manila folders holding Sandy's months of research on the phosphate plant were spread out on the table.

McNabb took the measure of Bill Wright. He interviewed him gently, learning about Wright's family. Wright's dad had worked for a few years as a first mate on a shrimp boat operating out of Georgetown, sometimes moonlighting as a bartender for private parties. His boat had traveled as far south as the Florida Keys in search of its sometimes elusive prey. When the steel plant had opened in Georgetown in the late 1960s, he went to work there. When the unionized workers went on strike in 1970 to protest the safety conditions, the other men had looked to Bill's father for guidance. But Jimmy Wright had been killed in a hit and run incident while walking by himself along a stretch of highway near his home. Many were convinced it was an ambush by strike opponents. A federal investigation had never solved the mystery.

Bill Wright had been a decent athlete at Georgetown High School and won an academic scholarship to the University of South Carolina. A political science major, he had not applied to law school right away because he needed to save money to attend. Instead he landed a job at one of Columbia's large law firms as a paralegal and had worked there for the past four years, sending some money home to his mother and saving some for law school.

McNabb's confidence in Bill Wright grew as he heard his story. Finally, he quit interviewing him and turned to the matter at hand.

"Bill, we have published hard stories before. The First

Amendment protects newspapers because it's important in this democracy that somebody hold our elected and appointed officials accountable. Newspapers have a duty to do that, but powerful people like Buck Ravenel know how to push back hard. They control a lot of levers of power, and they can afford to hire damned good lawyers. Hell, Ravenel even controls the appointments of all the judges. So, we need to keep our eye on this ball and be sure we've got our facts right.

"And I have to say," McNabb continued, "Ravenel's a likeable man as long as you don't cross him. He's been more progressive than most on racial issues, he's been strong on education issues. And he can gin up his charm when it suits him. I've seen it work on voters, and I hear it works on jurors. Now, tell me what you remember about that evening at Bowman's Forest."

Bill Wright didn't hesitate, but he spoke carefully as he recounted in detail what he had told Sandy.

McNabb was back in his cross-examination mode.

"Did you call Sandy here because you stand to profit if the phosphate plant gets stopped?"

"That's a good question," Bill said. "I'm not sure I'd stick my neck out so far on this if my family wasn't going to get screwed by this plant coming in here. But it's also the fact that this is my home, too. The Wrights have lived on the Waccamaw River since we were slaves growing rice for the white folks here. We earned this land and shouldn't have to give it up because these politicians think it's a good idea for them and their friends."

"Let me ask you this, Bill," Wade said. "If we print this and Ravenel or Carolina Phosphate sues us, we will defend it to the hilt. But if they come back and say there was never any dinner and never any investment deal discussed, we will need you to back us up. I'll make you this deal – we'll go with the story as it is. If we get sued, we protect your identity unless the judge orders us to identify you. If that order comes down, we need to be able to identify you as our source and have you tell the judge and jury what you've told Sandy and me. Can you live with that?"

Wright drummed his fingers on the table and popped the joints in his neck from side to side.

"I hear what you're sayin', man. You're risking your skin, and you need me to risk a little bit of mine, too. So, you don't put my name in the story. If you get sued and the other side asks you in a deposition who your source is, you're gonna refuse to give me up. Only if the judge orders you to identify me, that's when you need me to step up and tell my story. Have I got that right?"

"You got it cold, Mr. Wright," Wade answered.

Wright walked over to the window and gazed out at the river flowing by in the dusk. He bowed his head slightly, resting his forehead against the windowpanes, eyes closed. The two minutes of silence slowly filled the room right up to the corners of the ceiling, making it hard to breathe.

Finally, Wright turned back to the other two and met their eyes.

"I can't do that," he said finally. "I'd never get into law school if they found out. It would ruin me and it would ruin my uncle's life. Everything I've told you is absolutely true. It's up to you whether you want to publish your story or not."

He caught Sandy's eyes straight on and held them hard. Then he looked at McNabb.

"But publish or not, Mr. Editor, I expect you both to keep the promise Mr. Anderson made me earlier."

11

The Lawsuit

Vince Stone greeted Buck Ravenel just inside the tall double doors of Carolina Country Club.

Stone led the unhappy Senator to a quiet corner table in the club's Grill Room. A copy of the Sunday edition of the *Georgetown Pilot* was tucked under Ravenel's arm. When the two reached their table, he tossed it onto the tablecloth in front of Stone. Stone calmly folded it over and pushed it to the side of the table.

"Buck, I read it last night," Stone said in a soothing tone. "It's not that big a deal. Remember, this is just a story in yesterday's newspaper. They publish another newspaper every damn day, and people will forget about this one by tomorrow. It's just a blip on the screen, the crisis of the day."

Ravenel didn't hear a word Stone said.

"Who in the name of hell do you think leaked this shit?" Buck asked angrily.

"Buck, keep your voice down a little, okay?" Stone said, patting the Senator's forearm. "This really isn't as bad as you think it is."

"That's easy for you to say, sitting up here in Raleigh," Ravenel said. "Your name's not plastered all over the pages of every major newspaper in South Carolina, with everybody assuming you're a goddam crook."

Stone stayed cool, nodding at Buck.

"Who do *you* think leaked it?" Stone asked.

"First thing this morning, I had Tripp pull the telephone records of that guy Myer who wrote the draft report. There's no indication he ever telephoned Sandy Anderson, or any other reporter for that matter. Tripp grilled his ass this morning, and he's convinced that Myer had never even heard of Sandy Anderson before today. Tripp asked him for permission to get the telephone company to turn over his home telephone records, and Myer agreed to that on the spot. He doesn't seem to have anything to hide."

"I assume plenty of people could have had access to an early version of the report on the agency's computer system," Stone said. "That doesn't worry me so much, and it's something Tripp can explain to the press. I'd be more worried about the comments relating to the investment opportunity."

"Nobody in that room at the Forest had any incentive to breathe a word of this," Ravenel said. "When that reporter called me and asked me to comment on all this last week, I was almost paranoid enough to think maybe somebody had bugged the private dining room, but I know that's impossible. And, I guess if they did, we would've seen a lot more detail than this story has."

"Buck," Stone said. "One possibility occurs to me. We thought about cutting Chip Brantson in on this deal. He bird-dogged some key tax rebate issues through the Senate for us the past two sessions, and I floated this deal by him to see if he wanted in. But he's a such a damn Boy Scout. He's so honest you could play poker with him over the telephone. And his wife's family is so rich he doesn't need the money anyway. Her momma's people owned all that land near Kiawah Island before the Kuwaitis developed it. You know what they say: 'You can marry more money in thirty minutes than you can make in thirty years.' Chip sure did."

"You're right," Ravenel said. "Brantson's got all the coin he's ever gonna need. He's like old Scrooge McDuck, just sitting in his money bin, counting his dollars every day.

"And Brantson would love to see me squirm," Ravenel said. "He's been wantin' to chair the Judiciary Committee or move ahead of me on the Appropriations Committee. He's an uncommonly ambitious man."

"Buck, I think we need to leave this alone," Stone said. "This will blow over and the newspaper won't be able to dig up the details. They can't trace the ownership of the companies, even if they knew about the purchase of the property. You're the only one who's got a copy of the shareholders' agreement and the summary sheet, right? And if we need to, we can substitute in our files new documents that don't mention you guys anywhere. In fact, I'll take care of that today. Your fingerprints won't be anywhere to be found. We'll wait a few months and do a different deal."

Ravenel thought for a moment, waiting for the waiter to take their iced tea orders.

"Yeah. I didn't give copies of any of that stuff to Art or Tripp," Ravenel said.

He scanned the elaborate descriptions on the menu. Beef tenderloin medallions, topped with sautéed Chesapeake lump crab and artichoke hearts. Fresh strawberries and whole cream. Thick lobster bisque with a touch of sherry. Waiters talked all around him in soft voices, deftly dropping warm cheese biscuits on bread plates, offering black napkins for those wearing dark suits or skirts to avoid a deposit of white lint.

A trim woman in a white tennis dress spotted Vince from the doorway across the room, shot him a cheery smile and gave him a big wave. As she approached, Ravenel calculated her age as mid-forties, but he guessed she could still fit into her high school cheerleader outfit with no trouble. Vince noticed the light tan line on her right wrist which usually wore a sparkling David Yurman bracelet. As Vince half-rose to greet her, she swept down and planted an antiseptic kiss in the air in the vicinity of his cheek.

"Hello, Darlin'," Vince said with a warm smile and his best Conway Twitty bass drawl.

"Can't stop to talk, handsome," she chirped. "The ball machine is waiting for me, just wanted to say hello."

She smiled at Ravenel, and when his face didn't register and Vince didn't introduce him, she turned brightly back to Vince.

"I know you must be into some serious business talk here, so let me go."

She lowered her voice a little.

"Now, I am so pleased that sweet wife of yours is chairing the Terpsichorean Club deb ball this fall. Last year's was a bit of a disaster, and I think the chair was just *a teeny bit* over her head, bless her heart."

Ravenel smiled to himself at that most southern of incantations. Adorning a critical comment with that gentle phrase let one disclaim all malice toward the object of the observation. As in, "Bless her heart, I'm not sure that bathing suit fits her anymore."

"Angela will be just great," she continued. "Tell her I'm happy to help. I know these things don't just happen by themselves, not if they are going to turn out *just right*."

She scrunched her eyes and gave him another lightning-white smile and a pat on the hand.

"So good to see you, Sug-ah," she said.

Then, with a whirl of her blonde hair, she was gone, her tennis dress swishing behind her.

Ravenel could never fully understand why his visits to Carolina Country Club left him feeling vaguely ill at ease. Everyone certainly seemed, well, very nice. The dining room looked like an Easter egg basket – well-tanned men and women in pink and green and white and robin's egg blue polo shirts, lots of starched khaki pants, seersucker Bermudas, with cloth belts bearing ducks or whale patterns, cordovan penny loafers, a madras shirt here, a pair of lime green slacks there. There were enough LaCoste alligators, Polo ponies, and Brooks Brothers golden fleece to start a zoo.

The women all seemed slim and determinedly cheery, with expensive-looking, fashionable haircuts. Most of the men sported slight, satisfied paunches. Buck would notice the men patting them occasionally, like small pets.

The mood was casual and social, with a hint of business and commerce just below the surface. It was a country club for those who had Raleigh roots or clearly intended to plant them, different from the *perfectly fine* clubs peopled by transient executives on their way up the corporate ladders, stopping in Raleigh for a year or two. The waiting list was always long, although the right connections would leapfrog some quickly to the top. Still, no one ever bragged about being "a member of Carolina Country Club." If asked, a member's response was usually more subtle, as in, "Oh, we belong out at *Carolina*," accompanied by a knowing, satisfied smile. A slight distancing from those other perfectly fine country clubs.

It was hard at first glance to tell the strivers – the doctors and lawyers and bankers who had scratched out good *incomes* – from the second or third generation possessors of significant *assets*. Some of the latter group had married their money, some had inherited it. At second glance, the assets crowd – whose financial advisors had safely secured their nest eggs while leaving them some walking around money to invest and business to talk about on the fairways and across the poker table – looked a little more tanned, a little more relaxed because of those safety nets. The young princes, Vince sometimes called them.

Vince easily bridged both groups – he was the respected legal counselor to many in that room and had some established Raleigh money of his own, thanks to the sale years ago of his family's school photography business.

Here, Ravenel always felt like the outsider, a disorienting position. He struggled to make himself focus.

"Vince, you are wrong on this one," he said finally. "I want to sue the *Pilot*. I don't care about the money, but I do want to know who their source is. I want to know who's trying to take me down."

"You'll never get the source, Buck. South Carolina has a reporter's shield statute. It lets newspapers protect their sources. There's lots of hoops you'd have to jump through before a judge would make them turn over their source. That's just the way it is. The law lets newspapers shoot at us from behind a rock. And there's not a damn thing we can do about it."

Ravenel buttered the cheese biscuit the waiter had placed on his bread plate.

"I know all about the damn shield statute," Ravenel said. "I fought it quietly when it was in my committee, used every procedural trick I knew trying to keep it from being reported out for a floor vote. The guy who sponsored it, in fact, was a Senator from Georgetown County named Greg Smith. No one wanted to have to actually vote publicly against the damn thing because the newspapers had all agreed they would stick the editorial knife in anyone who fought it.

"Smith was one of those goo-goo types, a good government

Democrat who was always getting a free ride in the media. He wrote the shield statute, introduced it, wrapped it up pretty in the First Amendment.

"Well, we got him back for it. Before the next election we re-districted his ass. We redrafted his Senate District lines, put all the black voters in Georgetown County in one district and turned it into a minority district. The district map looks like a drunk snake that grew about six legs, but it pulled in the neighborhoods we needed. Smith's liberal friends couldn't oppose that because the Black Caucus was all for it. No white Democrat could win the primary in the new district. And *no* Democrat of any shade could win Smith's old district because it's full of older white folks who moved from up North to the South Carolina coast to retire. They only vote for Republicans who have taken the pledge to never raise taxes. Last time I checked, Smith was back down at the beach running a real estate business.

"And you're wrong about one thing," Ravenel said. "Our shield statute does not provide protection when the newspaper is sued for libel. I made sure of that when the bill was in my committee. We'll figure out who they've been talking to since July the first, and I bet we can figure out who's trying to screw us.

"It'll be a good brush back pitch, high and inside, for that Wade McNabb. It might give him second thoughts about pursuing this story any further. You know, sometimes when you make folks feel a little heat, they start to see the goddam light. And it might just remind McNabb of what happened to his daddy when he got too far out ahead of himself."

"Vince, I want one of your hard-ass litigator types to draft me up the best complaint they can against the *Pilot*. I want it to scare the shit out of McNabb. I want to sue that reporter and McNabb and not just the newspaper. I want them to understand that Buck Ravenel doesn't want to own just the *Georgetown Pilot*. He wants to own their houses and whatever money they might have in the bank somewhere. And I'll sign that complaint as the lawyer, representing Tripp and Carolina Phosphate. I want everybody to know I take this real personal."

*   *   *   *   *

Wade McNabb was still pacing around his desk when he spotted Sandy Anderson just outside his door and waved him in.

"This is one helluva thing," McNabb said, tossing Sandy the civil complaint a Georgetown deputy sheriff had delivered to him as he returned to the newspaper office after lunch.

"These guys have twisted everything we've ever done into something evil."

Sandy read hurriedly through the fifteen-page legal document.

"Carolina Phosphate and Tripp Ravenel have both sued us," McNabb said. "They say our story implied that Carolina Phosphate had bribed them to get the wetlands permit approved. And they didn't just sue the paper, they sued you individually and me individually. They want $10 million in actual damages and $10 million in punitive damages."

Sandy looked up from the complaint.

"This thing reads like a novel," Sandy said. "It talks about your editorials endorsing Buck Ravenel's opponent in the last election. It mentions the paper's coverage of Carolina Phosphate's environmental problems in Louisiana. It even includes a copy of our political cartoon that had Carolina Phosphate's PR guy dressed up like Pinocchio with his nose growing and his arm around Tripp Ravenel."

"Did you read the last paragraph of the complaint?"

McNabb asked. "Some damn lawyer trying to be eloquent. Listen to this: '*Defendants, aware that a half-truth is more harmful than an outright lie, included in their article truthful statements about the business relationship between Senator Francis Ravenel and Carolina Phosphate. Then, using innuendo, insinuation and leaps of logic, they left any reasonable reader of the article with the clear – and false – impression that defendant Carolina Phosphate had bribed Tripp Ravenel in order to have its way with the South Carolina coastline.*'"

"Well, they sound like they're serious," Sandy said. "What do we do now?"

"First thing I did after lunch was call Jason Hart, the lawyer in Columbia who represents most of the newspapers around the state when they get in trouble. He's good, knows his stuff, was actually a reporter for a couple of years before he went to law school. He grew up in Columbia, went to law school at the University of South Carolina and knows most of the judges. The problem is, one of his partners got hired two weeks ago to represent Carolina Phosphate in a routine real estate transaction. That creates a conflict of interest for his firm, so Jason can't handle our case. That's too bad, because Jason knows newspapers, he knows the law, and he knows how to make jurors understand that they're better off when their local paper is being aggressive.

"He was very apologetic. Said he's sure the company had hired his law partner just to conflict his firm out of this case. Carolina Phosphate called his partner two days after we asked the company for comment for the story. These guys knew just what they were doing – conflicting out the best libel lawyer in the state so he couldn't represent us. This is the way Buck Ravenel and his crowd play the legal game. Jason told me that if you plan to play against Ravenel, you'd better wear a cup to protect your balls.

"Anyway, I asked him who he'd recommend to help us. His answer surprised me."

Sandy was listening while rereading the allegations of the complaint. When McNabb paused, Sandy looked up.

"He said we ought to hire Kate Stewart," McNabb said. "He thinks she's one of the smartest lawyers anywhere in the state. He said she's a great strategic thinker, has good peripheral vision, knows how to see the big picture, not just what's right in front of her. He did say she'd never been a big fan of newspapers. In fact, Jason said that a few years ago, she helped one of her partners try a libel case against one of the upstate papers and whipped them. But he thinks if we could get her on our side, get her to believe that we were right, there'd be nobody better."

"Well, that's an interesting thought," Sandy said. "I tell you, she's been pretty cool with me, and I really haven't had a chance to get to know her."

"Jason said she's tough as they come, and never gives up," Wade replied. "Not one of those litigators who gets weak knees when it looks like they might actually have to go to trial. Jason calls them 'pioneers,' you know, 'early settlers.' He said she'd know what to do in a knife fight with somebody like Ravenel."

Wade thought for a moment, leaning back in his desk chair.

"I've met her a couple of times. Sometimes I worry about women in the courtroom. It's tougher for them. Most of the trial lawyers and almost all the judges are men. It's like a damn fraternity house. But she's got a smart head and a sharp tongue. And she's not afraid to speak her mind. I've already been on the other side of that."

McNabb bowed his head and rubbed his eyebrows hard, searching his brain for the right answer.

"Well," he said finally, "I'll call her this afternoon. We'll see if she's the right one."

12

In the Arena

The 8 o'clock sun angled low onto the dark green wooden rocking chairs lining the porch of the century-old, two-story home that Kate Stewart had bought and refurbished into her law office. She had loved at first sight the way the porch ran across the full front of the house and wrapped around its left side. She had liked the way the old master bedroom at the back of the house – now her office – caught the rosy glow of the late afternoon sun.

Kate greeted Wade on her front porch, polite but cool.

"There's coffee brewing if you'd like some. My Fridays are always a little tight. I've got court at ten, but it sounded like you wanted to talk this out right away."

Kate was wearing what she called her "battlefield armor" for days she needed to appear in court – charcoal grey skirt, ivory silk blouse and a navy jacket. Her hair was pulled back, held by a tortoise shell clip.

"I'd appreciate a Diet Coke , if you have it," Wade said.

"I think I saw one in our refrigerator," Kate said.

She walked him back to the kitchen, rummaged around in the refrigerator, found one and opened a cupboard door looking for a glass.

"This'll do just fine." He took the silver and red can from her hand. "I like it cold, straight from the can. That first rush of cold, carbonation and caffeine hitting the back of my throat helps get me going in the morning."

He closed his eyes and took a full swig, like a smoker taking a long, satisfying drag on the first cigarette in a while. He let out a sigh and smiled.

Kate cocked her head at him. She loved the slightly bitter taste of strong coffee and couldn't understand how a grown man could start the day with something as sweet as a Coke.

"Suit yourself. I hung out with guys in college who ate cold pizza first thing in the morning and chased it with a beer. They thought it was the breakfast of champions."

Kate led him into a large room with a thirteen-foot ceiling, shiny, honey-hued heart pine floors, and a conference table made from the outside door of an old tobacco barn. Twelve feet long and four feet wide, it had been refinished and polished to a surface smooth as marble. Her conference room had once been the home's grand dining room.

"Have a seat," Kate said, hanging her jacket on the back of the chair next to her.

"I stayed up a while last night reading the article and the copy of the complaint you sent me. I looked over the plaintiffs' written discovery questions, and the request for documents they want from you. I also had a chance yesterday afternoon to look through the clips you sent me of what the *Pilot* has written about Buck Ravenel and his involvement with Carolina Phosphate."

Kate reached for a legal pad and tossed one to Wade.

"I know we haven't gotten to know each other much in my short time here," she said. "I'm not the big fan of the media that Jason Hart is. But he is a fine lawyer, and better yet, the kind of friend who will cover your back even when you don't know it needs covering. It's a shame he can't handle the case."

She eyed Wade for a moment.

"He says you're a good man, and he's usually not too free with the praise. That's why I'm willing to help out."

"Jason tells me a lot of lawyers don't want to cross Buck Ravenel because he's got a lot of political power and holds a grudge," Wade said. "He says you're smart and tough enough to handle Ravenel. That's why I wanted to hire you."

Their eyes met across the table, searching for clues, both nodding slightly, not looking away. Finally Kate tapped her pen on her yellow pad.

"Okay, let's talk about this case. Rule number one. From here on, you are my client – you, the *Pilot*, and the reporter. It's your duty to tell me the truth, and I mean the whole truth. Our communications are protected from discovery in the lawsuit. That means the Ravenels and their lawyers can't ask you about conversations you and I have. That's designed to give clients the confidence to tell their lawyer the absolute truth, every detail, no punches pulled. But if you tell others about the substance of our conversations – your wife, your best friend, it doesn't matter – you can lose that protection. Do you understand?"

"I believe I do," Wade said with a slight smile. "So you know, I'm not married. And there are some days after the paper comes out when I don't think I have *any* friends, much less a best friend. Thank goodness I have a dog that likes me, and I'll be careful what I tell her about all this."

Kate looked up from her legal pad, and gave Wade the briefest of smiles.

"One thing you asked me about yesterday was insurance," Wade continued quickly. "I checked into it. The *Pilot's* insurance company, Home Security, covers the paper and its employees, including me, up to $1 million. The bad news is the first $50,000 comes out of the *Pilot's* pocket."

"I've done work for Home Security before," Kate said. "The folks there know me, and they should be fine with my representing the *Pilot*. Now, have you ever been sued before?"

"No," Wade said. "I guess I've been lucky. I've never been sued, not once in two decades of being a reporter and editor. I've never even been a witness before."

"How about Sandy Anderson, your reporter? He ever been sued?"

"No. He's only been a reporter for a year or two. He's a little wet behind the ears, but he's a smart guy, and I think he's pretty tough for such a young fellow."

"Is there anything in his personnel file, anything about him being a sloppy reporter, you know, annual evaluations, that sort of thing, that could hurt us? Sometimes that's the soft underbelly, and Ravenel is already sniffing around there in his requests for documents. In a libel case I had some years ago against an upstate newspaper, we hit a gold mine in the reporter's personnel file. The string of reprimands from his editors was two pages long detailing his history of careless mistakes. The jury loved hearing about that."

Wade clasped his hands behind his head, leaned back, and stared through closed lids toward the ceiling in the old dining room.

"No," he said. "I can't think of a single thing."

Kate picked up her coffee cup and walked over to the conference room's bay window.

"What do you think the Ravenels really want out of this lawsuit?" she asked.

"I'm not sure," Wade said. "I'm confident the article is true. Our source is strong. The Ravenels haven't denied that this meeting at the Forest took place, or that the agency's decision got reversed right after that. What they don't like is the suggestion that they got paid for making it happen.

"My bet is Buck Ravenel thinks he can scare us into backing off our coverage of the phosphate plant debate," Wade said. "Or maybe he thinks he can squeeze the name of our confidential source out of Sandy or me so he can get a little political retribution. But I don't work that way. That's not going to happen."

Kate completed her slow cycle around the room and sat back down across the table from Wade. Just beneath her coffee cup, Wade could make out some faint lettering from an ancient cigarette advertisement on the tobacco barn door: "Reach for a Lucky instead of a sweet."

"Or maybe he wants to win this suit and take your newspaper away from you so he can be the new publisher," Kate said finally.

She saw a flicker of fear in Wade's eyes. He blinked, and it was gone.

Kate sat quietly for the next fifteen seconds, pondering what she had heard, curious if Wade would say more. He didn't.

"It's clear he wants to know your source," she said. "Maybe he thinks it's one of his political enemies. He's already demanded in the discovery requests that you identify your source. He's scheduled the depositions of you and Sandy for next month, and he'll ask you under oath to disclose the name. Your reporter's shield statute won't protect you in a libel suit, you already know that."

Wade was quiet, rubbing the top of his forehead. This was beginning to feel like a war.

"I don't understand how he can jerk us around like this," Wade said, anger rising in his throat. "Is there any way we can get this case thrown out of court quickly? And sue him for our attorneys' fees?"

Kate leaned back in her chair, holding her coffee cup with both hands, and sipped thoughtfully.

"I don't think you appreciate what's about to happen to you, Wade," she said. "Somebody once described a litigant as a person about to give up his skin in hope of saving his bones. Ravenel may be going after your skin and your bones. But it's too early to tell what his real motives are.

"I've known him slightly since I've been practicing. He's a good courtroom lawyer. He can tell a story that pulls on a jury's heartstrings. But between us, I think these past few years he's come to rely on his knowledge of the judges more than his knowledge of the law.

"Remember, he chose not to be named as a plaintiff in this lawsuit. That would have put his reputation at issue, and we could have asked him under oath about everything he's ever done or been accused of doing. You've got to have a pretty damn clean conscience to be a plaintiff in a libel suit. He didn't want you to be able to delve into his business dealings or find out how much Carolina Phosphate has paid him in legal fees. Whatever he's after wasn't worth risking that. But he gets to represent his son and Carolina Phosphate in the lawsuit.

"Anyway, right now he's hell bent on getting the name of your source. I guess we'll just have to wait and see if he's also trying to get your newspaper."

Wade saw the lawyer's eyes dart toward her watch, and he looked at his own. It was 9:15.

"Okay," Wade said with a deep sigh. "You need to know that I am a catastrophic thinker. I can immediately imagine the worst in any situation. If my phone rings in the middle of the night, I automatically assume somebody I care about has died. I can't help it. Then I work backward from that, working through the less drastic possibilities. Deep in my heart, though, I'm a secret optimist. Once I have a plan, I work pretty hard to make good results happen. So what do we do next?"

"Let's focus on how we defend this," Kate said. "The first thing Tripp Ravenel and Carolina Phosphate have to prove is that you published statements about them that were false and hurt their reputation. They'll say that the *Pilot* has accused Carolina Phosphate of bribing Tripp Ravenel to approve the phosphate plant.

"Tripp Ravenel is a public official and the company is deeply involved in a public controversy over whether a state agency will grant it a wetlands permit. This is really important because both of them will have to do more than persuade a jury that what you published was *false*. They also have to prove that you published a false statement *knowing* it was false or at least with serious doubts about whether it was true or not."

Wade's frown eased a little.

"Well," he said, "I think that should give us pretty good protection. Both Sandy and I were confident that every single fact in that story was true. We checked it out as carefully as we knew how. I think our source is solid as a rock."

Kate's hazel eyes met Wade's and stayed there.

"Tripp Ravenel and his cronies will testify that the gist of your story, the 'sting' as lawyers like to say, is false." Kate said. "He'll swear he never took a penny, and the Carolina Phosphate folks will back him up. I suspect that it will be hard for us to prove that they took a bribe. These guys are too smart to have let traceable money change hands. And if the grease for the permit was a shot for Tripp and Buck at a no-lose 'investment opportunity,' they've probably aborted that project and covered their tracks. My bet is there won't be a paper trail now."

Kate stood and slipped on her jacket.

"Our key defense will be to show that the *Pilot* had a perfectly good reason to print this story – that you had the kind of information that a jury will think you should have relied on, even if we can't prove it's true. If you can show you had good reason to believe they took a bribe, I know the jury speech. Her voice suddenly grew deeper and more solemn: 'Ladies and Gentlemen, do you want to live in a community where the newspaper can print these facts alongside Ravenel's denials and let *you* decide where the truth lies? Or would you rather live in a community where a powerful public official like Tripp Ravenel can scare the press into silence with the threat of a libel suit?"

Her voice returned to a conversational tone, and she smiled at Wade.

"That's a case we can win," she said. "But Wade, that's where the rub's going to come. If you can't identify your source to the Court, it will be hard for you to put up that defense, to show why it made perfect sense to print that story. This isn't just about going to jail to protect a source. If you refuse to identify the source, the judge has the power to strike your defenses. That means he can simply enter a judgment for the plaintiffs for whatever amount of damages they can prove to a jury, plus maybe some punitive damages. That's what's got me worried about this case."

"Would a judge really do that?" Wade asked.

"A judge could, and I'm pretty sure the judge we're going to get would. Your case has been assigned to Judge Dupree Jones. He owes his seat on the bench to Buck Ravenel. And in this state, nobody thinks there's anything wrong with ruling on your hunting buddy's case. Or on the case of the state senator who got you appointed and gets to say whether you keep that seat when you come up for re-appointment again in six years. They just call it 'The Code of the Forest.'"

"What's the Code of the Forest?" Wade asked.

Kate shook her head.

"It's about having the right connections. But it's too long a story for now. Why don't we get together tomorrow and dig into all this a little deeper. Right now I've got to get to court. Come with me back to my desk and let me get you a copy of a law review article I found last night on protecting confidential sources in libel cases. It'll help you understand what we're facing here."

Wade followed Kate through a hallway to an office that was sparsely furnished with a dark red oriental rug, some bookshelves, and a wingchair across from the antique table she used as her desk.

"I'm still getting moved in here," she said. "Have a seat while I make you a copy of this. I'll be right back."

Wade's reporter's eyes quickly surveyed the room. On one wall was a photograph of an old brick building, a 1940s vintage auto parked in the front. The sign on the building said "A.H. Stewart & Co. – Tobacco Merchants." Beside it was a framed photograph of a family standing on the ocean-side steps of a 1950s style beach house. The parents had their arms around each other's waists, laughing. The young girl and her teenaged brother were smiling and squinting into the sunlight. They all looked happy.

Wade glanced at the opposite wall at a framed quotation, in careful calligraphy. From his chair, he could read Teddy Roosevelt's name at the bottom. He strolled over for a closer look.

> It is not the critic who counts: not the man who
> points out how the strong man stumbles, or where
> the doer of deeds could have done better. The credit
> belongs to the man who is actually in the arena,
> whose face is marred by dust and sweat and blood,
> who strives valiantly, who errs and comes up short

again and again, because there is no effort without error or shortcoming, but who knows the great enthusiasms, the great devotions, who spends himself for a worthy cause; who, at the best, knows, in the end, the triumph of high achievement, and who, at the worst, if he fails, at least he fails while daring greatly, so that his place shall never be with those cold and timid souls who knew neither victory nor defeat.

Kate returned carrying a copy of the article she had promised and saw Wade studying the quote.

"That's obviously one of my favorite thoughts," she said, nodding toward the wall. "I told you that I'm not the biggest fan of the media. I've seen careless reporting, sometimes mean-spirited stories, really hurt people close to me. Frankly, I've always thought that newspaper types are critics who never get down in the arena. They stir things up, simplify the world into a headline. They make everything seem black or white, no half-tones, no shades of gray. It's always good versus evil, never pretty good versus less good, or real bad versus less bad, the way most of the real world is. They write editorials telling everyone how it ought to be done in the perfect world, and then leave it to the politicians, the lawyers and the judges to deal with the details, the hard decisions, the tough compromises. With reality."

She took his elbow and led him down the hall toward the front door.

"Now, I don't know you well, and that may not apply to you. In any event, you're fixin' to be in the arena whether you like it or not. You've published a story that gives a glimpse under the bedcovers of South Carolina politics. You were brave to do it. But the good old boys club is tryin' to teach you a lesson."

"Kate, I know about newspapers," Wade said. "They have their flaws, and they don't always get it right. That's one reason I came back here to run my own paper. I want to get it right. And I think we did on the Buck Ravenel story."

"Well, I look forward to learning more about all this, but I've got to get to court right now, or the judge might put *me* in jail."

Kate tugged at her jacket, smoothing a wrinkle and checked her hair in the mirror near the front door.

"Kate, one thing I'm already worried about is Judge Jones," Wade said. "He hates the newspaper. Right after I came back here, we ran a series on housing code violations by landlords in Georgetown, and Jones was near the top of the list. He owns a couple dozen run-down rental houses, and he was pissed at us. He didn't like the stories, he didn't like the editorial about the "City's Top Slumlords," and he hated the editorial cartoons that made fun of his eyebrows. He made all that very clear to us. He made some rumbling noises about suing the paper that got back to us, but nothing ever came of it."

Kate paused at the door, pondered a moment, and nodded at Wade.

"Let me give that some thought," she said. "Maybe we could persuade the good Judge he should step aside and let a judge who hasn't threatened to sue you before hear this case.

"Why don't you and Sandy come by tomorrow about 10 o'clock and let's work on our strategy. I'll see you here tomorrow morning. Now, I'm off to court."

13

The Defense

At 10 o'clock the next morning, Sandy and Wade joined Kate Stewart in her conference room. Kate had brought a plate of oatmeal cookies and pecan-peach spins, her favorite treat from Kudzu Bakery. She set them in the middle of the conference room table beside a stack of yellow legal pads and a cardboard banker's box, already filling with research notes, copies of articles from the *Pilot*, and cases Kate thought might be relevant.

"You two will be glad to know that I skipped my Friday night dinner at Sliders. I stayed here reading cases and thinking about our strategy," she said. "I don't expect applause, but please don't tell me how great the grilled tuna was."

"You didn't miss a thing," Sandy said. "I hung out with the POETS crowd, and they were all abuzz about the libel suit. The courthouse crowd thinks the fix is in with Judge Jones. They think Buck Ravenel is going to end up owning the *Pilot*, no matter what we do."

"They don't have a damned clue, Sandy," Kate said. "The chattering class just loves to see other folks fight. And let's face it – everybody's got an ax to grind with their local newspaper, whether it's in Georgetown or New York City. Everybody at one time or another believes they've been misquoted or quoted out of context or had their aunt's name spelled wrong in an obituary. Lawyers, especially, think newspapers are a blunt instrument and that the people who run them are a little smug and a lot whiny.

"But, hey," she said brightly. "I'm on your side on this one, and it looks like you're wearing the white hat."

Sandy spent some time walking Kate through his background, his political science studies, and his late-blooming attraction to newspaper journalism. Kate was grudgingly impressed by his intelligence and by his quiet demeanor. He didn't give off the spark of a young punk trying to make a name for himself. He struck her as a reporter who had gone looking for facts and found a story, not someone who had started with a story and looked for just the facts that fit it. When they stopped for a break, Kate asked Sandy about his bow tie.

"I'm a big bow tie fan, by the way,' she said. "The best lawyer I ever knew never wore any other kind of tie. He could tie them while driving his car without even looking in a mirror, and they always came out just right. When did you start wearing them?"

Sandy's face turned red, and Wade started laughing. He had heard the story, and knew Sandy hated telling it.

"Come on, lover boy," Wade said. "Tell her the truth, the whole truth and nothing but the truth."

"If you promise this is covered by the attorney-client privilege, and you won't tell everybody who knows me," Sandy said.

"Nope, my lips are sealed," she said.

"Okay, when I was a freshman in college, I had my first serious girlfriend. We had been dating a couple of months, and we planned this big romantic Valentine's evening," Sandy said, shaking his head at the memory. "We splurged and went to this expensive bed and breakfast up in the North Carolina mountains. We dressed up and went out for a wonderful dinner at a fancy restaurant. We hadn't talked about it, but we both knew this was going to be our Big Night."

Sandy put "Big Night" in finger quotations.

"When we got back to the room, she lit all these candles. I opened a bottle of champagne, and we curled up on the bed and opened our presents. Things were going very, very well. I wanted one more glass of champagne, and I leaned across the bedside table to get the bottle.

"All of a sudden, I smelled something burning. I looked down and my damn tie was on fire! It had dipped into the candle flame while I was fumbling for the bottle. That silk tie went off like a fuse on a firecracker. I dumped half a bottle of champagne all over my front to dowse the flames. My shouting scared the couple in the room next door, and they came banging on our door. The manager showed up with a fire extinguisher. I was pretty embarrassed. And all that sort of killed the romantic mood. It didn't turn out to be the Big Night.

"Anyway, I made up my mind the next morning that I would never wear anything but a bow tie again."

Kate laughed.

"My old partner Cart Cooper would never tell me why he started wearing them. He always joked that it was cheaper to launder shirts with spilled soup on them than to dry-clean a tie."

As Kate quizzed Sandy and Wade about their backgrounds, she shared some of her own with them. When Wade told her that at thirty-five, he had turned down a job in the *New York Times* Washington bureau to take advantage of the chance to run a small daily newspaper in Virginia, Kate told them about her summer in Manhattan clerking for a big law firm.

"I understand your decision, Wade. I knew early on I wanted more control over my own life than that."

Wade nodded, surprising himself by his mental note that

Kate looked even better in her blue jeans than she had in her blue jacket. He filled in some of the blanks on his resume for her. He had dropped out of college in the fall of his junior year, 1971, to work for George McGovern's presidential campaign. Two years later, he moved back to South Carolina to help lay the groundwork for Pug Ravenel's come-from-nowhere campaign for the Democratic nomination for South Carolina Governor. It was still one of the most famous political campaigns in the state's history and he got a kick out of recounting it to Kate. The 36-year-old New York investment banker had grown up in South Carolina and earned the nickname "the Riverboat Gambler" as Harvard's cocky quarterback. A year after showing back up in his home state, the political unknown – a distant cousin of Buck Ravenel – surprised everyone by announcing he'd seek the Democratic nomination for governor. With disarming candor and a flashy television advertising campaign, the wisecracking challenger shocked the state's political establishment by outmaneuvering five other candidates – including the incumbent lieutenant governor – with direct attacks on the state's tradition of backroom politics. By late summer, he was in a head-to-head primary runoff with thirteen-term Congressman William Jennings Bryan Dorn. The Congressman, still partial to white suits, windy oratory and old-style political cronyism, looked even older as he and Ravenel stumped across the state in a series of debates. On election day, the Democratic primary voters tossed out the past and pinned their hopes on Ravenel and the future.

But the political gods weren't ready for that change. Two weeks after Ravenel's primary victory, a state court judge ruled that he didn't meet the state's residency requirement: he hadn't lived in the state for the five years before he filed for the seat. The state Supreme Court quickly upheld the decision, and the defeated Dorn was suddenly the Democratic nominee. In the resulting political turmoil, South Carolina elected a Charleston dentist as its first Republican governor since the post-Civil War Reconstruction era.

"I learned a lot in that campaign," Wade said. "I decided I might not be cut out for the brass knuckles of politics. But I thought it was important to help people understand political power and how it gets used. I went to work for the *Charlotte Observer*, covering South Carolina politics for them for a couple years. It was a great time. Pete McKnight and Jim Batten were my editors, and they were fearless. I never got back to college for that diploma, though."

"Do you regret that?" Kate asked.

"Not for me, maybe for my folks. My mother died in early 1977. I think she had just been holding on, hoping to see me get that degree, something my father had never done. After her funeral, I put our river house on the rental market and took a job with the *Chicago Tribune*. I worked in Chicago for eight years, covering state and local politics.

Wade took a bite from one of the oatmeal cookies and a sip of a Diet Coke.

"Now that was an education. I thought I knew a little about cronyism and corruption from my South Carolina days, but that was something else. I told a grizzled old editor up there one time about 'vote-buying' in the rural counties down here, how each candidate would give drivers' money to 'get out the vote' on election day. They called it 'walkin' around money.' The drivers would chauffeur all those folks who couldn't get there, or didn't care, to the polls and show them how to mark their ballots for the driver's candidate.

"In those days, South Carolina used a paper scratch ballot. You didn't circle the name of the candidate you wanted.

Instead, you scratched out the names of every candidate you *didn't* want. It was actually an emotionally satisfying process. Anyway, the drivers and poll workers would show their riders a sample ballot with the 'bad' names scratched out and the 'good' name in bold letters. The voters would take it into the voting booth with them to be sure they got it right. And somewhere along the way, the voters would get a dollar or two. The drivers paid for their gas and kept the rest.

"This old, tough, cynical Chicago editor looked at me like I was a Girl Scout. He said that was stupid, that you didn't know how people actually voted if you did it that way. He said in Chicago, it was more businesslike. The first guy who went in to vote in the morning would stuff a blank piece of paper in the voting box and walk out with his actual ballot, unmarked. He'd bring it back to the front door and give it to a poll worker who would mark it for the candidate they were backing. The poll worker would give him a George Washington, and send the marked ballot in with the next cooperative voter. That voter would put the marked ballot in the box and bring out a blank one, give it to the poll workers and get his "tip." Then the process would roll on like that all day. That way, the old guy told me, they knew they were getting the votes they had paid for. The only fair way to do things, he said."

"When did you leave Chicago?" Kate asked.

"In the mid-eighties. I got a little tired of those winters. I still had this thin Lowcountry blood, and I wanted to be back in the South. The *Times* job was tempting, but I decided I wanted to put my own stamp on a newspaper. So I took a job editing a small daily paper in Virginia. I did a pretty good job, and the Brackett chain hired me a couple of years later to run their paper in Pittsburgh.

"I did that for four years before I had burned out on the

demands of big chain newspapers. It got to be less about get-ting good reporting into the paper and more about managing budgets and maintaining the paper's comfortable profit mar-gin. In the old days, the publishers – the ones who decide how much money the newsrooms get to do their jobs – were former editors who had moved to the business side. They understood what the news side of the business was all about. By the time I left in the early 1990s, most folks on the business side were always looking over their shoulders trying to please the bean counters at headquarters.

"We all should have seen it coming. In the fifties and six-ties, locally owned papers around the country got bought by newspaper chains, and at first, that was a good thing. It gave them more resources and capital to put out a better paper, and they had enough independence to stand up to local advertis-ers and others who might not like what they were saying on their editorial pages. I can remember when local car dealers threatened to pull their ads every time Ralph Nader's name was in the paper. But by the eighties, these chains had all gone public, and they had to answer each quarter to the Wall Street stock analysts. Those guys don't care if you sell newspapers or nuclear waste, they just want to know how much money you made last quarter. It put some tough pressures on newsrooms.

"The *Pilot* came up for sale early in 1992, and I had been keeping my eye on it. One of my old college buddies had cashed out well when he sold his software business. He put up a chunk of money, and we bought the paper. Mostly his equity, entirely my sweat, but I own 51 percent. And we make enough money to be happy, but we don't have to squeeze out every dollar of profit. That's just not our main goal. We don't have hungry bankers and stock analysts breathing over our shoulder every quarter. The first thing I did when we bought the paper was to remove the newspaper's old slogan in the top right corner of the front page that said 'Pull for Georgetown or Pull Out.' I replaced it with my favorite quote from Justice Louis Brandeis: 'Sunlight is the best of disinfectants.'"

By early afternoon their attention had turned to strategy.

"The plaintiffs' focus will be on the bribe issue," Kate said. "They'll agree that the agency changed its report to approve the Carolina Phosphate permit. But they'll say it was because it was the right thing to do, not because there was a payoff. Your article pretty much says this investment opportunity was a payoff to the Ravenels.

"What exactly do we know about that?" Kate asked. "Remember, I don't want you to tell me who your source is, just what he or she told you."

Wade nodded at Sandy, who told Kate about his meeting at Sliders with his source.

When he was done, Kate pondered his story for a minute, rubbing her temples with both hands, her eyes squeezed shut. She spoke without opening them.

"How are you sure the draft report was authentic, not just something made up to embarrass the Ravenels and the company?"

"It has an official stamp of the ERA on it, with a date of June 15 and the initials FM – Frank Myer – the guy who wrote it," Sandy said quickly. "And I checked some other official agency documents to be sure the stamp was the official one."

"Are we sure the source and both Ravenels were at the Forest that night?" Kate asked, eyes still closed.

Wade answered this time.

"We don't have any paper backing up the story. But the travel expenses checked out, indicating the Ravenels were in Georgetown that weekend for a 'legislative strategy session,' and we can't find any official meetings that weekend," Wade said. "And we haven't been able to find anyone named Vince among the top brass on Carolina Phosphate's organizational chart. But I've met the source. He's not a regular at the Forest, but he's clearly been there. He described the main lodge and the dining room perfectly, based on my one brief visit there years ago to interview Senator Strom Thurmond."

When Kate opened her eyes, they were twinkling. It was the closest to a full smile either Wade or Sandy had ever seen from her.

"When you were there, did you notice a large-mouth bass, about twenty-five inches long, fat as a football, mounted on the wall near the porch?"

She didn't wait for an answer.

"I caught that fish when I was thirteen years old."

Wade crinkled his eyes as though he didn't believe her.

"What in the world were you doing there? I didn't think they allowed any girls or women at the Forest back then, unless they were, uh, there on private business, if you know what I mean."

Kate laughed.

"That's a story for another day," she said. "It's almost 4 o'clock and we've been at it long enough. I need to rest my brain a little and let all of this settle in."

Sandy looked relieved. He had plans to be in Columbia that evening, and he had a two hour drive ahead of him.

"I want to think some more about asking Judge Jones to step down from handling this case because of the slumlord stories you told me about," Kate said. "That, plus the fact that everybody knows he and Buck Ravenel are tight as ticks might do it. Wade, I need you to get me copies of all the stories the *Pilot* ran about Jones. And I need to know how to get in touch with anyone who heard Jones complain about them or talk about suing you."

"Copies of the stories are no problem," Wade said. "Getting anyone to say in court that they heard him threaten to sue the paper will be pretty damn tough."

Wade looked over at Sandy, who was beginning to fidget.

"You better hit the road if you want to get to Columbia to see your friends tonight," Wade said.

Sandy nodded and looked at Kate.

"Kate, I could go back to my source and try to get more details from him about the night of the meeting at the Forest," he said. "I'll be in Columbia this weekend and could try to set it up.

"I've called him a couple of times since the suit was filed," Sandy said. "He hasn't returned my calls, and I'm wary of leaving him a voicemail. Don't know who might have access to his phone. I'm afraid the media spotlight on the lawsuit may have spooked him."

"Do you think there's any chance that he would consider coming forward if the judge ordered you to go to jail or said he would enter a big money judgment against the newspaper?" Kate asked.

"I don't think so," Wade interjected. "We tried to get him to commit to that before the story was published, but he was dead set against it. It's worth a shot, but I don't think it'll happen."

"Sandy, these folks play hardball, and you may be under surveillance," Kate said. "I'm sure Buck Ravenel knows a private investigator or two who would do a good job of tailing you for a few weeks just to see who you might be meeting with. I think you should hold off for now on meeting with the source in person."

Kate began putting her notes and materials back in the cardboard box.

"So, here's where we are," Kate said. "The first thing we do is make Tripp Ravenel identify in discovery in the lawsuit everyone at the Bowman's Forest dinner meeting. Then we depose everyone who was there and ask them about this business deal. Maybe we can keep the judge from putting the heat on you two and your source."

"But my guess is that Tripp Ravenel will lie under oath about the payoff scheme if that's what it takes to save their skins," Kate said. "Who knows about the other guys? But folks in this kind of situation don't break ranks too easily and rat on one another."

Kate paused for a moment, going through her mental checklist of things to do. Suddenly her eyes brightened.

"Guys, I think I might know who this Vince fellow might be. A few years ago I met a Raleigh lawyer named Vince Stone. He's as politically wired in North and South Carolina as anybody I've ever met. His firm has some good environmental lawyers and a sophisticated corporate practice. If somebody needed to set up a private company, disguised by a few layers of shell companies and partnerships to make it untraceable in the public records, Stone's firm would know exactly how to do it."

Kate walked to the computer in the corner of the conference room and quickly logged onto the American Bar Association's national lawyer directory. In three clicks of her mouse, up popped a thumbnail profile and photograph of Vince Stone, complete with his puffed and polished biography. She scrolled over to the law firm's list of representative clients, and there it was, third on the list: Carolina Phosphate, Inc.

"What do you think, Woodward and Bernstein?" Kate asked triumphantly. "I believe this is our co-conspirator."

She hit the "print" button and handed copies of Stone's biography and photo to Sandy.

"Let's give this some thought, but I think he might be our bag man for the Ravenels."

Kate walked them out to the porch. Sandy hurried for his car. Wade lingered for a moment.

"Kate, can I buy you a beer or a cup of coffee?" he asked.

"Thanks, Wade, but I can't right now," Kate said.

Wade liked the way she said "cain't" with a long "a," like it rhymed with "faint." Law school and a stint in New York hadn't washed all of the small town out of her.

"Tonight is my friend Carolyn's birthday, and some of us are cooking dinner for her," Kate said. "I'm headed up to Winyah Bay Seafood to pick up some shrimp. If you're heading back toward Front Street, I'll walk with you."

It was three blocks from Kate's office to Front Street, which ran for several blocks along the Georgetown Harbor, with shops on both sides. The ancient live oaks forming a green tunnel over Broad Street provided little relief from the August sun.

"I think I was a little naïve about the prospects of a libel suit when we published this story," Wade confessed. "Even if I win this lawsuit, it could cost me a fortune. And it's already distracted Sandy and me from doing our day-to-day jobs."

They walked along in silence for half a block. On their left was a four-foot tall brick wall protecting the cemetery of the Prince George Winyah Episcopal Church, the second oldest Episcopal church in South Carolina. Two and a half centuries of Georgetown County Episcopalians lay nestled in that shaded cemetery, under hundreds of headstones. Their inscriptions hinted at powerful stories – some tragic, some heroic – of devoted marriages, infant deaths, commitment to church, soldiers killed, sailors lost, statesmen mourned, lives well lived.

Kate nodded as they passed the church's front door.

"You know I love the history here," she said. "But I haven't had time to learn enough about it. I walk by this church every day, and I've been meaning for weeks to check it out. It looks beautiful."

Wade smiled.

"That's my family's church. It's been here since 1747. It's taken its licks. In the Revolutionary War the Brits stabled their horses here when they came through. The Yankees did the same thing during the Civil War. Five generations of McNabbs are buried in that cemetery, including my parents. I'll give you a tour one day, if you'd like."

Five minutes later, they were on Front Street, busy with summer visitors checking out the antique shops and gift stores. The visual sores of the steel mill and the paper plant were still tough obstacles to Georgetown's blossoming into a robust tourist destination. The storefronts had a worn look.

As Kate and Wade were about to head in opposite directions along Front Street, Wade put his hand on her forearm, stopping her.

"Kate, I've been thinking about this all day. It looks like I'm about to put my newspaper in your hands. Far as I'm concerned, that pretty much amounts to putting my life in your hands. It occurs to me we need to know a little bit more about each other."

Kate eyed him warily, not sure where he was headed.

"How about going with me to my church tomorrow," Wade suggested. "It's a late afternoon service, very casual, shorts and polo shirt sort of thing. I can pick you up at 3 o'clock at your office. Bring a bathing suit and some sandals."

"Wade, I'm not much on church stuff," Kate said. "And I'm real busy with work. Maybe another time."

"Kate, I insist."

She hesitated again.

"Okay, I'll come along. We can talk a little more about the case. I'm sure there's some more background I don't know yet. Three o'clock, you said?"

Wade nodded and smiled, backed away with a wave, and headed toward the newspaper office.

Kate walked the two blocks to Winyah Bay Seafood, wondering whether she should have begged off the next day's gathering. She wasn't sure about spending a Sunday afternoon with her new client. And she was worried about where this case was heading. Taking on Buck Ravenel might not be the smartest thing she had ever agreed to do. She might never win a case again in front of one of Ravenel's hand-picked judges.

Kate turned down a short street that dead-ended at Georgetown harbor. Winyah Bay Seafood purchased the shrimp brought in on the boats that docked along the harbor. The building was a squat, one-story cinder block structure with a cargo door that opened right onto the docks. Inside it smelled of well-iced shrimp and fish.

A shrimp boat had just docked and was unloading its catch. At one end of the low-ceilinged room was a long wooden table lined on either side by a dozen older black women, pinching the heads off shrimp like they were snapping fresh green beans. At one end of the table stood a short, pudgy white man in stained khaki pants and a short sleeved shirt, calmly smoking a cigarette. The top two joints of the index finger of his right hand were missing, and he held his cigarette between the second and third fingers. He watched impassively as the women, fingers flying, tossed the headless shrimp bodies into plastic buckets. Every now and then he wagged his finger stump to silently signal the shirtless black man at the other end of the room to shovel more shrimp onto the table.

The scene had fascinated Kate each time she had seen it that summer. It seemed like some flashback to the 1950s. She found it vaguely offensive but still mesmerizing.

It was hard work in the mid-August heat and humidity, and the slight breeze from the two window fans hardly helped. One of the older women, who looked to be in her seventies, her salt and pepper hair peeking from a tightly bound purple bandana, hummed low and deep in a familiar cadence. Kate leaned her ear closer, picking up shards of what sounded like "What a Friend We Have in Jesus." Several of the women began to hum and moan notes, not words, along with her, still snapping head after head.

"Oh, what pain and grief we bear," the words leaked for a moment from the hums. The voices rose in unison on the next line.

"All because we do not carr-eee, everything to God in prayer." There was some snuffling and a few muttered "amens" and "all right nows."

The woman with the purple bandana was the first to fill her bucket. She immediately took it to the white man, who dropped it on the scale for a second, squinted through the smoke of the cigarette now clamped in the corner of his lips, scribbled a number on a white piece of paper, and handed it to her as her receipt. He dumped the bucket of headed shrimp into a large basket and gave her back the bucket. They didn't exchange a word or a glance. She tucked the chit into her apron pocket and returned, proud-backed, to the table to resume the heading.

Kate had learned that each bucket held about seventeen pounds of headed shrimp, and the owner paid twelve cents a pound for heading the shrimp. About two dollars a bucket.

The fastest headers could fill a bucket in ten minutes, making twelve dollars an hour. Most took fifteen minutes to fill a bucket, making eight dollars or so an hour. Not bad money for piece work, leaving aside a little for the Band-Aids and ointments to ease the pricks from the shrimps' sharp antennae and tails. When the boat's hold was empty and the last shovelful of shrimp was gone from the table, the women would cash in their receipts, then wander away, the group dissolving toward their small wooden houses a few blocks away, waiting until the word spread of another shrimp boat docking.

Winyah Bay Seafood sold the headed shrimp by the pound to its local customers and to the nearby restaurants whose chefs insisted on fresh shrimp. They didn't come any fresher than these unless you caught them yourself.

Kate bought four pounds of large shrimp, firm and clean-smelling, twenty to the pound. The young man helping customers shoveled a little ice into the bag, just enough to keep them cold for her short walk home.

14

Carolyn's Party

Kate strolled up the walk of Carolyn's small wood frame home on Salt Creek, balancing a platter of pink boiled shrimp and a bowl of red cocktail sauce. Most of the guests were gathered on the creek-side deck, enjoying the early evening breeze from the water. Kate spotted a few lawyers she knew and a couple of environmental types she had met with Carolyn. She located a bare spot on the dining room table and arranged the shrimp on the platter, then took a Heineken from the cooler. As she looked for an opener, Carolyn waved from the doorway.

"Kate, I'm so glad you could come. When you said you were working this weekend I was afraid you wouldn't make it."

"Hey, you're the birthday girl. Get out of that kitchen and let me open those wine bottles. And I'll stick around later and help you clean up."

Carolyn gave her a grateful look, put down the corkscrew and headed toward the deck.

"If you don't join me in five minutes, I'm coming back after you," Carolyn said.

Carolyn's musical tastes leaned to Paul Simon, Van Morrison and Bruce Springsteen, with an occasional dose of early Ray Charles. As Kate surveyed the group on the deck, she could hear Van Morrison's voice singing one of her favorite songs – "*I can feel her heart beat from a thousand miles...*"

Kate finished opening the wine bottles and put on the game face she saved for court and talking with strangers. She was humming "Crazy Love" as she plunged into the group looking for a friendly face.

It was hours later before Kate and Carolyn found time to talk. The guests had finally departed, the cleanup was finished, and the two women sat barefooted in chairs on the deck. The night was bathed in the full moon's soft yellow light, and the highest tide of the month slapped lightly against the deck's pilings.

"Kate, I have been thinking hard about this new law practice of yours. I talked last night with Charlie Pinckney. He was very interested to learn that you had left the Devereaux firm. He wants to talk with you about representing the Coastal Conservation League on two of its toughest environmental projects."

Kate leaned back in her chair and put her feet up on the deck rail.

"What would those be?" Kate said, taking a sip from her wine glass.

"One is trying to stop the new highway connector that would open up the whole western part of the county to development, wetlands and all. The second one is stopping this phosphate plant that Buck Ravenel and his cronies are trying to push through. Charlie would love to have you on board."

A mullet made three quick jumps, slap-splashing back into the water each time.

"He remembers how good you were when he was trying to close down the paper mill during the dioxin fight," Carolyn said. "You beat him pretty good. He hasn't forgotten that. I guess there's no bigger compliment than having one of your former opponents try to hire you to represent him."

Kate was quiet for a minute, trying to decide how much to

tell Carolyn.

"Charlie Pinckney's a good South Carolina boy, and he's being kind to me with those words," Kate said. "Under other circumstances, I might even give that some thought, but the timing isn't so good."

Kate sipped her wine slowly.

"You have to keep this absolutely quiet for now, okay?"

Carolyn leaned forward, curious.

"You got it, friend. Delta Love. My lips are sealed."

"I've just agreed to represent the *Pilot* in the libel suit Tripp Ravenel and Carolina Phosphate filed against the newspaper this week. I met with Wade McNabb today to talk about taking the case. That would knock me out of getting directly involved in the phosphate mine matter."

"You are representing the newspaper?" Carolyn said with a clear tone of surprise. "I know you aren't the biggest fan of newspaper types."

"You're right about that," Kate said. "I hate the way they oversimplify everything then hide behind their 'freedom of the press' and 'public's right to know' mantras when they screw up. A few years ago, Cart and I took on a libel case against an upstate newspaper. They had written a story claiming that Cart's cousin was about to be indicted in connection with a huge embezzlement from a local bank. The cousin had denied it and begged the paper not to print it. They did anyway, relying on what they said were unnamed sources close to the district attorney. Spread it all over the front page, and it got picked up by every daily and half the weeklies in the state. They got it flat wrong. Turned out Cart's cousin was an informant for the FBI who blew the whistle on the crooks."

Carolyn nodded.

"It's like that saying," Carolyn said. "A lie can travel halfway around the world before the truth can get up and put its pants on."

Kate smiled.

"The paper eventually ran a half-hearted correction, tucked way inside," she said, "but there were plenty of people who knew the man's name and thought he was somehow mixed up in the embezzlement. He kept asking us: 'Where do I go to get my reputation back?' He was a recovering alcoholic, and it pushed him right off the wagon. It was a terrible time for the whole family.

"It was the paper's arrogance that motivated us," Kate added. "First, they said they had run a full correction and that was enough. So we filed a lawsuit. Then they said they didn't settle libel suits as a matter of principle. So we took them to trial. The jury awarded our client $250,000 in damages and another million in punitive damages. We took a fee of $250,000, our client kept $250,000, and he gave the rest to the USC Journalism School to start a program in journalistic ethics. The first thing the students study every year is his case."

"You think you'll be okay on the other side of the 'v,'" representing a newspaper instead of a plaintiff?" Carolyn asked.

Kate thought for a minute.

"I'll admit, I'm a little worried about taking on Buck Ravenel. He takes no prisoners, and he owns most of the judges. But I know what Cart would do. And what he would want me to do."

"Has Wade told you much about the lawsuit?" Carolyn said.

"Just enough to know that he needs a good lawyer. I think the newspaper did the right thing with its reporting, but he's in for a fight."

"Now I'm even gladder that you're here," Carolyn said. "I think you might be saving your soul. And you might just manage to help us save this estuary. Defending Wade McNabb is a good start. We need him to be an honest broker on these issues. If he's intimidated by the likes of Ravenel, they will have won the real battle whether or not they win their lawsuit. I'm glad he's got you on his side."

"Wade's a good man," she added. "As the editor here, he's had a hard line to walk on environmental issues. His advertisers always want more growth, more development, just more, more, more. And that growth does mean more money for the paper. To his credit, he's still raising the right questions about the phosphate plant. But let's face it. The power of the pen is not an even match for the power of Buck Ravenel. You've got a tiger by the tail, sweetheart.

"And by the way, Wade told me about meeting you at Sliders a few weeks ago. He thought it was pretty funny the way you called him a pompous ass without knowing he was sitting there. And he was impressed that you didn't apologize for it. He could be a tough client, though. He plays his cards close to the vest. He's easy to talk to, but not easy to know."

Carolyn paused for a moment and sipped her wine.

"Trust me, I've tried," she said, shaking her head.

"I guess I'll get a chance to learn a little more tomorrow," Kate replied. "He said if he was putting his newspaper in my hands, I needed to get to know him better. So we are going to some church event. I can't believe I agreed to do that, but he caught me off guard."

Carolyn gave her a puzzled look.

"Wade McNabb at a church event? Now, *that* would make the front page of the *Pilot*. What church is he taking you to?"

"I guess it's the Prince George church, that really old one on Highmarket Street. He said it was his family's church."

"I thought Wade went only to the Church of the King

Mackerel. Maybe this new lawsuit's given him some real religion. Anyway, spending time with Wade won't be a chore. I'm not the only woman who thinks he'd be the best catch in town if he weren't married to that newspaper of his."

Carolyn finished her wine. For awhile the two women were quiet, listening to the cicadas buzzing in the cedar trees.

Kate broke the silence.

"Carolyn, I want to finish that conversation we started at Sliders a couple of months ago. I've thought a lot since then about questioning that witness in the dioxin hearings with the information you gave me."

Kate hesitated for a moment. Apologies were not familiar ground for her.

"I've learned a little about life since that case. That was the wrong thing to do, no matter how I've tried to justify it to myself. That was a big case for me. I wanted to win it and prove I was as good a lawyer as any of those good old boys I practiced with. But I wouldn't do that again. I'd step away from the case and let someone else handle it. You trusted me as a friend. I shouldn't have breached that confidence, and I am sorry for it. I would appreciate it – actually I would love it – if you would accept my apology."

Carolyn smiled in the darkness.

"Kate, of course I accept it. I understand why that was a tough call for you to make back then. Thank you."

Carolyn leaned back and looked at the full moon.

"You also said you'd tell me one day the second reason you moved to Georgetown and gave up that fancy big-firm law practice. I don't think you were just running away from something you didn't like. I think you were running toward something better. You said it started with something your Daddy told you."

Kate thought for a minute, the truth serum of wine, dark-ness and a full moon pulling her along.

"You didn't know this then," she said finally, "but my dad found out just before those dioxin hearings began two years ago that his lung cancer had spread. He wouldn't say so, but he wanted me to come home and stay with him. I kept putting him off until the hearings were over. I'd get over on weekends, but I thought we had more time.

"He died the week after the hearings ended. I never got to tell him a lot of the things I wanted to tell him. That's a big regret for me in this life. He had some things to tell me, too, and he found a way to do it. In his bedroom, he left a neatly organized box of letters for me. The first was dated in late December of 1960, still sealed in an envelope postmarked the last day of that year. It was from Daddy, and he told me about things that had happened to me and to our family in that first year of my life. Beneath it were letters dated and postmarked every December until I was 20. At the end of every one of those years, he had written me a letter, with tidbits about how I was changing, funny stories about things I had done. He gave me advice about what he was still learning each year of his life. He thought it would help me know him better and help me understand myself, and maybe even my own children one day. He sealed them up each December and mailed them to me at our home address, with a postmark stamp from the Mullins Post Office and the date. He intercepted them in our mail and then saved them for me all those years.

"The last letter was one he had written two weeks before he died," Kate said. "He told me about one thing that had troubled him greatly the past few years, and it made me rethink where my life was heading."

Carolyn walked over to pour Kate more wine, and Kate sat

silently for a moment, her Dad as real as life to her. He had loved the tobacco export business he had built in Mullins. He loved the people side of the business – the tobacco farmers who could get by pretty well if the dry weather or the hail storms or the tobacco worms didn't kill their crops. He appreciated the clever warehousemen who brokered the farmers' tobacco to the cigarette companies. He liked the teams of buyers who worked for him, jovial men who lived away from home five months a year, seemingly happier for it, staying in boarding houses in sleepy tobacco towns. He got along well with the black workers in the tobacco factory, who moved tobacco from the warehouses to the Stewart plant and then through the giant steam driven re-drying machines, packed it in huge wooden hogsheads and loaded it onto railroad cars. He even liked the stuffy British and German cigarette company executives who thought he was some kind of tobacco wizard.

Carolyn sat back down, breaking Kate's reverie.

"In the '40s and '50s, everyone smoked and no one thought much about it," Kate said. "Hell, he had smoked cigarettes since he dropped out of the Citadel, long before anyone thought smoking was a big deal. Back then, it was romantic, a social icebreaker, a poor man's luxury. The Depression and World War II made people worry about dying young, so nobody worried much about how you might die if you were lucky enough to get old. By the 1940s, Mullins was the largest tobacco market in South Carolina. Almost everyone depended on it one way or the other.

"People were proud of being from Mullins. On each of the four main roads into town, there was a large wooden sign that read simply: 'Mullins: South Carolina's Largest, World's Best.' Didn't even mention the tobacco market, just had a big gold tobacco leaf and a dollar sign in the center. Everybody knew what it meant."

A smile tugged at her lips. "Not, by the way, what some of those Mullins boys suggested it meant when they were down at the beach, trying to pick up girls."

Carolyn laughed.

"In that letter, my father told me that for the past few years, he had wondered if he had spent his life doing the wrong thing. Knowing what we know now about smoking, he worried that he had been helping people, including his friends, commit slow suicide. He told me that he knew he was a gifted tobacco buyer and that people in the industry had praised him and paid him well for his talent and his hard work. But he said he wished he had quit when he was thirty and done something that helped people instead of hurt them.

"And then he said, as gently as he could, that I should give that some thought myself. He told me he knew I was good at what I did. He just wondered if I would be happy about spending my life that way when I looked back thirty years from now."

"And now," she said brightly, "here I am, in Georgetown, doing something I love, for people who need it."

15

Wade's Church

Kate was waiting on the front porch of her office when Wade appeared on Sunday afternoon in his red Jeep Wrangler, canvas top off, ready to go. His khaki shorts, blue polo shirt and boat shoes made her wonder about the church meeting.

He tossed her bag into the back of the Jeep, and she climbed in.

"Nice ad on your license plate," Wade said, nodding at the rear plate of her dark green Miata.

"NOTGLTY," the personalized plate read.

"Vanity of vanities, as the old prophet said," Wade smiled.

"I promise you I was not cocky enough on this new venture of mine to do that myself," Kate said. "It was a surprise going away present from some of the lawyers in my office. Anyway, I've heard those words a lot from my clients these past few weeks, but I haven't heard them much from the judges and juries just yet."

"No, I like the tag. It's better than the one I saw last week revving up at a stoplight. It was a red Stingray convertible driven by a tough-looking blonde. The license plate said 'Topless.' I bet she had four on the floor and a fifth under the seat."

Wade drove down Highmarket Street, past the Prince George Church, and never slowed down. The church grounds looked quiet. Kate gave him that puzzled look he had seen before. He gave her a quick glance and a mock dead-pan.

"I told you I was taking you to *my* church. I didn't say my family's church. I want to show you where I worship. Just relax, I think you'll have fun, and I'll have you back by 11 o'clock tonight. That work okay?"

Kate sat back in her seat, bracing herself against the jolts of the Wrangler. She reminded herself that Jason Hart and Carolyn Brown had both vouched for this guy.

"That works fine. Besides, I'm really intrigued now. I thought newspaper editors worshipped only themselves."

He glanced at her, looking for a twinkle in her eye. He wasn't sure he saw one.

Wade wheeled into the Georgetown Marina, just off of Front Street, and led Kate down to the dock, stopping near his Boston Whaler. There was a cooler in the back, two beach chairs and some fishing gear. Sitting patiently erect on the bow, tongue hanging out, left front paw raised in greeting, was a liver and white English springer spaniel.

"Kate, meet my first mate, Molly. She's granting you permission to board. You take that soft seat on the back. Molly likes the bow. She's ten years old – seventy in dog years – but she's pretty frisky and still loves to go to church with me."

Wade stowed Kate's bag in the hold, untied the boat's dock lines, and in five minutes, they were leaving Georgetown Harbor headed toward Winyah Bay and the Atlantic Ocean.

It was the first time Kate had viewed the restaurants and shops lining Front Street from the water. From this angle, the town had a Cannery Row appeal to it – a little shabby, but plenty authentic. Clearly not a Disney-designed resort with all the rough edges sanded off.

Wade had said little since the boat had left the harbor. It was clear neither wanted to be the one to break the silence.

As both good reporters and good lawyers know, silence is a powerful investigative tool. A thirty-second pause in a conversation makes most people nervous, apt to blurt out something to break the silence. Some of the best information Wade had ever learned as a reporter had come after the person being interviewed had answered his last question, and Wade had simply sat quietly, doodling in his notepad, then looked up expectantly, finding the eyes across from him. Kate used the same technique in questioning witnesses.

They motored out Winyah Bay for the next ten minutes. Finally, Wade geared the engine down, reducing the noise, and pointed to his left. He handed Kate his binoculars.

"See the dock over there?" he asked. "That's Bernard Baruch's old estate, Hobcaw Barony. Baruch made a huge fortune in the early part of the century buying and selling stocks. He bought several thousand acres here as a hunting retreat for himself and his friends. That's where F.D.R. spent a month relaxing just weeks before D-Day. Winston Churchill used to visit Baruch here. You should take the tour."

Kate nodded.

"So where are we heading? Not to England to see Churchill's grave, I hope."

"No, we're gonna head out to the end of Winyah Bay, about another twenty or thirty minutes. The tide's going our way. Then we'll pull up on the inlet side of North Island. It's a six-mile stretch of beach that's owned partly by the state and partly by a private foundation. It doesn't have a thing on it except an old lighthouse, and it'll never be developed. You can only get there by boat. It's one of the most peaceful places I know. I think you've figured it out – this is my church out here. This is what soothes my soul."

Kate looked around. He had picked a good day for this

visit. The sky was clear, there was little wind and the bay's surface was almost mirror smooth. Behind her, she could see the tall plumes of condensation from the paper mill rising over Georgetown as the town receded into the distance. Ahead of her, she could see occasional flashes of silver, a sign that schools of menhaden were nearby.

"You know a little about this bay," Wade said. "You represented the paper plant during the dioxin fight."

Kate pondered his comment for a moment, not sure if it was a challenge or just a casual observation.

"Those hearings were tough on everybody," she said. "There was one black gentleman who testified that he'd fished Winyah Bay almost every day for twenty years. He'd caught his own bait with a casting net, pulling in minnows and menhaden to use as bait for puppy drum or sea trout. He said he'd managed to feed his family in tough times that way, but after what he'd heard about what the chemicals in the water were doing to his grandchildren, he'd never let them eat another fish from that water.

"I remember exactly what he said: 'I don't even want to hold the edge of my castin' net in my mouth in order to throw it anymore.'

"That got my attention," Kate said. "But those folks kept their jobs, and the plant doesn't put dioxin into this water anymore. Both sides won."

They sped along in silence for a while, enjoying the wind and the gentle bounce of the boat across the water. The salt marshes around them looked like endless fields of lush green wheat. Wade was eating boiled peanuts from a small paper sack on the seat beside him, tossing an occasional wet, salty treat to Molly.

Kate's keen eyes spotted something on the right.

"Wade, 2 o'clock, dolphins, I think," she said.

Off the boat's bow and to the right, two large dolphins, dark grey, were rolling slowly through the water, blowholes wheezing, feeding on the tail end of a school of menhaden. Alongside one of them, a small grey calf was bobbing and swimming in unison with its mother. Hearing the engine, they sped up and played in the wake of the boat's bow, almost close enough to touch. Molly lay across the bow, her back legs splayed out behind her, her head hanging over the boat's edge, eyeing the dolphins suspiciously.

"Those guys are even smarter than most people give them credit for," Wade said, slowing the boat so Kate could hear him. "There's a spot in the main creek south of McClellanville, behind Capers Island, where I've seen a pod of dolphin fishing together like a team. They call it strand-feeding."

"I've heard Carolyn talk about that, but I've never seen it," Kate said.

"It's amazing to watch," Wade said. "Dolphin love to eat striped mullet, but the smaller fish can almost always out-maneuver a single dolphin. At low tide in the creek, though, the dolphin can improve the odds. Three or four of them will swim in circles around a school of mullet, like they're herding cattle. They move the school toward the creek bank, until they're near a stretch of exposed beach. Then one of the dolphins flashes broadside into the school, splashing dozens of fish onto the shore. As the fish flip-flop along the bank, the dolphins come right up on the shore, halfway out of the water, feasting on them. Somehow these ocean mammals have learned how to communicate with each other better than most people can."

Wade revved the engine, and they sped toward the ocean. It was hard to hear over the engine's drone, so they talked little the rest of the way to North Island. By 4 o'clock, they had found the southern tip of the island and eased the boat close to shore on the inlet side. Molly immediately leapt from the bow and swam ashore. She shook herself, then sprinted down the beach, leaping like a deer in the small waves.

Wade set the boat's anchor in the sand, checked the status of the tide and satisfied himself that the boat was secure. He waded the cooler, the chairs and the fishing gear ashore, then reached into the hold and unfolded a small dolly with short, wide tires.

"We'll put our stuff on this, and roll it down the beach a way so we can find a breeze, take a swim, and cook up a little dinner. How's that sound?"

It was a five-minute walk around the inlet shoreline to the beach side, and Kate had not expected to see something this exceptionally beautiful unfold in front of her. The sand dunes were fifteen feet high, capped by stands of green-stalked, tan-topped sea oats. At low tide, the beach was wide and flat and full of shells. Kate immediately spotted dozens of whelk shells. She remembered how excited her mother had been when she found the rare one at Ocean Drive. When they were away from the beach, her mother had sometimes held a whelk shell to Kate's ear, convincing her she could hear the sound of the ocean in the shell.

Wade found a spot just above the high-tide mark, parked the cooler, set up the chairs and planted his fishing rod holder in the sand. Kate opened the cooler. At first she saw only Bud-weisers, then spotted a few Amstel Lights.

"Take your choice," Wade said. "I'm a domestic guy, but I thought you might like something else."

Kate pulled out two Buds and opened them, handing one to Wade. He quickly gathered several whelk shells in a circle and placed a small metal grill over them. He produced a plastic bag holding a couple dozen ready-to-light charcoal briquettes.

The light breeze from the ocean was just enough to keep the no-see-ums and horseflies back in the marsh behind the dunes. There was not another person on the beach as far as Kate could see. Just beyond the breakers, a dozen or so pelicans were circling above a school of menhaden or mullet, finding their mark, plunging, wings spread like ancient pterodactyls, head first into the ocean, crashing like cannonballs, then returning quickly to the surface to float, throw their heads back, perpendicular to the water, and gulp down a beakful of fish.

Kate looked over at Wade, patiently rigging up the tackle on his fishing rod.

"I have to say, Wade, I like your church service so far. So what happens next?" she asked.

"The usual order of worship includes a walk along the beach for a mile or two," Wade said. "That will tire Molly out pretty good. When we get back, she'll take a nap and you can sit and enjoy the scenery while I make a few casts and see if the pompano are hungry for some sand fleas. I see a few of them scurrying to bury themselves in the wet sand right now. If we're lucky, we'll have grilled pompano for dinner."

Wade adjusted the drag on his reel.

"There's a full moon tonight and a clear sky," he said. "I did check the weather forecast. I suggest we take a walk, have a swim, fish a little, eat some dinner, watch the moon rise over the ocean, then pack up for a quiet ride home. There will be enough moonlight to get us home after dark."

Kate kicked off her sandals.

"Praise the Lord," she said, smiling. "Sounds good to me."

"Tell you what, Kate," Wade said. "If you want to change into your bathing suit, I'll stroll on up the beach. I promise I'll walk slow and won't look back, but you can head up behind the dunes to change if that's more comfortable."

"I'm not as shy as you think I am, Mr. McNabb," Kate said and began unbuttoning her blouse, top buttons first. She unbuttoned four buttons then quickly unsnapped her shorts and started slipping them off right in front of Wade.

Before his eyes got too wide, Kate laughed and said, "Relax Wade, I wore my bathing suit under my clothes."

In ten seconds she had stuffed her shorts and her blouse into her bag and was ready to go. They headed north, watching the pelicans dive and scanning the sea's surface for dolphins.

They walked along in silence for a while. Molly ran ahead of them for a hundred yards or so, chasing shorebirds at full throttle, her brown, fluffy ears straight back. She slowed as the birds flew away, then made a wide turn and checked back in with Wade. Then she was off to sniff out ghost crab holes.

Wade remembered a comment Kate had made the day before.

"Kate, what was that story you started to tell us yesterday about catching a big bass? What were you doing at Bowman's Forest when you were thirteen anyway?"

Kate took a few more steps, pondering where to begin.

"My father was a great hunter and fisherman. And he loved to tell stories and to listen to them. Some were just funny, some were like little parables, with a nugget of wisdom. He was good company. One of his buddies used to take him to the Forest a couple of times a year.

"One year, they invited him to a 'father-son' weekend. He decided he'd take me along."

Kate paused for a few seconds, took a deep breath and continued.

"My dad decided if I was going to be a good South Carolina girl, I should know the basics of hunting and fishing. He was a patient teacher, and I was lucky to have him. Anyway, he brought me along to this father-son hunting and fishing weekend. He had that kind of defiant streak in him sometimes. When my tomboy self showed up, some folks gawked, but nobody said a word. I'd spent the last couple of falls learning to shoot wild quail, so poppin' some of those tame birds that had been raised in a pen and had never seen the sky before they were thrown out of a burlap bag was pretty easy for me. It was like an Easter egg hunt with guns.

"The second afternoon we were there, I caught a big bass in one of the stocked ponds. It was late spring, and the wild geese had laid eggs in nests on the ground all around the ponds. As we were taking my bass back to be weighed and measured, we noticed one of the geese strutting and hissing and flapping her wings at us. She made me nervous, and I told my dad we should take a different path.

"My dad was so stubborn. He said no goose was going to keep him from taking the path he wanted to. He said we should get a running start and sprint right by her. By then, that goose was going crazy, standing on her tiptoes, beating her wings at us and making little charges in our direction. She was almost hissing steam at us she was so mad. I wasn't about to take that goose on.

"My father told me to watch how he did it. He made a little head fake in one direction, then just jogged right by the goose, the bass cradled in his arms like a football. The next thing I knew that goose was chasing him as fast as she could go, and honking up a storm. My father glanced over his shoulder, saw the goose running after him, flapping her wings, so he picked up his speed. I know he was sure he could outrun any goose alive. And he was right. But what hadn't occurred to him was that the damn goose could fly!

"I couldn't believe my eyes. My father was running as fast as he could, but the goose was right behind him, flying right at the back of his head. It looked like an airplane was after him. My dad looked back one more time and saw that big old goose about to take a bite out of his head. He panicked, leaned forward as far as he could, running so hard it almost tore his toenails off. Suddenly he just tipped over forward and tumbled head over heels in a spectacular fall. He ended up flat on his back with his legs in the pond, stunned by what had happened so fast. The bass hit the ground and started flopping toward the water. By that time, the goose had flown away. I ran up, grabbed the bass by the mouth, pulled my father up by his arm and hustled us on out of there.

"I was laughing so hard, I had to pretend I was crying. And since some other fishermen saw the whole event, it became a pretty famous story at the Forest. And my fish won the prize for the weekend. It was mounted and put on the wall.

"That's a great story!" he said. "Did your father ever hear you tell it?"

"He did. He loved the fact that I enjoy telling stories almost as much as he did," Kate said.

About a mile up the beach, Wade spotted in the sand what looked like a set of prints from a small tractor running from the ocean up to the edge of the sand dunes and looping back toward the water.

"Kate, look at this. It's the tracks from a loggerhead turtle that laid her eggs on this beach last night. The tide has washed away some of the tracks, but you can see the part above the high water mark where she went up during the night to lay her eggs and then the track where she came back down to the water when she was finished. Let's walk up and see if we can find the nest."

Twenty-five yards away, just below the sand dunes, was an area where the sand looked like it had been dug up and smoothed over. Unless they had seen the tracks pointing like an arrowhead to the spot, they would never have noticed the slight disturbance of the sand.

"Have you ever seen a loggerhead come ashore to lay her eggs?" Wade asked.

"No, I've heard people talk about it, but I've never seen it," Kate said. "Why are they called loggerheads, anyway?"

"Just because their heads are so damn big," Wade said. "And it is a powerful sight to see the struggle and determination they have when they come ashore. I've only seen it once.

"I came out here a few years ago in late May and camped for a few days," he said. "In the late afternoon, I was fishing in the surf. It was smooth as glass, and I was watching closely for a patch of nervous water, any little shimmer or pattern that would signal a school of fish moving through. I kept seeing this brown head poke out of the water, then disappear. I finally figured out it was a female loggerhead scouting the beach for a nest site. About midnight that night, I walked up the beach, hoping she might come ashore. There was a half moon and not many clouds. Sure enough, about a mile away from my campsite, I saw this huge shape dragging itself out of the surf, right at the water's edge. She was about three feet long – they get to be nearly 300 pounds. I kept my distance so I wouldn't spook her.

"It took an hour for her to drag herself, one flipper at a time, across the beach to a spot just in front of the tall dunes. It's painful to watch – like a fat man crawling on his stomach for fifty yards, pulling himself along using only his elbows and ankles.

"Then she dug a hole in the sand with her flippers, turned

her back to the ocean, and began to drop her milky eggs into the hole. She probably laid about a hundred of them, like soft, wet ping-pong balls. I've always heard that tears run down their cheeks while they are laying their eggs, but I didn't get close enough to her face to see that. When she finished, she covered up the hole and smoothed the sand with her flippers. Then she dragged herself back to the ocean and slowly swam off into the surf. That's a dedicated mom."

"What happens to the eggs?" Kate asked.

"If the raccoons or the wild boars don't find them and eat them like caviar, they hatch in about two months. One day they pop out of those little white sacs, squirm their way to the surface and start skittering toward the ocean. There will be a hundred or more of these three-inch turtles trying to fight their way to the surf. Some get munched by birds, some get dragged by sandcrabs into their holes on the beach, some just don't have the strength to make it, and many of those who do get to the water are quickly eaten by fish and stingrays. But the ones who survive that first scary day head to the warm waters of the Gulf Stream, about twenty miles offshore. About one in a thousand live long enough to mate. And a couple of decades later, the females who survive will try their best to find that same beach again and lay their eggs. There is a constancy about it, a connection to a particular place, that I like."

By the time Wade had finished his story, they were back at their campsite.

"It's plenty warm for a swim," Wade said. "Want to get that bathing suit wet?"

Kate shook her head.

"Wade, as much as I love the beach, I'm not much for swimming."

Wade gave her a surprised look.

"I know," she said. "I don't panic when judges scold me in court or witnesses change their testimony in the middle of a trial. But deep water makes me nervous."

Kate stared out over the ocean, eyes focused on the horizon, her arms across her chest. Wade thought she was about to say more. He stood beside her, hoping his silence would encourage her to keep talking.

"It's a long story, too much for today," she said finally.

Her voice was steady, but Wade could see sadness in her eyes.

Kate took a deep breath and let it out, then forced a smile and looked over at Wade.

"Okay, Mr. McNabb," she said, her voice brighter. "Now, are you going to catch us some dinner or are you planning to grill us some of these little sand fleas I saw scurrying around in the waves?"

Wade took his cue, and answered cheerily.

"Don't worry, I brought some tuna filets just in case my hook comes up empty. I heard you missed your grilled tuna Friday night. And now that I know you're the big angler here, maybe you should do the casting."

"No, thanks," Kate said. "I'm gonna park in this beach chair for a little while and bury my feet in the sand. But I'll pretend to watch you fish."

Wade reached for his fishing rod.

"You know," he said, "there was a Scottish lawyer *and* journalist *and* trout fisherman named John Buchan who had the perfect thought about fishing. He said, 'Fishing is a perpetual series of occasions for hope.' Remember, I'm a secret optimist. We'll catch some fish."

Thirty minutes later, Wade had caught two keeper-sized pompano and cut four filets from them. He dipped them into a plastic bag with olive oil, wrapped a long strip of bacon around each one, then dropped them gently onto the grill. He salted and peppered them, then squeezed a lime over the filets. Out of the cooler came plates, a bag of salad, and two thick slices of sourdough bread, which Wade put on the grill beside the fish. Then from the bottom of the cooler, he pulled a bottle of Pinot Grigio, handed Kate a corkscrew and put her to work.

As they cleaned up after dinner, the last rays of the day streamed low through the feathers of the sea oats atop the sand dunes behind them, turning the ocean almost royal blue. The moon had not begun to rise over the ocean, but it wouldn't be long.

As the sky over the water darkened, Kate and Wade sat side by side in the low beach chairs, finishing the Pinot. Molly lay on the sand between them, her back legs stretched behind her, her head on her crossed front paws, dozing.

"Kate, thank you for coming with me to my church," Wade said. "I don't have much other religion. I figured out when I was about twelve that any god who sent people to hell because nobody had gotten around to telling them about the Bible wasn't the kind of god I wanted to believe in. Over the next few years, I watched our churches in Georgetown ignore the Golden Rule and use the Bible to explain why it was perfectly Christian to treat black folks like dogs.

"These were kind, well-meaning people who would give a church member their last piece of bread. But they couldn't believe that Jesus would have treated a black child just like a white one. It just hit me one day that a hundred years ago most of those good-hearted people would have been quoting scripture to justify slavery. I couldn't find my god in those churches."

Kate was nodding in the dark. They were lapsing into that

open conversation that sometimes sneaks up on two people driving through the night together, both looking straight ahead into the dark and straight into their own hearts.

"I think religion is mainly a way for us to figure out how to deal with the mystery of life and the knowledge that it will end," Kate said. "The certainty that our lives will end and the uncertainty of when they will end should make us live a little better, a little more intentionally each day. Thinking about that is what got me to Georgetown.

"I know this one thing for sure – the surface of the earth is a slippery place. Without an anchor to keep them grounded when life's tough times hit them, some people slide right off the face of the earth. When the sadness or loneliness or hope-lessness gets to be too much for them, they just let go and slip off into the void.

"For some people, religion is a good anchor to the earth," Kate continued. "For others it's a false hope, and they find a different anchor to keep them grounded. It might be family or friends or their work. Sometimes I think the best anchor is a sense that you are needed by someone. What gets me out of bed many mornings is the certain knowledge that a client is out there waiting for me to solve the problem he told me about yesterday. It helps when the folks who need you appreciate what you do, but that doesn't have to be part of the bargain."

Wade was quiet for a few minutes, staring out at the ocean. Then he laughed, trying to break the serious mood a little.

"Well, I decided years ago I'm just a cross between a Baptist and a Buddhist. Not those hellfire-preaching, no-dancing, no-drinking, drenched in the Blood of the Lamb Baptists, but the real Baptists who don't believe in a church or a doctrine stand-ing between them and whatever God is. I like that kind of Bap-tist's direct route to God, and I like the Buddhist's straight road to the natural world. Works for me.

"And you might be right about that anchor thing. I was born at sea-level, and I've never been happy when I was living very far above sea-level. And I'm pretty sure I'll die at sea-level and be buried at sea-level. Maybe I'm afraid I'll slip off if I stay at those higher altitudes."

Kate looked at Wade. The moon was rising just over the horizon, as deep red as an August plum and as big as a basketball. But it was too dark for her to make out Wade's face.

"Wade, your anchor is that newspaper and the good it lets you do in this community. I understand that better now."

"Well, maybe you're on to something, counselor," Wade said, standing up and offering her a hand to pull her up from the low chair.

"C'mon, we should head back. That moon will be as yellow and bright as a searchlight by the time we get to the boat. The tide has turned. It's coming in, and we'll have a nice ride."

A light breeze brushed their backs as they started toward Georgetown Harbor. Molly curled into a furry ball at Kate's feet, a fast friend. The full moon reflecting on the water paved an easy path home.

Kate sat quietly in the bow. The full moon's glow hid many of the stars in the sky, but the lights on either shore of the bay twinkled in the distance. She wondered if she should have told Wade more about how she learned that the surface of the earth is a slippery place. It was still a hard story for her to think about, much less tell.

PART II – OCEAN DRIVE BEACH
1970

16

Kate and David, 1970

Kate Stewart had been two weeks shy of turning ten on that August day.

Early in the morning Kate's mother, her eyes bright, and her voice as excited as a teenager's, shook her awake.

"Up and at 'em, punkin-head," Mary Stewart said, knowing it would make Kate groan.

She pushed back the curtains hiding the sunlight bouncing off the Atlantic Ocean along their stretch of Ocean Drive Beach.

"It's a perfect day for crabbing. It's supposed to cloud up a little bit, and the tide at the creek is almost dead low. If we leave soon, we'll hit Calabash Creek just as the tide starts in. The blue crabs will follow right behind it."

Kate burrowed deeper into her pillow, but she was awake enough to hear the break of the waves less than a hundred yards away. Crabbing was a ritual family expedition they took several times each summer, and a special treat for Kate's mother. Kate would rather have spent the day on the beach, reading her brother's old Hardy Boys books and catching rays.

"C'mon, darlin'," her mother whispered, leaning down to kiss her. "I want some of that warm neck sugar before it melts away."

Mary Stewart, the mother of a fifteen-year-old boy, knew that she had only a couple of years left of easy affection from

Kate. Then her daughter's hormones would kick in. The need for independence would rise, and Kate would start pushing her parents away. Mary knew it was a necessary part of the maturing process, nothing personal to them. Her son David's adolescent aloofness had hurt her feelings, but she feared that Kate's inevitable distancing would break Arch Stewart's heart. She got a quick nibble of the wrinkles on Kate's neck, topped it off with a tickle in the ribs, and left Kate giggling against her will.

"Your brother's dressed and ready to go. Put on some shorts and a T-shirt and your old tennis shoes. I promise we'll be back by mid-afternoon. Your Daddy will be here tonight, and we can surprise him with his favorites: crab cakes, a few ears of Silver Queen and some fresh peaches and ice cream for dessert."

Forty minutes later they were stopped outside Thomas Seafood Company, near the drawbridge over the Intracoastal Waterway. David was sent inside to get some flounder heads for crab bait. He picked his way carefully past the wooden tubs of white shrimp – heads still on, just off the boat from the Calabash docks – past the wood boxes of mullet, croaker, spots, tuna, dolphin, grouper, and soft-shell crabs, all neatly arranged in layers of crushed ice, to the tubs of flounder at the end of the line. The ample ice in the tubs and the frequent rinsing of the concrete floors from the freshwater hoses made the inside of the seafood market a cool haven from the August heat. The smell was fishy, but clean, with the hint of ocean salt. It drew smoothly through the nostrils without catching.

On a good day, Mr. Thomas would give David a toothy grin and say, "You're a lucky young man. I just filleted a bucket of flounder as big as doormats, and the heads are right here. I'll wrap them up for you."

They would still be cool from the ice, with hardly a fish smell to them. On a bad day, Mr. Thomas would shake his round, bald head, wipe his wet hands on the chest of his once-white apron, and point with the stub of his burned out cigar to the back door.

"Cleaned some yesterday, buddy-ro, and the heads are out back in the trash can."

It was David's job to dig out those stinky heads, wrap them up and bring them back to the car.

Mary preferred the day-old flounder heads. She thought the extra aroma attracted more, and perhaps bigger, blue crabs. She would scrunch up her nose as she pushed the crabbing twine through the gills on the bright-white, bottom-facing side of the flounder and then through and out the tight mouth, her slim fingers avoiding the tiny, needle-sharp teeth that could draw blood in a heartbeat. She tied on a one-ounce sinker, rolled out fifteen feet or so of twine, and tied that to an eight-inch stick. Ten of these, a long-handled crab net, and a bushel basket, and she had the makings of a successful day of crabbing.

It was another twenty minutes to Mary Stewart's favorite crabbing spot, and David entertained them along the way with his imitation of Mr. Thomas, using one of the extra sticks as a cigar prop and poking out his flat stomach to mock the fish seller's pot belly. Kate giggled the whole way, thrilled to have her brother's undivided attention. A natural mimic, he would often imitate their parents for Kate when they looked away. She loved it when he made her part of that gentle conspiracy. She would feel as old as he was, part of his team.

By ten-thirty, they had parked the car on the roadside near the two-lane wooden bridge over Calabash Creek and maneuvered their way down to the large sandbar, exposed at low tide and partly covered with oyster shells. At low tide, the salty creek and mud flats exuded a pungent mixture of the creosote-smell of the treated wood bridge pilings and the slightly sulphur, rotten egg scent of the fertile marsh.

Hundreds of tiny fiddler crabs scurried in and out of their holes in the wet sand. Each male had his oddly-outsized claw raised and ticking back and forth like a metronome, his normal-sized claw rhythmically crossing it, like a bow across a violin, sexual preening for the benefit of the pink-elbowed lady crabs, intimidation for the other male crabs.

* * * * *

Arch Stewart seldom joined the Calabash crabbing expeditions. He was a bit of a fishing snob and looked down his nose at the simple craft of crabbing. And that summer, as usual, he was traveling on business and made it to the Stewarts' Ocean Drive Beach house only on occasional weekends. He spent most of each May and June in Europe, plotting with the British and German cigarette companies how much of which grades of tobacco they needed for their products. This Mullins-born-and-bred boy – who had passed most of his growing-up summers in bare feet and left college after two years – had used his basic smarts and natural talents to good advantage. His receptive warmth and penchant for attentive, eye-meeting listening won the confidence of his tobacco company clients and turned them into trusting friends. His love of a good story, especially one told on himself, made him an easy companion, whether in a London restaurant, or in a small-town Georgia diner during the early part of tobacco season.

In late July, he would visit those hot south-Georgia towns, coaching his teams of tobacco buyers on this year's buying strategy. He was a patient teacher, always encouraging young buyers, helping them improve their skills in judging the golden leaf. He did not, however, tolerate poor performance born of laziness or inattention to detail, and he did not hesitate to fire those who repeated mistakes for those reasons. A hard-working young buyer who simply didn't display the necessary talent was gently directed to another career.

By early August, the South Carolina markets would open, and Arch Stewart would move north to the warehouses in Mullins and other parts of the Pee Dee section of the state. The North Carolina markets would open right behind them, and finally, by early fall, he would follow the markets in small-town Virginia. It was companionable work, much of it turning on subtle relationships: farmers who brought their tobacco to the warehouses owned by the sons of the men their fathers had trusted to get the best price for their tobacco – relationships between second-generation warehouse owners and second-generation tobacco buyers, communicating in their rapid-fire negotiations of winks, pulled ears and touched noses, where fast deals were sealed with a burst of eye contact and a final nod.

It was a ritual dance to the auctioneer's fast, nasal sing-song chant – "Seven-ty-ONE-one-one . . ." He spots a finger aside a buyer's nose, makes eye contact and nods. "I see TWO-two-two, seven-ty-TWO." He swings his head back and forth, looking up and down both lines of buyers, repeating the rapid, whiny chant, looking for response. An earlobe pulled, eye contact, he nods. "Seven-ty-THREE-three-three." He checks both lines. No signals, no eye contact. "I have seven-ty-three-three-three, do I hear four?" He swings his head quickly. No more winks, no more ear pulls, no more eye contact. "Seven-ty-FOUR, four, four . . ." he sings hopefully, looks around one more time, then ends with a shout, "SEVENTY-THREE, SOLD

AMERICAN!" or "Sold, Reynolds!" or "Sold, Stewart!" Then on to the next pile.

Beneath that human skin of every tobacco auction was a market calculus. Each player wanted a good deal for his principal – the warehousemen for the farmer, the buyer for his tobacco company. But each understood that if he cut too good a deal, the system would suffer: at prices too low, the farmers would sink too deeply into debt to produce another year's crop, at prices too high, the tobacco companies would consider more carefully the cheaper tobacco from new farms in Africa and South America.

Long before the auctioneer's rhythmic chant started, Arch Stewart would pull several golden "hands" of cured, bunched, and tied tobacco leaves from the bottom of a farmer's flat wooden basket. He would spread the leaves, hold them to his nose and inhale deeply. He would rub the leaves between his fingertips to test their flexibility. He would touch his tongue to the tobacco, then hold it under the sundevils dancing through the warehouse skylights in the tobacco-dust haze, checking it for just the right shade of gold – not too yellow, not too brown, not too green, not too cooked. Using just his senses, he could make instant decisions that cigarette company analysts would confirm – months later, after the re-grading and the re-drying – by their chemical tests. Archibald Stewart was the best judge of tobacco anywhere in the Southeast. His instinct was a natural gift, but he always reminded his children that it had taken hard work to perfect it.

On that August morning in 1970, Arch Stewart was in Conway working the Friday sales, planning to make the half-hour drive to the beach house that night. The weekend was in sight, and the buyers were looking ahead to their time off – some to slip into rocking chairs with their tired feet up on porch rails, others to find some mischief. The banter between the buyers and the auctioneer was quick and sharp. Arch watched as the two lines of buyers made their way down the last row of the Old Brick Warehouse's tobacco piles. All fifty piles in that row were the same grade, reviewed carefully and marked in advance of the sale by a Department of Agriculture grader. Normally, each similarly-graded pile would bring the same price per pound, each tobacco company buyer winning his share of bids at that price, boldly defying the principles of antitrust law.

As they approached the last fifteen piles of tobacco, Arch saw an ancient ritual begin. It was the job of Red Williams, one of the brothers who owned Old Brick, to call out the starting price for the bidding on each pile just as the buyers reached it. As the auctioneer started the bidding on the first of those last fifteen piles, Red clapped his hands and shouted out, "Help me out a little, boys. We're gettin' to the widow's tobacco. She needs shoes for the baby. Take care of her, now."

Without any exchange of conversation among the buyers, the price for each remaining pile of tobacco jumped a nickel, from 72 cents a pound to 77 cents. At the end of the row, Red Williams beamed at the buyers, wiping his sweaty forehead with his handkerchief, bobbing his flushed face in thanks. They smiled back and ducked their heads a little. The buyers clustered around the two older black men waiting there, one dipping iced water from a metal bucket into paper cones for the white men, the other offering small, wet paper bags of boiled peanuts for ten cents each. They shuffled, and smiled like they meant it.

Arch shook his head at Red Williams' pageant and hid his amusement. He remembered how touched he had been as a 12 year old, the first time he had heard the call for help for the "widow's tobacco." It had warmed his heart to see the quick response from the buyers, and he had looked around trying to spot the grateful face of the poor woman. It took him a second season to learn the code. The "widow's tobacco" – as all the buyers knew – in fact came from the warehouse owner's own farm, and he wanted a little boost in the price for *his* tobacco. In exchange for such friendly price hikes, the warehouse owners passed out small envelopes at the end of each week with gift certificates to the "Red Dot Store." The certificates – known in the buyer parlance as "likker tickets" – were used to purchase a little potion to ease the pain of a weekend far from home in a quiet South Carolina town. It was a few bucks out of the tobacco companies' pockets, shared between the warehouse owner and the buyers, but Arch Stewart understood it was part of the grease that lubricated the important relationships among these players.

Arch Stewart, in fact, was about to apply a little grease himself. He had been wondering why American Tobacco Company was unexpectedly bidding up the price of the leaves from the middle tobacco stalks just coming to market that week. He was planning to take one of American's buyers, and a bottle of the buyer's best friend Jack Daniels, fishing on the Little Pee Dee River that afternoon to see if he could find the answer.

* * * * *

David missed his traveling father more than he let on. Quiet as a child, David had absorbed his father's lessons by watching and imitating, only occasionally asking for help or direction. David had learned to catch fish and clean them, to shoot quail and dress them, and to always carry at least his share of any load. The father's Scot genes made him ration direct praise carefully, but he could not hide from his friends his pride in David. Only in recent months, as his body had begun to fill out his lanky skeleton, had David started to find his own voice. He was secretly proud of the fact that when his father was away, his sister and mother had begun to look to him as the man of the family, to do the things Arch Stewart usually did.

Mary Stewart was surprised by her reaction to this mix of boy and man who suddenly inhabited her home. She had been so protective of him as a child she had pretended not to notice the sprouting of the black, curly hair, first on his legs and in his armpits, then a sprig or two on his chest. At five-foot-nine, he towered over her by nearly a half-foot. This summer, when he put his arm around her shoulders and gave her a light squeeze as they walked together, she had felt for the first time that maybe he was the one protecting her. She could not understand exactly where this shy boy had found the beginnings of confidence to make playful banter, to tease her and even to make light fun of the father he adored.

*   *   *   *   *

Kate stomped her feet along the edge of the sandbar, scattering the fiddler crabs.

"Kate, careful on the oyster shells," David said sternly. He tapped a reminding finger on a two-inch scar on his right knee, earned three years ago on the same sandbar. She stopped and pouted.

"I want to be the netter today," Kate grumped. "I'm old enough."

Crabbing is a simple art, and David had learned it from his mother. Mary was a patient teacher and a strict disciplinarian, especially on issues of honesty and fairness. When teaching by example and coaching failed, she was quick to teach by the switch. As in, "That's enough, young man. Go pick me a switch right now and bring it here to me." A few quick switches across the back of the calves were powerful teachers, as both David and Kate could attest. And they were always followed by Mary's strong hugs.

David had learned how to find the best spots along the sandbar to set out the crab bait, usually the natural channels that funneled the rising tide up the creek. That day, he quickly spotted those, unrolled the twine on the first stick, and with an easy underhand pendulum swing, tossed the end with the weighted flounder head into the slow-moving current. He jabbed the stick into the wet sand at the edge of the waterline.

Mary and Kate helped set out the other seven lines, and by the time they were finished, the tide had begun to push its way back up Calabash Creek. The light cloud cover kept their shadows off the water, and they stood back, eying the lines carefully. Within minutes, David saw a slack line go taut, and he quickly picked up the stick. He was afraid he might be a little rusty, but he remembered how his mother had taught him to catch a crab. Patience and stealth were the keys.

He held the line between the thumb and index finger of each hand, the stick tight against his wrist, and gave the string a gentle pull. He felt the steady pressure from the end of the line and knew he had a keeper. He motioned to Kate to bring the long-handled crab net, and he tucked it snugly against his right leg. He started inching the twine in slowly, feeling the firm resistance from the two-clawed creature nibbling away on the flounder head, but still safely out of sight in the murky creek water. When he had retrieved about half the line, David's eyes narrowed to slits, trying to penetrate the reflections from the creek's surface. There was still no sight of the flounder head or the crab. He pulled in several quick inches of line, and it suddenly went slack.

His aggressive tug had spooked the crab, and it had released the bait, instinctively slipping back a few inches to the safety of deeper water. David mentally slapped his forehead, then remembered what he had seen his mother do so many times in that situation. She would stop dead still for a minute, letting the flounder head sit quietly where it was. She would look around serenely at the setting, the deep green marsh grass lining the creek banks, perhaps a yellow-beaked white egret walking stiffly on its black stilt-legs, stretching its elongated neck low over the water to eye a minnow or small crab beneath the surface, striking swiftly, retracting the neck and gulping down its prey.

She would plant one hand on a slim hip and wait patiently until the crab, more hungry than smart, would reattach both claws and begin its machine-like mouth movements on the bait's softest parts. The tension returned to the crab line. She would show a sly smile and re-start the inching process. Each time the crab sloughed off, she'd go through her patience routine. When the bait was about five feet away from shore, she could usually make out the shape of the flounder head and see its white side flutter slightly. Then she could see the white streaks on the inner sides of the crab's claws and the outline of its dark green shell, sharply pointed at each end. She would stretch out her left arm and lift the string, easing the flounder head a few inches off the bottom. The crab, lulled by its gluttony, would cling tightly to its meal. Mary would reach the net behind the crab with her right hand and with a fast flip of her wrist and scarcely a splash, dip it into the water, under the crab and the bait. The net would then erupt from the water full of string, flounder head, and a furious, claw-snapping crab. She'd flip the net upside-down, empty its contents into the basket and quickly retrieve the flounder head, leaving the crab to scurry around the basket's bottom. She could never resist a successful smile.

David had mastered those patience and stealth tactics. Kate had a pretty good handle on the patience part – inching in the crab – but was still learning the stealth-netting part. She missed more crabs than she caught, and made quite a splash when she went for a crab, often letting it drop backwards and escape the net as it hit the water. But, she was improving.

They had a good morning on the creek, and by 2 o'clock they had a bushel of good-sized blue crabs. Kate netted the last one, and as she tried to flip it into the basket, it catapulted over the side and scrambled toward the water. David moved in front of it, and the crab backpedaled furiously, then stopped and raised itself up on its eight legs, both claws swinging high and snapping, a fierce sight.

"Kate," David said calmly, "Come up behind this guy and put the toe of your shoe on the back of his shell. Quick."

Kate didn't hesitate. She could tell her brother wasn't teasing. As she put her rubber-toed foot on the crab's back, it reared high and reached as far back toward her with its claws as it could. David walked around quickly, reached down behind the immobilized crab and grabbed the right and left hind legs with one hand, pulled them together, and lifted the crab up in the air. No matter how wildly the crab swung its claws, it couldn't reach David. The boy turned the crab upside-down, exposing the bright white underbelly.

"Kate, give his stomach a rub."

She looked at him like he was crazy. But she trusted him with her finger, or with her life, for that matter, and did as she was told. She rubbed the white belly with a tentative index finger. In fifteen seconds, the crab's claws had closed and folded back to its body. It seemed to be asleep. David tossed it into the basket and grinned.

Several of the crabs they had netted were females with the slight swell across their bottoms indicating they were full of roe. On some trips Mary would keep a couple of these to make she-crab soup. Its critical ingredient was fresh crab roe. Today, she somehow didn't seem to have the heart for harvesting that roe, and she gently tossed those crabs back into the creek.

By the time the Stewarts were ready to leave, the crabs in the basket had settled down, no longer fighting with each other, just seething silently, blowing bubbles from their mouths. Here and there pairs of crabs had ended their close-quarter disagreements in stalemate, each crab's blue-streaked claws – which gave them their name – locked onto the other's.

As the Stewarts rolled up the lines and started back to the car, David could see that his mother was nervous. She held one handle of the basket of crabs, David the other. Kate carried the crab net and the bucket containing the crab lines. The sandbar had become a sand island as the rising tide had filled a channel between the Stewarts and the path back to the car. It was only knee-deep on David, but deeper on Kate and her mother. Mary Stewart had never been a good swimmer, and she could get panicky in fast water. She was scanning the bank looking for the shortest way across.

"Mom, I've got an idea. Let's put the basket down."

David kneeled down, put his arms out behind him like wings, and waved Kate up onto his back. She took the signal, and in thirty seconds he had carried her across the rising current. The water was a little swifter than he had expected. He put Kate down on the far bank, then waded back across. He smiled at his mother and put her arm through his, taking her hand.

"C'mon, Mom, let's just walk this one together. You hold onto me and I'll hold onto you – no problem."

Arms locked together, they made the ten-foot journey one careful, coordinated step at a time, their soggy sneakers fighting the suction of the soft creek mud and the strong current of the rising tide. While Kate and Mary scrambled up the bank to the car and took off their shoes, David made one last trip for the basket of crabs.

He slogged back across the current without breaking his stride, the basket of crabs balanced on his deeply tanned right shoulder. He carefully placed it in the trunk of the car, wedging it tightly so it wouldn't turn over. Mary watched him closely, smiling, proud of how he had learned to take charge.

David caught her look and frowned at her.

"Let's go," he said, his voice now impatient. "The surf should be up by now."

17

Arch and Mary Stewart

They were back at the beach house by 3 o'clock. Mary put three large pots of water on the stove and brought them to a rolling boil. Using a pair of long-handled tongs, she plunged the crabs one after the other, claws waving an angry goodbye, into the water, cooking them until they turned sunset red. She drained them and iced them down in two coolers, with plans to clean and pick out the chunks of succulent white flesh once they had cooled. Her favorite part was the sweet meat from the claws.

After lugging the crabs to the kitchen, David had quickly changed into his red bathing suit. He made himself a pine-apple sandwich – a touch of mayonnaise on the bread, crushed pineapple chilled in the refrigerator and drained, eaten quick-ly before the bread could get soggy, a cool meal for a hot day. Kate munched on Ritz crackers and pimento cheese and ate a bowl of sliced fresh peaches.

The tide at the beach in front of the house was just about at full-high. A brisk wind blew in from the ocean, pushing in breakers bigger than usual. Rough water for kids, but just right for body-surfing. That was one of the things David had learned from observing his father. David loved the thrill of catching a wave right at its peak, just before it broke, match-ing its momentum exactly and letting it hurtle him forward and down, his arms stretched straight, his feet together, his body stiff, his face down, his hands clasped in a sharp point, like an arrow headed to shore. On a perfect ride, he'd glide forward until he ran out of water, his chest and knees scraping the sand.

He had also devised another way to body surf. When he caught a breaking wave just right, he would clasp his hands behind him, arch his back and push out his chest, riding it with his head up and out of the wave, his eyes wide open, carving down the wave's shoulder like a seal. He had tried to teach his father that technique, but the old man couldn't quite master it.

"Mom, I'm going for a swim," David shouted to Mary Stewart as she was icing down the last of the crabs. "The waves look great."

"Honey, why don't you wait until I'm finished? I might sit out on the porch and watch."

"You don't have to watch me, Mom," David snapped with a clear note of irritation. "I'm fifteen years old."

"I know I don't have to watch you, I just thought I would put my feet up for a few minutes. Or I might walk down and see if the high tide has washed up any good shells."

David didn't buy that for a moment. He rolled his eyes and stomped around the living room. He was tired of her babying him all the time.

"Suit yourself," he said. "But you don't have to hover over me like some helicopter. Anyway, I'm leaving."

Before his mother could respond, David hustled out the screen door, letting it slam shut behind him.

Kate marveled at David's challenging tone of voice to their mother. It had emerged only this summer. The two seemed to be testing each other, looking for limits. Kate quietly found her newest mystery book and headed for the porch hammock. She climbed into the pocket of the rope swing, formed from hours of careful positioning, and gave a tug to the cord tied to a hook on the porch wall. The hammock's soft sway and the repetitious sound of the surf lulled her eyes shut before she could read four pages.

The surf was rougher than David had expected, with a persistent undertow clutching his legs when the waves ebbed. He was a strong swimmer, though, and it didn't worry him. The rides were powerful. Time after time he caught waves at their peak and rode them, arms back, head forward, rocketing across the breaking edges.

Mary took a quick shower to erase the boiled-crab smell, slipped on khaki shorts and a royal blue cotton shirt, and headed to the porch to check on Kate. She found her asleep in the hammock, her stuffed bear Fuzzy – her bedmate since birth – squeezed tightly in the crook of her right arm. Mary watched her for a minute, saw the deep breaths move her chest, and marveled at this wonder. When Kate was asleep, she became her mother's three-year-old toddler, bright-eyed and full of laughs. As a young child, Kate had seldom birthed an un-uttered thought. Her internal musings flew directly from her brain to her lips, uncensored, and were sown upon the world.

In the last two years, Kate had retreated more and more, forming and considering her own ideas, and beginning to keep them to herself. When Mary was thinking with her head, she knew that was a good thing, a necessary step toward in-dependence. But when she was thinking with her heart, she wanted nothing more than to have her three-year-old Kate back again, the sweet child Mary could coax into curling up beside her at naptime, who would drift off to sleep only after Mary had promised she would always be right there when Kate woke up again.

Mary wished she could give that three-year-old a bath,

wash her hair and hold her head back, pouring cup after cup of warm water over it while Kate giggled and squealed. She longed for that state of pure innocence and trust.

Kate snored gently and relaxed her grip on Fuzzy's neck. The unlatched screen door slapped softly in the ocean breeze.

From the porch, Mary spotted David in the water and worried that he was out too deep. The overcast skies and rough surf had chased most people off the beach. A few souls were scattered along the beach, sitting, reading, talking, or just soaking up peace of mind from the ocean.

At low tide, Ocean Drive had one of the widest beaches on the east coast, and even at high tide there was plenty of room to walk. The beach was flat and sloped gently away from the sand dunes in front of the houses. Ocean Drive was still a family beach – no high rise hotels, no condominiums, just unpretentious single family houses, most built in the late 1950s or early 1960s, after Hurricane Hazel had devastated the South Carolina coast in 1954.

In many ways, this stretch of sand had been the focus of her adult life. Mary and Arch Stewart had met on this beach almost twenty years ago. They were both in their early twenties, visiting friends at Ocean Drive, and were introduced at a boiled-shrimp-and-beer party. Just before midnight, Mary had strolled down by herself toward the beach to check out the huge yellow moon rising over the ocean. Slipping off her sandals, she saw Arch coming from the direction of his car carrying an empty minnow bucket. When he saw her, he looked a little sheepish.

"Wasn't meaning to be anti-social," he said. "But I'm supposed to take a fellow fishing tomorrow in the creek and show him how to catch a flounder. I'm just walking down to the pier to buy some minnows. Why don't you join me?"

They filled the half-mile walk with talk about the friends who had invited them there. Arch bought them each a beer at the pier's bait store, and they walked to the end of the pier, checking out the late-night catches by the hard-core anglers fishing under the full moon. They settled onto a high wooden bench facing the moonlit water and finished their beers, feeling the swells push against the pilings below them, making the pier creak and sway just slightly. After a second beer, Mary surprised herself by patting Arch's forearm to emphasize a point she was making. Arch, who often looked away when talking with people, found himself searching through the dark for her eyes, which seemed to laugh and be serious at the same time. When Arch ran out of money, they split one last beer, and their knuckles grazed lightly as each would reach for the can. Their stories tumbled out more easily than either expected.

She told him about growing up in the North Carolina mountains, in a crossroads community called Beuladean, the only child of doting parents. Her father had worked in a feldspar mine and raised Christmas trees on the side, determined to save enough money to send her to the University of North Carolina. Mary had won a partial scholarship to Chapel Hill. After graduation, she had found a job teaching high school English in Conway and had quickly fallen in love with the South Carolina coast.

Arch told her about his father, who had grown up in Moore County, in the North Carolina sandhills. The Stewarts were Presbyterians who had fled Scotland in the mid-1760s, helping settle the village of Aberdeen just after the American Revolution. Arch's father was the first American Stewart of that line who did not make his living as a farmer. In the early 1920s, he had followed Drowning Creek, which ran through the Stewart farm until it married with Naked Creek at the southern tip of

Moore County and flowed into the Lumber River. The Lumber meandered southeast until it met the South Carolina border and became the Little Pee Dee River. Farms had sprung up along the river, and the railroad had followed.

Arch's father had settled in Mullins, alongside the Little Pee Dee not far below the North Carolina line, and opened an insurance agency. In the early 1920s, he had started a tobacco brokerage company, right after the green gold had proved itself to be a reliable money crop. Arch had been the first Stewart to make it to college, but he had chafed under the Citadel's rigid military regimen and left the Charleston school after two years. His father had welcomed him back and put him to work learning the fast growing tobacco business. Since the 1920s, tobacco had been king, and the sweet, almost intoxicating aroma of cured tobacco had permeated rural communities from Virginia to Georgia as the lucrative cash crop was hauled in the late summertime from the farms to the warehouse floors. In those communities that thrived on tobacco, folks smiled and said it was just the smell of gold dust.

By the time they quit telling stories, Mary and Arch were leaning into each other as they talked, wondering where the night had gone. As they stepped off the pier's boardwalk to head home, Mary stumbled in the deep, soft sand. Arch caught her instinctively, grabbing her hand to keep her from falling. She didn't let go and neither did he. They wandered back down the beach hand in hand, smiling and finally quiet, enjoying the first pink glimpses of the sun over the water. They always said it was a full moon and an empty minnow bucket that brought them together.

Six months later they were walking that same beach together on a clear December night, cold, moonless, with no wind. Against the black sky, the stars were brilliant over the ocean. Arch stooped over to pick up a shell.

"Have you ever seen the reflection of a star in a seashell?" he asked Mary, holding the shell out to catch the starlight. "It looks like a shiny shark's eye."

He had taught her many things about the beach and the ocean in the past few months, but she never knew when he was teasing her.

"I don't think so," she said.

As he picked up the shell at his feet, he turned away slightly before handing it to her. When she turned it over in her hand, a gold band with a glistening diamond slipped out of the shell. She turned to find Arch on one knee, asking her to marry him.

They had walked this beach together now for over two decades. At a strolling pace, Mary could scan the shoreline for sand dollars, round, white and as large as the palm of her hand. At the slower "shark's tooth pace," she could look for the tiny fossilized teeth, hard to spot except for their polished black sheen. Their pace together depended on their mood. But after all these years, they still held hands as they walked.

In October 1954, with a rage unknown since William Tecumseh Sherman had blown through South Carolina almost a century before, Hurricane Hazel had laid waste to Ocean Drive Beach and the rest of the South Carolina Grand Strand. Virtually every oceanfront house at Ocean Drive was destroyed, and those on the second row were severely damaged. The storm surge at high tide crashed through the Tinker-Toy stilt legs supporting most of the houses, leaving their second story torsos flat in the sand like sad amputees. Some had simply torn loose from their foundations, leaving their now nude plumbing as the only claim to their property. Others stood bare-headed, their roofs blown blocks away by the 140 mile per hour winds. The wind had dug hard under the roof eaves, like an eager child's fingers on the tight lid of a cookie tin, until an extra-strong gust suddenly ripped the entire roof off and sent it sailing through the air as though it were a mere shingle. Surveyors struggled for months to reestablish boundary lines for the beach's property owners. Debris from Hazel and the angry storms that had followed her in the next decade still emerged from the sand during new construction or washed ashore in heavy surf.

Many saw Hazel as a reminder of Mother Nature's wrath and swore off ever owning beach property again. Arch Stewart, however, thought the odds were with him. There hadn't been a hurricane like Old Witch Hazel in half a century, and there shouldn't be another one for the next half century. A few eager speculators had quickly purchased lots and built new houses, but buyers were still scarce.

Without telling Mary, Arch quietly purchased one of those spec houses, a simple cottage on the ocean front row of Ocean Drive. It was a four bedroom wood-frame box built over a concrete block first story, likely, he thought, to withstand at least the average hurricane. It had no air-conditioning for the summer, no heat for the winter, no telephone.

The beach house was a surprise anniversary present for Mary, one they could barely afford in their fourth year of marriage. But Arch was wise enough to know that he could not afford not to buy it.

In October, as the eye of Hazel had roared over Mullins, reducing the barometric pressure to all time lows, virtually every woman carrying a baby anywhere near its term found the infant inside her fighting for release. Baby David arrived two days after Hazel left, one month premature.

For the first twelve weeks of his life, it looked like he might not survive. Mary stayed up with him night after night, her inability to soothe his constant cries and whimpers driving her nearly crazy. Dr. Jim Martin, who had cared for the town's babies for forty years, offered all the remedies in the black leather bag he brought for house calls and all the diagnoses his experience had stored up. But David's fevers returned every few days as his body fought the mysterious infection that had attacked him.

When the fever set in, his body heated like a small woodstove. He would cry until his voice croaked, then whimper, his squinched eyes scarcely opening, as if begging for help. After forty-eight hours or so, his fever would spike, his body would burst into a sweat, and he would be comfortable and quiet for two to three days. Then the cycle would begin again, and Mary's fears for her baby would build along with the fever and the cries, and she could feel her heart hurt.

She moved a metal cot into David's bedroom and spent the nights there. She had refused the nurses Arch had hired to spell her on occasional evenings, explaining with cold-blooded calm that if David died when she wasn't there to touch him, then the coroner would have to fill out two death certificates. A few nights, exhausted to the point of collapse, she asked her long-time black housekeeper Hope Rivers to stay with her. She knew Hope understood her need to be connected to David, and she could doze lightly with Hope present to watch over David's breathing.

As Mary had focused on David, she had withdrawn deeply into herself. Most nights, Arch tried hard not to take it as rejection of him. But he missed her smiling eyes even more than he missed the comfort of her warm body spooned against his in the night.

Three days after Christmas, David's fever broke and subsided and Mary expected the next cycle to begin around New

Year's Day. When it didn't come, Mary hardly knew what to do.

Dr. Martin said David had gotten well because his immune system had finally matured enough to fight off his infection without the need for the fevers. Hope attributed David's recovery to the three prayers a day she had said for him and to her earnest daily whispers of support in his infant ear. Mary, though, knew the real reason: she herself had breathed her own heart and life into him.

Still, for weeks afterward Mary would strain in the darkness for sounds from David's bed. She had rejoined Arch in their bedroom. But when she awakened and heard no sounds from David's room next door, she would rush through the dark blanket of night and put her face down to his until she felt his breath against her cheek.

Arch bought the beach house on a Friday in April 1955. After church on Sunday, Arch suggested to Mary that they drive the hour to the beach for a late lunch.

"I'd sure like some fried shrimp at Hoskins Restaurant," he said. "How about a drive to the beach? We could introduce David to the ocean."

"I'd love it. I could eat a few fresh oysters with a little butter. And if you promise to hold my hand when we walk on the beach, I'll share one of my oysters with you," Mary said with a smile.

She knew oysters were the one seafood Arch Stewart would never touch.

After lunch, they drove down the paved road behind what had once been an unbroken row of oceanfront houses, jammed side by side on lots fifty feet wide. The worst of Hazel's detritus had been cleared away, and a few new houses were under construction. Near Sixth Avenue, Mary noticed one that was nearly completed – a white cinderblock first story, a wood frame second story, and a wood fence around the driveway. The lots next door – which had once held houses – were vacant, littered with small piles of wood and brick not yet hauled away.

"Let's sneak a look at this one," he said.

"Okay," Mary said. "I am amazed people are brave enough to build back so quickly after Hazel, especially on the front row. How are they going to feel if we get another hurricane this fall just like Hazel? Some folks think the weather patterns are changing, and we'll get one just like that every two to three years."

Arch pulled into the driveway.

"Knock on some wood quickly," he said. "We sure don't want that."

They circled the new house, checking it out from all angles. They walked around and viewed it from the ocean side. Mary loved the second-story screened porch that faced the ocean and ran the length of the house.

"I'd have a hammock for the porch, and the green cane-bottomed rocking chairs from your grandmother's front porch, and a day bed for naps," she said.

They looked at each other and smiled. When they were first married and rented rooms at the beach for a few days in the fall, they would kid about saving time for afternoon naps. It was their code for "naked and playing."

Mary held David up and pointed his face to the ocean, where the waves were rolling toward shore in peaceful swells.

"The ocean will bring you great peace of mind, my sweet baby," she said. "It will help you think great thoughts. It will help you understand constancy and change. This beach played a great role in our lives, and I hope it will in your life."

Arch led her around to the streetside door.

"C'mon, let's be nosy. Let's see whose name is on the building permit. I'll hold David," he said. "You take a look."

She peered hard at the handwritten scribbles on the tiny piece of poster board nailed to the upstairs back door.

"This is odd," she said. "It says, 'Owner: J. McIntyre.' That's scratched out, and 'M. Stewart' is written in."

It took a moment for it to sink in, and then she saw Arch's silly grin and his face turning red.

"Happy Anniversary, darlin'," he said. "We may eat a lot of macaroni and cheese for a year or two to help pay for it, but we'll have a great place for naps. And David will love this beach."

Mary had moved to the beach house for that first summer, taking nine-month old David with her. Hope Rivers had come along, as much a companion as a baby sitter. They had added a small downstairs bedroom for Hope. It was private, but even hotter than the upstairs, which would catch whatever breeze there might be on the stuffiest summer nights. Arch would make it down most Friday nights, even if he couldn't get there until midnight, his body missing Mary almost as much as his spirit did, anticipating watching the dawn light up her face as she slept on Saturday morning.

Mary could still remember the first summer weekend they had spent together at the beach house. Arch had arrived late Friday afternoon, a bag of fresh peaches in one hand and three new records in the other. They had feasted on fried flounder, corn dodgers, fresh tomatoes and corn on the cob. During dinner they listened to young Ray Charles moan his blues and play his piano. When Hope was clearing the dishes from the table, she noticed that Mary had slipped her sandals off and was rubbing her foot against Arch's foot under the table. By that time, they were listening to Bessie Smith breathing a song in the background:

I need a little sugar in my bowl,
I wanna little sweetness down in my soul...

Mary was humming along, having serious, silent eye con-versation with Arch. Hope hid a smile. Some people kidded that Bessie's song had *two* meanings, but Hope was pretty sure it had just one.

"Why don't y'all let me keep David tonight," she said. "I'll walk with him on the beach 'til the sound of the waves puts him to sleep. He can stay in his crib in my room."

Arch winked at Mary and gave Hope a mock serious look.

"I guess we ought to see if Mary can make it through a night without shaking him awake to see if he's still breathing," he said. "Hope, that would be very nice. Mary and I haven't had much time to talk, and that would be wonderful."

"I'm happy to," she said, smiling to herself. "Who knows," she thought, "a little more of this belly-rubbin' music and those two liable to do so much talkin' we'll have another young 'un around here by next spring."

Arch and Mary sat on the screened porch after dinner, Arch sipping a second glass of Jack Daniels, Mary a Kahlua and cream on ice. They rocked and talked about David, about the prospects for a good financial year if Arch landed one more client from Germany, about plans for a new gazebo on the sand dunes, close to the beach.

Mary slipped downstairs to check on David – he and Hope were both sound asleep. When she returned upstairs, Arch had started the Bessie Smith album again. He took Mary in his arms, and they danced slowly, her head bent into his chest, her hand inside his shirt, grazing his backbone with her fingers.

"Some people say dancing is the vertical expression of a horizontal desire," she teased, and nibbled on his ear lobe. "What do you think?"

He smiled and pressed his forehead against hers.

"I have missed you more than I've been willing to tell you," she said quietly. "Your cards are wonderful, and they brighten my days. But the nights are hard without you. I do love you so."

Ever since David's illness, Arch had left Mary a card for every night he would be away for her to open before she went to bed. Sometimes the message was sweet, sometimes it was funny, sometimes it had a line from a song they both liked, sometimes it had a picture from a magazine of a place they had been or wanted to go.

Arch leaned back and looked in the moonlight for her eyes.

"Mary, because of you, I sometimes feel like I have two hearts. Mine, and yours right beside it. This may sound corny, but I think about it when we're apart. Whenever I see something interesting or hear a phrase I know you would like, I sort of glance at that other heart and say, 'What do you think, baby?' Wherever you are, we are connected, and what's in my heart is in your heart. I don't think many people have that, but we do."

"That's not corny. Who do you think you are talking to, anyway?" Mary said. "Thank you for wanting to know me and for letting me know you. You are my anchor in this world."

She stroked his neck with her fingertips. She liked the faint, familiar scent of the Mennen Skin Bracer he patted on each morning after shaving.

"I know I've been a little crazy because of David. I was so afraid of losing him. I prayed every night to God to take me if he had to take one of us. You and I made him, and he will be special because of that. He will be the best of both of us."

She squeezed her body tighter against his. The hand that had been stroking his neck slipped just inside the back of his trousers and pulled him toward her. She gave him a long exploring kiss.

"I'll meet you in the bedroom in two minutes," she whispered. Then she padded off barefoot to the bathroom.

Arch turned out the lights and pulled back the sheets on the bed. He took off his clothes and opened the blinds so any hint of breeze from the ocean could find them, but none did. The ocean was as smooth as a mirror, sending out only the soft lap of six-inch waves barely breaking on the flat beach. He walked naked back into the den, and brought the floor fan into the bedroom. He pulled a wood chair over beside the bed and placed the fan on it. He thought it might at least stir up the hot air in the room and make it a bit cooler.

Moments later, Mary slid into bed beside him, and Arch pulled her close. He kissed her mouth gently, his tongue teasing hers. When she returned the tease, he kissed her harder and his hand found her silky and ready for him. She pulled him quickly into her, arms tight around his back. She arched her hips against him and loved his urgent pulse and abandon inside her.

They lay together, her head on his chest, his hand stroking her hair, talking quietly of their time apart, of the weekend to come, of everything and nothing. After a while, when her wandering hand brushed against him, he was ready again and rolled toward her. He kissed her breasts, ivory in the moonlight, pulling each marble-hard nipple gently with his lips for a moment, then circling it with his tongue, teasing her. Mary sighed and shifted underneath him. This time they made love slowly, the tension building gradually. He tried to find her eyes, but they were closed, focused on an inner horizon. And when their pleasure came, it was from far away, like a slow sunrise over the ocean, a distant pink promise, then a spreading red sky, finally a blinding burst of brightness that left them both damp and breathless.

Later, they slipped into the shower together and let the lukewarm water cool them. Arch toweled Mary off slowly and kissed her on her forehead.

"It's still too hot," he said. "Let's see if we can find some breeze down by the water."

They both put on shorts and t-shirts and were on the beach, barefoot, in minutes. At two a.m., the tide was dead low. The late June moon was a giant orange ball, hanging low over the water, sending a shimmering flame across the calm water to them.

"You know," Mary said. "The first time I ever came to the beach I was about eight. One night my parents brought me out on the beach and there was a full moon over the ocean. No matter where I walked, the line of the moon on the water pointed directly to me. I thought that the man in the moon was doing this especially for me. I never told anyone because I thought it was just a secret between me and the man in the moon. I was probably twelve before I realized that the moonlight on the water looked that way to everyone, no matter where they were standing."

They were the only ones on the beach at that hour.

"How about a quick skinny-dip, baby?" Arch said with a smile. "I promise not to pinch you like a crab."

Mary hesitated. A mountain girl, she had never been comfortable in the ocean, or in any deep water for that matter. Even with no waves at all, the thought of going into the water above her knees brought a knot to her stomach. And skinny-dipping under a full moon required going out further than that.

"Not tonight, Sweets," she said. "How about if we go back and have a nightcap, play a hand or two of double solitaire and see if we can cool off enough to sleep."

She won the first game of double solitaire, he the second. They played one game of Spit for the playoff, and Arch slammed a king on an ace in one pile at the same time Mary slapped a two on an ace in the other pile, both of them out of cards. They called it a draw.

There was still no breeze in the bedroom. Arch tucked the bedsheet tightly in on one side of the bed and put the edge of the other side atop the fan on the chair. He weighted the sheet down on the fan with the dictionary they kept handy to referee Scrabble games. The fan pumped a steady stream of air under the sheet, puffing it up like an iron lung, keeping the sheet afloat just above their naked bodies.

They stayed just far enough apart to maintain the cool, only their hands and feet gently grazing.

When Arch heard Mary's slow, steady sleep breathing, he leaned over on his elbow and looked at her peaceful face. He loved to watch her sleep. He put his right hand lightly on her left breast. She stirred, not waking, and he smiled at the darkness of his hand against the pale skin inside her tan line.

"Thank you, my sweet baby, for opening your heart so wide to me and to our David," he whispered almost to himself. "Before I knew you, I was often lonely. Now I'm never lonely because I know you're in this world and connected to me. I'm lonesome for you when we're apart, but I never feel alone. I love you, and I thank you for loving me. Good night."

He wasn't sure she heard him, but her sleeping face seemed to smile.

18

Mary's Decision

Mary gave Kate's cheek a kiss, picked up her shelling basket, and let the screen door on the porch close gently behind her, trying not to wake Kate from her hammock nap. She saw David neck deep in the big swells, waiting for the right ride. Mary waved from the top of the stairway, but David wasn't looking her way.

She walked down the steps and out the boardwalk. When she reached the beach, she slipped off her sandals and headed north about a hundred yards, glancing back occasionally to check on David. She would spot him bobbing over and through the breaking waves. She saw a patch of crushed shells and rocks at the water's edge, the kind of spot which often held shark's teeth. Mary knelt, sifting the shells through her fingers, and found two tiny black teeth. She opened a metal film canister she kept in her shell basket and popped them into it. She continued spreading the shells, searching for shark's teeth, then looked up to catch a glimpse of David. She didn't see him.

Mary stood up to her full height and squinted for a better view. Still no David. Her heart quickened a little, and she scanned the surf above and below the place where she had last seen him. No sign. She began walking quickly back down the beach toward the house. She knew she was being silly – he was probably swimming low in the water or had headed for the house.

"No, I would have seen him if he had walked onto the beach."

On instinct, she started trotting down the nearly deserted beach. She saw no sign of him anywhere in the ocean. Her heart was beating fast, and she was suddenly scared.

"David, David!" she called loudly. "David, where are you?"

Running hard now, she tripped forward on the firm, damp sand, caught herself on her hands, scrambled back to her feet and half-ran, half-stumbled up the beach. She could barely get her breath. By the time she reached the spot in front of the beach house where she had last seen David, her shouts had attracted attention. A white-haired man was lumbering in her direction, a teenaged girl right behind him, both uncertain what the problem was or how they should help.

Mary waded out into the breakers, still shouting David's name. She jumped as each wave broke against her legs, nudging her a few yards back toward shore, the undertow then sucking her a few yards away from the beach. The waves began to crash around her waist, deeper now, and she lost her footing, then regained it, struggling against the force of the inbound waves and the outward tug of the undertow. She could taste the salt in her mouth, partially from the ocean, partially from her eyes.

"David!" she shouted. "David, answer me!"

Her mind flashed with snippets of her many admonitions to him about the ocean, that it was something to be feared, and how the invincible teenager had scowled at her.

She scanned the water in front of her, jumping as each wave hit her, trying to see further out. Still no sign of him. Mary wiped her eyes, looked back at the beach and saw the old man standing at the edge of the water, waving his arms. The girl was running away. Mary hoped she was going for help.

Thirty yards behind the old man, Mary saw Kate running down the boardwalk from the house. She heard Kate call for her.

"Momma, come back!" Kate shouted. "Please, Momma, come back."

Kate was running as fast as she could toward the water.

Mary turned her back to the beach, her life moving now in slow motion. Every detail stood out, every second seemed a minute, her tears stopped. Every sight was in perfect focus.

In a swell just beyond the breakers, she caught a glimpse of red. It disappeared, then she saw it again in the next swell. The water was now at her chest, the waves breaking over her head.

It was David, floating in the water, not moving, except for the rise and fall of the ocean swells.

Mary looked back once more to the shore. Kate was standing in the shallow water, screaming for her. Mary turned again toward David, twenty yards away. He seemed like a baby, her baby, and she could save him, she could breathe her life into him if she had to. She had done it before.

She searched again for Kate, who was no longer screaming, just holding out her arms, sobbing.

Mary's eyes locked for a few seconds with Kate's. In that look, Mary sent her a lifetime of love, but she didn't know if Kate would ever understand it.

Another breaker crashed into Mary from behind, buckling her knees, almost knocking her down. She turned toward the ocean and started half-swimming, half-lunging toward David.

*   *   *   *   *

By the time the rescue squad arrived twenty minutes later, an off-duty policeman had pulled them both from the water. He took one look at David's blue-hued body and the gash and swollen bruise on his forehead and moved quickly to try to resuscitate Mary. He tried his best to get her to breathe again, but she didn't respond.

The two bodies seemed somehow serene lying side by side on the sand. The onlookers gathered around them on the beach were almost silent, staring, nodding at the wound on David's head, careful not to point, turning away respectfully, but unable to keep from glancing back again. Someone finally brought two beach towels and covered the bodies.

A four by four inch piece of lumber about five feet long, once part of a washed-away set of beach steps, had been pushed up into the shallow water by the waves.

"I think that old piling must have been floatin' out there, under water a little bit," the policeman said, talking low, partly to a man standing beside him, partly to no one in particular. "The boy must have had his head throwed against it by a big wave and knocked hisself out. She weren't five feet from him when I got to her. Wasn't neither one of them breathin.'"

The Stewarts' next-door neighbor, a woman in her forties who had played with Kate on the beach since she was a toddler, wrapped her, sobbing, in a beach towel and took her up to her house. She sat Kate on her couch, put her arms around her and held her tight, rocking Kate's shaking body in her arms.

* * * * *

The gray-haired South Carolina Highway Patrolman finally located Arch Stewart's car parked near the Deer Crossing boat ramp on the Little Pee Dee River just outside Conway. It was almost dark, and most of the fishermen were off the river, headed home. Arch Stewart's car was the last one in the parking lot. The officer spotted a lone fisherman idling his motor at the concrete ramp, about to pull his boat from the water onto his trailer.

"You see any other folks out on the river?" he asked the fisherman.

"Yessir," he answered. "I seen two fellers fishin' over some bream beds about a mile up the river. One of them drives that car over there. They were laughin' hard when I passed by, you know, likker kinda laughin'. They had caught a big mess of fish, and one of them was saying he was the one who had sniffed out the bream bed. He was claimin' credit for findin' the fish the other feller had caught. They said they was about to head back."

The grim look on the patrolman's face shut him up.

"Is there something wrong?" he asked.

The patrolman stuck his hands deep into his pants pockets and looked away, shifting his weight from foot to foot. He rolled a toothpick from one corner of his mouth to the other, then made a little sucking sound with his teeth. He ducked his head and shook it sadly.

"I'm pretty sure that's a man named Arch Stewart fishing down there," the officer said, his eyes on the toes of his shoes. "His wife and son got drowned this afternoon over at Ocean Drive."

He was having trouble finding the words. At the same time, he understood the important role he played in this drama and seemed quietly proud of it.

"I'm the one who's got to tell him. In all my years, I've never had to do nothing as hard as this."

The fisherman looked down the river for a moment. The tannic-acid leeching from the cypress trees gave the water a tea-colored tint in the shadows of the early evening.

"They don't have no motor on their boat. They're paddling," he said. "It'll take them twenty minutes to get back here to the landing. You want me to run you down there in my boat to pick 'em up?"

The officer took off his hat, ran his hand through his thick gray hair and looked away. He shook his head.

"No," he said finally. "I'll wait here for them. Sounds like he's happy right now. Let him enjoy that twenty minutes. It might be the last happy time he ever has."

19

Hampton McNabb

Hampton McNabb, the 50-year-old editor and publisher of the *Georgetown Pilot*, rested his left elbow on his desk and rubbed his forehead, struggling to write the headline for the news story about the Stewart drownings.

He finally settled on "Mother, Son Drown In Heavy O.D. Surf," with a subhead of: "Mother Tried To Save Teen."

Most of the seven drowning deaths along the Grand Strand beaches that summer of 1970 had been caused by sudden rip currents near the inlet at the south end of Pawleys Island, the story noted. When Hampton's son was younger, his favorite surfing spot had been the southern tip of Pawley's, where the ocean pushed its high tides back through the inlet and into the creeks and salt marshes behind the beachfront houses. He suspected that Wade and his girlfriend had sometimes walked across the shallow Pawley's inlet at low tide to Debidue – a five mile stretch of undeveloped sandy beach with tall, sea-oats-covered sand dunes – and skinny-dipped on hot summer days. He had warned Wade sternly about surfing in the dangerous currents, but hadn't known exactly what to tell a teenager about the dangers of skinny-dipping.

Hampton hoped he had hit the right tone of drama, teaching and sympathy in the drowning article, which had included details of the Stewarts' civic contributions – Mary's honors as Best High School English Teacher, awarded to her for four straight years by the South Carolina Education Association, David's Eagle Scout and God and Country Awards, Arch's leadership in his church and two terms on the Mullins City Council.

But Hampton's main worry was another story running in the next day's paper.

On page fourteen, in the lower right corner, was a small, ten-inch article chronicling the wedding of William Duncan of Georgetown and Betty Jones of Manning. The article itself was unremarkable. It noted that the bride was a high school teacher in New York City and that Mr. Duncan was attending Union Theological Seminary. Her parents taught in the Manning schools. His father worked at the steel mill, his mother was deceased.

The article provided the usual wedding information – a description of the cake, a listing of the bridesmaids and groomsmen, and details about the bride's dress. It was the accompanying photo – a striking bride with dark hair, in a white wedding gown, smiling at the camera – that Hampton knew would immediately attract his readers' attention.

Mrs. Duncan was the first black bride whose picture had ever run in the *Georgetown Pilot*. Hampton had been careful to put no other wedding articles on the same page. The Duncan-Jones account was on a page with a feature about a large tarpon caught in North Inlet the previous week and a half-page advertisement for the local Piggly Wiggly grocery story. He thought it would probably be the last ad he'd have from the Pig for a while.

That week's *Pilot* hit the news boxes around town at nine on Wednesday morning, and the copies mailed to subscribers were delivered by early afternoon. By 9:30 that morning he had his first angry phone call. It was the mayor, Grant Webster.

There had been a time when Webster and McNabb had been close friends. The *Pilot* had endorsed Webster in the rare election years when the incumbent mayor had attracted opposition. The two had sometimes fished and hunted together and often raised a glass of scotch to celebrate something, or nothing.

There had been one prolonged chilly spell a few years back. Webster, angered over a particularly sharp editorial dig from the newspaper, had refused for a few months to pay the outstanding advertising bill his funeral home business had run up. When McNabb's spinster aunt had died that same spring, McNabb had used Webster's funeral home to handle the arrangements. When the bill arrived on McNabb's desk a few weeks later, it was just a few dollars less than the amount of the funeral home's outstanding advertising bill. McNabb sent back the bill with a handwritten notation: "Taken in trade, paid in full." They had eaten dinner together the next week and laughed about their feud.

The last two years, though, things had been different. They were having trouble even agreeing to disagree. It had strained their friendship, and they had begun to avoid social time together.

"Hampton," Webster said with the tight, controlled voice he used when he was angry, "You have crossed the line this time, but there may still be time to fix this. I don't know why you get this bee in your goddam bonnet about racial things. You have gotten people stirred up again, this time worse than I've ever seen.

"I've heard from half the City Council, and you might as well know, from two of your biggest advertisers, including Buzz Timmons at the Piggly Wiggly. They are ready to cut you off. You take those ads away, you lose the city and county legal advertising, and you'll be printing nothing but obits and weather reports," Webster said.

McNabb held the receiver at arms length for a few seconds. It wasn't like he hadn't expected something like this. He took a deep breath and spoke evenly to the mayor.

"Grant, calm down and think about this," McNabb said. "Forget for a minute whether treating black folks with a little bit of the same dignity we use for white folks is the fair, the right, the American, or even the Christian thing to do. Think about it from a sense of enlightened self interest."

"If you own The Pig or the drugstore and you sell stuff to black folks – do you want them to read your ad so they'll buy more from you? If I run stories about blacks, do you think the black community is more likely to read the newspaper? Do you think they're more likely to see the Piggly Wiggly ad? Do you think they might buy a little more from The Pig if they see the ad? Do you think they might even be a little more interested in the progress of this county?"

"Hampton, you're missing the point. People don't want to be mixing the races around here. I don't bury any colored people," Webster said. "They have their own damn funeral home. I tell you what, ever since those old boys up in Lamar turned over that colored school bus last spring, you've been a little screwy. You've gotten too focused on the coloreds, and a lot of people think you're on their side. I'm telling you, I've known you since we were in grammar school, and I love you like a brother. I love you when you're sober, and I love you when you're on a drunk. But you have really fucked up this time."

Hampton smiled as he remembered a late night with Webster in a Charleston bar when they had both exceeded their limits. Both of them enjoyed getting outside of a little too much brown liquor on occasion. Sometime after midnight,

McNabb had started asking the bartender for Grant Websters and calling the mayor Johnnie Walker, or so he was told later.

McNabb tried to calm the mayor down.

"Grant, I realized years ago that there are three things almost every man is sure he can do better than any other man: tend a good fire in a fireplace, make love to a woman, and edit a newspaper. Now, I can handle lots of criticism for my decisions about what to print in my newspaper."

"But Hampton, sometimes you're just too damned unrealistic," Webster said. "People don't change overnight. I've smoothed the waters for you before around here, and I might could do it one more time, but you're playing with dynamite."

"I think you just don't get it this time. People are furious about the court orders forcing the schools to integrate this fall. They are mad about your editorials supporting that. Now they're mad about this colored bride in your newspaper. Let me just put it on the table – the next big issue is the strike at the steel mill. You mix the race issue with the strike against the town's most important employer, well, you come down on the wrong side of that one and you can kiss your paper goodbye."

"Grant, I know how polarized this town is. I'm the safety valve to keep this boiler from blowing up. People here have got to start talking about this stuff. If they don't talk, they're going to fight."

"I don't think you get the real drift of what's happening here, Hampton," Webster said. "Listen, I've got some folks coming over to the funeral home tonight at seven-thirty to talk. If you know what's good for you, you'll show up. It'll be Buzz Timmons from Piggly Wiggly, the city attorney, and the banker who holds the mortgage on your building and on that fancy new printing press of yours – the one that printed such a lovely picture of Betty Duncan."

McNabb heard Webster's phone hit the cradle hard at the mayor's end and gently put his own down. He stared at the phone for a few seconds and thought about what he should do. Then he picked it back up and dialed his home number.

Hampton told his wife Sarah he wouldn't be home for dinner. He did not tell her why. He knew she would counsel him to be cautious. Their conversation was short, and when he hung up, he closed his office door. He sat down in his creaking wooden chair, opened a desk drawer and had a longer talk with his Scottish companion and confidant Johnnie Walker. Hampton knew Mr. Walker's brown tonic would provide him the courage he sometimes lacked.

*   *   *   *   *

Grant Webster had not intended to pursue the burial trade when he had graduated from Presbyterian College. His marriage three months later to Peaches Pearson, however, had made him the heir apparent to her father's "collection" – Mr. Pearson, afflicted with a funeral director's penchant for euphemism, hated the word "chain" – of funeral homes dotting the Pee Dee.

Webster had focused early on the outreach part of the funeral home business – the solemn greeting of the bereaved family member, the engulfing two-handed shake-and-hold, the earnest eye contact, furrowed foreheads almost touching, the soft hand on the shoulder, the quick offer of the clean, white handkerchief with the Pearson Funeral Home monogram, the quiet, hush-toned efficiency with which the cars were parked, the family seated, the casket moved. He made sure the final ceremonies for Georgetown's departed upper crust went off without a hitch. Webster did not, however, like

the clinical part of the business. He had witnessed one embalming his first week on the job twenty years ago and had
decided he never needed to see another.

Hampton understood that marrying money could sometimes be a hard way to make a living. In a moment of frustration, Grant had once told the editor that Peaches would have
been good at the embalming part of the business because she
preferred people who did not talk back to her.

Webster, though, was a born booster, an affable promoter
of progress and prosperity. He could have the local Rotary
Club vigorously nodding in agreement when he spoke with
passion about his hopes for Georgetown's future, or about the
importance of Pre-Need Planning for Eternity. He was always
eager to help others. Webster had quietly shown many an as-
piring politico just where to sit at funerals in order to be noticed by, and nod solemnly at, the largest number of sad-faced
attendees. He had been Mayor of Georgetown for ten years,
but still had trouble dealing with controversy. In fact, Webster
hated conflict as much as he hated cold bodies. And tonight,
he was in the heart of conflict.

* * * * *

When Hampton arrived at the handsome three-story white
frame building with the large double staircase outside, the funeral home was a tranquil scene. The Pearsons had tastefully
transformed the dilapidated Mansfield home into a cozy way
station for the recently departed. It had been built in 1775 by
William Mansfield's unmarried daughter who, finding spin-
sterhood on her father's Black River rice plantation stifling,
had moved into town.

There was no visitation that night, and the uplighting on

the live oaks and palmetto trees gave the stately old mansion a regal air. Hampton paused a moment before climbing the wide brick steps from the sidewalk to the front door. He was not looking forward to this conversation.

"Oh well, I'd rather they kick my ass for who I am than kiss it for who I'm not," he muttered to the wind or maybe to Mr. Walker.

Hampton was ushered to Webster's large clubroom on the second floor. It had been the Mansfield library, lined on three walls by floor-to-ceiling chestnut bookshelves, with an auburn heart pine floor. An English pub table anchored one corner of the room, ready for Webster's regular Thursday night poker game with a rotating group of local businessmen and politicos. In the center was a sitting area with two leather couches and several club chairs, arranged for easy conversation. On the far side of the room was a small mahogany bar. A black man in a dark suit, a white shirt and a skinny black tie was smiling, nodding, and pouring drinks for the four men already present.

Grant Webster looked over and smiled broadly as Hampton entered the room, the door shutting softly behind him.

"Hampton! Come in!" Webster called cheerfully. "It's good to see you. Thanks so much for coming."

Webster's head turned slightly in the general direction of the bartender.

"Jimmy, Mr. McNabb could use a little Johnnie Walker Black on the rocks, if I remember correctly. And some of these other gentlemen might like to have their drinks freshened."

Hampton sized up the room and nodded at the bartender. It was clear the others had arrived at least one drink earlier for a private caucus. Ed Cleveland, the Georgetown city attorney, a handsome man in his early thirties, came over and shook

Hampton's hand. The editor suspected that Cleveland was proud of his head of thick, dark hair, always carefully trimmed and perfectly parted. Hampton didn't know him well, but believed him to be reasonably bright, if somewhat plodding, and ambitious with a true knack for brown-nosing. He helped out the city on zoning issues and contracts, and the general interpretation of state statutes affecting municipalities. He liked Hampton and had been a good source of information on the inner workings of City Hall.

Hampton could tell that Cleveland was uncomfortable being here. Each time Hampton tried to catch his eye, the attorney smiled nervously and glanced away, combing his hair with his fingers.

Buzz Timmons, the owner of the Georgetown Piggly Wiggly grocery store, did not rise from his leather chair but simply lifted his cigarette-holding hand and waved it, briefly glancing in Hampton's direction. Timmons' thin face and hard black eyes hinted that he had not always been sure where his next meal or his next mortgage payment would come from. He had the air of a man still glancing over his shoulder to be sure tough times weren't about to catch him again. Timmons had in fact grown up hard on a small farm in a remote part of the county. His father had refused to marry Buzz's sixteen-year-old mother and declined to acknowledge that Buzz was his son, even in the tiny crossroads community they all lived in. Until he was eighteen, Buzz had been known as Buzzy Blanton and believed his mother – only sixteen years his senior – was his older sister and that his grandmother was his mother. They told him his father had been killed in France during the war, and other folks in the community never let on different to him. The charade might have survived forever had Buzz not discovered the truth on his birth certificate when he signed up for Army duty right after his senior year in high school. He spent two years in the Army, much of it pondering how to deal with the situation. Upon his return, he promptly paid a lawyer $25 and the clerk of court $40 to adopt the last name of his real father. So for $65, he became Buzz Timmons, and for another $35 took out an ad in the local newspaper announcing his new name. Just his way of letting the old man know Buzz knew the score.

Timmons soon opened a butcher shop and freezer plant in Georgetown, using the skills he had picked up in the Army. A few years later when the Charleston-based Piggly Wiggly food store chain saw opportunity in Georgetown, it had offered Timmons the franchise, and he jumped at it. His grandmother had mortgaged her farm to get Timmons the capital to make the investment, and it had turned out to be a good one. Timmons now saw himself as a self-made man, living proof that in this great country anybody with gumption and a strong work ethic could succeed if the government would stay out of the way. He was famously tight-fisted and known to look the other way when the dinner check was placed nearby. His companions always said he had deep pockets, but mighty short arms.

Timmons' grocery ads filled two pages of the Georgetown paper each week, highlighting specials on everything from fatback to canning jars. He had once complained to Hampton about all the money his store spent advertising in the newspaper and questioned whether it was really worth it. Hampton remembered with a smile Buzz's anger and obvious frustration: "Dammit, McNabb," he had spat out one day, sitting in Hampton's office. "Sometimes I think half the money I spend on ads in your newspaper is wasted."

Hampton had possessed the presence of mind to sit quietly for a moment, leaning back in his office chair. Then he re-crossed his feet on his desk, and said with a twinkle in his eye, "Dammit, Buzz, you just might be right. But the problem is, you don't know which half, do ya?"

The other guest was Ron Elliott, a smooth, fortyish, blue-suited banker. His grandfather had started Planter's State Bank just after the Depression, and Ron had recently taken the reins as president. His taproots ran deep in the George-town soil, but in recent years, he and his wife had traveled to banking conventions around the country and come back with a taste for California wines and New York theatre that some in Georgetown thought a little showy. Planter's handled the newspaper's payroll and day-to-day banking needs, and Elliott had personally approved the *Pilot's* recent $200,000 loan for its new printing press. Blaming the increasing scrutiny of state bank regulators, he had required both Hampton and Sarah to personally guarantee payment of the loan. He now understood more about the McNabbs' personal financial condition than they did.

The banker walked Hampton's glass of scotch over from the bar and handed it to him with a flicker of a smile. Webster, always the gracious host, gestured toward the sitting area, and the five men took their seats. For a moment the only sound in the room was that of the bartender leaving and returning through a side door to refill the ice bucket and straighten up around the bar.

"Hampton, let's cut to the chase," Elliott said, breaking the silence.

The banker fanned his hand around the small circle, mak-ing brief eye contact with each of the men in the room.

"Every man here likes you well enough, and we want you to succeed. We want the *Pilot* to succeed. But you need to know that we think you are becoming a divisive force in this com-

munity. The people in this room have nothing against the coloreds in this town, but you are pushing for too much, too fast.

"If you keep heading where you are going, you will lose
your readers. If you lose readers, you are going to lose advertisers. If you lose advertisers, you can't make your loan payments.
That won't do you any good. It sure as hell won't do my bank
any good."

He leaned his torso forward, toward McNabb, resting his
forearms on his knees, looking right into the editor's eyes.

"The truth is, Hampton," he said earnestly, "We are all in
this thing together."

He glanced around at the other faces in the circle to see if
they thought he had hit the right touch. Everybody was nodding, looking right at Hampton.

Hampton rattled the ice cubes in his half-empty glass,
thinking he should have passed on that third drink. He could
feel his wife Sarah and his friend Johnnie Walker tugging at
him from different directions. Finally, he spoke, slowly and
firmly.

"Boys, I don't know just what 'too much, too fast' means.
You sound like some high school sex education film. Sixteen
years ago, the United States Supreme Court said that South
Carolina had to integrate its public schools 'with all deliberate
speed.' Here it is, 1970. Half the students in Georgetown County are black and not one of them attends school with a white
student. A few months ago the federal courts ended the last
dodge the states have used to avoid integration and finally said:
'No more excuses, period, that's all she wrote.' It seems to me
we can either go to war with the federal government – like we
did a hundred years ago and lost – or we can do the right thing."

Buzz Timmons had been leaning forward in his chair like a
man pushing against a stiff wind. The blood rose up through

the veins in his neck until his face was fully flushed, the color of a ripe pomegranate about to burst. Finally he exploded like a balloon blown one breath too many.

"Goddam it, Hampton McNabb, let me tell you something. I have fought integration tooth and fuckin' nail ever since those niggers in Clarendon County sued their school board in 1950! At first, all they wanted was a school bus like the white folks to get to their own school. Before we knew it, that black son-of-a-bitch Thurgood Marshall was down here arguin' that separate schools were flat out unequal and unconstitutional."

He spat the hated name out of his mouth like he had tasted rat poison: "Thor-oh-good Mah-shall."

"The Supreme Court screwed us in 1954, and I must have put up five hundred 'Impeach Earl Warren' signs all over this part of the state. We used smart lawyers and our own judges to fight off integratin' our schools right up 'til now.

"Now, I like the colored folks in our community fine. Their dollar is just as green as a white man's dollar. It spends just fine. But they need to know their place," Timmons said.

His voice lowered to a growl that seemed to come straight from his large Adam's apple.

"I am not ready, do you hear me, not fuckin' ready to sit my fourteen-year old daughter down in a classroom next to some 15-year-old black buck. I personally want to hear from you right here, right now who you are backing for governor. If you are backing Albert Watson, we can talk. But if you're be-hind that nigger-lovin' John fuckin' West, then our bidness is gonna come to a halt, right here, right now. If that's the case, you can kill my ads in your piece-of-shit newspaper startin' yesterday."

Timmons glanced around at the other men and saw them staring at their feet, embarrassed by the starkness of his speech. But not one of them said a word. Hampton had heard this sort of racist rant from Timmons before. He took a deep breath and closed his eyes for a second. When he opened them, he looked straight into Timmons' eyes.

"Buzz, you know what happened in Lamar, not seventy miles from here, this spring. It should've been a wake-up call to every damned one of us. Watson went over there and told that bunch of rednecks they should stand up to the federal government and keep their schools segregated. Albert Watson should've known he was throwing gasoline on hot coals.

"A few days later, a mob of white men – a couple hundred of them – surrounded two school buses full of black children, throwing bricks at the windows, screaming at the kids, rocking the buses back and forth. Some of the teachers were brave enough to get the kids out of there before the mob flipped the buses over. It was pure luck they didn't kill any of those children," Hampton said.

He took a long, deep breath, trying to keep his voice down and his cadence measured.

"I'll tell you the truth, Buzz. Something snapped in me when I heard about that. It's time the sensible people in these communities stood up and said that kind of thinking is wrong. I've said it, and I intend to keep saying it. I can't support a man like Albert Watson who would do that. John West has his flaws, but he's trying to heal racial wounds in this state, not continue to pour salt in them."

Webster quickly stepped in, looking for middle ground.

"Hampton, you know we don't support that sort of thing here. But we've got some tough issues here right now. The strike at the steel mill is in its second week. Almost every one of the striking workers is colored. They have picketed the plant, marched up and down Main Street. They have boycotted businesses that don't put 'Support the Strikers' signs in their windows. You know the strike is about safety conditions at the plant, but it's becoming a racial issue in this town.

"And the strike is hurtin' us all," Elliott offered. "Those are some of the best jobs in this town, they pay above minimum wage and give health benefits. The steel mill has quit spending money in this town and that's hurtin' the merchants. It didn't start out as a racial thing, but the NAACP has got organizers down here now helping out with the strike and those northern union guys know how to stir things up. You know all this, and we need your help.

"Hampton, let me just level with you," Elliott said. "Here's the deal. If you come out in support of those workers, if you keep runnin' those full-page ads from the union about how bad the steel mill management is, this thing could blow up in our faces. The plant could shut down. Or, we could end up with some terrible violence between the strikers and the non-strikers. And it would be black against white. It would be a damn race war. We need you on our side, Hampton, so that won't happen."

Webster looked at the town's attorney and nodded.

"Hampton," Cleveland said, "We hadn't told you this because we didn't want to see it in the newspaper. But the manager of the plant had the tires on his cars slashed twice this week. He got a death threat last night on the telephone. The police chief tells me that the union leaders have taken to keeping pistols with them at all times. And half the non-strikers who are still going to work are doing the same thing."

Hampton drained the last of the amber liquid from his glass and looked around the circle.

"Grant, you know Janie Hall, the black woman who used to help out at our house and half-raised my boy Wade when his mother was sick for awhile. A few days after the Lamar incident Janie came into my living room with her face full of tears. Said she was scared for her son Robert. He's just turned twenty, same as my Wade. She was afraid that some white hot-head would treat him wrong and her boy would end up in a fight. And every black mother knows her son will lose that fight, if not right then, then later. No black mother in this country has ever forgotten the lynching of Emmett Till.

"It suddenly hit me that but for the luck of the draw, that boy could be my son. Wade could have been born in Janie's part of town, with black skin, and no chance for a decent education, no chance at any job that won't break his back. I wouldn't want that for Wade. Why should we want it for any-one? I decided Jesus wouldn't like this way of life, no matter how our preachers dodge that issue on Sunday mornings.

"It's my job to put the facts on the table and let people decide what they think. If I'm not getting my facts right in the newspaper, you need to let me know. But if I'm getting the facts right, I'm doing my job. You know, when people used to say that Harry Truman was giving them hell about something, he'd always say: 'I'm not giving them hell. I'm just telling the truth. Sometimes the truth just hurts like hell.' Now, if you – "

Elliott cut him off in mid-sentence.

"You're not getting it, McNabb! I know how you high and mighty newspaper-types think. You say you don't take sides. If a damn house is burning down, you're neutral as between the fire and the fireman, or so you say.

"Let me spell this one out for you. If you don't support the plant in this strike, if you keep stirring up racial issues in this town, I will personally see to it that every important advertiser you have will cut you off. Not just Buzz there, but everybody who matters. The bank will call your loans, foreclose on your building, take your precious new printing press, and sell it at auction to someone who understands this town.

"And if you ever tell anyone about this little conversation, I'll deny it ever happened and so will every one of our friends here," Elliott said, nodding at the men in the circle.

Hampton set his empty glass down carefully on the table beside his chair and looked at each man one at a time.

"I'm sorry we disagree about this," he said firmly. "We can't handle this by pretending it's not happening. Dammit, *you're* the ones who aren't getting it. This is something the people in this community have to sort out together, and it's my job to help that happen by printing the facts. I know you think you have my back up against the wall, but I can deal with that. Gentlemen, I will speak the truth, and the truth will set me free."

He stood and started toward the door.

"Grant, thank you for the whiskey. I'll let myself out."

*   *   *   *   *

Hampton's hands shook as he opened the downstairs door to leave the funeral home, and they were still shaking as he struggled to put his key in the front door of the newspaper office. He went straight to his desk drawer and poured himself a shot glass of calming tonic. He downed it in a single swallow and dropped heavily into his wooden desk chair, hearing its familiar creak as he leaned back to ponder his situation. He dripped a few beads of Johnnie on the spring, and it quieted right down.

Hampton saw no clear way out of this corner. He gazed up at his favorite quotation from an old newspaperman named Liebling. A friend with calligraphy skills had heard Hampton say it so often, she had written it out and framed it for him.

He hung it proudly on his wall, a reminder about who has the final say at any newspaper. His eyes were still watery from the quick shot of scotch, but he knew it by heart anyway.

"Freedom of the press is guaranteed only to those who own one."

He poured another glass and sipped this one slowly.

On the opposite wall was a small portrait of Robert E. Lee. He had always admired Lee for his pride and his sense of duty. When Hampton was wrestling with a tough decision, he sometimes consulted with the general. Lee, after all, had suffered the worst kinds of heart-heavy decisions, helping send more than 600,000 soldiers to their deaths. He always reminded Hampton how small his own worries were by comparison. On evenings like tonight, when he and Johnnie were the only ones around, he'd talk to General Lee as though he were just across the desk.

"If I stand up to these goddam bullies, they will make sure I don't own this newspaper much longer," he said to the unsmiling bearded face. "They think they have me trapped against the wall, and they will fuck me if they have to.

"But if I bend over and let them have their way, I'm not going to really own the paper anydamnway," he muttered. "Those bastards will know they own me *and* the goddam newspaper."

He toasted Lee with the scotch bottle and refilled his shot glass.

Hampton re-read the article about the black bride. He still liked it. He looked at the Piggly Wiggly ad on the same page. He knew he'd never see another one of those again.

He looked at his watch. It was 10 o'clock. He reached for the telephone and dialed his son's number. Wade was spending the summer in Chapel Hill, living with friends and doing some research for his senior thesis.

The telephone in Wade's dorm rang a dozen times before Hampton heard his son's breathless hello, sounding like he had been running.

"Son, it's Dad. Was just thinking about you, and wanted to say hello and see how you're doing."

They had talked only every other week or so since Wade had started his junior year at college.

"Dad, you sound like you've been drinking," Wade said, with a wariness born of past liquor-laced conversations with his father. "Where are you?"

"I'm at the office, son. One of the advertisers didn't like the way his ad came out in today's newspaper, so I was tryin' to figure that out so I can explain it to him tomorrow. And I've had some pretty strong reaction to that story about the colored bride I told you I was going to run."

Hampton sent Wade each week's edition. Some of the articles embarrassed Wade – the photos of locally grown eggplants that looked oddly like Richard Nixon; the stories about moonshine stills being raided in the woods by federal revenue agents – when his college buddies from more cosmopolitan places read them. But Wade was grudgingly proud of his father for his unpopular stands on racial issues.

"Dad, why don't you just go home and deal with that tomorrow. It's Thursday night – there's not another paper until next week. I know you must be tired. We can talk another time."

The slight music of the scotch bottle brushing glass tinkled through the phone line.

"Son, I need to tell you that things are a little tough here right now," Hampton said. "I've scared the hell out of some of our local changephobics by writing some truth about the steel mill troubles. And a few of our advertisers didn't much like the bride story. That son of a bitch Buzz Timmons and our candy-ass mayor tried to take me to the woodshed tonight. Cowards and bullies can be pretty dangerous when they get scared."

The editor paused for a moment, then asked the question he needed to.

"If you are about finished up in Chapel Hill, I could use you here for the rest of the summer," he said. "I need to be mendin' fences with some of our advertisers. I'd love to have you helping me get the paper out for a few weeks."

Wade took a deep breath and let it out slowly.

"Dad, we've had this conversation before. I need to finish up what I'm doing here this summer. If I can get this work done on my thesis, I can take the spring semester off next year and work for one of the Presidential candidates opposed to the war. That's where I need to be, not down in Georgetown writing about some new leash law or some damn zoning ordinance."

"Well, goddamit, son, I may just need you to be here."

"That's not going to happen, Dad. I'm sorry, but it's just not. I'm going to lead my life, not yours. Look, I can hear the whiskey talking in your voice. Please go home and talk to Mom about this. I will call you tomorrow."

Hampton eased the receiver back onto the cradle and tried to stand up, but he was shaking, not just his hands this time, but his legs as well. He crossed his arms on his desk and laid his head over them. He decided he would just sleep right there for awhile. Sarah wouldn't call. She would know exactly where he was and why he wasn't home. He had slept many nights with Mr. Walker, and she had given up worrying herself to death about him.

It was the high-pitched squeal of tires and the crash of glass shattering in his front door that broke Hampton's drugged sleep. The fear-driven adrenalin sobered him immediately. He scrambled to the door and saw a pickup truck's taillights flash by and heard the screams of "niggerlover" as it sped away.

Hampton stalked back to his office and unlocked the closet behind his desk. He took out his shotgun and thumbed five shells into the chamber. He put away the bottle of brown liquor and rolled his desk chair to the steps just outside the front door. He kicked away the brick that had smashed his door, and took a seat, his shotgun across his lap.

His hands were rock steady. He planned to own this newspaper for the rest of his life.

PART III – THE LAWSUIT
1995

20

Motion to Recuse

K ate slammed the thick Sunday edition of the Columbia newspaper down on her desk so hard that Wade could hear it through the telephone connection.

"Dammit, I hate it when lawyers try their cases in the newspaper," Kate said loudly. "They say they're just trying to get their story out to protect the good names of their clients, but I know they're trying to influence Judge Jones, and they're hoping to get a few licks in with potential jurors."

"I read the story in the *State*," Wade said. "The Ravenels have great friends at that newspaper, and they've let the Ravenels tell their version of the story."

Wade looked down at the 1A story. It jumped to an inside full page spread about the lawsuit and the Ravenels' long time involvement in South Carolina politics. Under a bold headline "Ravenels Deny Bribery Charge, Vow to Clear Name," the newspaper had given the Ravenels and Carolina Phosphate ample space to refute the claims made in the *Pilot's* early August article. They had laid out their plans for pursuing their libel action against the newspaper. The article included a long quote from Buck Ravenel:

> Tripp Ravenel and I did meet with Carolina Phosphate in early July to get the company to commit to higher wages and tougher environmental controls if the state approved that permit.

The *Pilot* got its story flat wrong and is going to
pay for it. Either they don't have a source, and the
reporter made all this bribery malarkey up. Or their
source lied to them.

We are not going to let them destroy our reputations
while shooting from behind a rock. I am confident
any good judge will require them to identify this so-
called 'source' and let a jury decide who to believe.

If this was a hundred years ago, I would invite
Editor Wade McNabb to join me at dawn for a duel.
I guess these days we just have to make do with a
libel suit.

"Kate," Wade said. "It's just the way newspapers operate.
I'm trying to do better on our end and hit it straight down
the middle. I'm not letting any of our staff cover this. I hired
a reporter from the *Greenville Press* to write a down the middle
story about the libel suit and the underlying controversy. I had
him quote directly from the Complaint and from the Answer
we filed – no spin, no speculation, no bright comments from
the usual "political observers."

"That sounds reasonable," Kate said. "Sorry I blew off so
much steam, but some days the Ravenels really do get to me.

"Anyway, I've got some other news for you. This morning
I reviewed the materials you gave me about Judge Jones. I've
drafted a motion asking the judge to remove himself from this
case for two reasons. First, we'll rely on his quotes to you in
your own newspaper after you ran the 'slumlord' stories. He
said your stories were poorly researched, false and libelous. He
said he was planning on suing the newspaper. Second, we'll do
something no one has ever done before in South Carolina. We
will question whether a judge with such close political ties to a

lawyer representing a party should rule on that case. I suspect it will stir things up pretty good."

"I need a couple of affidavits establishing that Buck Ravenel was one of Jones' key supporters when Jones was elected by the legislature both times he ran. I'll have those in a couple of days, and we'll get this motion to recuse filed before the week is out. The judge will need to hear it promptly before any other issues in the case come before him," Kate said.

"Wade, I'm fixin' to get right down in the arena with you. Taking on one of Ravenel's favorite judges head-on is something most lawyers won't do. This case is about to get pretty damn interesting, for me and for you."

*   *   *   *   *

Just before three p.m. on the following Thursday, Kate quietly entered the main courtroom of the Georgetown County courthouse through the rear double doors and led McNabb and Anderson to a seat in the second row. A reporter for the *Pilot* was already sitting on the row in front of them, just behind the short wood railing that separated the courtroom spectators from the counsel tables, the jury box and the judge's bench.

The Georgetown County courthouse had been built two years after the Great Hurricane of 1822. That wooden structure had floated away in the flood, but the elegant brick courthouse that replaced it had withstood repeated bouts with nature's fury. It was still home to justice in the county. The craftsmen who finished the interior of the main courtroom had taken it upon themselves to etch the Ten Commandments in gold letters in the mahogany wall behind the judge's bench. The Commandments flashed yellow to defendants accused of theft or murder: THOU SHALT NOT STEAL. THOU SHALT NOT MURDER. They promised a biblical punishment along with the state's secular sentence.

Judge Jones was on the bench, appearing to listen to two young lawyers argue, with emotion but without precision, about what documents one side had asked for in discovery but the other had refused to turn over. Kate could read in the judge's eyebrows and body language his boredom with the dispute and his annoyance at its poor presentation by the lawyers.

When Buck Ravenel entered the courtroom minutes later, Kate was surprised to see that he was alone. She had met him only a few times, years ago when she and Cart Cooper had been on the opposite side of a trade secrets dispute with Ravenel. The senator's client had been accused of stealing his former employer's secret formulations for a new soybean pesticide and sharing it with his new employer. In the depositions they had taken before the case settled, and in the court hearings she had attended, Ravenel had always traveled with an entourage – a younger partner, at least one associate, and a paralegal. Kate had decided his strategy involved a maximum show of force, a demonstration that the case was of major importance to his client, and an outward commitment to fight the legal war to the death – millions for defense, not a penny for tribute, no matter how bad the law and the facts might really be for his side. The strategy cowed many of his adversaries into a quick settlement to avoid the costs of total warfare. Ravenel had clearly decided that today's hearing was one he wanted to handle with a more delicate touch.

Kate had pondered hard whether to take Judge Jones on head-to-head with a motion to have him recuse himself from the case. Most judges voluntarily removed themselves from cases when the parties might question their ability to be impartial. It was a rare case when one party's lawyer took the risky step of formally asking the judge to step aside and have the case assigned to another judge. As Cart Cooper had once cautioned her, if you shoot at the king, you'd better kill him, because the payback from a failed attempt is likely to be deadly.

Kate knew it put her personally at risk. Judges were used to lawyers disagreeing with their rulings, arguing hard that the judge was mistaken on a point of law, or appealing their decisions, hoping to get them reversed by a higher court. That's how the law normally ground its way to a final result. But judges hated being told that they couldn't rule fairly on a case. Kate knew they took that personally. She knew Judge Jones, and other judges, would keep her decision to make this motion in their memory banks, and it would come back to haunt her. As calm as she tried to be on the outside, she worried hard about the risk she was taking.

But she had decided to go for it. If Jones refused to remove himself from the case despite the evidence of his anger toward the newspaper over the "slumlord" stories, it would probably signal he was already determined to look out for Ravenel and his cronies in the libel case. That would be apparent to anyone interested in the case. And she thought getting the bias issue into public view would at least remind the judge that others would be watching the case closely for signs that he was being unfair to the newspaper.

The judge's voice interrupted her thoughts.

"All right," the judge said loudly, stopping the then-speaking lawyer in mid-sentence. "I've heard enough, actually more than enough. I'll read your briefs and see if you are any more clear or persuasive there than you have been in this courtroom. I'll take this matter under advisement and let you know how I rule."

Judge Jones leaned down and whispered to the courtroom clerk for a minute as the two lawyers cleared the counsel tables and left the courtroom. Then he nodded in the general direction of Ravenel and Stewart, took the file folder the clerk handed to him, and motioned to the lawyers.

"It appears the only thing left is the motion in the Carolina Phosphate case. Counsel, I'll see you in chambers."

Before the judge could rise, the *Pilot's* reporter stood, as if on cue, and cleared his throat loudly.

"Your honor, my name is Jim Ellis," he said in a shaky voice. "I'm a reporter for the *Pilot.*"

He began to read from the printed card he kept in his wallet for just such an occasion.

"On behalf of the *Pilot*, I respectfully object to the exclusion of the public from this court proceeding. The United States Supreme Court in Richmond Newspapers v. Virginia ruled that the First Amendment guarantees the public a right to be present...."

"Young man, you may sit down," the judge said in a voice that was not shaky. "I am quite familiar with the notion of open courtrooms. I was simply planning to meet in chambers to get a handle on the procedural posture of this case, not to address the substantive aspects of the motion."

The judge gestured to the otherwise empty courtroom.

"Citizen Ellis, it appears that you are the only member of the public interested in this motion, other than the parties. Very well, let's just stay here and chat about this. Counsel, please come forward and let me hear what you have to say."

Once the lawyers were settled at the counsel tables, Judge Jones turned and looked directly at Kate.

"Ms. Stewart, I have read your motion and the exhibits attached to it," the judge said solemnly. "You and your clients take the position that I should recuse myself from sitting on this case because I had a bit of a disagreement with the newspaper a few years ago. And you note correctly that Senator Ravenel, who represents his son and the other plaintiff in this case, voted for me in the General Assembly in both my elections to the bench. Based on that, you assert that I could not rule fairly in this case. Do I mis-state your position?"

Kate's heart was beating fast, and she took a quiet, deep breath to steady her voice.

"Your Honor, I would respectfully like to clarify a point or two. As the affidavits show, Your Honor didn't just have a disagreement with the newspaper, you threatened to sue the paper over the articles about you. And Senator Ravenel didn't just vote for Your Honor, he was a key supporter and the chair of the Judiciary Committee that nominated you. The critical point...."

"Ms. Stewart, let me get a few things straight right now," Judge Jones cut in sharply, his voice booming, his eyebrows rising. "Number one, it's true that I don't like your client."

The courtroom was so quiet she could hear the judge wheeze slightly as he gathered his breath for his next angry salvo.

"Number two, it's true that I don't trust your client. But I have people in my courtroom every day I don't like or trust – murderers, rapists, crooks, lawyers who don't tell the whole truth about their cases. But I rule on their cases fairly because that's my job. That's the oath I took when I became a judge."

Kate's adrenalin was flowing now, clearing her head.

"Judge, I respect that. And as a lawyer and an officer of this court, I understand that Your Honor can be objective and impartial in any case you have before you," Kate said in her most sincere, soothing voice, one she had practiced just before court, anticipating this very exchange. She hoped her nose wasn't growing.

"At the same time, we both know that is not the legal standard that must be applied. The issue is not actual bias, but whether the Court has the *appearance of bias.* It's important that my clients, and the public, will believe that this Court can rule fairly," Kate said.

She took one more deep breath before firing her final shot.

"I respectfully submit that there is enough evidence here to give those who don't know you the impression that you might have a bias in favor of Mr. Ravenel and against the newspaper. The real issue is the public's confidence in the fairness of our courts. That's why we believe the Court should have this case re-assigned to another judge who has less history with Mr. Ravenel and with the newspaper."

The judge leaned forward on his elbows and laced his fingers. He rested his chin across his knuckles and peered down straight into Kate's eyes.

His voice was calm, but his face was red and his eyebrows erect.

"Ms. Stewart, never in my twelve years on the bench has a lawyer suggested I should step down from a case because I could not be fair. Let me be sure you know that Senator Ravenel was not the *only* person who voted for me in those legislative elections for this seat on the bench. I was elected unanimously each time – 170 Senators and House members voted for me. Not *one* Senator, not *one* House member voted against me."

Kate knew the right response to that statement, but she couldn't say it in the courtroom. Once Ravenel's Judiciary Committee nominated someone for a judgeship, the battle was over. It was in his committee that the horse-trading took place and the final deals were cut. That was where Ravenel flexed his political muscle. Once the nominations were released, the floor vote was always a polite formality. No one ever voted against the committee's nominees.

"As to the newspaper articles, let me say this. I have heard Mr. McNabb explain to my Rotary Club how his newspaper can be objective in its news coverage of this public official or that official at the same time his editorial page is endorsing one of them for election and calling the other one an idiot or a crook. I respect his professionalism and his ability to be objective, and I feel confident he can respect mine."

He looked over at Buck Ravenel.

"Do you have anything you'd like to say, Senator Ravenel?"

Ravenel rose and spoke with a voice of honey and silk.

"Judge, as Ms. Stewart may know, I have appeared many times before you as an advocate. As this Court knows, Your Honor has sometimes ruled for my clients, and I'm sure you have sometimes ruled against them. Whether we left your courtroom happy at the result or disappointed, we never left feeling that you ruled for anyone other than Justice herself. That's all I have, Your Honor."

He looked directly at the judge with the most solemn of faces, stole a sideways glance at Kate, and slowly took his seat at the counsel table. Judge Jones didn't give Kate another look. She felt like she had a fist balled up inside her stomach.

"All right, thank you both for your briefs and your argument. Ms. Stewart, your motion is denied."

He turned to the bailiff sitting in the far corner of the jury box.

"Bailiff, please adjourn this session of court."

The judge gathered his file, nodded at the lawyers, and shuffled through the door to his chambers.

* * * * *

"Judge Jones also denied our motion to postpone your depositions," Kate said as soon as Sandy and Wade sat down at
her conference table the next Monday morning. "The written
order was in this morning's mail. No big surprise. The judge
said the plaintiffs have the first shot at gathering evidence, and
that's pretty routine. He's moving this case along real fast."

She glanced at Sandy.

"You're first up next week," she said. "We've turned over
all your notes that didn't identify your confidential source, so
they'll have plenty to ask you about."

She looked back at Wade.

"We've spent a good bit of time trying to anticipate everything they might ask either of you. You two are as ready to testify as you'll ever be. I don't think there should be any surpris-
es. They'll hammer you on your refusal to identify your source,
and you're ready for that. There's no judge at a deposition, so
if Ravenel gets out of line, I'll jump in and make objections. If
there are any segments of your deposition testimony that they
particularly like, they can read those to the jury at trial.

"So remember – straightforward answers, no sarcasm, and
be respectful. We want the jury to like us and trust us more
than they do those guys. What's the theme of our case?"

Wade smiled and remembered their careful discussions.

"We want to be able to ask the jury at the end of the case
the key question: 'Do you want to live in a state where a newspaper can print what the *Pilot* knew and let its readers decide
where the truth lies? Or would you rather live in a state where
a newspaper with information about public corruption would
be scared to print it because the politicians would tie them up
in court?'"

Kate tapped her pencil on the table.

"I do like the sound of that," she said.

"Before you go, some quick thoughts on our strategy. After we received Tripp Ravenel's responses to our written discovery requests identifying Vince Stone and State Senator Arthur Long as the other participants in the Bowman's Forest meeting, I contacted them. Neither will agree to an informal interview, so we'll have to wait until we take their depositions to see what they will say. Stone is a serious lawyer, and normally I wouldn't think he would be willing to lie under oath just to protect Buck Ravenel and his son. But his career is on the line here, too, and a bribery conviction carries more time in the steel hotel than a perjury conviction would. So who knows?

"And I've saved the best for last," Kate said. "Bowman's Forest has turned over to both sides its complete guest list for July first, along with a list of all of the employees on its dining room payroll that month."

She handed Wade and Sandy copies.

"My guess is Ravenel will question them and ask each of them if he or she is your source. I don't want to know if your source testifies under oath that he is not your source. I am an officer of the court, and it puts me in a bad position to know that a witness may have perjured himself. I may have an obligation to tell the judge if I'm aware of a "fraud upon the court.""

Wade's eyes narrowed a little, and Kate detected anger in them.

"I thought you told me at the outset that anything we told you was protected by the attorney-client privilege. If we were to tell you the name of our source, and that's the only way you knew it, how could you tell the judge who our source is?"

Kate put both hands on the conference table and pushed

back in her chair so she could see Sandy and Wade in one glance.

"It's a difficult issue," Kate said. "I'm not sure of the answer. I wouldn't have to reveal the identity of the source, but I might have to resign from the case. I'd probably have to go find some ethics professor and explore it. That's why I don't want to know the name of the source if I don't have to know."

The two men were silent as they read through the names on the two lists. After a few seconds, they looked up and glanced at each other.

"You can rest easy for the moment, counselor," Wade said. "It may not be an issue any time soon. Our source isn't on here."

Kate furrowed her brow, not sure what to make of that answer. They didn't offer more, and she decided it wasn't time to ask. She wanted to think about that a little more.

"Okay, guys," she said. "You're ready. Both of you get plenty of sleep. You need to be alert. Wade, they'll start your deposition as soon as they finish Sandy's."

She walked them to the front door of the office.

"Sandy, that story in Sunday's newspaper may finally persuade your source he should call you back. It would sure take the pressure off if he'd be willing to come forward and testify in the event the judge decides to order you to identify him. I know you don't want to do it without his permission. So keep your ears peeled and be sure you check your voicemails."

21

A Few Questions

Sandy's blue and white seersucker suit and navy bowtie with small sea turtles on it stood out among the dark blue suits and red-striped power ties of the lawyers on the other side of Kate's conference room table.

Buck Ravenel had two young lawyers from his firm beside him, scurrying about organizing exhibits, talking in hushed tones, trying to look necessary. Carolina Phosphate had its in-house counsel and a young lawyer from a pedigreed Charleston law firm in attendance. Tripp Ravenel sat near the end of the table. He seemed oddly detached, more of an observer than a participant. When Sandy first noticed him, he was sitting alone, picking stray pieces of lint from his navy blue suit coat.

The court reporter was stationed at the head of the conference table, her wrists poised over the stenography machine, ready to take mechanical shorthand and record every syllable spoken in the room once the proceedings began. She was from Intercoastal Court Reporting Services and handled all of Ravenel's deposition work.

Buck Ravenel began his questioning of Sandy in the folksy manner he was famous for, a gentle, almost friendly inquiry into the reporter's education and experience, punctuated by a slight barb here and there.

"You'll be twenty-four years old next month, is that right, Mr. Anderson?

"Yes, sir, it is."

"Now you went to college up in North Carolina, didn't you, son?"

His dismissive tone made it sound like North Carolina was as foreign to South Carolina as North Dakota might be.

"Yes, sir," Sandy responded.

"I take it you didn't grow up around here either, did you?"

"No, sir. I grew up in Maryland."

"Well, part of Maryland's on this side of the Mason-Dixon line. We don't need to ask which side you grew up on, though, do we? You didn't study journalism up there at Chapel Hill, did you?"

"No, sir."

When it suited him, Ravenel could slow his voice to a drawl as thick as left-over grits. He managed to make "journalism" come out in four long, syrupy syllables.

"They teach courses on libel law at jour-na-li-zum school, don't they, Mr. Anderson?"

"I don't really know, sir."

"If you'd gone to journalism school, you'd know a little more about libel law, wouldn't you?"

"Objection," Kate said quietly.

"Withdraw the question," Ravenel responded. "Now, Mr. Anderson, they have a pretty good student newspaper up there at Chapel Hill, don't they?"

"Yes, sir."

"And while you were a student up there, were you ever a reporter or an editor for the student newspaper?"

"No, sir."

"Well, now, you didn't study journalism and you didn't work on the school newspaper. Let me ask you this, Mr. Anderson, while you were in college, did you get any training or experience of any kind whatsoever in the field of journalism or news-reporting?"

"No, sir, I did not. I was interested in political science in those days, and I did most of my studies in that field."

Ravenel's eyes lit up and his face broke into a pretend grin. "Po-li-ti-cal Science?"

He looked around the room, smiling at everyone as though he had just learned about the discovery of a new planet.

"I've been involved in politics for the last thirty years. I didn't know there was such a thing as political *science*. I've always thought that politics was an *art*.

"So I'll be sure I understand this, did you have *any* experience or training whatsoever in the newspaper bidness before you came to work here in Georgetown at the *Pilot*?"

Sandy took a deep breath and wondered just where Ravenel was going. He straightened his bow tie, then put his hands out of sight below the table. He could feel them beginning to sweat.

"No, sir. I came here because everyone told me that Wade McNabb was a great journalist, and I could learn everything I needed to know about news reporting and newspapers from him."

"Well, Mr. Anderson, that's a very generous thing for you to say about your boss, the man who signs your paychecks and pays your legal bills."

Ravenel turned toward the editor and gave him half a salute. Then he turned to the court reporter.

"Madame Court Reporter, please let the record reflect that Mr. McNabb is sitting right here, and this high praise from his young employee is making him blush just a little."

"Objection," Kate said firmly. "I move to strike Mr. Ravenel's comments from the record. We don't need your testimony in this deposition."

The Senator smiled and turned back to the newspaper reporter.

"Has Mr. McNabb ever been kind enough to send you up to the University of South Carolina to its fine journalism school for any continuing training or education?"

"No, sir, I've been right busy covering things for the newspaper, and I have not been to any courses like that."

"Are you familiar with an organization called Investigative Reporters and Editors ?"

"Yes, sir, I've heard of that."

"Do they have meetings or seminars where they teach folks investigative reporting techniques?"

"I understand that they do, but I have never been to any of their meetings."

"Mr. Anderson, is it fair to say that before you went to work on this story about my son and me you had never done any of what some people refer to as 'investigative reporting?'"

"I don't know exactly what 'investigative reporting' is, Senator Ravenel. I think all good reporting is investigative. It's asking questions, reviewing documents, finding facts and checking them as carefully as you can."

"Is it fair to say, Mr. Anderson, that a good bit of your reporting this past year has focused on Carolina Phosphate and its plans to put a plant along the Waccamaw River near Georgetown?"

"Yes, sir."

"And, would it be fair to say that you have covered the so-called 'environmental issues' involving locating such a plant here?"

"Yes, sir."

"Do you have any background in environmental science?"

"No, sir."

"Would you say you are an environmentalist?"

"I don't know what you mean by that. I do think we should take care of our physical environment around us."

"Do you know what the Sierra Club is, Mr. Anderson?"

"Yes, sir. It's an organization that supports efforts to protect wilderness areas and to improve the quality of our water and air. I know that much."

"Have you ever heard anyone describe Sierra Club members as 'Druids'?

"Objection!" Kate interjected sharply. "You are heading way off on a tangent that has nothing to do with this case. The Sierra Club is not on trial here."

"Objection noted," he said quietly. "I'll continue in this vein for another minute or so."

"Please answer the question, Mr. Anderson."

The reporter glanced at Kate, who shrugged her shoulders and nodded.

"Yes, sir. I've heard some people refer to them as Druids."

"And can you explain to the rest of us here why they are sometimes called Druids?"

"Because in England, a couple of thousand years ago, the Druids were a nature-worshipping sect. They used to sacrifice humans to please the trees. I've heard people who don't like the Sierra Club describe them that way."

"Now, Mr. Anderson, have you ever been a member of the Sierra Club?"

"When I was in college, I was a member for a year or two. I found it a great way to meet young women who like to go hiking on weekends. I confess I never read the newsletter very carefully."

"Did you ever belong to an organization called Students for Clean Air while you were up at Chapel Hill?"

Sandy paused for a moment and looked up at the ceiling.

"I don't remember, sir."

Ravenel leaned across the table and snared one of the hard candies from the dish the court reporter placed on the table at the beginning of the day. Each peppermint candy had the company's initials on it: ICRS. Ravenel twisted the clear wrapper off his candy and held the sugary nugget in front of Sandy's face.

"You know what we call this, Mr. Anderson?" he said with a tight, mean grin. He looked at the court reporter. "Evelyn, this is off the record."

"We call this an 'I Can't Remember Shit' pill. Some witnesses have eaten one too many. That ain't gonna play in a real courtroom, son."

"Objection," Kate said loudly, slapping the table. "That is improper conduct, improper questioning, and I want it read back to be sure it's in this record, so the court can get a feel for your bullying, Mr. Ravenel."

Kate looked at the court reporter.

"Please read Mr. Ravenel's comments back to us."

"I didn't get down what Senator Ravenel said," the court reporter said softly. "He said it was off the record."

Ravenel smiled sweetly at Kate.

"Now, if we can move along, Ms. Stewart.

He turned to the witness.

"Let me show you something that might refresh your recollection, Mr. Anderson."

Ravenel handed the reporter a sheet of paper and slid one across the table for Kate to review. It was a membership list from the 1991 Students for Clean Air, Chapel Hill Chapter, and Sandy's name was near the top of the alphabetical listing.

"Well, I guess I must've been a member, but I don't remember ever attending a meeting. This may be something that I agreed to support but never got too involved in."

"You know this organization was started by Ralph Nader and his acolytes?"

"No, sir, I didn't know that."

"But it's fair to say that you would consider yourself an environmentalist?"

"I'm not sure what you mean by that."

"Well, wouldn't you agree that your background - Sierra Club, that Clean Air group - shows you have a bias in favor of those who call themselves environmentalists, like those people right here opposing the Carolina Phosphate plant."

"Objection to this entire line of argumentative questions," Kate said. "But he can answer if he understands your question."

Sandy paused and thought about that question for a moment.

"Once I decided to become a reporter, I realized I had to look at everything I covered from all sides and let everybody involved have their say. If I have any biases, I keep them out of my reporting."

"So your position is that you have biases but you can cut them on and off like a light switch?"

Kate leaned forward on her elbows and looked straight at the court reporter.

"Objection to the form of the question. Mr. Anderson, you need not answer that one."

The deposition continued in this fashion for the rest of the morning, Ravenel teasing out Anderson's testimony, trying to suggest at every turn biases, inexperience and lack of training as a reporter. Before the lunch break, Ravenel walked Sandy through the numerous articles he had written about Carolina Phosphate, marking each as an exhibit. When they started back after lunch, Ravenel's tone changed abruptly. His playful needling disappeared, and his voice and face hardened.

"Mr. Anderson, you have tarnished the good name of my son and the reputation of an upstanding company, not to mention my own reputation. Do you understand this?"

Kate quickly put her hand on the table, signaling Sandy not to utter a syllable.

"Objection," she said firmly. "Please rephrase your question, Mr. Ravenel. You know that's testimony from you, not a question. We'll be happy to put you under oath and take some testimony from you today, though, if I can do the questioning."

Ravenel did not even look in her direction. He stared straight at Sandy.

"Were you at Bowman's Forest on the night of the meeting you wrote about in your news article?"

"No, sir."

"Have you ever been to Bowman's Forest in your life?"

"No, sir."

"So you have no firsthand knowledge whatsoever of what may have taken place during that meeting at Bowman's Forest, do you Mr. Anderson?"

"No, sir, I have no firsthand knowledge."

Ravenel's voice got slightly lower.

"So, Mr. Anderson, everything you put in your article about this meeting at Bowman's Forest came from your so-called confidential source, is that right?"

Sandy kept his voice as even as he could. But he couldn't keep his eyelids from fluttering just a little.

"No, sir. Not everything. You'll remember that I had a copy of the draft report that Tripp Ravenel's office told me didn't exist."

"Did you get a copy of that draft report from your source?"

Sandy hesitated. He looked at Kate and back at Senator Ravenel.

"It came from a source, yes, sir."

Ravenel paused, leaned back from the table and spread both hands wide gesturing at the other people in the room.

"Mr. Anderson, I would like you to tell this court ...," he caught and kept the eye of the court reporter taking down the testimony as though she was the judge and jury, "and everyone here the name of your confidential source. Tell us that name here and now."

"I think you know, Senator, that I can't do that. I promised my source I would not disclose his or her name."

Ravenel paused for thirty seconds before he asked another question. When the room was absolutely still, he leaned forward across the table to make close eye contact with the reporter.

"Mr. Anderson, this is a very serious matter we are dealing with here today. I ask you one more time to tell me the name of your source, or we will take this issue straight to the judge."

Sandy was having a hard time keeping his cool. He looked away from Ravenel's steady gaze.

"I can't tell you that, sir."

Ravenel's voice was hard, his volume louder.

"And why can't you tell me the name of your source? Is it because you don't *have* a source, Mr. Anderson?"

"Sir, I have a source. But I promised my source I would not do that. I gave my source my word."

"Do you claim some kind of testimonial privilege that the law recognizes? If so, I'd be pleased to hear about that."

"Mr. Anderson claims no statutory privilege at this point," Kate said. "He has promised his source not to reveal that person's identity, and his conscience requires that he honor that promise."

Ravenel still refused to acknowledge Kate with a look. He continued to glare at the reporter.

"Let me be sure I understand, son," he said.

"I object to the form of your question. Do not call my client 'son' again, Senator. His name is Mr. Anderson."

"All right, Mr. Anderson, is your so-called source now, or has he ever been, an employee of Bowman's Forest?"

"I can't answer that."

"You mean you *won't* answer that question. Was your so-called source a guest of Bowman's Forest on the night of the meeting?"

"I respectfully decline to answer that question. That's just another way of narrowing down the list of possibilities."

"Are you telling the court that you refuse to answer a request for relevant and critical information and that you have no legal basis for that refusal?"

"Objection," Kate said firmly.

Ravenel ignored her, but didn't wait for an answer from Anderson. He slid across the table two sheets of paper, one containing a list of Bowman's Forest employees, the other the guest list from the evening in question.

"Let me show you two lists, one of Forest employees, one of Forest guests that night. I'm not asking you to name your so-called source. I'm just asking you if he or she is on either of those lists."

"I cannot answer that, sir."

Ravenel's eyes narrowed as he fixed them on the reporter's eyes. His voice rose a little more.

"You know some people believe you don't have a source for this story, don't you? People who believe you made it up."

"If that's a question, my answer is no, I don't know that there are people who think I made it up."

"Other than your so-called source, has anyone ever told you that there was any kind of bribe or payoff related to the permit?"

"No, sir."

"Have you ever found any evidence of any bribe or payoff other than what your so-called source allegedly told you?"

"No, sir."

"Do you know that your lawyer requested all records from me, Tripp Ravenel and Carolina Phosphate that would have anything to do with the permit or any kind of investment with Carolina Phosphate?"

"Yes, sir, I know that."

"And you all asked for all copies of any records of any ownership interest in any business or property acquired by any one of us in the past twelve months?"

"Yes, sir."

"And you've reviewed the records we produced, have you not?"

"Yes, sir, I have."

Ravenel paused, and the room slowly fell silent. The stenographer's fleet hands caught up with the fast-paced testimony and hung suspended over her keyboard, waiting for the next flurry of words. The lawyer lowered his voice just a little, enjoying the drama.

"And there's not *one single* document that refers to *any* investment of *any* kind made in the past twelve months by me or Tripp Ravenel or anyone else at the meeting, is that right?"

"That's right, sir."

"Mr. Anderson, who else besides you knows the name of your source?"

"Wade McNabb."

Ravenel for the first time took his gaze off of Sandy Anderson. He stared hard at Kate Stewart without smiling.

"How about your lawyer, Ms. Stewart? Does she know who your source is?" he said, asking Anderson the question while staring straight at Kate.

"Objection! To the extent a response would invade the attorney-client privilege, I advise my client not to answer."

Sandy looked at her, then at his interrogator.

"I decline to answer."

"You claim no statutory privilege, Mr. Anderson," he said gently this time. "You simply refuse to answer my questions, is that right?

Anderson sat quietly, hoping no one would see him squeezing his own hands under the tobacco barn door.

"Yes sir," he said.

Ravenel smiled.

"I have no more questions for this witness. We are off the record, unless Ms. Stewart has some follow-up."

Kate shook her head. Ravenel spoke in the direction of the stenographer.

"Please provide me a transcript of the last ten minutes of Mr. Anderson's testimony by tomorrow morning."

Ravenel leaned back in his chair and looked around the room. To no one in particular he said with a bemused smile, "I find this refusal to testify simply fascinating, and I suspect Judge Jones will, too."

*   *   *   *   *

At 9:30 the next morning, Wade McNabb took three quiet, deep breaths to relax, waiting for Senator Buck Ravenel to question him about his experience in the newspaper business.

Ravenel nodded to the court reporter, who nodded to the

witness, and McNabb placed his left hand on the Bible and swore to tell the truth. A part of him actually looked forward to describing his career story, starting with his first newspaper job, at fourteen, helping his father translate high school baseball scorebooks into box scores for the next day's paper.

Ravenel instead went straight to the heart of the matter.

"Mr. McNabb, are you the Editor and Publisher of the *Georgetown Pilot?*"

"Yes, sir," McNabb answered, a little startled, but trying not to show it.

There was no charm or folksiness evident today. The senator was all business. He didn't have a note in front of him.

"On August 5 of this year, you held both those positions?"

"Yes, sir."

"You had the ultimate authority to print or not to print any article submitted to you by one of your reporters, is that right?"

"Yes, sir."

Ravenel's questions came rapid-fire. The editor would barely finish one answer before the next question came from the lawyer.

"On August 5, the *Pilot* published the article that is the subject of this lawsuit brought by Carolina Phosphate and by Tripp Ravenel, is that right?"

"Yes, sir."

"And you read it thoroughly before its publication?"

"Yes."

"And you approved its publication, didn't you?"

"Yes, I did."

"Part of the August 5 article purports to describe a meeting in early July between Tripp Ravenel, a representative of Carolina Phosphate and myself, among others, down at Bowman's

Forest, is that correct?"

"That's right."

"Neither you nor your reporter were there, were you?"

"No, sir."

"Everything in the August 5 article about that meeting came from your so-called confidential source, did it not?"

"Yes."

"You have no other information – firsthand or otherwise – about what took place at that meeting, do you?"

"Only that the newspaper obtained a copy of a draft report that Tripp Ravenel's Environmental Resources Agency had told us did not exist."

"Mr. McNabb, I am not going to belabor this point with you. We went over it at some length yesterday in Mr. Anderson's deposition. You were present at Mr. Anderson's deposition, were you not?"

"Yes, I was."

"And you heard him refuse repeatedly to identify the newspaper's source, didn't you?"

"I did."

"I think we have enough testimony on that point to get Judge Jones' attention, but let me ask you briefly about that.

"Do you know the name of the source for the information published in your newspaper on the fifth of August relating to the alleged substance of an early July dinner at Bowman's Forest?

"Yes, sir, I do know the source's name," McNabb responded.

"What is the source's name?"

McNabb smiled at the lawyer's directness.

"I can't tell you that," he said. 'I personally promised we would protect the source's confidentiality."

"So you maintain, right here, under oath, under penalty of

perjury that you really had one single source for the information about this dinner meeting?"

McNabb cocked his head and stared at Ravenel from a different angle, hoping he could understand the Senator a little better.

'Yes, I do. I'm not trying to be mysterious about that," McNabb said.

"But even though I need to know the name of any such source in order to prove that you had no business relying on that person, you refuse to let us know the source's name?

"You are right in saying that I will not identify the source."

"And if you don't identify the source, we will never even know that you *had* a source, will we, Mr. McNabb? You just want the rest of us to trust you on this, don't you?"

"Objection," Kate said quietly. "Counsel is just arguing with the witness. You know he doesn't have to respond to that kind of question."

Ravenel ignored Kate's comment and moved on quickly.

"So you, like Mr. Anderson, simply refuse to provide us with this information which is crucial to pursuing our lawsuit against you and your newspaper?"

"I decline to name the source."

"You think you can just destroy the reputations of my clients with your newspaper's lies and sit there mute when I ask you to name the source of these lies? I don't think Judge Jones is going to cotton to that, my friend."

"Objection," Kate said firmly. "There's no need to answer that, Wade."

"Madame Court Reporter," Ravenel said nodding in her direction, "Please mark this portion of the deposition so we can have it transcribed and ready for Judge Jones on Monday afternoon."

The Senator looked back at McNabb and changed subjects.

"Now, Mr. McNabb, you were born in 1950 as I recall, and that would make you forty-five, is that right?"

"Yes, sir."

"And you've been in the newspaper business for quite some time, haven't you?"

"Yes, sir. In one way or another, I've been involved with newspapers since I was a teenager. I picked up obituaries from the funeral homes and things like that until I was in high school. When I was fifteen or so, I began to write sports stories for the local newspaper, and the occasional small news story."

"Your father was Wade Hampton McNabb, and you are a Junior?"

"That's right."

"And your father bought this paper right after World War II and owned it for about twenty-five years, didn't he?"

"Yes, sir, he did."

"Now sometime around 1970, the newspaper hit some hard times, as I recall. Do you have any recollection of that?"

Kate placed both hands on the conference table and looked at the court reporter.

"Objection. Who the owner of this newspaper was twenty-five years ago or what problems it may have had then are of no relevance to this lawsuit. I object to this line of questioning."

The Senator never took his eyes off Wade McNabb.

"Objection noted, Ms. Stewart," he said. "I believe this information is relevant to the editor's state of mind when he published the article about my son. It may help us understand just why he may have harbored some ill will toward the subjects of the August five article. I have just a few more questions in this vein, and unless you get Judge Jones on the telephone and have him order me to stop, I will continue."

Kate sensed Wade's nervousness and considered telling him not to answer and waiting for the judge to rule on these questions. But she knew the more questions her witnesses refused to answer, the more intrigued Judge Jones might be. She decided to let the questioning continue a little further.

"Did your father ever tell you why he had to file for bankruptcy?"

McNabb met Ravenel's gaze steadily.

"I was away at college when all that happened, but he told me a little about it. He said some of his key advertisers boycotted the newspaper and cut off his ad revenue. He said they were mad at him for treating black people like they had equal rights in this country and for suggesting that others should do the same."

"So your father lost this newspaper twenty-five years ago because of what he published in it? Is that your understanding, Mr. McNabb?

"Yes, sir, it is."

"Now your paper published editorials opposing the granting of the phosphate plant permit, didn't it, Mr. McNabb?"

"That's right, we did."

"Did any of your advertisers threaten to quit advertising with you because of those editorials?"

McNabb nodded.

"Yes, two or three did. That kind of stuff happens all the time. I try not to take it too seriously. I like to think their businesses need me as much as I need them. If not, I'm not doing my job."

"Did you tell one of them that you took the same position your father did: you were going to print the truth and it would set you free?"

"I said something like that."

"Did you consider before you published the August 5 article that your family might get to lose this newspaper a second time?"

"Objection," Kate said, slapping her hand on the table. "That question is inappropriate, and I move to strike this entire line of questioning from the transcript."

"I withdraw the last question," Ravenel said quietly. "I don't have any other questions for you, Mr. McNabb.

Ravenel paused a moment and waited for McNabb to meet his eyes. Ravenel nodded at the court reporter.

"Let's go off the record."

The court reporter let her fingers rest, and the lawyer turned back to McNabb.

"I want to tell you that I was sorry about your father's death. I always thought he was a progressive voice in this state, just as I have tried to be. It was a terrible thing, and it didn't have to happen. He didn't understand that politics is the art of the possible, and you can't get too far ahead of your own times."

The lawyer shifted his attention to the stenographer.

"Madame Court Reporter, I have no further questions of this witness. Please have the transcript of these last few pages ready by Monday afternoon. We are concluded."

22

The Shell Game

The early dusk of mid-September had married a light breeze, cooling Sliders' bayside patio. Wade and Kate ducked around the POETS crowd inside and found a secluded table at the patio's far end.

The fall hurricane season was in full swing, but not a single storm had threatened the South Carolina coast. The mayhem inflicted by Hurricane Hugo six years earlier was still evident, especially along the undeveloped barrier islands south of Georgetown. Hugo's ferocious gusts had snapped off pine trees and utility poles at half mast, and its storm surge had flattened McClellanville. Georgetown had largely recovered from a potent but less direct blow.

Wade sometimes felt these powerful storms – spawned on Africa's north coast and empowered by the Atlantic's warm currents – might be a form of cosmic payback for the cruelties of slavery. They seemed to seek the Confederate states – Virginia, the Carolinas, Georgia, Florida, Mississippi, Alabama, Texas, Louisiana – that had fought so hard to keep Africans in chains.

Kate sipped her martini, savoring that first icy blast of clarity. Wade nursed a Budweiser, watching the door for Sandy.

"Do you ever drink anything else?" she asked, nodding at the brown longneck in his hand. Other than the white wine he had brought to their beach outing, she had never seen him drink anything other than a red, white and blue Budweiser.

"I guess it's a form of reverse snobbery," he said. "I got fed up over the years with guys talking about exotic 'local' beers from some little crossroads in Ireland or from an obscure village in Germany. It seems sort of affected. So I've stuck with Budweiser. I've had my share over the years. You know what the fine print says, don't you?"

He didn't give her a chance to respond. He tapped the tiny blue-script legend on the paper label on the longneck and launched right in. Wade looked at Kate as he recited with a mock serious tone: "This is the famous Budweiser beer. We know of no brand produced by any other brewer which costs so much to brew and age. Our exclusive Beechwood Aging produces a taste, a smoothness, and" – he paused for dramatic effect – "a *drinkability* you will find in no other beer at any price."

"How about that?" he laughed.

She wasn't sure if she was impressed or depressed.

"Okay, how about you?" he asked. "What do you know by heart? You're a great lawyer. Maybe you have the First Amendment memorized."

Kate hesitated. Wade didn't. He was having fun.

"Congress shall make no law respecting an establishment of religion, or prohibiting the free exercise thereof; or abridging the freedom of speech or of the press; or the right of the people peaceably to assemble and to petition the Government for a redress of grievances."

"Not bad for a non-lawyer, huh?" he said with a tease in his voice. "Two very important statements of principle – almost exactly the same number of words. Pretty amazing, don't you think?

Kate shook her head, smiling.

"Okay, I do know a poem or two," she said. "If you must

know, I wrote my college thesis on Robert Frost, and I know some of his poems by heart. My mother was an English teacher, and she made me memorize all sorts of things and then perform them for our family. You know, things like *The Midnight Ride of Paul Revere* and *Casey at the Bat*."

Kate drained the rest of her martini, leaned her head back and closed her eyes as though reading from the inside of her eyelids:

> *Oh, somewhere in this favored land the sun is shining bright.*
> *The band is playing somewhere and somewhere hearts are light.*
> *Somewhere men are laughing and somewhere children shout.*

Kate opened her eyes and smiled at Wade.

"But there is no joy in Georgetown: Mighty Rav-nel has struck out."

"Let's hope it ends that way," Kate said with a mock bow.

Sandy's head appeared through the patio door, and he spotted their table. The sound of Ray Charles singing *You Don't Know Me* spilled through the open door for a moment, then faded. Sandy set his Heineken on the table, reached for a chair, turned it around, straddled the seat, and crossed his arms across the back.

"Those reporters in there are full of questions about our depositions," he said. "It's a funny feeling being on this side of things and having to say, 'No comment.' But the questions keep coming anyway. It's more obnoxious than I had realized."

Kate tried to hide her smile, then changed the subject.

"Here's where we are as of late this afternoon," she said. "Judge Jones has scheduled a hearing for a week from next Friday on plaintiffs' motion to compel you two to disclose your sources. Ravenel filed today sworn affidavits of Senator Long and Vince Stone saying that they are not your source and that they 'do not recall' any discussion during 'any portion of the meeting in which they were present' of a 'sweet deal' or any kind of an 'investment opportunity' for the Ravenels."

Kate made quotation marks with her fingers around the careful language from the affidavits.

"Just between us, my guess is that they decided that a bribery rap carries a significantly longer sentence than getting caught giving perjured testimony. So they have hunkered down with the Ravenels. I guess they figure if they all stick to their story, they'll be okay.

"Today Ravenel also filed one-page statements from every person named on the Bowman's Forest guest list and dining room employee list. All of them said that they were not your source. You told me the other day that your source was not on the list, so that makes sense. But I think I need to know more about this."

Sandy jumped in, eager to talk.

"Kate, let me tell y'all first about my conversations with the source today. There's a gym where the source plays basketball at lunchtime some days, and I took a shot at finding him there. Sure enough, he was shooting hoops by himself. I grabbed a ball, dribbled over and shot with him. There was nobody else on the court, and we had a chance to talk a little.

"He's not gonna come forward for us," Sandy said. "I understand his position. This guy grew up poor and black, he's busted his hump to get where he is. His dream for years has been to go to law school. If the Ravenels find out he's the source of their troubles – no matter how this turns out – they'll keep him out of law school in South Carolina. And he thinks that even if he did testify, no one's gonna believe the word of a twenty-five-year-old black man against a bunch of powerful white guys. He thinks they'll convince a jury he made up the story to protect the value of the black-owned property at Wright's Landing. And he thinks he might end up a defendant in this lawsuit."

Sandy noticed Kate was studying him closely.

"Do you still believe he's telling you the truth about the conversation that night at the Forest?"

Sandy didn't hesitate.

"Absolutely. I gave him a chance to back away from any or all of his story. He didn't budge one bit. I believe he was there, I think he heard the conversation, and I think he told us what really happened that night. I think the Ravenels have just covered their tracks well."

Kate frowned and tapped the table with her fingernails.

"Is there a chance that your source was not actually at the Forest that night and just repeated what someone told him about the dinner? You know, maybe he's just told you what he *thinks* happened. We don't have any confirmation that he was really there, do we?"

"I'm confident he was there," Wade said. "If not, he's the biggest con man I've dealt with in twenty-five years of reporting."

"So why isn't he on any of the lists the Forest provided of guests and employees?"

Wade leaned forward. Despite his show of certainty, that same thought had occurred to him a few times during his pre-dawn worrying.

"Kate, this is where it gets tricky. Without telling you his name, I'll tell you this much. He was not a regular employee of the Forest. He was visiting relatives in Georgetown that weekend, and he was asked to fill in for an employee who was absent. He knows some of the people who work at the Forest, and they just asked him to fill in. He wasn't even paid out of the Forest's payroll. The guy he replaced just paid the source out of his own pocket for the night's work."

Kate stared out at the docked shrimp boats fading in the dusk, bobbing gently on the water.

"You can see why Judge Jones may get the idea that no source exists. Everyone who's been listed as being at the Forest that night has said under oath that they were not your source. At a minimum, I think the judge is going to find that the name of the source is critical to plaintiffs' case and that they have tried all other reasonable ways to find out this information. Here's the worry that's keeping me up at night."

She lowered her voice a little and spoke low across the table.

"If Judge Jones orders you to testify and you refuse, he could hold you in contempt of court. If he levies a daily fine against the newspaper – say $5,000 a day – your insurance company doesn't cover that. If he enters a default judgment because of your refusal to disclose the source, your insurance company will claim you have 'ceased to cooperate' with them in the defense of your case. They won't pay any judgment against you in that event. You are in a damn tough spot.

"Ravenel knows he has you in a corner. And he's pretty confident Judge Jones isn't going to give you an easy way out."

It was quiet around the table for a minute. Finally, Sandy looked at his watch and stood up from his chair. He hooked his seersucker jacket on his index finger and hung it over his shoulder. He looked defeated.

"It's 9 o'clock," he said. "It's been a long week. If you don't need me for anything else, I'm heading home."

Kate and Wade stood up just as Bobo Baxter stopped by their table to say hello. It was never easy to tell when Baxter was being serious and when he was kidding. He had an odd sense of humor and a killer deadpan.

He put one arm around Sandy and the other around Kate

and Wade and pulled them into a tight huddle. He looked around at them like a quarterback calling a play in the final seconds of a big football game.

"Guys, I've been reading about your case. You're up against some tough customers. Be careful And remember the line from *The Man Who Shot Liberty Valance*: 'When the final showdown came to pass, a law book was no good.' Don't forget, the lawyer – Jimmy Stewart – won, but he needed a little help from John Wayne's rifle."

Baxter smiled cryptically, patted their backs, turned quickly and disappeared through the patio door.

Kate and Wade walked in silence for a half a block, heading back to Kate's office where Wade's Jeep was parked. Both were still sobered by the thought of what Judge Jones might do if the *Pilot* refused to disclose its source.

They paused at the next corner to let pass a horse-drawn carriage full of tourists. They listened to an animated female guide tell them about "famous ghosts of Georgetown" and point out the old houses where gory, if apocryphal, deaths and supernatural events had occurred.

Kate turned and faced Wade.

"Wade, I wanted to talk this source issue over with you without Sandy present because you have more at stake than he does. If the judge orders you two to reveal your source and you refuse, it's possible he could go to jail and so could you. Or the judge could order you and Sandy or the newspaper to pay a huge daily fine, more than you could ever pay without bankrupting you and the paper. Even worse, you could lose the paper if the judge enters a default against the *Pilot*.

"When you decided to print this story, I don't think you ever believed anyone would squeeze you this hard for the source. It doesn't happen often. If they did, you thought you'd eventually be able to locate a paper trail of corporate documents to back you up. But these guys are tough and smart, and they've covered their tracks."

The carriage had rumbled by, and they kept walking, Kate still talking, low, but with firmness in her voice.

"When we first started talking, it was clear to me that you thought the worst that could happen to you would be the judge ordering you to reveal your confidential source. You'd refuse, and you might get sent to the lockup for a few days, or maybe a few weeks 'til everyone was convinced you and Sandy would stick by your principles. I don't think you understood you could lose the paper."

Kate took a deep breath.

"You won't like hearing this, but it's my job as your lawyer to say it. You don't have to lose the paper to protect this source. That was not the bargain you made. No one could have contemplated that you would get backed into this corner. I've looked carefully at the law in this area. Your source wouldn't have a strong legal claim against you if you identified him to comply with a court order. From what you've told me, he wouldn't be in any physical danger. He might end up being a damn hero in this state.

"And here's something else. Simply defying a court order is something no one should do if there's an alternative. The press in this country looks to the courts for protection day in and day out. What if everyone defied court orders they didn't agree with? You have the option to identify the source if the judge orders you to and we can't win an appeal of his order. We have fought it hard. You've done your job on this. I don't want to see you lose the paper, and I sure as hell don't want to see Buck Ravenel own it."

She finally stopped to catch her breath and looked at Wade.

He was quiet for a minute, then gave her a tired smile.

"Kate, I'm not some kind of martyr. I don't even want to risk going to jail over this. I'm too old to think that's somehow romantic and heroic. And the last thing I want to do is put the newspaper at risk. Don't think I haven't lain awake at night the past few weeks, ever since you explained all this to me about the default judgment stuff, and tried to figure out how to avoid this train wreck. I've even had a few middle of the night mental chats with my dad about this. I've tried every way I know to persuade the source to come forward. And I've played out in my head every angle of giving the court his name anyway. But every time, I come back to this: we didn't put any conditions on the promise we made to the source. He relied on that promise."

Wade looked away, somewhere above the live oaks along the opposite side of the street, then looked back at Kate's face in the faint light of the street lamp.

"My mother was a quiet, but wise woman. She must have told me a hundred times: "Wade, two of the most important things in life are your reputation and your character. It's very important what other people think of you. That's your reputation. But it's even more important what you know yourself to be. That's character.

"I think you're telling me that we could give up this source and put a good face on it, explain it to the world in a way that didn't make us look bad. I can't tell you how tempting that is. In fact, I've been wrestling with my conscience pretty hard over this, and I almost won a couple of times. But that's not something I can do. Some days I wish I'd never made that promise to him, but I did. I've got to live with it and play this thing out."

They had reached the corner of High Market Street, and

finally Wade could clearly see Kate's worried face.

"Hey, didn't I promise you a cemetery tour of the five generations of McNabb tombstones?" he asked. " C'mon, graveyards are much more interesting and mysterious after dark. We just might see some of those ghosts that guide was talking about."

Wade opened the black wrought iron gate and took Kate's elbow to steady her down the two brick steps to the cemetery. He escorted her along a cobblestone walk for about thirty yards, then stopped, his left arm sweeping in front of him at a couple dozen headstones in an area surrounded by a six-inch tall brick border. Rain and time had worn smooth many of the once heartfelt inscriptions. Some of the headstones had fallen and lay awkwardly atop the graves of their subjects.

Wade was quietly proud of his strong South Carolina lineage, and the name that came with it. The Wade Hampton family had played a powerful role in South Carolina politics and public life since the 1700s. Wade's mother's great grandfather had been Governor Wade Hampton who had led the "Bourbons" after the Civil War in fighting the federal government's toughest Reconstruction rules. In the tenor of those bitterly racist times, Wade Hampton stood for relative moderation, appointing blacks to office and assuring funding for black schools. Wade's father's family had been in Georgetown almost as long, first as rice merchants who brokered and shipped rice for the plantation owners, later as timber owners. Wade's immediate family had lost most of their land and savings in the 1930s as the Great Depression had killed the timber sales but not the government's thirst for property taxes.

Kate and Wade settled onto a wood bench his parents had donated to the cemetery. The glow from the spotlight illuminating the church's stained glass window on the rear of the main building filtered dimly through the leaves and the Spanish moss on the live oak trees.

"What was Ravenel talking about this afternoon, Wade?" Kate asked. "He asked you about your father's death. Is that anything I need to know about?"

Wade stared directly ahead at his father's headstone.

"I don't know whether he was taunting me or not," Wade said after a few moments. He cut his eyes toward Kate, but she was looking straight ahead.

Wade looked back at the tombstone, remembering the weariness in his father's eyes the last time he had seen him.

"In the fall of 1970, I was in my junior year at college. I knew my father was having some problems with the newspaper, that he had made some of his advertisers mad because of what he had written in the paper about racial issues. He told me that it was hurting the paper but that he couldn't give in to the pressure from his advertisers.

"The truth is I was pretty absorbed in my own life. The Vietnam war was raging, and I was against it. I wasn't all that big on protests, but I did have a column in the student newspaper, and I poured my energies into that. I had all the drama and self-focus of a twenty year old. I wasn't paying much attention to Dad's problems.

"Kate, some things you never forget. Not one detail. At about 9:30 on the morning of December 13, the phone in my dorm room rang. It was my mother. She was crying, but like nothing I'd ever heard. It was more like wailing, almost like a wounded animal."

Wade's voice had dropped into a monotone. He was talking like a reporter giving an editor a matter-of-fact preview of the deadline article he was going to write about a terrible accident that had happened to someone neither of them knew.

"It took her a long time to calm down enough for me to

understand her. She told me my dad had gone hunting the day before. When he hadn't come home by dark, she got worried and called a family friend. He and the sheriff spent most of the night looking for where my father may have gone, and finally found his car parked at the end of a dirt road outside of town. They looked for hours in the dark and couldn't find him. At dawn, they went back with a search dog who found him about a half-mile away.

"He had been hunting alone. They found his body lying across a wire fence between two fields. They said he must've tripped as he swung his legs over the fence and that his shotgun discharged when it hit the ground. The shot hit him in the head and killed him instantly.

"When I got home that evening, my mother took me down to my father's office. She had been afraid to go by herself, afraid of what she might find there. His office door was locked, but we used the extra set of keys he kept at home.

"His desk was messy, as always. The usual stuff – letters, bills, to-do lists, that sort of thing. But in his locked desk drawer, there was a sealed envelope with my name on it. There was a scribbled note in his handwriting. It said: "Wade, Just in case something happens to me." I tore it open, not sure what I was expecting. The only thing in it was the name of an insurance company and a long number, which I realized was an insurance policy number. Other than that, his office looked like it always did."

Wade stood up, walked over to his dad's tombstone and put his hand on it. He looked back at Kate.

"He had been a high-functioning alcoholic for decades – a good newspaper man with strong principles. He and my mother had been living more as housemates than husband and wife for years, as best I could tell. They didn't fight, but they didn't talk much either. They had somehow learned to navigate their separate courses around the house, careful not to bump into one another too much. They had slept in separate bedrooms for years. They told me it was because of my father's insomnia. They were lonely souls.

"When I grew up enough to start pushing my parents away, trying to find my own self, I think it hurt my father more than I could see, more than he would let on. He wanted me to come back home one day and run that paper with him. I made it clear to him that was the last thing I'd ever want to do. I understand all that better now, that the newspaper was his anchor in this world. It had become what he was living for. And he wanted it to live on after him. We all look for immortality in different ways."

He walked back over to the bench and sat down beside Kate.

"After my dad's death, I used to come here with my mother during holidays, and we would talk about him. As far apart as they had grown, she still knew how it had broken his heart to see the newspaper slipping out of his hands because of the boycott.

"I went by to see the coroner the day after I got home. He was very careful in his explanation of what happened. He told me that as far as he could tell, my father had been hunting alone. He had been drinking – the coroner had found an empty pint of scotch in his car and essentially confirmed what the police had concluded. Somewhat awkwardly, though, the coroner asked me if I had found anything that suggested the death was other than accidental. I told him no.

"I was sure, though, that he had killed himself. He had taught me to hunt when I was a boy, and he had several strict rules. No drinking while hunting. No hunting alone. And when you cross a ditch or a fence, you take the shells out of your gun and put your safety on. No exceptions. He violated all those rules that December day.

"I am certain that my father knew that his sole insurance policy would not have paid off in the event of a suicide. Thus, the carefully orchestrated hunting accident. And that's why there was no note, no explanation, no goodbye."

Wade took a deep breath, and then another one.

"The insurance money wasn't enough to pay off the newspaper's debts. It was enough to help my mother make ends meet after the newspaper filed for bankruptcy. There was a discreet inquiry from the insurance company sniffing around on the suicide issue, but nothing came of it. My mother lived another five years or so. She slowly lost interest in the world immediately around her. She took to her room, reading, getting through the long nights listening to talk radio, committing slow suicide with her unfiltered Pall Malls and the sugar filled mugs of coffee that wouldn't fill the hole in her heart. I tried to get her out, keep her interested in life, but she had given up."

Kate sat quietly beside him, knowing not to interrupt. She slipped her arm through his and slid closer beside him.

"To this day, I wish I could have talked with my father and helped him get through it. I go for months without thinking about it. Then all of a sudden, twenty-five years later, I find myself overwhelmed by the loneliness, the sense of utter desperation he must've known just before he pulled that trigger. What would make someone take that step that ends everything you know? What kind of hurt would make you leap into that darkness?

"The hardest part in all of this is that several times in the months before his death he and I had gotten into big arguments on the telephone. Earlier that week, I told him I wanted to drop out of school at the end of the semester and work for George McGovern's Presidential campaign. He told me that was a stupid thing to do. He said I needed to finish school and that there'd be plenty of time to be involved in politics after that.

"I was angry. I told him that he had never understood me and never would, and that I had to lead my own life. That's how our last conversation ended, with both of us angry. He must have decided that his marriage was a failure, his newspaper was a failure and now I had pretty much told him he was a failure with me, the only child he had. I think I pushed him over the edge, and I'll live with that all my life."

Wade fell silent and slumped back on the bench.

"Wade, I didn't know your dad," Kate said quietly. "But I know a lot about people. Your father was clearly suffering from depression, but people didn't talk about that openly back then. It sounds like he saw troubles everywhere he turned and no clear way out. Depressed people can slide down into a silo of isolation, and suddenly suicide looks rational to them. Death looks like peace. It's not meant to hurt anyone else, just to get them to what they think will be a better place."

Kate patted his arm lightly.

"One tragedy of a suicide is that it leaves everyone behind wondering what they could have done differently. Wade, even if you could have changed the timing, I don't think you could have stopped him from following that path eventually. It sounds like he had crossed the line and made the decision. He was just waiting for the right moment."

"In my head, I understand that. But in my heart, I wish that he had left me a note to say it wasn't my fault. That would have helped.

"Some days when I think about it, I get a little crazy. I start wondering if maybe he *didn't* commit suicide, that maybe some political enemy shot him and made it look like an accident. Maybe that's what he meant by "in case something happens to me." Or maybe it *was* an accident. I used to call people who saw him in those last few days, trying to see if he said anything that would tell me if I caused this to happen. Or that I didn't."

Wade leaned forward, put his elbows on his knees and his face in his hands.

"Kate, I'm sorry. I think the strain of this lawsuit has gotten to me. I don't need to burden you with all of this."

"Wade, it's not a burden. Every one of us has a story that shapes our lives. I think you already know that I do. I almost told you about it on the beach that night.

"But those things don't have to control how we end up leading our lives. Look what you have done with your life. You played an important political role in South Carolina in your twenties. You became an award-winning journalist – I know you didn't tell me about that, but I did a little research on you myself. I know about the awards you won for the vote-buying stories in Chicago, and about the death threats you ignored. And about the county commissioners who went to jail in Virginia after your paper wrote about the kickbacks they got from architects who got rich on public projects.

"You worked hard, you bought back your father's newspaper, and every day you make this community a better place because of your voice. Your parents would be very proud of you today."

Kate looked toward the faint reflections from the church's stained glass window.

"I told you on the beach that night that my Dad taught me how to hunt and fish a little. For awhile he needed me to be both daughter and son to him. There was a reason for that."

She took a deep breath and let it out.

"I had a brother who drowned when he was 15," she said. "I was 10. He was body-surfing in rough waves in front of our beach house and hit his head on a piece of lumber, a real freak accident. I worshipped him, as younger sisters do."

The whole scene came flashing back to her, and her eyes filled with tears.

"Everything was so good for us before that day. My mother had taken us on a great crabbing trip that morning. I remember how excited my brother David was about the big waves rolling in. I remember my mother kissing me as I was dozing off in the hammock on the porch. I woke up thinking my dad would be coming down that night and I was so happy about that. Then I heard this girl shouting for help, and I ran down to the beach to see what was happening."

Kate blinked hard, tears rolling down her face.

"I saw my mother standing in the ocean screaming for David. She could barely swim. I saw her look back at me. Then she went deeper and deeper. She drowned trying to save him."

Kate was crying now.

Wade took her hand and tried to find her eyes.

"I begged her not to leave me. But she did."

They sat in silence for a few minutes. The sweet night scent of Carolina jasmine drifted from the yellow blooms draped across the cemetery's brick wall.

She squeezed Wade's hand, took the handkerchief he offered and wiped her eyes.

"Our stories aren't all that different," she said softly. "My mother leaving me. Your dad leaving you. When something like that happens, you either toughen up and make a go of it anyway, or you lose the will to take control of your life. You and I toughened up and moved forward. It doesn't mean that those events don't affect the way we lead our lives. They write an early chapter. But they don't have to write the rest of the book."

Kate dug into her purse and pulled out her key chain. Attached to it was a smooth, purplish-brown shell the size of a small chestnut and the shape of a snail shell.

"That's a shark's eye shell," Wade said. "And a pretty one."

Kate rolled the shell around in her fingers, staring at it.

"A few months after my mother died," she said, "my father and I were going through my mother's jewelry box, and I found this shell. He told me about the cold December evening he had proposed to my mother on the beach and how he had hidden the ring in this shell. It was a magical story to me, and I've kept this shell as a good memory of my mother. But sometimes, I think of it as a shield. When life gets too tough, when I feel too exposed, I can go there and be safe. I used to call it the shell game."

Kate sat back on the bench and closed her eyes, afraid she had said too much. Wade moved closer and put his arm across the back of the bench behind her. She reached up and patted Wade's hand. They sat quietly that way for a while, listening to the clip-clop of a horse-drawn carriage move slowly by, hearing the faint murmur of the tour guide telling his visitors about the old church. Finally, Kate gently disengaged herself.

"Wade, we'd better go. It's really late, and I've got a long weekend ahead getting ready for Judge Jones.

23

Everyman's Evidence

Judge Dupree Jones smoothed his eyebrows as he looked down at his docket sheet, then announced the case of *Carolina Phosphate, et al. v. the Georgetown Pilot, et al.* He glanced toward the table closest to the jury box, where plaintiffs' counsel always sat. His eyes brightened.

"I see Senator Ravenel is here. Welcome, Senator. Always a pleasure to have you in my courtroom."

The judge looked to his left at the table of defense counsel and saw Kate Stewart. "Ms. Stewart. Glad to see you again. I hope you've been well."

The judge surveyed the nearly full courtroom, noting to himself that this hearing was better attended than most. He spoke to the courtroom generally.

"I am assured by the quality of the counsel for the parties to this action that this matter will be handled ably and with great civility." Then, nodding to the lawyers, he continued.

"I have read all of your briefs and supporting documents. I will hear any additional oral elucidation you may have on this matter. These are important issues, and I will give you time to discuss them thoroughly."

He shuffled the papers before him and looked toward plaintiffs' table.

"Senator Ravenel, I believe your motion to compel is before the court. I understand you would like to require certain testimony from the *Pilot's* editor, Mr. McNabb, and from its reporter, Mr. Anderson. I'll hear you first."

Buck Ravenel stood as tall as his six-foot frame would allow. He wore a two-button navy blue suit with an almost imperceptible herringbone pattern – a gift from a grateful client whose problem had been deftly handled by a combination of Ravenel's legal skill and political touch. Ravenel had never sent the client a bill, but one quiet telephone call to Ravenel's legislative assistant had turned up the name of the Senator's Charleston tailor. The client had picked a lightweight wool that he knew Ravenel would like – soft as warm butter, one the tailor said had a "nice hand." The suit had been delivered to Ravenel's law office on his birthday, along with a bottle of twenty-five year-old port and a handwritten thank-you note from the client. Just a gift to a good friend, tax-free and a perfect fit.

His white shirt had pencil-thin blue pinstripes. The shirt cuffs peeking from the dark jacket showed a small notch, and the tiny blue initials "FMR" just below the ivory buttons, were sure signs the shirt was custom-tailored. His deep red tie – the underside loop bore the logo of Ben Silver's men shop, Charleston's best – sported small, dark blue ducks with green heads. Like most courtroom lawyers, Ravenel was secretly superstitious – he had never appeared in court without a tie that had at least some red in it.

Ravenel buttoned his suit jacket with his left hand, smoothed it against his flat stomach and gestured with his right hand toward the judge, smiling.

"Judge Jones, as the Psalmist wrote, a single day in your courtroom is better than a thousand elsewhere. I thank Your Honor for scheduling this matter on such short notice for us. I'm sure counsel for the defendants appreciates that as much as we do. Before I address the precise merits of our motion, I would like to set the stage for the Court, Your Honor, just a bit."

Judge Jones nodded, and Ravenel continued. Years of courtroom and senate oratory had taught him that bearing his voice down on the occasional verb and adjective enhanced the impact of his delivery.

"This case involves claims for libel, for the defamation of the character of an upstanding corporate citizen of this state – Carolina Phosphate – and for the *defiling*, Your Honor, of the reputation of Francis "Tripp" Ravenel – director of the South Carolina Environmental Resources Agency – a fine public servant of this state. Their reputations were *eviscerated* by the *Pilot's* publication of false assertions that Carolina Phosphate in effect *bribed* Tripp Ravenel to ensure that the Environmental Resources Agency would issue a wetlands permit for a plant here in Georgetown.

"My clients warned the newspaper before it published its story that those assertions were false and should *not* be published," Ravenel continued. "Those warnings and pleas fell on closed ears. Not *deaf* ears, Your Honor, but *closed* ears. They could *hear* us, Judge, but they callously *refused* to listen.

Ravenel looked over at Wade McNabb and Sandy Anderson. He made a dramatic pause between each of the words of his next sentence.

"Judge …. they…. published …. these …. lies …. *anyway.*

"And Judge, what they wrote was *worse* than lies. They were half-truths. It's like bait on a hook, Judge. The bass sees that worm dangling and bites it. It tastes pretty *good*, so he just gobbles down the rest, hook and all. That's how the half-truth works.

"We brought this action against the newspaper *immediately*, one week after the article was published, so we could announce to the public that these statements were false. We wanted to act quickly to set this record straight. We immediately asked the newspaper to tell us the name of the so-called source they claim gave them this false information."

Ravenel looked one more time at McNabb.

"Judge, they refused."

His voice was low and firm.

"We simply want to know the name of that source so we can continue with our lawsuit. We are *entitled* to examine that witness and find out why he would have told them such a lie. Maybe the so-called source simply thought he had a free shot at damaging my family by making these false charges while hiding behind the newspaper. Or maybe that source had his own reasons for trying to stop this plant even if it took fabricating this wild story. But let me assure the Court that this source will be the *next* defendant in this lawsuit, and we will be entitled to have a jury decide whether this source is the type of person that the newspaper should have relied upon."

Ravenel paused and turned sideways to eye McNabb and Anderson. He lowered his voice a little.

"Or maybe, Judge, we'll find out there was no source at all. But that's why we're here. To get this court to order them to answer our questions."

Ravenel's eloquence made McNabb nervous. And Ravenel's Biblical reference made the editor recall the Psalm his father used to quote when he heard a persuasive but calculating speaker: "The words in his mouth were smooth as butter, but there was war in his heart."

"The legal basis for our motion and the pertinent factual background are both in the record before the Court," Ravenel continued. "Judge, this is not the kind of case a court often gets to hear. This case does not involve a broken contract be-

tween two businesses. This case does not involve a broken leg
arising from a car accident. Those cases – as important as they
may be to the participants – *pale* in public significance to a
case like this one – the *destruction* of a public servant's good
name through the deliberate and reckless misuse of the power
of the press."

Ravenel began to rock back and forth slightly, bringing a
bit of body English to bear, addressing not just the Court and
the defendants' table, but occasionally turning back slightly
toward the audience in the courtroom, emphasizing his verbal points with a hand gesture here, a cocked head there. As he
reached his conclusion, he squared up and addressed the judge
directly, eye to eye, as though the two of them were having a
private conversation. He made his voice firmer without raising
it. The courtroom audience sat absolutely silent, no legs crossing, no feet shuffling, intent on the Senator's final comments.

"Shakespeare said it best, Your Honor: 'Good name in man
and woman is the immediate jewel of their souls. Who steals
my purse, steals trash. But he that filches from me my good
name robs me of that which enriches him not, and makes me
poor indeed.'

"Judge, we respectfully ask that you order Mr. McNabb
and Mr. Anderson to provide plaintiffs with the name of their
source no later than next week. We ask that you instruct them
that if they fail to disclose their source, you will hold them in
contempt of court and impose the civil and criminal penalties
the law requires. That's all, Your Honor."

"Thank you, Senator Ravenel," Judge Jones said, glancing
up at the clock at the back of the courtroom. "That was an
eloquent argument. I expected no less. And, I suspect that Ms.
Stewart will respond in kind."

Judge Jones swung his head in her direction, his eyebrows

quivering. Kate stood, nodded at her opposing counsel, and addressed the court firmly.

"Your Honor, Senator Ravenel has made a powerful statement about the importance of reputation. Nobody worth his salt would disagree with that."

Kate picked up a copy of a law book open on the counsel table before her. She tapped the book with her index finger and set it back on the table.

"But Judge, the United States Supreme Court has taught us that the protection of reputation must be balanced carefully against the critical importance of wide-open, robust debate about public affairs. The success of any democracy depends on that debate – about public issues and about the officials who do the public's business. Public officials can't be allowed to win libel suits every time a citizen or newspaper writes something critical of them, even if they make an honest mistake. That would discourage public debate because newspapers would be constantly afraid of being sued by deep-pocket plaintiffs like Carolina Phosphate and Tripp Ravenel. They'd never print anything controversial. The content of our newspapers would be reduced to long obituaries, Aunt Margie's favorite recipes, and photos of politicians cutting ribbons. There would be very little reporting about who has political power in this state and who they use it for.

"This case involves serious allegations that one of this state's most important public officials – Tripp Ravenel – and a company subject to some of our state's most critical environmental regulations were involved in political bribery."

Kate reached down and took a sip of water from the paper cup on the table. She stepped back and took a look around the courtroom before returning her gaze to the bench.

"It is no secret that our democratic government is made up

of men and women, flesh and blood, who are often tempted by the power they possess. This country has always counted on a free, cantankerous, nosy, and often downright obnoxious press to act as a watchdog on our public officials. Who else, after all, in this busy world of commerce and daily life, has the time, the energy, the motivation, to shine a searchlight's beam into the corners and back rooms where the sometimes shady sides of government and business intersect?

"Plaintiffs' strategy is to persuade this court to force this newspaper to identify its confidential source. Plaintiffs know that Mr. McNabb and Mr. Anderson are principled professionals who will honor their pledge of confidentiality to their source. Plaintiffs simply hope they can punish them and this newspaper, make them knuckle under, and send a message to other newspapers not to pursue stories like this.

"Plaintiffs also know that these tactics will put fear in the hearts of other potential sources and whistleblowers who might have evidence about possible governmental corruption. Imagine being a source with that kind of information and feeling afraid to approach the State Law Enforcement Division or even the attorney general because those high officials may be politically connected to the very people whom the source is blowing the whistle on."

She paused for a moment, gathering her final thoughts, and glanced casually at Buck Ravenel.

"So maybe that source can muster the courage to go instead to a newspaper reporter and offer a tip about a corrupt official. Is he going to risk his job, or maybe his life to do that? Of course not. But if he can get a promise that the newspaper will protect his identity, he may tell them what he has seen and heard. These plaintiffs would have this court force this source into the open, where his or her life or livelihood would most certainly be in danger. By forcing the disclosure of this source, they want to scare into silence other potential sources of information about possible government corruption.

"Your Honor, these plaintiffs have complained that the *Pilot* published 'bad speech,' speech that was false about them. In this country, the best remedy for bad speech is more speech. Give the citizens, the voters, the full back-and-forth, both sides of the debate, and let them decide what is right, what is true. In fact, Tripp Ravenel and Carolina Phosphate have had ample access to the media to tell their side of this story."

Kate held up the copy of the September 3 edition of the Sunday *State* newspaper with a large color photo of Senator Ravenel and Tripp Ravenel, standing in the well of the South Carolina State House, smiling and shaking hands.

"Judge, there is abundant authority in our law – under the First Amendment, under the Rules of Civil Procedure – to allow plaintiffs' case to go forward without forcing the disclosure of the newspaper's source. If we ever reach a time in the lawsuit where it becomes critical that plaintiffs have this information, then the Court could revisit the issue. But there is no need to force this disclosure at this time.

"I respectfully submit that this court should deny the motion to compel with leave for plaintiffs to renew their motion later in this case if necessary. Thank you, Your Honor."

Judge Jones sat thinking for the next thirty seconds, a long time in a quiet courtroom. His hands were clasped together in front of him, his index fingers tapping against each other slowly, his eyes closed. Finally he sighed and spoke.

"Ms. Stewart, I have heard the Senator's eloquent words about the importance of reputation, and your persuasive discourse on why free speech is sacred in our democracy. I agree with you both. But we all learned way back in evidence class in law school that the parties to a lawsuit are entitled to 'everyman's evidence.' You know the old saying – if the Prince of Wales and the Archbishop of Canterbury and the Lord High Chancellor were all in the same horse-drawn coach and witnessed a simple chimneysweep and a poor woman fighting over an apple and one of those two thought it was necessary to bring those three august gentlemen into court to give their evidence about what they saw, even they could not refuse to come.

"Ms. Stewart, you suggest strongly that our democracy could not exist without almost absolute protection of a newspaper's confidential sources. If that is the case, it is for our legislature or our Congress to pass a law that will protect that information. Neither has done so.

"Our courts demand a full search for the truth. These plaintiffs, I think, are entitled to a fair chance to prove their case."

Judge Jones nodded at Kate, then looked away, a sure sign he had heard enough from her. He did not look back in the direction of plaintiffs' counsel. He turned over a few pages in his legal pad, found some notes he had written, and began to recite from them.

"I'm going to grant plaintiffs' motion to compel Mr. McNabb and Mr. Anderson to reveal the identity of their source for the August 5 article. I find that no reporter's privilege applies in this libel case, but even if such a privilege existed, it appears to have been overcome by the facts of this case. The information sought is critical to plaintiffs' case, and the plaintiffs have been unable to obtain it from any alternative source.

"I want to be sure, however – in all fairness to Mr. McNabb and Mr. Anderson – that plaintiffs have exhausted all other reasonable ways of obtaining the information they need before I order these gentlemen to disclose their source."

Judge Jones looked out at the lawyers and the parties.

"I want to see all of you here in this courtroom on Monday morning. Senator Ravenel, I want you to have here the manager of Bowman's Forest to talk about the guest list he turned in for July 1. And I want the head of the dining room familiar with the employees who were there that weekend. I want to be sure they have identified everyone who might have been present at the Forest that night.

"I want to give Mr. McNabb and Mr. Anderson the weekend to consider where they find themselves. If I am satisfied on Monday that they should provide plaintiffs the name of their source – and right now, I'll tell you, that's where I'm headed – I will order them to provide that information. If they refuse to do so, I will hold them in contempt of court. I will strike all their defenses and enter a finding that they are liable to plaintiffs. Then we can set a trial date and let a jury decide what damages – actual and punitive – plaintiffs may be entitled to recover from them."

He banged his gavel. His eyebrows relaxed and lay down flat like small sand dunes.

"Court is adjourned. I will see you all Monday. Have a nice weekend."

He gathered his robes and disappeared through the door to his chambers.

24

Like the Moon Pulls on the Tide

Kate, Sandy and Wade had been meeting for two hours in her conference room when Bobo Baxter appeared on her front porch holding two grocery bags of take-out. They had not been up to facing the inquisitive POETS crowd at Sliders that Friday night, and Bobo had insisted on bringing them dinner.

Bobo spread out several layers of that morning's edition of the *Georgetown Pilot* at one end of the conference table and dumped a couple pounds of fresh shrimp – boiled, pink, and iced – on top of it. He set out three small bowls of his signature cocktail sauce – ivory shards of freshly ground horseradish flecked the rich tomato base. An ample first taste of his sauce could make the eyes water, the nostrils burn, the head clear, and the scalp tingle. He laid out platters of cole slaw, sweet potato fries and fresh corn bread. Bobo quickly arranged the food, gave firm, friendly pats on the back to each of them and returned to his pick-up truck for a small cooler. He set it down on the floor at one end of the table and took out two Heinekens, two Budweisers and a silver-sided martini shaker.

"Kate, I'll shake these for you and pour you one now. The other will be good for later. As Old Blue Eyes might say, 'One for my baby and one more for the road.'" He glanced at his watch. "It's seven-thirty, and the POETS crowd will be getting rowdy. I need to head back. You guys hang in there. I'm pulling for you."

And then he was gone.

Sandy loaded a shrimp with a full dollop of cocktail sauce, bit the whole thing off at the tail and began chewing. In a split-second, his eyes widened, watering and blinking rapidly, and he sat straight up in his chair, slapping the conference table with his left hand and rubbing the top of his head with his right.

"Damn, it *does* make your scalp move," he said. "It's the closest thing to hard drugs I've ever done."

They lingered over dinner, avoiding the tough subjects at hand. Finally, Wade cleared away the shrimp shells and other detritus, wrapped it up in the newsprint and took it to the kitchen. Kate drained the last of her martini, and resisted joking about the highest and best use of newspapers. Sandy untied his bowtie, leaving it hanging down his shirt, too tired to remove it. Kate pulled out a clean yellow legal pad and started another outline in her neat handwriting.

"Kate," Wade said as he walked back into the conference room. "I hate to tell you this, but for someone who thought journalists were just leeches on society who buy newsprint for fifty cents a pound, spread trash on it and re-sell it for a dollar a pound, you sounded like a true believer in court today. You did a great job, no matter how the judge rules."

"Thanks," she said. "You guys have taught me a little something these past few weeks. Anyway, here's where I think we are. Behind that good ole boy banter of his, Judge Jones is a smart and practical lawyer. He doesn't want this to look like he is picking on the newspaper, or like he's favoring Buck Ravenel. He's bringing those two guys in here from the Forest so the record will show that plaintiffs had a chance to ask everyone present that night if they were the source, and that they all said no. Then the plaintiffs will have shown that the only way to find out the name of the source is from you. It won't leave us much room for an appeal.

"He gave you two the weekend to think this over. Maybe he thinks if your source sees the bind you're in he'll volunteer to come forward. Or maybe he thinks you'll figure out a way you can reveal the source without breaking your promise. In any event, he's holding your feet right next to the fire.

"On Monday, you'll have to decide whether to step into that fire."

Sandy and Wade looked the glummest they had since the suit began. Neither had really let himself believe they could end up losing the newspaper.

"So what do you think the judge will do on Monday?" Wade asked.

"It sounds to me like he is going to hold the two of you and the newspaper in contempt of court. And he says he's planning to strike your defenses and enter a default judgment against you and the newspaper. Then the only issue is damages. He'll give us a chance to do some discovery – take depositions of Tripp Ravenel and Carolina Phosphate to see if they have any evidence they have actually been damaged by your story. And he's likely to give them a shot at punitive damages. He'll probably set the damages part of the case for trial early next year."

"Is there any way we could appeal an order requiring us to reveal our sources and holding us in contempt of court?" Sandy asked.

"We can try, but given the careful way Judge Jones has handled this, I think the Court of Appeals will deny any attempt to have it reviewed at this stage. They'll probably let it go to trial on the damages issue first. And in the meantime, your insurance company's likely to jump ship and leave you paying for your defense and on the hook for any verdict the jury comes back with."

The room was silent, and they could hear the faint pealing of the bells of the Prince George Episcopal Church, signaling the 9 o'clock hour.

"You know I'm not going to abandon you, no matter what the insurance company does," Kate said. "I'm here for the duration, and we'll work out a way to keep us in boiled shrimp, beer and martinis 'til this thing's finished. I respect you two for sticking to your principles. And I'm with you, right there in the arena."

She doodled on her pad for a moment and looked up at the two men.

"By the way, you'll remember that I've avoided finding out who your source is. Do you recall at the end of the day yesterday, when Judge Jones asked the lawyers to approach him at the bench?"

Sandy and Wade nodded absently.

"We had a discussion outside the presence of the court reporter and the audience. The judge looked at me hard and told me in no uncertain terms that he expects me to inform the Court if any of the individuals listed on the Bowman's Forest lists are lying when they say under oath they are not your source. I told him in careful terms that I intend to follow all applicable rules of law and all ethical requirements. I think he was trying to raise my discomfort level as high as he can."

The lines in Wade's forehead had grown deeper as the evening had gone on, and his eyes had a dull look to them. Kate wondered if he was reconsidering his decision not to reveal his source if the court ordered him to. Sandy was staring out the bay window, focused on nothing in particular.

"In any event, I think that's all we can do tonight," she said finally. "I know you folks still have a newspaper to put to bed. I'll check in with you over the weekend."

Kate let them out the front door, giving each of them what she hoped was a reassuring pat on the shoulder. She went to the kitchen and finished cleaning up the remains of their dinner. She spent a little while in the conference room organizing her notes, then decided she'd focused all she could that evening. She turned out the downstairs lights, paused for a moment, thought about the second martini still chilled in the cooler, but decided to leave it there. She turned out the porch lights and climbed the stairs to the portion of the house she had refurbished as her bedroom, bathroom and den. She turned on her CD player, found a favorite Bonnie Raitt song and sang softly along to "Dimming of the Day" as she undressed, husking herself of her court uniform.

"You pull me like the moon pulls on the tide..."

Kate took a hot shower, hoping to wash the worries of the week from her body and soul. She knew that a late night shower should give her a clean burst of energy that would last for an hour or so, then help her sleep soundly. She toweled off, pulled a nightgown over her head and climbed into the queen-size sleigh bed she had found and fixed up. It had been built in the 1850s as a wedding gift from one of Georgetown's plantation owners to his son and his bride, and Kate had spotted it, in need of great repair, in a yard sale in McClellanville. On her bedside table were two stacks of books and papers. In one stack were legal materials – articles from law reviews, copies of newly decided cases from the South Carolina Supreme Court, an article by a law school friend about current issues on indigent representation. She tried to read one piece from that stack each evening before going to bed. The other stack contained her current pleasure reading: issues of *The New Yorker*, a novel by Wallace Stegner, and a collection of Robert Frost poems.

She read a little of the article on lawyering for the indigent, but even that didn't make her sleepy. She felt one of those nights coming on when her body was weary but her mind was wired, and sleep might be elusive. She turned out the bedside light, lay flat on her back and closed her eyes, trying to relax her body one limb at a time, starting with her toes and working up her body. This routine would often trick her mind into sleep submission. Tonight, it didn't work. Her thoughts returned again and again to what she might tell Judge Jones on Monday to keep her clients from losing the newspaper.

She wondered what Buck Ravenel's strategy would be with the witnesses from the Forest. Neither had been willing to talk with her ahead of time. Ravenel's courtroom style was usually straightforward, linear, a direct attack with no subtlety. Some lawyers had the gift of indirectness, teasing out the truth from reluctant or evasive witnesses, occasionally setting traps along the way that gently herded a lying witness back to an inevitable choice between an obvious contradiction of earlier testimony or an unpleasant truth. At its best, courtroom lawyering was like a chess game, requiring an ability to think several steps ahead, to anticipate the opponent's next few moves, to see around corners, never giving away too soon the fact that you were closing in. Cart Cooper had possessed that knack in spades, a natural talent that seemed to spring from his genetic makeup. Kate had struggled to acquire that skill through hard work.

She had learned that courtroom lawyering was not for the timid. You had to be bold, and you had to be willing to take chances. In the courtroom, you needed every sense, every antenna to be alert for detail, for nuance. You had to be able to take a shot to the gut when a witness turned on you and gave unexpected testimony that hurt your case, never letting the court, the jury or even your client see you wince. Most of all, you had to walk into every courtroom with a show of confidence and an air of being in charge. You had to always look like a lawyer who expected to win.

Kate finally gave up on sleep, went back downstairs and made herself a mug of Earl Grey tea, no caffeine. She knew she had a reading night ahead of her, and climbed back into bed.

She reached for the poetry book. Sometimes that would distract her brain's legal lobe and let her drift off. Then she thought for a moment and slipped out of bed. She walked to her desk in the den, found the key to the right hand set of drawers, unlocked the large drawer on the bottom and pulled out a stationery box. She took it back to her bed, stuffed an extra pillow behind her, sat up and slipped the top off the box. Inside were the letters her father had written to her, still bending at the creases from their years in their envelopes.

She found the one dated December 30, 1968. She skipped over the paragraphs about their weeks at the beach that summer, her learning to body surf, the paragraphs about her years in second and third grade, about her love for books. She read the part she liked most, carefully written in his neat, slightly cursive print. She had read them many times over the last two years, knew them almost by heart, but each time she read them, it was like hearing her father's soft, deep voice talking to her.

Kate, at eight years old, you are already a determined soul. I watched you this summer as you were learning how to dive at the swimming pool. When you finally got brave enough to dive from the diving board, you leapt, time after time, belly-flopping loudly with a slap heard by everyone, until your tummy was as red as a cooked crab. On your eighth or tenth try, you finally got your head down and your feet up, and cut into the water like a knife. You came up with a smile – to yourself. It was so clear you didn't need the praise of those at poolside who were clapping any more than you had cared about their chuckles while you were belly-flopping.

You are a strong, independent young lady already, my sweet Kate. That determination will take you far. I'm proud of you for always trying, never giving up, always having hope. You remind me of a quote from e.e. cummings your mother read me years ago: "To be nobody but yourself – in a world which is doing its best, night and day, to make you everybody else – means to fight the hardest battle which any human being can fight, and never stop fighting."

You may learn one day that a parent will try to step between his child and any kind of pain or disappointment and take it on himself in order to keep the pain away from the child. But life doesn't work that way. Parents can't keep some disappointments and pain – sometimes little, sometimes big – from striking. The best we can do is to help you learn to overcome adversity and sadness, to get back on your feet and to seek out the good and the joy in this world. By the time you read these words, years from now, you will probably have experienced your share of pain and disappointment. I'll protect you from as much of that as I can, but I hope I can also teach you how to deal with it when it comes.

I love you,
Daddy

Kate took a sip of her tea and smiled. She remembered the belly-flopping day. She held the mug close to her nose, smelled the hint of citrus in the tea, and found the letter dated December 30, 1970.

Kate,

For nine years, I have looked forward each year to writing this letter to you, and this year my heart is so full of sorrow I can barely push my pen across the paper.

I will never know why you and I have had to suffer this way. I will never know why two people as fine and as joyful and as good-hearted as your mother and David had to die so young. Their absence has left huge holes in your heart and mine.

I have tried my best to be strong for you. When you read this as an adult, you will have a better understanding of how hard this was, how close I was to letting go myself. If I had not had to be here for you, I think I would have died one way or another of a broken heart.

I have held you in my arms so many nights as you have cried yourself to sleep. And I have woken up with a start in the middle of the night to find you fleeing your bed, crying like some wild animal. You would have awakened from a dream that your mother had drowned. You would be shaken by that dream, but suddenly be relieved, thinking it was just a bad dream. And then the second shock would hit, and you would remember that it was not a dream at all, that she was gone and there was nothing you could do that would ever bring her back. And then you could not stop crying. I understood it completely, because I've had that same dream many times, and I know this sadness has scarred our hearts.

We will keep your mother and David alive in our hearts. I wish I could tell you honestly – I do tell you dishonestly – that I know they are with a loving God. But it is hard beyond words to understand a God who would take these two away. I do hope, though, that the connections we make on this earth are our doorway to a God of good intention. There are certain people we meet in life, and we know almost immediately that they are special people, closely attuned to what is right with the world, somehow more connected to others and to what is important in this life. I've often thought these people are glimpses of God. And we move toward that God, I hope, by working hard to know these others beyond the superficial, beyond the daily tasks of life, and by connecting in ways that transcend life and death. Your mother and I had that.

Kate, I have seen so much of your joy fade these past few months. I hope with all my heart your sense of joy returns, and I think it will over time. You have gone so deeply inward, and I understand that this is a normal way to grieve. But I hope you will bring that joyful side back into the sunlight. I miss your smile so much sometimes, it makes my bones hurt. I long for the day you find it again. Please know that I will always be here to help.

I love you.
Dad

She flipped over to a letter dated December 30, 1978 and found the part she was looking for.

You are doing well in your first year at USC, and being apart has been tough at times. I do miss your company, and I miss making those pancakes for you and your friends on Saturdays. The house is quieter than I'm used to. I miss you telling me what you're reading about and what's bothering you. But I'm doing better, and I love hearing the independence and happiness in your voice when you call.

*You asked me just before you left for school why I had
not found someone else to share my life with. (I hope you
weren't feeling guilty about leaving home. I promise you
that I'm doing fine.) After all, it has been eight years since
your mother died. I have been fortunate to spend time
in these years with a few very fine women, divorced or
widowed, who have dealt with their own sadnesses and
tragedies and come out on the other side. But every
time I try to open up this tough old heart, it just doesn't
happen. Your mother and I did not have a marriage of
convenience, the kind of household-and- income-sharing,
child-raising partnership many couples fall into. We lucked
into that kind of soul-connectedness that few people ever
know, and many people doubt even exists. So I've enjoyed
the companionship and the warmth of some wonderful
women these past few years, but I've never thought it fair
to them, or to the memory of your mother, to pretend to
love them the way I loved her.*

*You know I always try to include a quote that's meant
something to me or your mother. This one is from Carl
Sandburg. Kate, when Sandburg wrote this, it was a father
talking to his son. But it clearly applies to a daughter, too.
"A father sees a son nearing adulthood.
What shall he tell that son?
'Life is hard; be steel; be a rock,'
And this might stand him for the storms
and serve him for humdrum and monotony
and guide him amid sudden betrayals
and tighten him for slack moments.
'Life is soft loam; be gentle; go easy.'
And this too might serve him.
Brutes have been gentled where lashes failed.
The growth of a frail flower in a path up
has sometimes shattered and split a rock.*

A tough will counts. So does desire.
So does a rich soft wanting.
Without rich wanting nothing arrives.
Tell him too much money has killed men
and left them dead years before burial:
the quest of lucre beyond a few easy needs
has twisted good enough men
sometimes into dry thwarted worms.
Tell him time as a stuff can be wasted.
Tell him to be a fool every so often
and to have no shame over having been a fool
yet learning something out of every folly
hoping to repeat none of the cheap follies
thus arriving at intimate understanding
of a world numbering many fools.
Tell him to be alone often and get at himself
and above all tell himself no lies about himself
whatever the white lies and protective fronts
he may use amongst other people.
Tell him solitude is creative if he is strong
and the final decisions are made in silent rooms.
Tell him to be different from other people
if it comes natural and easy being different."

Kate, I have tried to give you wings as well as roots. You will
always have a home here with me and in my heart, but I
know it's time for you to find your own place in this world,
and you are doing that well. I am prouder of you than I
know how to tell you.

I love you, sweetie, Dad

Kate thought for awhile about how hard it must have been for her father to let her go when it was time for that first year of college. But he had never let on, dropping her off and unloading her suitcases and boxes, joking around with her new roommate, avoiding saying the word "goodbye," just reminding her that he was only two hours away and would be up there soon to bring anything she had forgotten. Like she was just going to camp for a couple of weeks, when she was really going away forever. He had put on a good game face.

She kept looking through the box until she found the last letter he had written her. It was dated August 20, 1993, two weeks before he died.

Kate,

I know I usually write these letters to you in December, at the end of the year, but this year's different, of course, and I'm writing on your birthday. I have been blessed with the opportunity to tell my friends goodbye these past few weeks. Summer is not a bad time to say goodbye to life. I had the chance to see a final spectacular show of springtime dogwoods and daffodils and smell the perfume from the clematis armandi. I've savored this summer's bounty from the farmer's market —the May strawberries, the fresh pulled ears of Silver Queen, some of the sweetest peaches I've ever eaten, tomato sandwiches of perfect texture and taste. Rich, ripe, sensuous figs from that tree in the backyard. And I've had the chance this summer to walk the beach where I met and fell in love with your mother, and I can still find the exact spot where I handed her a shell with a ring in it and asked her to marry me that cold December night.

Kate, I want you to know that I have had a wonderful life. It was largely because I was lucky enough to have an empty minnow bucket one July night forty-some years ago at the very moment your mother had a hankering for a full moon. She and I connected in a way that was amazing. I loved her mind, I loved her heart, I loved her laugh. I loved her willingness to give everyone the benefit of the doubt and not judge too quickly. I loved her gentleness, her toughness, her generosity and her passion. I loved the way she would wake me deep in the night to tell me what worried her or what excited her. Sometimes I think connections between two people are at their best at 3 o'clock in the morning. And for those who aren't truly connected, lying awake at three in the morning is the most desperately lonely time in life. You don't have to be alone to be lonely.

All these years without your mother, I've missed her more than I can say. But I've not been lonely, because she and I always carried each other in our hearts. I carry her in my heart today, and wherever she is, I believe she carries me in her heart. And I think we will both live on in your heart, my dear sweet Kate. That may be as close to immortality as any of us can get.

I was sorry you didn't have a mother around to teach you the things girls need to learn – about the terminal cuteness and dumbness of teenage boys, about the silliness and meanness of teenage girls, about make-up and training bras, about prom dresses, about all of the things that dads have no clues about.

You were so loyal to me, seldom showing any anger about what I didn't know, at least pretending to listen to my simple, sometimes simple-headed, advice.

I taught you to be independent and to take care of yourself, and sometimes I fear that you learned the lessons of independence too well. So let me leave you with these pieces of advice.

First, it is important to balance independence with

vulnerability. For many reasons, you have never let yourself be vulnerable to anyone or depend on anyone. You were hurt so much when your mother died, Kate, that you have never been willing to risk being hurt again. You have put your heart and your energy into your work, and you have done so well, and I am so proud of you. You are admired by everyone who knows you, and you have many good friends, but you only let them know you so far.

You think so well with your head, but I hope you will learn to think with your heart more, and I hope you find a man you can trust with your heart. I have watched several fine men try to open that heart of yours. They wanted to know you and to be known by you, but you couldn't quite let that happen. When I've watched you over the years gently fend off their attempts to get closer than you wanted, I've thought of how you dealt with Wilson Walker when you were twelve or thirteen.

That cute, earnest little boy would come over and sit on the glider with you on our front porch in the summertime, playing you little tunes on his Sears-bought guitar, sliding a little closer as the daylight dimmed. You could always sense when Will couldn't stand it any longer and was about to lean over and try to kiss you. You knew just when to hop up and say brightly:

"Will, I bet you'd like a Popsicle!" And off you'd run to the freezer and dig around with your hands until you found a chocolate Popsicle. You'd run back and hand it to him, knowing it would keep his mouth occupied for a while, gently knocking him off balance, postponing the next kissing attempt for another day.

I bet the sight of a Popsicle depresses him to this day!

Kate, my second piece of advice has to do with your work. You are so good at what you do. Judges and lawyers and clients all across this state look to you as a powerful advocate I must say, though, that I have worried these past few years that I spent my own life being the best in a business that hurt people badly, giving them a little daily pleasure in exchange for their heart and lungs. We didn't know everything back then that we know now, but we suspected smoking was unhealthy long before the tobacco companies owned up to it publicly.

You are young, and you have great talents. Let me gently suggest that sometime before long you consider whether you want to be a lawyer for the rest of your life defending those who harm the environment. I think if you look deeply into that warm heart of yours, you'll decide there's a better way to use those talents.

Thank you, Kate, for being the light of my life for so long. You and I have kept your mother and David alive in our hearts, and there's not a day that passes that I don't think of them being absolutely connected to us, aware of us, worrying for us, proud of us and somehow waiting for us. I have taken great comfort from those thoughts these past few weeks.

I confess to being a little scared about what's on the other side of this life, this consciousness, this light. I worry sometimes that it will be just darkness and nothingness. I lie here and wonder how it will be to lose everything and everyone I know. Then I think hard about how I connected with Mary, with David and with you, and I know what comes next will be larger than just me. I think those incredible connections gave me a glimpse of what connection to that unknowable God may be. I am almost ready.

Kate, know always in your life that you were as loved as a person can be. We find love best by giving it, and that generous heart of yours, once it opens, will connect as tightly with your chosen one as mine did with your mother's years ago. Go look for that full moon. There's a good man out there with an empty minnow bucket.

It is hard to say goodbye, but know always how much I have loved you, and always will.

I am always with you.
Dad

Kate closed the notebook, dropped it to the floor beside the bed, and turned out the light. She slid down in her bed and pulled the sheet up under her chin. She could hear the quiet click of her ceiling fan and feel the hint of the breeze it stirred in the late September air. It felt good to sleep with her windows open. As she closed her eyes, finally sneaking up on sleep, she could hear the chimes from the Prince George Episcopal Church tolling 3 o'clock in the stillness of the night.

25

Webster's Appeal

By 1 a.m., the Saturday edition of the *Pilot* was printed and on its way to news boxes and subscribers' doorsteps. Sandy had left around midnight, headed for his apartment on Front Street above one of the riverfront watering holes, and the two man printing crew departed with him on their way to a late beer. Wade was sitting with his feet propped on his desk, not ready for sleep and wondering what Monday would bring.

The sharp rap at the newspaper's front door startled him, stiffening his neck hair. He dropped his feet and walked a wary gait toward the door. He could see a silhouette against the translucent glass door, but had no idea who it was.

"Who's there?" Wade asked loudly through the closed door.

"Grant Webster," a husky voice said, faintly audible through the glass. "I'm looking for Wade McNabb. His father Hampton was a friend of mine."

Wade unlocked the door and pulled it open. A thin, grey-haired man who appeared to be in his mid-seventies stood on the top step of the porch. Time had forged deep wrinkles in his face, and his sad eyes suggested the creases had not all been born of laughter. His sharply pressed white pants, well-fitting blue blazer and carefully combed hair would make him look at home in any country club in South Carolina. Wade suspected he carried a comb in the inside pocket of his blazer, always ready for a quick swipe.

"Please come in," Wade said, trying to remember what he had once known of Webster. His father had mentioned twenty-five years ago that the mayor had sided with the newspaper's enemies in the boycott struggle, but Wade could not recall more than that.

The man stepped inside and held out his hand.

"Son," the man said, "I'm sorry to show up like this in the middle of the night, but I was close by and decided this might be the best way for us to have a little conversation."

Webster appeared to be watching Wade's face closely for any sign of recognition.

"I don't know what your Daddy may have told you about me, but I want to set a couple of things straight with you. My wife's family used to own Pearson Funeral Home. Maybe you remember that. I ran it for her daddy for thirty years or so until I got just goddam tired of dealing with him and with dead bodies. Sometime after your daddy died, we sold out and moved to the North Carolina mountains. Suits us better there in a lot of ways, a damn sight cooler that this place."

Wade nodded, wondering just where this was going. But he also knew that older folks can sometimes ramble before they circle back to the point.

"Mr. Webster, why don't we walk back to my office," Wade said. "We can sit and talk there."

Webster sat, pulled a handkerchief from his pocket and absently cleaned the arms of the chair. He stared across the desk for a moment, his gaze fixing on the wooden chair where Wade was about to sit.

"I had many talks with your father in this room, with him sitting in that very chair. Sometimes we were laughing, sometimes we were arguing, sometimes we were drinking and doing both. I think of him often, and some days I still miss him like a lost tooth. We had a lot of shared memories, the two of us did. Most of them were real good, even near the end."

He smiled at Wade.

"I bet that damn thing still squeaks like a banshee."

Wade leaned back and the chair spoke its creaky voice. He waited for Webster to explain why he was here.

Webster tapped his fingers on the arm of his chair and glanced around the room, then finally looked back at Wade.

"You just need to listen a little to an old man clear his head and his heart.

"I'm staying over at Litchfield Beach with some friends for a few days. I decided tonight to head over to the Dunes Club to see if a poker game was going on back in the Men's Grill. I like to see if I still have a poker face when I need one. There were five or six fellows in the Grill, one of them somebody you know – Buck Ravenel. He was pretty likkered up, and had thrown in his cards. He was sitting at the table beside me with one other guy.

"Now, I've paid some attention to this libel suit you're in, read a few stories in the newspaper. When I overheard him mention the name McNabb and say something about the newspaper, I decided to listen sort of closely."

He gave Wade a wink and tapped a plastic tube behind his ear.

"When I turn this damn thing up, I hear better than a puppy listening for his momma.

"He told the fellow with him that he had you and your newspaper by the balls, and he didn't plan to let go. He said you were a proud man just like your daddy was, and you were going to lose the *Pilot* just like your daddy did. He thinks you'll refuse to reveal your source, and the court will enter a huge verdict against you. He wants to send a message to folks that – if you will pardon my language – they shouldn't 'fuck with Buck.'"

Wade looked straight at Webster, but stayed silent.

"Wade, I lost track of you after your teenage years, once you went off to college. You know that your daddy and I got sideways over the racial stuff and the steel mill strike. Hell, the businessmen here were just trying to protect our jobs and our families. I thought your father would see the light and meet us partway. I didn't know he'd dig his heels in and run the newspaper into the ground.

"I loved your daddy like he was my brother. He was smart, and he was stubborn. Too much so for his own good a lot of the time. He loved your mother, but the liquor got in their way in the later years. I am sorry beyond words for what happened to him. I wished everyday for years that I could bring him back, that I had handled things a different way.

"I saw him a few days before he died. I came to this office and sat right here looking at him just like I'm looking at you. I begged him to find some middle ground with that son of a bitch Buzz Timmons and the others. But he said if those bastards wanted to own his paper they'd have to take it from him. He said they weren't going to own *him*."

The grey-haired man stopped talking and took a deep breath.

"Son, what I came to tell you is this. Don't let Buck Ravenel have his way. If there is any way you can get the name of your source out so the judge won't have an easy way to screw you and the newspaper, do it. If you don't disclose that source, I think they are going to squash you. If you can keep this newspaper, you'll do this community a lot of good for a long time."

He leaned over desk and looked hard at Wade.

"I helped your daddy lose this newspaper, and it cost me my best friend. It's given me years of regret, almost like I was the one who pulled the trigger on his shotgun. Wade, I don't want you to lose this newspaper."

Wade rubbed his chin for a minute, and leaned back in his chair.

"Mr. Webster, I thank you for being willing to come share this with me. And I appreciate the kind words about my dad. And there's plenty of worry to go around about not keeping him from pulling that trigger. I've lived with it for twenty-five years myself."

"Wade, you need to know this, too. I talked to your dad several times that fall just before he died. I don't think there was a time he didn't go out of his way to tell me what you were up to at school and how proud he was of you. Sometimes dads aren't as good at telling sons that as they should be. He was especially proud of your stands against the Vietnam War, even though he disagreed with you on that. The last night I saw him he told me that very thing."

"Mr. Webster, that means a lot to me. I promise you I'm trying hard to save this newspaper. And I'm trying to do that without losing my conscience."

Grant Webster stood and reached across the desk to shake Wade's hand.

"Well, it's almost 2 o'clock, I need to go. I drove over here thinking you might be here tonight. Would have left you a note to call me if I had missed you. Peaches will be wondering if I've met some sixty-year-old slow-dancin' sweetie. I may need you to vouch for me tomorrow morning."

Wade walked Grant Webster to the door, then found himself following the old man to the front steps.

"Mr. Webster, did you recognize the fellow Senator Ravenel was with, by any chance?"

"Son, I've been gone from around here too long. He seemed to be with a fellow who came in and sat with him at the table at the Grill for a little while. But he left separately from Ravenel."

Wade tried to recall a photograph Kate had shown him and the description from Bill Wright.

"Was he a tall, lean fellow, in his fifties, sort of distinguished looking?"

Webster thought for a moment, rubbing his temple.

"No," he said, shaking his head. "He was an older fellow, heavy-set, white hair. He had the bushiest eyebrows I've ever seen. I never heard Ravenel call him by name. I just remember when he was leaving, the senator said something like, 'Night, do good. I'll see you next week.'"

Wade tried to smile.

"Thanks, Mr. Webster. All this is very helpful. You drive carefully. And if Mrs. Webster wants to know who you were dancing with tonight, have her call me."

26

Dewey Wright

On Monday morning, Dewey Wright moved stiffly around his cabin at Bowman's Forest, his long, thin fingers slowly buttoning his white shirt. He brushed lint from the shoulders of the navy blue suit coat he wore only to church. In the years since his wife Rose had died, his church visits had been mostly limited to funerals.

Wright kept an eye out through his curtains for Earl Pittman's old blue Cadillac. Pittman, the Forest's general manager, had offered Wright a ride to the courthouse. Their subpoenas called for their testimony to begin at half past nine.

Wright stood before the mirror that hung above his dresser and evened the ends of his string tie. He pulled the small silver clasp - in the shape of a saddle - up close to his top button and straightened it. The string tie was a nostalgic nod to his years in Texas and Wyoming with the railroad. The silver clasp was a long ago Christmas gift from his brother Jimmy. Wright's young body and spirit had taken to bronco riding at weekend rodeos back then. He had liked being a bit of a curiosity - the lone black cowboy competing. The early morning stiffness in his back and ankles was a long-term dividend of those rides and spills. The stiffness hit with a special vengeance on mornings after he had slept poorly.

He ran his hand over his smooth ebony scalp and straightened Rose's photo on the dresser top. They had met just after he'd moved back to Georgetown in the early 1970s. She had suffered in her last decade from what she called the "sugar diabetes." Not long after her death eight years earlier, Wright had moved from town to a two-room cabin at the Forest. He still missed her sassy company. And even though he had quickly attracted the attention of some of Georgetown's prettiest widows, he had never had the urge to marry again. In recent years, when he had occasionally been persuaded to stay overnight in town, he always made it respectfully clear that another marriage was not in his plans.

Wright glanced at his watch, then fumbled with his key ring to find the small key to his desk drawer. He opened it, pulled out the thin manila folder he needed for today's hearing and slid the drawer shut.

Promptly at eight-thirty, Pittman eased his Cadillac to a stop in front of Wright's cabin. The twenty-year-old DeVille with the high tail fins sported an unusual shade of blue -- a rich, but not quite royal, blue, more like the back of a male bluebird in the springtime sun. Pittman called it "Pabst blue." He had bought the car used, straight from Mosby Bowman, and treated it like a newborn.

Wright slid gingerly into the front seat of the car and said a quiet good morning to his supervisor. Wright was old enough to remember the days just thirty years ago when no black man – a "nigra" or a "colored" or a "darkie" or worse – would even think of sitting in the front seat of a vehicle with a white man. Instead, he would slip into the back seat, hat pulled down shading the eyes, and slide down a little low, quiet-like, speaking only if spoken to. Wright's responses had always been short, vague and noncommittal, seldom inviting further conversation.

Wright had often wondered how many times in his years he had been addressed as "Boy," and how many times he had pretend-grinned and hustled to answer, secretly hating both the speaker and the responder.

He had been witness to the racial changes the last quarter-century had brought. He heard the young black men he saw on television or in town angrily asserting that "nothin' had changed" in the last forty years, despite *Brown v. Board of Education*, despite Martin Luther King, Jr., despite Rosa Parks, despite Malcolm X, despite the civil rights and voting rights acts of the 1960s, despite affirmative action. But he had lived the apartheid life of the 1950s' South. He knew which things had changed, and which hadn't.

Back then, he had sneaked sips from the "Whites Only" water fountains, curious to see if the white folks' water tasted somehow sweeter than the water in the "Colored" water fountains. He had used the Colored toilets, sat in movies in the "Colored" balconies, stood around back at restaurants, waiting at the "Colored" take-out counter until all the white customers were served before his order could be taken. He had watched his mother, who had cooked and cleaned house for the same white family for twenty years, fix her plate of leftovers and eat it in their kitchen, while the white folks ate together at their table ten feet away. She would pull her own glass, an old peanut-butter jar, from the kitchen cabinet to hold her iced tea. It was simply understood that the white family – however generous they might be with their hand-me-downs and cast-offs – didn't think it would be quite right for her to drink from the same glasses they drank from. Soap and hot water could not cleanse her blackness from that glass.

No one ever said that. It was simply understood. She had cooked their breakfasts and suppers, wiped their babies' asses and dressed their children up nice and clean for Sunday School, but they didn't want her drinking out of *their* iced tea glasses. As a boy, it had made him think that white folks must somehow *be* better than black people. Why else would God let things be this way?

He couldn't remember exactly the first time he had heard the word "nigger." But by the time he was eight, he had heard it about every way it could be said, spat from the mouth of white men, riding an anger rooted somewhere strange and deep: stupidnigger, lazynigger, drunknigger, shiftlessnigger, fuckinnigger, worthlessnigger. He heard "dumbnigger" so many times he thought for a long while it was the real word for black people. Sometimes a white man would refer to someone as a "good nigger." That had sounded okay to Wright at first. But he soon figured out that it meant only a black man who shuffled, chuckled, and never challenged a white man, not even with a cold glance. A good nigger "knew his place." A bad nigger still had a man inside who might cross a mean white man one day or maybe kill one.

Wright had watched the white politicians try to "out-nigger" each other, playing on the frustrations of poor whites barely holding onto the lowest rungs of the economic ladder, the sixth-grade dropouts, the illiterate adults who could read little more than their names and the Bible verses learned from Sunday School repetition. Those poor souls desperately needed someone below them to look down on, and they fought hard to pry loose the fingers of any "niggers" clutching at the bottom rung.

Wright had escaped South Carolina a few years after high school, wandering west with the railroad, because he could not stand that racist culture. He found the discrimination out west more subtle, somehow less stressful. Folks there seemed to give an independent, hard-working black man grudging respect instead of instinctive hostility. He had stayed away from

Georgetown for years. His first trip back was to attend the funeral of his younger brother Jimmy. A steel mill worker who openly supported the strike at the mill, Jimmy was the victim of a fatal hit-and-run one month into the strike. No one had ever been charged in his death. Without his quiet, behind-the-scenes leadership, the mill workers had eventually caved in on most of their demands and gone back to work.

Knowing his brother's family needed him close by, Dewey Wright had found a safe niche at the Forest. His cooking talents and ability to manage the dining room staff had won him job security with a succession of bosses, including Earl Pittman. His dignified, deliberate manner, combined with his ability to banter when necessary with important guests, had earned him a good measure of respect and affection. He had made his personal peace with the politics of his home state. He kept his political opinions carefully to himself.

27

The Truth Will Set You Free

As Kate swung her leather briefcase onto defendants' counsel table in Georgetown County's main courtroom, she could hear the faint chimes of the Prince George Episcopal Church signaling the 9 o'clock hour. The bailiff nodded at Kate as he stopped to add ice and water to the clear plastic pitcher on the counsel table and leave a short stack of paper cups. Kate glanced over her shoulder at the clock above the rear courtroom doors just in time to see Buck Ravenel stride in with his entourage – Tripp Ravenel, two younger male lawyers, a paralegal and a buttoned-up looking representative of Carolina Phosphate. Ravenel wore a strong smile and a confident look on a ruddy face. Kate wasn't sure if it reflected a weekend in the sun or a last-minute cheek pinch in the men's room. One of her Devereaux partners had been known to rub his cheeks red just before court to give himself a healthy glow.

Ravenel's group was all smugness and nudges, like a group of seventh grade boys heading to recess. As they made their way to plaintiffs' counsel table, Ravenel put his arm around Tripp's shoulders, leaned his head down close to his son's ear and stage-whispered to him, just loud enough for Kate to catch the gist of it.

"That little candy-ass reporter would look real cute in an orange jumpsuit. His jailhouse roommate would tie that bow-tie in a knot around his dick for him," the Senator said.

He looked up, caught Kate's eye and smiled broadly.

"Good morning, Kate," he said. "Hope you're doing well this morning."

"Mornin', Mr. Ravenel," Kate replied, with a half-smile. "You've brought quite an entourage. You do know we aren't starting the trial today?"

Ravenel's only response was a frozen grin and a cold stare.

Kate let her eyes roam the courtroom as casually as she could. She recognized a few local lawyers who nodded, or lifted a finger from the bench back in front of them in silent greeting. The courthouse regulars were anticipating a good show with the possibility of some serious fireworks, depending on Judge Jones' mood. Like fans at a stock car race or a Saturday night cockfight, they were hoping for a spectacular collision and maybe a little blood, and they knew it wouldn't be their own. Several Coastal Conservation League members who had vigorously fought the granting of the permit for the phosphate plant at Wright's Landing chatted in a corner. Kate spotted Wade McNabb as he came through the courtroom door and saw Carolyn pat him gently on the shoulder and brush away a stray hair on his jacket. She straightened his tie and whispered something that made him smile.

Minutes later, McNabb and Anderson walked up and stood awkwardly beside Kate, uncertain if they should be chatting with well-wishers in the courtroom. McNabb looked glum, like he'd taken a swig of sour milk, the strain apparent in the dark circles painting the underside of his eyes. This was clearly not an event he had contemplated when he purchased the *Pilot* two years earlier. He looked like a man in the path of a hurricane with no high ground in sight. Sandy's nervousness was obvious. He kept clearing his throat and straightening his bowtie, reflexively glancing around the courtroom with his reporter's hawkish eyes.

His scan of the courtroom identified several lawyers he knew from the POETS gatherings at Sliders. He nodded at Charlie Pinckney, the long time director of the Coastal Conservation League.

Seated on one row of the dark wooden benches was a group of a dozen or so black men and women. Sandy recognized one of them as a lawyer representing several owners of the property at Wright's Landing. He knew why they were interested in the outcome of all of this. If the permit for Carolina Phosphate was granted, the value of their land would plummet. Anderson saw the bailiff stick his head in the doorway to the judge's chambers, then walk importantly to the side of the courtroom.

The reporter turned around to find his spot to stand stiffly when the judge would enter. The courtroom rituals had become like stage directions for a play, and they had all learned their parts. As Anderson turned, he glimpsed a young black man slipping quietly through the courtroom door to take a seat by himself in the back row. It was Bill Wright, dressed in a blue suit. Sandy tried to catch his eye, but Wright looked right through him as though he had never seen him before. Sandy gently nudged his editor and whispered to him.

"Don't turn around now, but we have an unexpected visitor."

Before Wade could respond, the bailiff stood at attention and shouted his "Oyez, Oyez" chant, signaling that court was in session. Everyone in the courtroom stood. Buck Ravenel instinctively buttoned his suit jacket. Kate unconsciously pushed her hair behind her right ear. McNabb's hands slid to his sides to be sure his coat flaps were not tucked in, as his mother had always reminded him. Anderson smoothed his bowtie with his thumbs and forefingers. All stared intently at Judge Jones as he lumbered through the doorway from his chambers and took his seat behind the high wooden desk. He nodded to those facing him.

"Be seated," he said, looking down at the papers he placed on the desk before him.

The judge made no immediate eye contact with either Ravenel or Stewart. Instead he peered at the papers, shuffled them for a few moments, then raised his head, deep in thought. He was clearly in a somber mood. His bushy eyebrows were flat against the bottom of his forehead, and his face was stern. He pursed his lips and stared down at his papers for a few more seconds. On this day, when he finally addressed the lawyers, he offered no flowery salutations.

"All right, Mr. Ravenel, I understand you have subpoenaed Mr. Earl Pittman and Mr. Dewey Wright from Bowman's Forest to be here with us this morning. Are they present in the courtroom?"

Senator Ravenel stood and half turned, extending his hand toward the two men seated on the front row of the courtroom.

"Judge, Mr. Pittman and Mr. Wright are here."

"You can keep it short. I just want to be sure that the plaintiffs in this case have had a chance to ask every person known to be at the Forest on the night of July 1 if they were the source for the *Pilot's* article. If they've all denied being the source, then our members of the local Fourth Estate will need to share the name of their source with us. All right, call your witnesses, Mr. Ravenel."

Earl Pittman stepped up into the witness box and placed his hand on the judge's small black Bible with gold-edged pages. The only Bible Judge Jones had thought much of since his college days was Thomas Jefferson's bible, the Virginia Gentlemen's version of the New Testament, edited to exclude the parts that Jefferson, scribbling away by candlelight with his quill pen, thought untrustworthy or unnecessary. But the courtroom Bible was the palm-sized copy Judge Jones' grandfather had used at his own swearing-in as the Chief Justice of the South Carolina Supreme Court in 1925. The Chief Justice had always carried the tiny Bible in the inside breast pocket of his suit coat. One corner of the volume was now frayed and partly missing where, aided by a strategically inserted, page-sized piece of thin steel, it had deflected a pistol shot aimed at the Justice's heart. The newspapers had described his assailant – shot dead by Justice Jones – as a crazed political fanatic. His family could never completely dispel the rumor that the exchange of shots had occurred in a late night confrontation with the jealous husband of the Justice's young mistress. Judge Dupree Jones always waved the story away without a complete denial, enjoying the whiff of ancient scandal, and insisted the Bible be used for all ceremonial occasions in his courtroom, including the swearing of witnesses.

Ravenel stood and stepped a little to the side of the plaintiffs' counsel table, directing his full attention to Earl Pittman.

"Mr. Pittman, I have just a few questions. You submitted an affidavit in this case, did you not?"

"Yes, sir, I did."

"And in that affidavit you listed everyone you saw register or you otherwise knew to be a guest at Bowman's Forest on the evening of July 1, 1995? Is that correct?"

"That would be correct, sir."

"And you stated in your affidavit that Francis Marion Ravenel III, Senator Arthur Long and Vince Stone were all guests of the Forest that evening, as was I? Is that correct?"

"Uh, yes, sir, that would be correct."

"Mr. Pittman, were you yourself ever in the dining hall or

the private dining room at Bowman's Forest on the night of July 1?"

"No, sir."

"Did you ever overhear any conversations in the dining hall or anywhere else regarding any form of business deal between me, my son Tripp Ravenel, Mr. Long or Mr. Stone?"

"No, sir, I did not."

"Ever hear anyone mention the name "Carolina Phosphate" that night?"

"I've heard of that company, but I don't recall anybody there at the Forest mentioning it that night, no."

"Have you ever heard anyone else at the Forest mention that they overheard any conversations about any such business deal?"

"No, sir, I have not."

Ravenel walked slowly over to the edge of plaintiffs' counsel table and picked up a copy of the *Pilot*. He glanced at the judge, who nodded, signaling permission to approach the witness. Ravenel shook the folded newspaper open as he walked forward so that Pittman could see the full front page. He handed it to the witness, then walked back toward the counsel table.

"Mr. Pittman, did you read this story published in the *Pilot* back in August about my clients?"

"Yes sir, I did."

"You see where it says the newspaper "has learned" that Carolina Phosphate had discussed a business investment with Tripp Ravenel and me at a dinner at the Forest?"

"Yes, sir, I see that right here in the story."

"Mr. Pittman, were you a source of Mr. Anderson, or Mr. McNabb or the *Georgetown Pilot* for their story that was published August 5 in that newspaper?"

"No, sir, I was not the source. I've never talked to Mr. Anderson or Mr. McNabb."

"So they did not learn this piece of so-called information from you?"

"No, sir. They certainly did not."

"All right, then. Let me be sure I'm clear on this one thing. You are absolutely sure that you listed in your affidavit every single person who was a guest at the Forest on the night of July 1?"

"Yes, sir, I did."

Ravenel walked back up to the witness and took the newspaper from him.

"Thank you, Mr. Pittman."

Ravenel shifted his gaze back to Judge Jones.

"That's all I have for this witness, Your Honor," he said, satisfaction drenching his words. "As the Court knows, everyone on that list has given a sworn statement that they were not the newspaper's source."

He turned smugly to Kate Stewart.

"Your witness, counselor," he said sharply. "Ask him."

Kate stood and addressed Judge Jones.

"We have no questions of this witness, Your Honor," she said calmly.

"All right, Mr. Ravenel. What else do you have?" Judge Jones asked.

Ravenel stood again, buttoning and unbuttoning the middle button on his suit coat.

"Your Honor, I call Dewey Wright to the witness stand."

Wright stood up stiffly to his full height. He walked slowly and with dignity to the front of the courtroom. His back straight, he took the witness stand, raised his right hand and put his left hand on the Bible.

"Do you swear to tell the truth, the whole truth and nothing but the truth, so help you God?" the courtroom clerk asked.

"Yes, I do," Wright answered.

Ravenel quickly began his questioning.

"You are the dining room director at Bowman's Forest, are you not, Mr. Wright?"

"Yes, sir. Been doin' dat for 'bout twenty-five ya-ahs, yes sir, maybe twenty-six."

"And, Mr. Wright, you cook some pretty good meals over there at the Forest, don't you?" Ravenel asked with a smile and a quick glance over his shoulder to those seated behind him in the courtroom.

"Well, sir, folks seem to come back for seconds most evenins'."

Ravenel half-turned to those in the benches behind him and forced out an actor's chuckle.

"Now, Mr. Wright, you don't need to tell everybody here about how many pieces of your pecan pie I have been known to eat," he said with a broad smile, looking up at Judge Jones.

Ravenel pronounced it "pee-can" with the accent on the "pee." He had often been tempted to change his pronunciation to the more genteel "pe-kahn," but had refused to do so partly on principle. He had grown up saying pee-can and thought it poor form to change because folks at Vince Stone's Carolina Country Club smiled when he said it that way. Besides, to connect with his jurors, a good trial lawyer wanted to talk like them.

Ravenel's tone turned serious again.

"Mr. Wright, in that position, do you also manage all of the employees at the dining room of Bowman's Forest?"

"Yes, sir."

"And is it true that you would know better than anyone else who was employed in the dining room on the evening of July 1?"

"Yes, sir, but I wouldn't be knowin' dat right out of my own head. Different people worked different nights and different shifts. But I checked the payroll records of the dinin' room for the night of July 1."

"All right. And have you submitted an affidavit in this case, Mr. Wright?"

"Yes, sir, I sure enough did."

"And in that affidavit you listed the names of the employees working that night. Is that right?"

"Yes, sir. Everybody on the payroll. I have a copy of it right here."

He lifted the manila folder in his right hand.

"Mr. Wright, were you yourself present in the dining room on the evening of July 1?"

"Yes, sir, you know I was. You and I talked a little that evenin'. You kidded me 'bout my old bald head."

"That's right, Mr. Wright. We did kid around a little. And most of that conversation occurred in the bar area, did it not?"

"Yes, sir, that'd be right. I came out to the private dinin' room for a minute or two where you and the other gentlemen were. You introduced them to me and bragged on my cookin' a little. That was 'bout it, best I remember."

"Do you recall who the other gentlemen present were?"

"Uh, yes, sir, I believe I do. It was you, Mr. Tripp Ravenel, Senator Long and another gentleman, a lawyer, but I don't rightly recall his name."

"Could it have been Vince Stone?"

"Could have been, could have been, sir, I just don't recall. Don't think I'd ever seen him before."

Ravenel pointed at the man sitting at the far left end of plaintiffs' counsel table.

"Mr. Wright, the gentleman I am pointing to at the end of

our counsel table – raise your hand, please – is that the other gentleman who was present in the dining room at the Forest that evening?"

Wright peered in that direction and nodded.

"Yes, sir. I believe it is."

Ravenel looked to the court and then to the court reporter.

"Your Honor, if there is no objection, let the record reflect that the gentleman whom Mr. Wright has identified is Vince Stone."

Ravenel glanced at Kate Stewart, and she nodded. Ravenel turned back to the witness.

"Your full name is Dewey Wright, isn't it?"

"Yes, sir. Been that way all my life."

"And out at the Forest, do folks have a nickname for you?"

The witness gave a bashful smile, and turned his head down and sideways a little.

"Yes, sir, some folks do."

"They call you Mr. Do-Right, don't they?"

"Some of them do that."

"And they call you that because you have a reputation for doing the right thing whenever you can, don't they?"

Kate considered objecting to the blatant leading of the witness on direct examination but knew it would look silly to the judge.

"Others can say about that better than I can, Senator."

"Now, Mr. Wright, you and I have known each other for some years, have we not?"

"Yes, sir, Mr. Ravenel. Be mo' like decades than years. I have seen you on many occasions at Bowman's Forest."

"And you saw me on the night of July 1, did you not?"

"Yes, sir, like I already said."

"Did you hear any discussions that evening among Senator Long, Tripp Ravenel, Mr. Stone or me about any kind of a business deal?"

Wright paused for a moment, thinking about the question. Then he answered softly.

"No, sir, I did not hear any discussions like that."

"Did anyone ever tell you that they had heard any such discussions?"

"No, sir."

Ravenel again made eye contact with the judge, saw his nod, and walked up to the witness to hand him the August 5 copy of the *Pilot*.

"Mr. Wright, did you read the story published by the *Georgetown Pilot* back in August about my son, Tripp Ravenel, and me?"

"Yes, sir, I did."

"The story said the newspaper 'had learned' about a dinner at the Forest where we had a big discussion about some kind of investment?"

"Yes, sir, I remember it said that."

"Mr. Wright, were you the source for that story written by Mr. Anderson?"

Ravenel turned and pointed toward the reporter.

Wright looked over at Sandy Anderson, then at Wade McNabb, and shook his head.

"No, sir. I've never met or talked with either of those gentlemen before."

Wright looked back at Buck Ravenel.

"Now mebbe I should say that I once met Lawyer Stewart. I have read about her in the newspapers, and I know she is the lawyer for the newspaper in this case. But it was a long time ago when I met her, and she was so young she probably don't remember it. But I thought I should say that since you askin' about who all I know."

Wright nodded in her direction with a slight smile. Kate smiled back.

Ravenel seemed to be about to ask another question, then saw Judge Jones staring at him. The judge's eyebrows suggested he had heard enough. Ravenel walked back to his spot at the counsel table.

"Well, Mr. Wright, that's a reminder that this is a small state we live in, isn't it? Thank you for your time."

He looked up at the judge.

"No more questions, Your Honor. As this record reflects, every individual on that list has given a statement swearing he or she was not the newspaper's source. I turn this witness over to the defendants."

"All right," Judge Jones said. "I think I've heard what I needed to. Ms. Stewart, do you have any questions of this witness?"

Kate wasn't sure if she did or not. She looked directly at Dewey Wright and saw him staring right back at her eyes. Her instincts, born of questioning hundreds of witnesses in the last ten years, told her she should begin a conversation with him. She had learned that cross-examination is a powerful engine of truth. She stood up slowly.

"Yes, Your Honor. I have a few," she said, not knowing yet what they would be. "I will be brief."

Judge Jones looked at her, his eyebrows arched, with no smile.

"I already knew that, Ms. Stewart," he said curtly. "I'm glad you do."

Kate's stomach fluttered but her calm expression remained unchanged. Wade had told her about his conversation with Grant Webster, and she wondered what the judge might have promised Ravenel Friday night. And what Ravenel might have promised the judge.

"Mr. Wright, I didn't know if you would recall meeting me so long ago, but it's good to see you again."

The witness's serious gaze didn't change, but Kate detected no hostility in his eyes.

"Yes, ma'am, you was just a little girl. You caught yo'self a big ole bass at the Forest, and your daddy got chased by a wild goose and about let that fish get away. I mounted yo' fish and put it on the wall of the dinin' room, and I put yo' name on it. And I've seen yo' name in the newspapers many times since then and that fish would make me smile ever'time. You done real well. I knew your daddy, and he would be right proud of you."

"Thank you, Mr. Wright, for saying that. Now, Mr. Wright, I want to understand a little better what happened on July 1 at Bowman's Forest if you'll help me. You said you were present in the dining room that evening, is that right?"

"Yes, ma'am."

"How long were you there that night?"

"I was around all night, a little in the dining room, mostly in the kitchen," Wright said. "We let some of the cooks knock off and go home once everybody's been served, but I always stay to the end. I'm the last one out the door. That's my job."

"And you said Senator Ravenel introduced you to several gentlemen in the private dining room, including Senator Ravenel's son Tripp, Senator Arthur Long and Mr. Stone, the man down at the end of the other table, is that right?"

"Yes, ma'am."

"And did you testify that you heard no discussions about any sort of business deal between any of these gentlemen?"

Wright did not answer immediately. He stared straight at Kate for several seconds before he responded, expressionless.

"I did not hear any discussions about any business deal."

Kate pondered that response for a moment. She felt like

her crab had just let go of the bait. She could feel her mother telling her to be patient, to take it inch by inch.

"Did you hear any part of their conversations in the private dining room?"

Wright did not move his gaze from her.

"Yes, I did," he said quietly.

Kate felt her crab line go taut again.

Before Kate could begin her next question, Senator Ravenel rose slowly from his chair and caught Judge Jones' eye. He cleared his throat.

"Your Honor, I object to this line of questioning. Mr. Wright has already been asked the relevant questions and has answered them. This is tangential and well beyond the scope of the issues relevant to plaintiffs' need for the identity of defendants' confidential source. Mr. Wright has testified that he was not the source, and he has testified that he has correctly and fully identified everyone who was working for him in the dining room that night. The rest of this is simply not relevant."

Judge Jones, eyebrows now at attention, addressed Kate Stewart directly.

"Ms. Stewart, I'm glad to see that you and Mr. Wright have gotten reacquainted after all these years, but I do have to ask you whether this questioning is going anywhere at all. I hope you are not just stalling for time until you think of a theory that might possibly help your case."

"Your Honor, I assure you that I'm not. Plaintiffs' counsel opened this door by asking Mr. Wright about what discussions he himself had heard, and I am just probing a little further on that issue."

"It seems to me, Ms. Stewart, that you may just be on a fishing expedition, but I'll give you a few more questions to wrap it up."

Kate turned her attention back to the witness.

"Mr. Wright, do you recall any part of the conversations you heard these gentlemen engage in that evening?"

"I heard them talk about a permit for the Carolina Phosphate plant. I had read about that issue in the newspapers. Some of my kin-people own property out there. I was interested, so it caught my attention a little bit. I do remember they talked about the permit and that Carolina Phosphate really wanted the permit to be approved."

"All right," the lawyer said. "Do you remember anything else any of them said about the Carolina Phosphate plant or about the permit?

Wright paused again and rubbed his forehead hard for a few moments, deep in thought.

"No, that was about all of the discussion I remember. I did talk with Senator Ravenel later in the evenin'. He asked if I would give him a ride to the railcar down the street from the Forest, where he was stayin'. I told him I'd be glad to take him as soon as I had finished cleanin' up. He sat out on the porch and had some port and smoked a cigar. We were the last two to leave the dinin' room that night."

"And did you give him a ride back to the railcar?"

"Yes, ma'am, I did. He'd had a right smart to drink. He was feeling pretty good, you know. I helped him get settled in the railcar that evenin'. I had done that for him before."

"When you say 'get settled,' what do you mean?" Stewart asked.

Wright glanced over at Ravenel, who started to stand and object, then thought better of it.

"Helped him get his shoes and britches off, and get him in the bed so he'll go to sleep. He was singin' a little and laughin' and I was getting him to quiet down and go to bed."

"Was that the last time you saw Senator Ravenel that weekend?"

"No, he came by the dining room the next morning when he was fixin' to leave."

Wright was talking calmly, slowly and Kate sensed he wanted her to keep asking questions. She felt like he understood the oath he had taken and wanted to tell the whole truth, but wasn't going to tell it unless she asked the right questions.

"What do you remember about your conversation with him that morning?"

Wright paused for a moment. He looked over at Buck Ravenel, then scanned the folks seated near the back of the courtroom. He didn't let his gaze stop on his nephew.

"He came by to see if I had found any papers he had left in my car the night before when I had given him a ride home. I told him I had found a folder of his on the front seat and put it in a safe place because I figured he would want it. I handed him his folder. He thanked me for finding it."

Buck Ravenel stood up again, this time more quickly.

"Your Honor, I hate to keep making objections to defendants' questions, but this line of inquiry seems to be going nowhere."

He turned and looked behind him at the clock over the rear courtroom doors.

"We've been at this for over an hour, and we've clearly established that plaintiffs have exhausted the possible alternative sources of this information, that is, the identity of defendants' confidential source. I believe the Court has indulged defendants' counsel enough, and we should move this matter along."

Judge Jones turned his gaze back to Kate Stewart.

"Well, Ms. Stewart, I feel like I have given you ample opportunity to fish this pond. I believe Senator Ravenel has a point. You haven't caught a big bass this time. I don't see the relevance of all this. Please wrap it up now."

"Now" boomed out like a rap of the judge's gavel.

"Yes, sir, I will. I am just about through."

"Mr. Wright, did you have any further conversations with Senator Ravenel or any of the other gentlemen before they left?"

"No, ma'am."

Kate paused for a long moment before she circled back to the question she wanted to ask.

"Mr. Wright, one thing I'm just a little curious about. How did you know that the papers you found in your car that night belonged to Senator Ravenel?"

Kate saw a slight smile at the edge of Dewey Wright's thin, straight lips.

"Well, as a matter of fact, I did glance at 'em to be sure they belonged to Mr. Ravenel. I had hauled a bunch of those men in my car that day, driving them out to hunt. I knew those papers weren't mine, and I needed to see who it was they did belong to," Wright said. "So I looked at them. One of the documents talked about somethin' called Bluefish and the other one had a bunch of numbers on it with different names beside them. I sure didn't know what all that meant. But at the bottom of one page, I saw the signatures of Senator Ravenel, Senator Long and some other folks. I figured it must be his."

Before Kate Stewart could ask another question, Buck Ravenel stood straight up from his chair and walked around to the front of plaintiffs' counsel table to get Judge Jones' attention. His voice was louder and firmer this time.

"Your Honor, I object to this line of questioning. Whatever the contents of these documents may be, they are not relevant to the issue now before the court – the identification of defendants' confidential source. Your Honor, these papers could be legislative documents, they could be documents from a legal client, protected by the attorney-client privilege, they could be personal papers. With all due respect, Mr. Wright had no right to look at them, and he certainly should not be allowed to testify here about what he thinks he might recall weeks later about their contents. I object vigorously to this line of questioning."

"Your Honor, I will wrap this up quickly," Kate said. "Judge, I do think we need to hear what Mr. Wright has to say."

Before the judge could say anything else, Kate shot another question at Dewey Wright.

"Do you recall anything about what the documents said, Mr. Wright?"

"Well, I can recall a little bit, but I could make this easier for you. It was just about five or six pages, and I made a copy that night of what was in the folder."

He reached for the manila folder beside him and offered it to the judge.

"I'll be glad to read it out loud. Or I could give you this copy."

Ravenel exploded from his chair this time.

"Objection! Your Honor, may we approach the bench or be heard in chambers on this evidentiary issue?"

Judge Jones' eyebrows were dancing now, and he looked back and forth from Ravenel to Stewart and then down at the witness who was still sitting expressionless in the witness box, holding out the manila folder toward the judge.

"Mr. Wright, let me have those documents, and I will see if this line of questioning should proceed further."

Judge Jones studied the documents for several minutes, as

the spectators waited in uneasy silence. As a whispering buzz like summer cicadas began to rise, he reached for his gavel and looked up, his eyes wide, his eyebrows high. The audience quieted immediately, and he finished his reading. Finally, he looked up at the silent courtroom, his face strawberry red and grim.

"All right, I'll see Mr. Ravenel and Ms. Stewart in my chambers right now. And, Mr. Wright, would you be so kind as to join us?"

As soon as Judge Jones and his three guests had disappeared through the door to his chambers, the courtroom began to stir. The bailiff stepped to the rail and barked to the crowd to come to order or leave the courtroom, and the buzz subsided to whispers.

Sandy looked quickly behind him at the back row of the courtroom. There was an empty spot where Bill Wright had been sitting. Sandy leaned over, put his arm around his editor and whispered to him.

"What in the world do you think is going on back there?"

"I don't know," McNabb said. "I just hope that those papers don't get lost somewhere between Judge Jones and Buck Ravenel. I think we may have our smoking gun. We may have the *quid*, the *quo*, and the goddammed *pro* all wrapped up here."

Back in chambers, Judge Jones plopped down into his tattered leather desk chair. He pulled out his lowest desk drawer and propped a low-heeled cowboy boot on it. Kate noticed that the ear pulls at the top were engraved with the South Carolina state seal.

The judge gestured toward Ravenel as the lawyer came through the door.

"Push that door to," he grumbled. Then he tossed the manila folder on the desk before him.

"This is a hell of a development, counsel. We have two documents here. The first appears to be incorporation papers for a company called Bluefish, the owners of which appear to be Senator Buck Ravenel, Francis Marion Ravenel III and Senator Arthur Long. The other document suggests that Bluefish is one-third owner in another company called Osprey. The other owners of Osprey are Vince Stone and another individual named James Sullivan. Mr. Sullivan, if I recall correctly, is the president of Carolina Phosphate. Is that right, Senator?"

Ravenel nodded.

"Senator Ravenel, come look at this signature and tell me whether it's yours," the judge said. "Looks to me like it is."

Buck Ravenel walked over and took a grim-faced look at the documents.

"Yes, sir, it appears to be, Judge."

Kate Stewart caught the judge's eye.

"Judge Jones, could I please see the documents?"

The judge handed them over to Kate. Buck Ravenel got up and walked over to the far corner of the judge's chambers and stared out the window. Kate quickly understood what she saw. A document signed by the three men designed to create a company called Bluefish, Inc. The other document made it clear that Bluefish, Inc. would own one-third of a company called Osprey, Inc. The other owners of Osprey were Vince Stone and James Sullivan. The summary sheet showed large cash infusions from the Phosphate folks, none from the Ravenels or Long.

It was a clear paper trail to Carolina Phosphate's no-money-down, no-risk "investment" for the Ravenels, signed one week before Tripp Ravenel's agency had reversed itself and granted the permit to the company.

Judge Jones had needed less time than Kate to figure it out. He reached over and took the documents back from her.

He carefully surveyed Dewey Wright, who sat with his fingers laced across his belt buckle, waiting to see what these folks wanted of him.

"Mr. Wright, will you tell me why you thought it necessary or proper to copy these documents? You knew they didn't belong to you. Did it occur to you that you may have committed a crime of misappropriating another person's personal property?"

For the first time that day, Dewey Wright looked nervous. He looked down at his hands for a moment, then lifted his head up and looked in the judge's direction, but not at his eyes.

"Judge, I can only tell you what I did. My people own some of the property out at Wright's Landing. It's heirs' property, Judge, and nobody really knows who owns exactly what. But I been followin' that issue in the newspapers, and I heard these men talking about the Carolina Phosphate permit. All of the Wrights know that if that permit goes through, the property is going to be worthless to us. So when I heard these men talking about it all quiet-like, and I saw these pieces of paper, I thought it might be something I should look into. I thought I might show 'em to one of the lawyers representin' some of the families who own the property out at Wright's Landing. But I never did. I was too scared to. They've stayed locked up in my desk drawer since the day I got them."

He looked down, and muttered, almost to himself.

"I've been Tommin' for these white men for twenty-five ya-ahs. I was scared, Judge. They's some powerful people mixed up in all this. I'm ashamed to say I just decided to leave it alone."

He looked over at Kate Stewart.

"But I decided last night I wasn't gonna tell no lies about it neither," Wright said. "My brother Jimmy told me once that he had seen Mr. McNabb's daddy stand up to a bunch of the white men in this town. Said those men were trying to keep him from printing stories in his newspaper about black folks and about the steel mill strike. He said old man McNabb stared them down and said: 'I will speak the truth, and the truth will set me free.'"

Wright's lips made a tight smile.

"Well, I'm feeling pretty free right now."

Wright looked over at Kate, then back at the judge.

"The black people in this town knew that Hampton McNabb had stood up for us. After my brother Jimmy was killed twenty-five years ago, Mr. McNabb came to see me. He told me he thought my brother was murdered by the people who wanted the steel mill strike to end, and he was tryin' hard to learn more about that. That was two weeks before they found him dead out in the woods. Today, I thought it was time to pay Mr. McNabb back a little."

That was a lot of talk for Dewey Wright. He fell silent, staring down at his hands.

Judge Jones stroked his eyebrows for a moment, pondering all he had heard, nodded at Wright, then spoke crisply to Ravenel and Stewart.

"Counsel, here is what I'm going to do. We are going to go back into the courtroom, and I'm going to have Mr. Wright identify these documents as papers Senator Ravenel left in his car. We're going to mark them as Exhibit A to his testimony. I'm going to order them placed under seal for three days, and then I'm going to adjourn this hearing."

He rocked for a moment in his leather chair and looked hard at Buck Ravenel. He thought for a few seconds, calculating whether there was a way to save him. Finally, he shook his head and let out a deep sigh. Even Ravenel didn't have enough ducks in his freezer for that.

"I assume that plaintiffs and defendants will resolve this lawsuit in a way that will result in its dismissal before those three days expire. But settlement or no settlement, three days from today, these documents will be unsealed, and people can figure out for themselves what they mean. I expect the *Georgetown Pilot* and the rest of the South Carolina news media will be interested. The South Carolina State Law Enforcement Division might even want a copy. Or the FBI.

"All right, Mr. Wright, thank you for your candor. Counsel, let's go back outside."

Ravenel slumped through the doorway into the courtroom, followed by Dewey Wright. The pink was gone from Ravenel's cheeks. As Kate started toward the door, Judge Jones touched her shoulder to get her attention.

"Ms. Stewart, that was the finest piece of lawyerin' I've seen since the last time your old partner Cart Cooper stood in my courtroom," he said to her quietly. "He'd be real proud of you today."

28

The Right Connections

Wade leaned back in the tall wooden chair on Sliders' patio and stretched his arms and legs as far as they would go, like a dog rising stiffly from a long nap. The low-angled October sun shimmered off the surface of the bay, making him squint. He took a slow pull from the long neck of his Budweiser and surveyed the supporters who had gathered to help celebrate this morning's victory in court. It occurred to Wade that many of them had been a little quiet about that support when it had looked like Ravenel held all the cards and might be the *Pilot's* new publisher.

Kate sat across from him, jacket off, arms bare, feet propped on a chair in front of her, eyes closed, face turned up to the sunlight. A few freckles had already begun to punctuate her cheeks, like the jeweled spots on a brown trout when its back hits the air.

Bobo Baxter's beer was on the house. It was flowing freely and the keg taps were running like water faucets. His jukebox was at full volume, piped to the outside speakers. The POETS crowd was loudly handicapping the odds of Buck Ravenel becoming a houseguest of the federal government for a few years. The silky sound of Sam Cooke singing *Let the Good Times Roll* floated above the conversations.

"*Sha-la-la-la-la-la-tee-da*," Wade found himself humming right along with the late Mr. Cooke.

Carolyn Brown sat on a bench near the water, telling a favorite old joke to one of her ex's. She spotted Bobo and waved him over.

"I heard you were looking for me," she said.

Bobo gave her his best slow deadpan.

"Baby, I've been looking for you, exactly you, since about 1963," he said with a smile.

Carolyn laughed.

"Okay, I fell for it. Nicely done."

"I might not be kidding, you know," Bobo said. For the life of him he couldn't think of a song lyric that fit.

Nearby, Wade opened a Budweiser and handed it to Kate.

"You couldn't get Sandy to join us?" Kate asked, her eyes still closed, her cheeks showing pink. "He tried hard not to let on to you, but I think he's been more worried about losing the newspaper than you've been. He felt like this was his fault, that he had found the source, that he was the one who convinced you to run the story."

Wade leaned forward in his chair and put his elbows on his knees so Kate could hear him with his voice low.

"I never saw it that way," he said. "I met the source. And I heard him tell his story. I believed him. And it turns out our instincts were absolutely right. I'm sorry I doubted him a little these last couple of weeks. It shows you what the stresses of a lawsuit and the fear of losing something you've worked your whole life to get can do to you.

"Sandy, by the way, insisted on going straight to the newspaper office," Wade added. "He's not writing any of the stories about this. We still have the Greenville reporter covering this for the paper. But Sandy's there to provide some background. He wouldn't miss this for anything."

"Wade, don't you need to get back? I can't imagine you not

wanting to be in the thick of this," Kate said.

Wade took another sip of his beer, rested his head against the back of his chair, and folded his arms across his chest.

"No, I'm too damned close to this story anyway. If I were there, the reporter might feel pressured to give special attention to my point of view. What I want is good journalism. I want this covered just as if it was about the *New York Times*, and not about us. The reporter knows he can ignore Sandy if he wants to, but it'd be tougher if I were there. So, I'm gonna stay clear of the office this afternoon," Wade said. "I might drop by the paper later tonight when they put it to bed. I'll read the first copy that comes off the press tonight."

Bobo stopped by and left Wade another Budweiser.

"Here's another bottle of The Famous for you. High damn time somebody shined a little light on the back-scratchin' politics of this state. These guys know exactly how to change political power into personal profit. They don't even think of it as stealin'. It's like Woodie Guthrie said, '*Some men will rob you with a six-gun, some with a fountain pen.*' Anyway, I'm proud to know you two. All these beers are on me."

Wade smiled at Kate.

"How does he keep all that stuff in his head? Maybe I should get him to write a weekly column on life's lessons from lyrics," Wade said.

They sat quietly for a few minutes, soaking up the breeze from the harbor and listening to the pleasant buzz of nearby conversations and the background beats of music from Bobo's jukebox.

One of Bobo's passions was the music on his jukebox. It had all the shagging standards, from the Dominoes' *Sixty-Minute Man,* to the Showmen's *39-21-46* to Marvin Gaye's *Stubborn Kind of Fellow* and Maurice Williams' *Stay.* And the box

had great range. It had the country soul of Hank Williams
– the hillbilly Shakespeare – singing *Setting the Woods on Fire*.
It had the energy of Jackie Wilson, the smoothness of Sam
Cooke, the sadness of Willie Nelson, the soul of Otis Redding,
the passion of Aretha Franklin, the guitar ballads of Chuck
Berry, the New Orleans heat of Irma Thomas, the romance of
Etta James, the blues of Ray Charles, the saxophone of Can-
nonball Adderley, the silkiness of the Iceman, Jerry Butler, the
rock n' roll of Buddy Holly and Elvis, the anarchy of Little
Richard and Jerry Lee Lewis, the poetry of Smokey Robinson,
the harmony of the Temptations, the Texas twangs of Jerry
Jeff Walker and Guy Clark, the New Jersey brashness of Bruce
Springsteen, the story songs of Randy Newman and Paul Si-
mon, and the prophecy of Bob Dylan.

His favorite song – A-1 on the jukebox – was The Killer,
Jerry Lee, singing his own improbable version of *Somewhere
Over the Rainbow*. It was what Bobo said he wanted played at
his funeral: "Way above the chimbly tops, that's where you'll
find me."

"You know your source is not out of the woods yet, don't
you?" Kate said after a while. "If there is a criminal investigation, we may see the federal prosecutors looking for grand jury
testimony from you and Sandy about your source. And there's
no federal shield statute to protect you."

Wade thought about that for a moment.

"I don't think I'll worry about that today," he said. "I suspect somebody in that crowd is going to decide he doesn't
want to leave his wife or his children or his mistress alone for a
few years while he vacations at the Federal Hilton. Somebody's
gonna flip and agree to nail the others in exchange for a Get
Out of Jail Free card. In fact, I bet they are meeting with lawyers this very afternoon and by tomorrow morning we'll hear

them trying to outrun each other to the prosecutor's office to see who'll get to be the first rat to get a sweet deal."

Wade chuckled.

"This is going to be a lawyers' full employment act," he said. "I'll bet the boat salesmen and the BMW dealers are already getting excited."

He looked over at Kate.

"How about you? What's your afternoon look like?"

Kate's eyes stayed shut, her face still turned to the sun. She had pulled her hair back in a ponytail to give the sun more of her face. In the sunlight, Wade could make out traces of red in her brown hair.

"I don't know," she said. "I may just take it easy. I always have telephone calls to return, but I had thought I'd be spending the next few days on an emergency appeal of an order holding you in contempt of court. So maybe I'll just reward myself with a free afternoon."

Wade put his beer on the table beside him and stood up. He held his hand out to Kate.

"Well, in that case, I think we should take a short road trip. I want to see if you can really catch a fish."

Kate opened one eye and gave him a wary stare.

"This little trip won't be like going to see your church, will it? I'm feeling pretty good right here, you know."

Wade didn't sense full conviction in her dodge. He heard the beginning of the Del Vikings' most famous beach song start up from the jukebox. He reached down and grabbed Kate's hands to pull her up from her chair.

"Come go with me," he said with a laugh.

This time, she didn't hesitate. She reached for her jacket, swung it over her shoulder, and they headed down the outside pathway back to Front Street. She glanced back and saw

Carolyn, in her best Biblical attire, laughing and dancing with Bobo. She could almost hear him singing the words of *Sixty Minute Man* – "*I rock 'em, roll 'em, all night long, I'm a Sixty Minute Man...*"

They were quiet as they walked toward Kate's place. As they passed the church cemetery, Wade paused a moment, then took her elbow and steered her through the iron gate and toward his parents' gravesite. He stopped a few feet from his father's headstone. In the sunlight, she could read for the first time the inscription carved on the tombstone: Wade Hampton McNabb. 1915-1970. Publisher and Editor, The Georgetown Pilot. *The Truth Has Set Him Free.*

"Kate, I'm going to have a long-overdue chat with my dad."

Kate nodded gently. Wade walked closer and placed his hand on his father's headstone. For the first time since she had met him, he looked completely at peace, comfortable in his skin. He closed his eyes and bowed his head. He spoke very softly, almost to himself, but Kate could overhear part of what he said.

"Dad, I want to finally thank you for all you have done for me. When we got into this fix, I found myself trying to figure out just what you would do. I realized you would've printed the story and stuck to your guns, and that's what I did. You wouldn't have revealed your source even if it meant risking the paper. And thanks to our friend Kate Stewart here, we didn't lose our newspaper, yours and mine."

Kate heard his voice break a little on the last few words. She didn't say anything, but slipped her arm through his and pressed her head against his shoulder. Wade turned slightly to face her. He cupped her cheeks in his hands and leaned down to kiss her. A light kiss, soft, all lips. Kate didn't turn away as he had feared. Instead, she kissed him back gently and put her hands on top of his.

When they opened their eyes, they were smiling.

"I promised you a road trip, didn't I? Why don't you change out of that courtroom costume, and we'll drive out to my place at the river."

"That sounds good to me," Kate said.

*   *   *   *   *

Molly met them in the driveway to Wade's house, jumping and wagging her bobbed tail, throwing her head back and woo-wooing, bending in against their legs to be rubbed, glad to have some company so early in the afternoon.

Wade headed quickly to his bedroom to change clothes. Kate wandered the den, looking for clues about him – books or photographs that might reveal a side she had not yet seen.

Their cemetery kiss lingered awkwardly. She wasn't sure whether it was just the moment that had broken a barrier between them and whether that barrier had gone right back up. And it was clear Wade didn't know what to do next, either. They had retreated a little ways back into their shells.

On one bookshelf, she found a yellowed baseball signed by most of the 1961 Yankees – Mantle, Maris, Berra, Boyer, Kubek, Richardson, Howard, Ford, Lopez, Arroyo.

Wade walked up behind her, dressed in frayed khaki shorts, a dark blue untucked polo shirt, and well-worn leather boat shoes.

"No Skowron autograph. Moose didn't much like children, best I could tell," he said. "My dad took me to a few days of spring training in Florida when I was eleven. We got to the ballpark early the first day, and I got all these guys to sign my baseball. It was a big day for a little boy from Rural Route 2, Georgetown, South Carolina."

"Was your dad a big fan?" Kate asked.

"Not really. He didn't care all that much for baseball, but he loved to spend times like this with me. He tried hard to be a good dad. Actually, it was my mother who was the baseball fan. On summer Saturdays back then, when it was too hot or too rainy to play outside, I would sit in the den with her watching the Game of the Week on our little black and white television, listening to Dizzy Dean and PeeWee Reese swap stories. The Yankees were always on, and she became a big fan. Frankly, being a good South Carolina boy who back then thought *Dixie* should be the national anthem, it seemed a little disloyal or maybe even sacrilegious to be pulling for a team called the Yankees. But the second baseman, Bobby Richardson, was from Sumter, about fifty miles away. He was a local hero, so that made it a little better.

"When the games got a little dull, old Diz would burst into a chorus of *Wabash Cannonball*, and Mama would look up from her crocheting or from shelling peas – she couldn't stand to have idle hands. She'd shake her head, fingers still busy, and say with a frown: 'Wade Hampton, I'm afraid our Dizzy has been drinkin' again.'"

Wade pointed to a small framed photo of a young woman with a bobbed haircut and a pretty face with high cheekbones. The camera's lens had captured a slightly sultry look in her dark eyes. By the time Wade was old enough to remember her, she was older and plumper. By then, sultry had given way to wisdom tinged with sadness.

"I think she had an old soul," Wade said. "Like she had been here on earth many times. She was gentle and funny in an understated way. She didn't ruffle easily. She seemed to take a long view of life."

"She must have been a great companion," Kate said.

"Yes, and she was the fairest person I've ever known," Wade said. "She was a small-d democrat. She never judged anyone on how much money they had. She had grown up in a small town in south Georgia. Her father ran a little drug store, didn't make a lot of money. She always told me not to think anybody was better than me just because he had more money. And she told me I had better not ever think I was better than someone else if I happened to have more than they did. She believed you judged people by what they had accomplished using what they had started with.

"Somehow, like the white people all around her, she couldn't quite apply that thought to people whose skin was a different color," Wade added. "She thought she treated black people with compassion, but it never occurred to her to treat them as equals. It's hard, looking back twenty-five years, to understand that blind spot."

"She still sounds like she had a big heart, Wade," Kate said. "I think you learned some good things from her."

"Well," Wade said, "I didn't mean to get so serious. One thing she told me pretty often was that there are lots of things in the world I should take seriously. But she always instructed me not to take myself too seriously. It bores others, she said. Sorry if I've bored you these past few weeks."

He picked up a photograph near the autographed baseball. Standing next to what looked to be a boyish Wade was a man in his early forties with a ruddy face and soft, honest eyes, hinting a history of hurt. They were both wearing Yankee caps and grinning at the camera.

"That's my dad and me in Florida," Wade said. "When he was happy, he had a great smile. It made everyone think they knew him well. But no one really did."

Wade handed Kate some black running shorts with orange

trim and a t-shirt with a drawing of a baby turtle and a legend that read: "The Turtles Protect *Us*." "A gift," Wade said, "from one of the loggerhead turtle protectors with a sense of humor."

"Why don't you put these on? I'll get us a beer, and we'll catch some sun on the deck while I rig up my spinning reel. Mr. Bass and Mr. Bream are out there waiting for us."

"Well, if you're pouring, I'd actually love a martini. I don't think I've ever had one this early in the day before. But then again, I don't think I've ever had a day like today."

"I'm happy to do that, but I warn you, no Grey Goose on the premises. You'll have to do with one of those house brands I use for the occasional Bloody Mary."

She smiled and nodded.

"That sounds great."

Changing into the shorts, she could hear the rattle of a martini shaker full of ice, then the sound of Marvin Gaye singing *Stubborn Kind of Fellow*. Wade was singing along as he shook the martini.

When she emerged from the bathroom, Wade handed her a full martini glass and led her out onto his riverside deck. For the first time, she had a full view of the Pee Dee. Wade's house sat in a sharp curve of the river, giving him a long unobstructed view west and southeast. Thirty yards from the house was a small area of sandy beach with a dock that extended twenty-five feet out from the shallow river's edge.

"Wade, this is so beautiful. When I think of people coming to the beach or to Georgetown, I never envision this kind of beauty on the river. No wonder you've hung onto it all these years."

"For me, this is one of those anchors to the earth we've talked about," Wade said with a smile. "I'm glad you like it. I hoped you would. I'm as comfortable here as I am anywhere on earth. And I'm as free as a dolphin when I want to be. I can

hop in my boat and follow the Black River inland. Or I can follow the Pee Dee or the Waccamaw out to Winyah Bay and into
the ocean and as far north or south along the Atlantic coast
as I am brave enough to go. I can snake through these creeks
blindfolded on a good day. This spot gives me stability. And it
gives me freedom."

Kate accepted Wade's offer of a seat in the green wooden
rocker on his deck, facing the river. She propped her feet on
the porch rail and leaned back, sipping the martini cupped
in her hands. Wade leaned his elbows on the rail, one foot
crossed behind the other, and stared out at the river. For a
few minutes, they listened to the quiet of the river flow, punctuated only by bird chatter and warbles in the trees and the
tat-tat-tat of a distant woodpecker. A flock of ten or so white
wood storks glided over, broad, black-tipped wings extended,
their long, reed-like legs stretched behind them. They were
ready to roost for the night in the tall trees along the river, as
they followed autumn's southward pull. They were pre-histor-
ic looking birds, awkward, almost bald and nearly ugly when
perched. But they were graceful and beautiful in flight, their
pink feet dangling below them, almost like human hands.

Finally Kate spoke.

"Wade, why do you think Dewey Wright brought those papers with him to court today? He didn't have to do that. He
could've let this whole thing just pass him by. Now he's going
to be smack in the middle of it. You think it was because he
wanted to protect the property owned by all those members
of the Wright family? If so, his plan worked. Carolina Phosphate's permit is dead in the water now. That's a certainty."

Wade turned and began pacing the deck.

"I don't think that's what was driving his train today," he
said. "I think he figured out that our source might be the guy

who filled in at the Forest that Saturday night and didn't show up on the payroll records. And that could be someone who matters a lot to him, and he wanted to be sure to keep him out of this fray. Maybe he was afraid that Sandy or I would get cold feet and rationalize a way to give up our source in order to keep from losing the paper, so he decided to take the heat himself. It'll probably cost him his job at the Forest."

"True that, as some of my clients might say," Kate said. "But I think he made that decision before he showed up in court. He may have finally decided his job wasn't worth his soul. He was probably tired of dancing to the tunes of a hundred Buck Ravenels. My guess is that he'll find a place to do his art. In fact, Bobo took me aside this afternoon and said he could use a little more magic in his kitchen. He said he was going to talk to Dewey Wright about joining him."

"The Ravenels, on the other hand, are in big trouble," Kate said, shaking her head. "The feds will have to make an example of one of those guys. And federal judges have lifetime appointments, and they aren't so partial to Democrats these days. Unlike state court judges, they don't have to go back to the Senator's legislative buddies every few years to ask to keep their jobs."

"You know the code of the political fixers – never speak when a nod will do, never nod when a wink will do, and never put anything important on paper," Wade said. "Buck Ravenel thought the only paper in this deal would never see the light of day. He didn't figure on the likes of Dewey Wright and Kate Stewart."

Wade was still pacing, trying to organize his thoughts enough to say them. He wished he could type them out, that would be easier. Finally he stopped, took a deep breath, and started his speech.

"Kate, I don't have a clue how to thank you for what you've done for me these past few months. It was you who made this turn out the right way. Ravenel had us cornered just the way he planned it. There's no way Dewey Wright would've told the whole story if you hadn't coaxed it out of him. I don't think he came to court today planning to tell all he knew unless he saw we were going to identify our source. It was your instincts, your sense of knowing exactly what questions to ask, that persuaded him to put the finger on a man as powerful as Buck Ravenel. You saved my newspaper for me."

Kate smiled and took a sip of her drink. Wade had started pacing again.

"Those are kind words, Wade, and I thank you for them. But I'm not sure you're right. I think Dewey Wright had figured out over these past few weeks that he might just have to stand up against that kind of power, that kind of *misuse* of power.

"Wade, I need to tell you about something that happened while we were back in the judge's chambers this morning. The judge was pressing Wright on why he decided to come forward with those papers after sitting on them for months. Wright said he remembered his brother Jimmy telling him years ago about how he had seen Hampton McNabb stand up to a group of white businessmen who wanted him to quit writing about racial issues in the newspaper. Dewey Wright quoted your father to the judge '*I will tell the truth and the truth shall set me free.*'"

Wade stopped pacing and looked at Kate.

"Yeah, he used to say that whenever he felt like anybody was backing him into a corner. Maybe you saw it on his tombstone."

Kate nodded.

"I saw it this afternoon," she said gently.

Neither spoke for a while. They watched as a slate-blue

kingfisher darted from Wade's dock to the water for a snack, showing a flash of ruby and white under its wings, then perched on a dead tree limb.

Kate looked down at the turtle on the t-shirt Wade had given her and smiled.

"Wade, I have thought a lot about that loggerhead turtle story you told me when we were at North Island, about how the mother turtle laid her eggs. That mother turtle has a tough job. She has to find the beach *her* mother laid her eggs on decades before. Then she trudges up the beach to the sand dunes to find just the right spot to lay the eggs. She digs the hole, lays the eggs, then painstakingly covers them up, hoping nothing will find and eat them. Then she drags her body all the way back down to the water. But the poor thing never gets to see a single one of her babies. She doesn't get to teach them how to dig their way out of the sand, how to get back to the ocean, how to swim, how to survive, what to eat, how not to get eaten. She doesn't get to teach them how to find that same beach again and have their own babies. No wonder the mother turtle has tears in her eyes when she is laying her eggs. I would, too. I'd cry all the way back to the ocean."

Kate stared down at her hands. Wade didn't say anything right away.

"I know why that story is so sad for you," he said finally. "But your mother did get to teach you a lot, and your dad picked up right where she left off. I think their genes gave you some pretty good instincts about how to take care of yourself. And you do a great job of taking care of the rest of us. They would be proud of who you are."

Kate smiled at him.

"You do a good job of listening between the lines, Wade McNabb," she said.

Wade smiled and rose slowly to his feet.

"I'm going to have another beer," he said. "Can I bring you anything?"

Kate handed him her glass.

"I'll take another martini, if you don't mind," she said.

When Wade returned, they sat for a few minutes watching the sun meet the tops of the trees west of them. The late afternoon rays were turning the sky pink and giving the river a deep red, almost purple hue. Kate sipped her drink.

"Wade, I was scared for you these past few days. I was afraid of what would happen to you and your paper if you didn't disclose your source. But I was impressed that you decided to risk losing the newspaper to keep the promise you had made. That took a lot of courage."

Wade's eyes were still on the spot where the sun had just disappeared.

"At first, I was more scared than my conscious self would admit, to you or to myself. I never told you about the dreams. Right after you told me about how we could lose the paper, I dreamed I had fallen off my boat in a storm out in the ocean. I got turned around underwater, unsure which way was up. I guessed and started fighting in that direction, hoping I was headed to the surface. Like every dream, it was all in slow motion. I had held my breath as long as I possibly could, and I finally exploded, sucking for air the same second I broke the surface. Another second, and it would have pulled salt water into my lungs. I gasped so loud and flinched so hard, Molly woke up barking beside the bed. I had soaked my t-shirt right through with sweat. I had that one more than once. This past weekend, I almost called you to say I had changed my mind about revealing the name of the source.

"But I figured this all out. One of the reasons I worked so

hard to buy this newspaper a few years ago was to pay my father back for the good things he taught me. He lost the paper
because he chose to stand up for what he believed. People can
always find a reason to compromise their principles, to live to
fight another day, as they always say. My father would've wanted me to do just what I did. Once I realized that he would've
preferred me to stick to my guns at the risk of losing the paper,
the rest wasn't so hard.

"My mother tried to explain to me once how happiness
comes from appreciating something or somebody without holding on so tightly you squeeze the life out," Wade said. "Might be
a puppy, might be a friend, might be a newspaper. I didn't want
to lose the paper, but I didn't want to keep it at all costs."

Kate smiled and shook her head.

"Your momma was a wise woman, Wade. And you were
smart enough to listen and remember. But I don't think you're
giving yourself enough credit. Most people I know would've
found a way to justify revealing the source. They would have
taken the newspaper out of Judge Jones' gun sights."

Wade raised his beer and clinked Kate's glass.

"Well, here's to Kate Stewart and Dewey Wright, my two
new heroes," Wade said. "And a toast to my smart momma and
my brave dad."

He set his beer on the rail, walked over to the end of the
deck and picked up his spinning rod. Pulling his tackle box
from under a bench, he fumbled in it for the right size hook,
then slipped the fishing line through its eye. He looked up
brightly at Kate.

"Let's go down to the dock and check the minnow trap, see
if we have any tasty minnows down there. Maybe you can show
me how you caught that big bass that made you so famous at
the Forest."

Wade picked up his rod, and they crossed the narrow strip of grassy lawn to the thin swath of sandy beach. Setting the fishing gear on the edge of the dock, Wade walked to the end of the pier.

"Sad report," he called out, kneeling to lean over the side of the pier. He pulled the bucket up and set it on the dock.

"No minnows to be found, but I bet those fish might be tempted by a little Roostertail Spinner. You want to give it a try, Kate?"

"The truth is," she said, "I'd rather dangle my feet off the edge of this dock in the water for a little while."

Kate tossed her canvas bag onto the dock and slipped off her sandals, then pulled a small bottle of sunscreen from the bag.

"Well, I've got an even better idea," Wade said. "Let's go for a quick swim. This is bound to be one of the last warm afternoons of the fall. The water around the dock is only a few feet deep, and the sun keeps it pretty toasty."

Kate's face turned suddenly serious, and her body stiffened a little. Wade looked in her eyes and took both her hands.

Kate didn't pull away, but she didn't move any closer to the water.

"Kate, you are an amazing woman," Wade said quietly. "And it took me a while to understand that you are not quite as tough as you need the world to think you are. We are a lot alike in that way. We're like pecans or oysters – tough as we need to be on the outside, softer on the inside."

Kate's key ring was visible in her bag, and Wade reached in and pulled it out. He held up the purple-ish snail shell looped onto the ring.

"Let me keep this for you for a while. I want you to understand that you don't need this for a shield anymore."

Wade took her hands again and walked slowly backward

from the shore, gently pulling Kate with him into deeper water. She tensed, squeezing his hands tightly. When they were
waist-deep, Kate stopped.

"I can't do this," she said.

"You can," Wade said firmly. "Close your eyes and lean
back into me."

She was shaking, but she leaned back into the crook of his
arm. He wrapped one arm around her waist and put his other
arm under her knees, lifting her high in the water. Kate closed
her eyes and gripped his arm, and Wade could feel her rising
panic.

Flashing behind her eyelids, Kate saw waves crashing in
the ocean, a red bathing suit, her mother's sad eyes saying
goodbye, two grey-blue bodies side by side on the sand, people
staring and nodding, her ten-year-old self wrapped in a towel,
rocking, sobbing, her head exploding, screaming inside. What
could be so wrong with me that my mother would leave me?

Then she heard Wade's voice saying quietly, "Breathe, Kate,
breathe."

Kate felt Wade's hands under her back and her legs. She
closed her mouth tight, inhaled deeply through her nose, filling her lungs with the deepest breath she knew how to take.

"Now let your muscles relax, one at a time."

She leaned her head back as far as she could and let her
arms and legs drift.

She had never felt more vulnerable.

And then she was ten again, crossing a rising salt creek riding on David's back, laughing, her arms tight around his neck.
She was relaxed; she was safe. Then she was nodding off to
sleep in the hammock on the porch at Ocean Drive, the waves
breaking in the background, her mother's kiss still warm on
her cheek. She was waiting for her dad to arrive for the week-

end, with a smile and a hug, smelling faintly of tobacco, bourbon, bream and after shave.

She opened her eyes and saw Wade, smiling, his arms by his side. She was floating on her own.

She had never felt more independent.

Behind Wade she could see the full moon rising just above the trees across the river and the silhouette of his empty minnow bucket resting on the edge of the dock.

She had never felt more connected.

Author Acknowledgements

I want to thank my family and friends who contributed in important ways to this long-gestating story of South Carolina political intrigue and human connection. Family members Suzette Buchan and Caroline Buchan, Geoff and Sara Eloge, I thank for their careful reading, constant patience, kind encouragement and sound advice. Thanks to friends Corby Anderson, Derb Carter, David McClintock, Ray Owens, Alex Sanders, Greg Smith and John Wester – for sharing their favorite stories, experiences and quotes with me, and to Bob Mottern for reminding me that mallard drakes don't quack. I owe deep gratitude to Karen Garloch, Carolyn Karpinos, Dannye Romine Powell, and the late Doug Marlette, who encouraged me to believe in this story enough to make it happen. I thank Lori Burr, Beth Carroll and Karen Laubach for taking their time to translate my words into pages, and editors Alice Peck and Susan Kammeraad-Campbell for pushing me to make a good story better. Finally, thanks to my lifelong friend, Wade Hampton Townsend Jr., that South Carolina gentleman full of stories, laughter, friendship, generosity and heart, who truly understood South Carolina. His friends everywhere miss him fiercely.